SHE WHO BECAME THE SUN

SHE WHO

BECAME THE

SUN

SHELLEY PARKER-CHAN

TOR

A TOM DOHERTY ASSOCIATES BOOK

New York

SHE WHO BECAME THE SUN

Copyright © 2021 by Shelley Parker-Chan

A Tor Book
Published by Tom Doherty Associates
120 Broadway
New York, NY 10271

www.tor-forge.com

Tor® is a registered trademark of Macmillan Publishing Group, LLC.

Library of Congress Cataloging-in-Publication Data

Names: Parker-Chan, Shelley, author.
Title: She who became the sun / Shelley Parker-Chan.
Description: First edition. | New York : Tor, 2021. | A Tom Doherty
    Associates book.
Identifiers: LCCN 2021009142 (print) | LCCN 2021009143 (ebook) |
    ISBN 9781250621801 (hardcover) | ISBN 9781250837134 (Canadian) |
    ISBN 9781250621795 (ebook)
Subjects: GSAFD: Fantasy fiction.
Classification: LCC PR9619.4.P369 S54 2021 (print) |
    LCC PR9619.4.P369 (ebook) | DDC 823/.92—dc23
LC record available at https://lccn.loc.gov/2021009142
LC ebook record available at https://lccn.loc.gov/2021009143

Our books may be purchased in bulk for promotional, educational, or
business use. Please contact your local bookseller or the Macmillan
Corporate and Premium Sales Department at 1-800-221-7945, extension
5442, or by email at MacmillanSpecialMarkets@macmillan.com.

First U.S. Edition: July 2021
First Canadian Edition: July 2021

Printed in the United States of America

0 9 8 7 6 5 4 3 2 1

All things, O priests, are on fire . . . And with what are they on fire? With the fire of passion, say I, with the fire of hatred, with the fire of infatuation; with birth, old age, death, sorrow, lamentation, misery, grief, and despair are they on fire.

ADITTAPARIYAYA SUTTA: The Fire Sermon

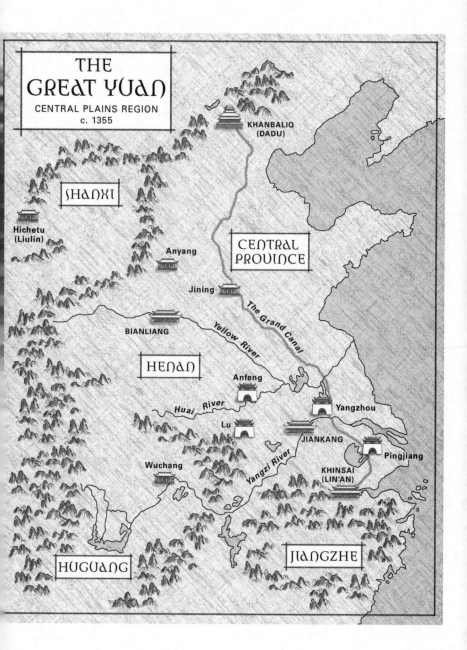

THE
GREAT YUAN
CENTRAL PLAINS REGION
c. 1355

KHANBALIQ
(DADU)

SHANXI

Hichetu
(Liulin)

Anyang

CENTRAL
PROVINCE

Jining

The Grand Canal

BIANLIANG

Yellow River

HENAN

Anfeng

Huai River

Lu

Yangzhou

JIANKANG

Pingjiang

Wuchang

Yangzi River

KHINSAI
(LIN'AN)

HUGUANG

JIANGZHE

PART ONE

1345–1354

1

HUAI RIVER PLAINS, SOUTHERN HENAN, 1345

Zhongli village lay flattened under the sun like a defeated dog that has given up on finding shade. All around there was nothing but the bare yellow earth, cracked into the pattern of a turtle's shell, and the sere bone smell of hot dust. It was the fourth year of the drought. Knowing the cause of their suffering, the peasants cursed their barbarian emperor in his distant capital in the north. As with any two like things connected by a thread of qi, whereby the actions of one influence the other even at a distance, so an emperor's worthiness determines the fate of the land he rules. The worthy ruler's dominion is graced with good harvests; the unworthy's is cursed by flood, drought, and disease. The present ruler of the empire of the Great Yuan was not only emperor, but Great Khan too: he was tenth of the line of the Mongol conqueror Khubilai Khan, who had defeated the last native dynasty seventy years before. He had held the divine light of the Mandate of Heaven for eleven years, and already there were ten-year-olds who had never known anything but disaster.

The Zhu family's second daughter, who was more or less ten years old in that parched Rooster year, was thinking about food as she followed the village boys towards the dead neighbor's field. With her wide forehead and none of the roundness that makes children adorable, she had the mandibular look of a brown locust. Like that insect, the girl thought about food constantly. However, having grown up on a peasant's monotonous diet, and with only a half-formed suspicion that better things might exist, her imagination was limited to the dimension of quantity. At that moment she was busy thinking about a bowl of millet porridge. Her mind's eye had filled it past the lip, liquid quivering high within a taut skin, and as she walked she contemplated with a voluptuous, anxious dreaminess how she might take the first spoonful without losing a drop. From above (but the sides might yield) or the side (surely a disaster); with firm hand or a gentle touch? So involved was she in her imaginary meal that she barely noticed the chirp of the gravedigger's spade as she passed by.

At the field the girl went straight to the line of headless elms on its far boundary. The elms had once been beautiful, but the girl remembered them without nostalgia. After the harvest had failed the third time the peasants had discovered their gracious elms could be butchered and eaten like any other living thing. Now *that* was something worth remembering, the girl thought. The sullen brown astringency of a six-times-boiled elm root, which induced a faint nausea and left the inside of your cheeks corrugated with the reminder of having eaten. Even better: elm bark flour mixed with water and chopped straw, shaped into biscuits and cooked over a slow fire. But now the edible parts of the elms were long gone, and their only interest to the village children lay in their function as a shelter for mice, grasshoppers, and other such treats.

At some point, though the girl couldn't remember exactly when, she had become the only girl in the village. It was an uncomfortable knowledge, and she preferred not to think about it. Anyway, there was no need to think; she knew exactly what had happened. If a family had a son and a daughter and two bites of food, who would waste one on a daughter? Perhaps only if that daughter were particularly useful. The girl knew she was no more useful than those dead girls had been. Uglier, too. She pressed her lips together and crouched next to the first elm stump. The only difference between them and her was that she had learned how to catch food for herself. It seemed such a small difference, for two opposite fates.

Just then the boys, who had run ahead to the best spots, started shouting. A quarry had been located, and despite a historic lack of success with the method, they were trying to get it out by poking and banging with sticks. The girl took advantage of their distraction to slide her trap from its hiding place. She'd always had clever hands, and back when such things had mattered, her basket-weaving had been much praised. Now her woven trap held a prize anyone would want: a lizard as long as her forearm. The sight of it immediately drove all thoughts of porridge from the girl's head. She knocked the lizard's head on a rock and held it between her knees while she checked the other traps. She paused when she found a handful of crickets. The thought of that nutty, crunchy taste made her mouth water. She steeled herself, tied the crickets up in a cloth, and put them in her pocket for later.

Once she'd replaced the traps, the girl straightened. A plume of golden loess was rising above the road that traversed the hills behind the village. Under azure banners, the same color as the Mandate of Heaven held by the Mongol ruling line, soldiers' leather armor massed into a dark river arrowing southward through the dust. Everyone on the Huai River plains knew the army of the Prince of Henan, the Mongol noble responsible for putting down the peasant rebellions that had been popping up in the region for more than twice the girl's lifetime. The Prince's army marched south every autumn and returned to its garrisons in northern Henan every spring, as regular as the calendar. The army never came any closer to Zhongli than it did now, and nobody from Zhongli had ever gone closer to it. Metal on the soldiers' armor caught and turned the light so that the dark river sparkled as it crawled over the dun hillside. It was a sight so disconnected from the girl's life that it seemed only distantly real, like the mournful call of geese flying far overhead.

Hungry and fatigued by the sun, the girl lost interest. Holding her lizard, she turned for home.

At midday the girl went out to the well with her bucket and shoulder pole and came back sweating. The bucket got heavier each time, being less and less water and more and more the ochre mud from the bottom of the well. The earth had failed to give them food, but now it seemed determined to give itself to them in every gritty bite. The girl remembered that once some villagers had tried to eat cakes made of mud. She felt a pang of sympathy. Who wouldn't do anything to appease the pain of an empty stomach? Perhaps more would have tried it, but the villagers' limbs and bellies had swelled, and then they died, and the rest of the village had taken note.

The Zhu family lived in a one-room wooden hut made in a time when trees were more plentiful. That had been a long time ago, and the girl didn't remember it. Four years of desiccation had caused all the hut's planks to spring apart so that it was as airy inside as outside. Since it never rained, it wasn't a problem. Once the house had held a whole family: paternal grandparents, two parents, and seven children. But each year of the drought had reduced them until now they were only three: the girl, her next-oldest brother Zhu Chongba, and their father. Eleven-year-old Chongba had always been cherished for being the lucky eighth-born of his generation of male cousins. Now that he was the sole survivor it was even clearer that Heaven smiled upon him.

The girl took her bucket around the back to the kitchen, which was an open lean-to with a rickety shelf and a ceiling hook for hanging the pot over the fire. On the shelf was the pot and two clay jars of yellow beans. A scrap of old meat hanging from a nail was all that was left of her father's work buffalo. The girl took the scrap and rubbed it inside the pot, which was something her mother had always done to flavor the soup. Privately, the girl felt that it was like hoping a boiled saddle might taste like meat. She untied her skirt, retied it around the mouth of the pot, and splashed in water from the bucket. Then she scraped the circle of mud off the skirt and put it back on. Her skirt was no dirtier than before, and at least the water was clean.

She was lighting the fire when her father came by. She observed him from inside the lean-to. He was one of those people who has eyes that look like eyes, and a nose like a nose. Nondescript. Starvation had pulled the skin tight over his face until it was one plane from cheekbone to chin, and another from one corner of his chin to the other. Now and then the girl wondered if her father was actually a young man, or at least not a very old one. It was hard to tell.

Her father was carrying a winter melon under his arm. It was small, the size of a newborn baby, and its powdery white skin was dusty from having been buried underground for nearly two years. The tender look on her father's face surprised the girl. She had never seen that expression on him before, but she knew what it meant. That was their last melon.

Her father squatted next to the flat-topped stump where they had killed chickens and placed the melon on it like an offering to the ancestors. He hesitated, cleaver in hand. The girl knew what he was thinking. A cut melon didn't keep. She felt a rush of mixed emotions. For a few glorious days they would have *food*. A memory boiled up: soup made with pork bones and salt, the surface swimming with droplets of golden oil. The almost gelatinous flesh of the melon, as translucent as the eye of a fish, yielding sweetly between her teeth. But once the melon was done, there would be nothing except the yellow beans. And after the yellow beans, there would be nothing.

The cleaver smacked down, and after a moment the girl's father came in. When he handed her the chunk of melon, his tender look was gone. "Cook it," he said shortly, and left.

The girl peeled the melon and cut the hard white flesh into pieces. She had forgotten melon smell: candle wax, and an elm-blossom greenness. For a moment she was gripped by the desire to shove it in her mouth. Flesh, seeds, even the sharp peel, all of it stimulating every inch of her tongue with the glorious ecstasy of *eating*. She swallowed hard. She knew her worth in her father's eyes, and the risk that a theft would bring. Not all the girls who died had starved. Regretfully, she put the melon into the pot with a scatter of yellow beans. She cooked it for as long as the wood lasted, then took the folded pieces of bark she used as pot holders and carried the food into the house.

Chongba looked up from where he was sitting on the bare floor next to their father. Unlike his father, his face provoked comment. He had a pugnacious jaw and a brow as lumpy as a walnut. These features made him so strikingly ugly that the onlooker's eye found itself caught in unwitting fascination. Now Chongba took the spoon from the girl and served their father. "Ba, please eat." Then he served himself, and finally the girl.

The girl examined her bowl and found only beans and water. She returned her silent stare to her brother. He was already eating and didn't notice. She watched him spoon a chunk of melon into his mouth. There was no cruelty in his face, only blind, blissful satisfaction: that of someone perfectly concerned with himself. The girl knew that fathers and sons made the pattern of the family, as the family made the pattern of the universe, and for all her wishful thinking she had never really expected to be allowed to taste the melon. It still rankled. She took a spoonful of soup. Its path into her body felt as hot as a coal.

Chongba said with his mouth full, "Ba, we nearly got a rat today, but it got away."

Remembering the boys beating on the stump, the girl thought scornfully: *Nearly.*

Chongba's attention shifted to her. But if he was waiting for her to volunteer something, he could wait. After a moment he said directly, "I know you caught something. Give it to me."

Keeping her gaze fixed on her bowl, the girl found the twitching packet of crickets in her pocket. She handed it over. The hot coal grew.

"That's all, you useless girl?"

She looked up so sharply that he flinched. He'd started calling her that recently, imitating their father. Her stomach was as tight as a clenched fist. She let herself think of the lizard hidden in the kitchen. She would dry it and eat it in secret all by herself. And that would be enough. It had to be.

They finished in silence. As the girl licked her bowl clean, her father laid out two melon seeds on their crude family shrine: one to feed their ancestors, and the other to appease the wandering hungry ghosts who lacked their own descendants to remember them.

After a moment the girl's father rose from his stiff reverence before the shrine. He turned back to the children and said with quiet ferocity, "One day soon our ancestors will intervene to end this suffering. They *will*."

The girl knew he was right. He was older than her and knew more. But when she tried to imagine the future, she couldn't. There was nothing in her imagination to replace the formless, unchanging days of starvation. She clung to life because it seemed to have value, even if only to her. But when she thought about it, she had no idea why.

The girl and Chongba sat listlessly in their doorway, looking out. One meal a day wasn't enough to fill anyone's time. The heat was most unbearable in the late afternoon, when the sun slashed backhanded across the village, as red as the last native emperors' Mandate of Heaven. After sunset the evenings were merely breathless. In the Zhu family's part of the village the houses sat apart from one another, with a wide dirt road between. There was no activity on the road or anywhere else in the falling dusk. Chongba fiddled with the Buddhist amulet he wore, and kicked at the dirt, and the girl gazed at the crescent moon where it edged above the shadow of the far hills.

Both children were surprised when their father came around the side of the house. There was a chunk of melon in his hand.

The girl could smell the edge of spoil in it, though it had only been cut that morning.

"Do you know what day it is?" he asked Chongba.

It had been years since the peasants had celebrated any of the festivals that marked the various points of the calendar. After a while Chongba hazarded, "Mid-Autumn Festival?"

The girl scoffed privately: Did he not have eyes to see the moon?

"The second day of the ninth month," her father said. "This is the day you were born, Zhu Chongba, in the year of the Pig." He turned and started walking. "Come."

Chongba scrambled after him. After a moment the girl followed. The houses along the road made darker shapes against the sky. She used to be scared of walking this road at night because of all the feral dogs. But now the night was empty. Full of ghosts, the remaining villagers said, although since ghosts were as invisible as breath or qi, there was no telling if they were there or not. In the girl's opinion, that made them of less concern: she was only scared of things she could actually see.

They turned from the main road and saw a pinprick of light ahead, no brighter than a random flash behind one's eyelids. It was the fortune-teller's house. As they went inside, the girl realized why her father had cut the melon.

The first thing she saw was the candle. They were so rare in Zhongli that its radiance seemed magical. Its flame stood a hand high, swaying at the tip like an eel's tail. Beautiful, but disturbing. In the girl's own unlit house she had never had a sense of the dark outside. Here they were in a bubble surrounded by the dark, and the candle had stolen her ability to see what lay outside the light.

The girl had only ever seen the fortune-teller at a distance before. Now, up close, she knew at once that her father was not old. The fortune-teller was perhaps even old enough to remember the time before the barbarian emperors. A mole on his wrinkled cheek sprouted a long black hair, twice as long as the wispy white hairs on his chin. The girl stared.

"Most worthy uncle." Her father bowed and handed the melon to the fortune-teller. "I bring you the eighth son of the Zhu family, Zhu Chongba, under the stars of his birth. Can you tell us his fate?" He pushed Chongba forwards. The boy went eagerly.

The fortune-teller took Chongba's face between his old hands and turned it this way and that. He pressed his thumbs into the boy's brow and cheeks, measured his eye sockets and nose, and felt the shape of his skull. Then he took the boy's wrist and felt his pulse. His eyelids drooped and his expression became severe and internal, as if interpreting some distant message. A sweat broke out on his forehead.

The moment stretched. The candle flared and the blackness outside seemed to press closer. The girl's skin crawled, even as her anticipation grew.

They all jumped when the fortune-teller dropped Chongba's arm. "Tell us, esteemed uncle," the girl's father urged.

The fortune-teller looked up, startled. Trembling, he said, "This child has greatness in him. Oh, how clearly did I see it! His deeds will bring a hundred generations of pride to your family name." To the girl's astonishment he rose and hurried to kneel at her father's feet. "To be rewarded with a son with a fate like this, you must have been virtuous indeed in your past lives. Sir, I am honored to know you."

The girl's father looked down at the old man, stunned. After a moment he said, "I remember the day that child was born. He was too weak to suck, so I walked all the way to Wuhuang Monastery to make an offering for his survival. A twenty-jin sack of yellow beans and three pumpkins. I even promised the monks that I would dedicate him to the monastery when he turned twelve, if he survived." His voice cracked: desperate and joyous at the same time. "Everyone told me I was a fool."

Greatness. It was the kind of word that didn't belong in Zhongli. The girl had only ever heard it in her father's stories of the past. Stories of that golden, tragic time before the barbarians came. A time of emperors and kings and generals; of war and betrayal and triumph. And now her ordinary brother, Zhu Chongba, was to be great. When she looked at Chongba, his ugly face was radiant. The wooden Buddhist amulet around his neck caught the candlelight and glowed gold, and made him a king.

As they left, the girl lingered on the threshold of the dark. Some impulse prompted her to glance back at the old man in his pool of candlelight. Then she went creeping back and folded herself down very small before him until her head was touching the dirt and her nostrils were full of the dead chalk smell of it. "Esteemed uncle. Will you tell me my fate?"

She was afraid to look up. The impulse that had driven her here, that hot coal in her stomach, had abandoned her. Her pulse rabbited. The pulse that contained the pattern of her fate. She thought of Chongba holding that great fate within him. What did it feel like, to carry that seed of potential? For a moment she wondered if she had a seed of potential within herself too, and it was only that she had never known what to look for; she had never had a name for it.

The fortune-teller was silent. The girl felt a chill drift over her. Her body broke out in chicken-skin and she huddled lower, trying to get away from that dark touch of fear. The candle flame lashed.

Then, as if from a distance, she heard the fortune-teller say: "Nothing."

The girl felt a dull, deep pain. That was the seed within her, her fate, and she realized she had known it all along.

The days ground on. The Zhu family's yellow beans were running low, the water was increasingly undrinkable, and the girl's traps were catching less and less. Many of the remaining villagers set out on the hill road that led to the monastery and beyond, even though everyone knew it was just exchanging death by starvation for death by bandits. The girl's father alone seemed to have found new strength. Every morning he stood outside under the rosy dome of that unblemished sky and said like a prayer, "The rains will come. All we need is patience, and faith in Heaven to deliver Zhu Chongba's great fate."

One morning the girl, sleeping in the depression she and Chongba had made for themselves next to the house, woke to a noise. It was startling: they had almost forgotten what life sounded like. When they went to the road they saw something even more surprising. *Movement*. Before they could think, it was already rushing past in a thunderous press of noise: men on filthy horses that flung up the dust with the violence of their passage.

When they were gone Chongba said, small and scared, "The army?"

The girl was silent. She wouldn't have thought those men could have come from that dark flowing river, beautiful but always distant.

Behind them, their father said, "Bandits."

That afternoon three of the bandits came stooping under the Zhu family's sagging lintel. To the girl, crouched on the bed with her brother, they seemed to fill the room with their size and rank smell. Their tattered clothes gaped and their untied hair was matted. They were the first people the girl had ever seen wearing boots.

The girl's father had prepared for this event. Now he rose and approached the bandits, holding a clay jar. Whatever he felt, he kept it hidden. "Honored guests. This is only of the poorest quality, and we have but little, but please take what we have."

One of the bandits took the jar and looked inside. He scoffed. "Uncle, why so stingy? This can't be all you have."

Their father stiffened. "I swear to you, it is. See for yourself how my children have no more flesh on them than a sick dog! We've been eating stones for a long time, my friend."

The bandit laughed. "Ah, don't bullshit me. How can it be

stones if you're all still alive?" With a cat's lazy cruelty, he shoved the girl's father and sent him stumbling. "You peasants are all the same. Offering us a chicken, expecting us not to see the fatted pig in the pantry! Go get the rest of it, you cunt."

The girl's father caught himself. Something changed in his face. In a surprising burst of speed he lunged at the children and caught the girl by the arm. She cried out in surprise as he dragged her off the bed. His grip was hard; he was hurting her.

Above her head, her father said, "Take this girl."

For a moment the words didn't make sense. Then they did. For all her family had called her useless, her father had finally found her best use: as something that could be spent to benefit those who mattered. The girl looked at the bandits in terror. What possible use could she have to them?

Echoing her thoughts, the bandit said scornfully, "That little black cricket? Better to give us one five years older, and prettier—" Then, as realization dawned, he broke off and started laughing. "Oh, uncle! So it's true what you peasants will do when you're *really* desperate."

Dizzy with disbelief, the girl remembered what the village children had taken pleasure in whispering to one another. That in other, worse-off villages, neighbors would swap their youngest children to eat. The children had thrilled with fear, but none of them had actually believed it. It was only a story.

But now, seeing her father avoiding her gaze, the girl realized it wasn't just a story. In a panic she began struggling, and felt her father's hands clench tighter into her flesh, and then she was crying too hard to breathe. In that one terrible moment, she knew what her fate of *nothing* meant. She had thought it was only insignificance, that she would never be anything or do anything that mattered. But it wasn't.

It was death.

As she writhed and cried and screamed, the bandit strode over and snatched her from her father. She screamed louder, and then thumped onto the bed hard enough that all her breath came out. The bandit had thrown her there.

Now he said, disgusted, "I want to eat, but I'm not going to touch that garbage," and punched their father in the stomach. He doubled over with a wet squelch. The girl's mouth opened silently. Beside her, Chongba cried out.

"There's more here!" One of the other bandits was calling from the kitchen. "He buried it."

Their father crumpled to the floor. The bandit kicked him under the ribs. "You think you can fool us, you lying son of a turtle? I bet you have even more, hidden all over the place." He kicked him again, then again. "Where is it?"

The girl realized her breath had come back: she and Chongba were both shrieking for the bandit to stop. Each thud of boots on flesh pierced her with anguish, the pain as intense as if it were her own body. For all her father had shown her how little she meant to him, he was still her *father*. The debt children owed their parents was incalculable; it could never be repaid. She screamed, "There isn't any more! Please stop. There isn't. There *isn't*—"

The bandit kicked their father a few more times, then stopped. Somehow the girl knew it hadn't had anything to do with their pleading. Their father lay motionless on the ground. The bandit crouched and lifted his head by the topknot, revealing the bloodied froth on the lips and the pallor of the face. He made a sound of disgust and let it drop.

The other two bandits came back with the second jar of beans. "Boss, looks like this is it."

"Fuck, two jars? I guess they really were going to starve." After a moment the leader shrugged and went out. The other two followed.

The girl and Chongba, clinging to each other in terror and exhaustion, stared at their father where he lay on the churned dirt. His bloodied body was curled up as tightly as a child in the womb: he had left the world already prepared for his reincarnation.

❋

That night was long and filled with nightmares. Waking up was worse. The girl lay on the bed looking at her father's body. Her fate was nothing, and it was her father who would have made it happen, but now it was he who was nothing. Even as she shuddered with guilt, she knew it hadn't changed anything. Without their father, without food, the nothing fate still awaited.

She looked over at Chongba and startled. His eyes were open, but fixed unseeing on the thatched roof. He barely seemed to breathe. For a horrible instant the girl thought he might be dead as well, but when she shook him he gave a small gasp and blinked. The girl belatedly remembered that he couldn't die, since he could hardly become great if he did. Even with that knowledge, being in that room with the shells of two people, one alive and one dead, was the most frighteningly lonely thing the girl had ever experienced. She had been surrounded by people her whole life. She had never imagined what it would be like to be alone.

It should have been Chongba to perform their last filial duty. Instead, the girl took her father's dead hands and dragged the body outside. He had withered so much that she could just manage. She laid him flat on the yellow earth behind the house, took up his hoe, and dug.

The sun rose and baked the land and the girl and everything else under it. The girl's digging was only the slow, scraping erosion of layers of dust, like the action of a river over the centuries. The shadows shortened and lengthened again; the grave deepened with its infinitesimal slowness. The girl gradually became aware of being hungry and thirsty. Leaving the grave, she found some muddy water in the bucket. She scooped it with her hands and drank. She ate the meat for rubbing the pot, recoiling at its dark taste, then went into the house and looked for a long time at the two dried melon seeds on the ancestral shrine. She remembered what people had said would happen if you ate a ghost offering: the ghosts would come for you, and their anger would make you sicken and die. But was that true? The girl had never heard of it happening to anyone in the village—and if no one could see ghosts, how could they be sure what ghosts did? She stood there in an agony of indecision. Finally she left the seeds where they were and went outside, where she grubbed around in last year's peanut patch and found a few woody shoots.

After she had eaten half the shoots, the girl looked at the other half and deliberated on whether to give them to Chongba, or to trust in Heaven to provide for him. Eventually guilt prodded her to go wave the peanut shoots over his face. Something in him flared at the sight. For a moment she saw him struggling back to life, fueled by that king-like indignation that she should have given him everything. Then the spark died. The girl watched his eyes drift out of focus. She didn't know what it meant, that he would lie there without eating and drinking. She went back outside and kept digging.

When the sun set the grave was only knee deep, the same clear yellow color at the top as it was at the bottom. The girl could believe it was like that all the way down to the spirits' home in the Yellow Springs. She climbed into bed next to Chongba's rigid form and slept. In the morning, his eyes were still open. She wasn't sure if he had slept and woken early, or if he had been like that all night. When she shook him this time, he breathed more quickly. But even that seemed reflexive.

She dug again all that day, stopping only for water and peanut sprouts. And still Chongba lay there, and showed no interest when she brought him water.

She awoke before dawn on the morning of the third day. A sense of aloneness gripped her, vaster than anything she had ever felt. Beside her, the bed was empty: Chongba had gone.

She found him outside. In the moonlight he was a pale blur next to the mass that had been their father. At first she thought he was asleep. Even when she knelt and touched him it took her a long time to realize what had happened, because it didn't make any sense. Chongba was to have been great; he was to have brought pride to their family name. But he was dead.

The girl was startled by her own anger. Heaven had promised

Chongba life enough to achieve greatness, and he had given up that life as easily as breathing. He had *chosen* to become nothing. The girl wanted to scream at him. Her fate had always been nothing. She had never had a choice.

She had been kneeling there for a long time before she noticed the glimmer at Chongba's neck. The Buddhist amulet. The girl remembered the story of how her father had gone to Wuhuang Monastery to pray for Chongba's survival, and the promise he had made: that if Chongba survived, he would return to the monastery to be made a monk.

A monastery—where there would be food and shelter and protection.

She felt a stirring at the thought. An awareness of her own life, inside her: that fragile, mysteriously valuable thing that she had clung to so stubbornly throughout everything. She couldn't imagine giving it up, or how Chongba could have found that option more bearable than continuing. Becoming nothing was the most terrifying thing she could think of— worse even than the fear of hunger, or pain, or any other suffering that could possibly arise from life.

She reached out and touched the amulet. Chongba had become nothing. *If he took my fate and died . . . then perhaps I can take his, and live.*

Her worst fear might be of becoming nothing, but that didn't stop her from being afraid of what might lie ahead. Her hands shook so badly that it took her a long time to undress the corpse. She took off her skirt and put on Chongba's knee-length robe and trousers; untied her hair buns so her hair fell loose like a boy's; and finally took the amulet from his throat and fastened it around her own.

When she finished she rose and pushed the two bodies into the grave. The father embracing the son to the last. It was hard to cover them; the yellow earth floated out of the grave and made shining clouds under the moon. The girl laid her hoe down. She straightened—then recoiled with horror as her eyes fell upon the two motionless figures on the other side of the filled grave.

It could have been them, alive again. Her father and brother standing in the moonlight. But as instinctively as a new-hatched bird knows a fox, she recognized the terrible presence of something that didn't—*couldn't*—belong to the ordinary human world. Her body shrank and flooded with fear as she saw the dead.

The ghosts of her father and brother were different from how they had been when alive. Their brown skin had grown pale and powdery, as if brushed with ashes, and they wore rags of bleached-bone white. Instead of being bound in its usual top-knot, her father's hair hung tangled over his shoulders. The ghosts didn't move; their feet didn't quite touch the ground. Their empty eyes gazed at nothing. A wordless, incomprehensible murmur issued from between their fixed lips.

The girl stared, paralyzed with terror. It had been a hot day, but all the warmth and life in her seemed to drain away in response to the ghosts' emanating chill. She was reminded of the dark, cold touch of nothingness she had felt when she had heard her fate. Her teeth clicked as she shivered. What did it mean, to suddenly see the dead? Was it a Heavenly reminder of the nothingness that was all she should be?

She trembled as she wrenched her eyes from the ghosts to where the road lay hidden in the shadow of the hills. She had never imagined leaving Zhongli. But it was Zhu Chongba's fate to leave. It was his fate to survive.

The chill in the air increased. The girl startled at the touch of something cold, but real. A gentle, pliant strike against her skin—a sensation she had forgotten long ago, and recognized now with the haziness of a dream.

Leaving the blank-eyed ghosts murmuring in the rain, she walked.

☼

The girl came to Wuhuang Monastery on a rainy morning. She found a stone city floating in the clouds, the glazed curves of its green-tiled roofs catching the light far above. Its gates were shut. It was then that the girl learned a peasant's long-ago promise meant nothing. She was just one of a flood of desperate boys massed before the monastery gate, pleading and crying for admittance. That afternoon, monks in cloud-gray robes emerged and screamed at them to leave. The boys who had been there overnight, and those who had already realized the futility of waiting, staggered away. The monks retreated, taking the bodies of those who had died, and the gates shut behind them.

The girl alone stayed, her forehead bent to the cold monastery stone. One night, then two and then three, through the rain and the increasing cold. She drifted. Now and then, when she wasn't sure whether she was awake or dreaming, she thought she saw chalky bare feet passing through the edges of her vision. In more lucid moments, when the suffering was at its worst, she thought of her brother. Had he lived, Chongba would have come to Wuhuang; he would have waited as she was waiting. And if this was a trial Chongba could have survived— weak, pampered Chongba, who had given up on life at its first terror—then so could she.

The monks, noticing the child who persisted, doubled their campaign against her. When their screaming failed, they cursed her; when their cursing failed, they beat her. She bore it all. Her body had become a barnacle's shell, anchoring her to the stone, to life. She stayed. It was all she had left in her to do.

On the fourth afternoon a new monk emerged and stood over the girl. This monk wore a red robe with gold embroidery on the seams and hem, and an air of authority. Though not an old man, his jowls drooped. There was no benevolence in his sharp gaze, but something else the girl distantly recognized: interest.

"Damn, little brother, you're stubborn," the monk said in a tone of grudging admiration. "Who are you?"

She had knelt there for four days, eating nothing, drinking only rainwater. Now she reached for her very last strength. And the boy who had been the Zhu family's second daughter said, clearly enough for Heaven to hear, "My name is Zhu Chongba."

2

The new novice monk Zhu Chongba woke to a thud so deep she thought it came from inside her own body. Even as she startled it came again, and was answered by a clear tone of such volume that it rang in her bones. Light flared on the other side of the dormitory's window-paper. All around her bodies were in motion: boys already in their trousers and undershirts were throwing on peasant-style short inner robes, then over them the wide-sleeved gray monastic robes, and running for the door. Straw sandals slapped as the mass of them burst from the room like a school of bald-headed fish. Zhu ran at the rear, her gray robe tangling between her legs. To be Chongba she would have to run as fast as he would have run, think faster than he would have thought, look how he would have looked. She was smaller than the boys, but the enveloping robes made her otherwise identical. She touched her newly shaved head. Her hair was too short to even have a nap; it was as unfriendly to her fingers as a scrubbing brush.

As they ran their panted breath and slapping feet added their own music to the pounding of the drum. Gaping as she followed, Zhu thought she could have risen into the Heavenly realm of the Jade Emperor and not found it any stranger. They were crossing a dark courtyard. Ahead rose a towering black-beamed hall, lanterns casting light under the golden eaves. Behind, stairs climbed into darkness. Without the clarity of day the monastery seemed a world without end, vanishing forever upwards into the shadow of the mountain.

The boys joined a serpentine line of monks ascending to the hall. There was no time for Zhu to look around as they entered: monks were peeling left and right from the front of the line, each finding some space particular to themselves and sinking onto crossed legs. Zhu, coming in last, saw the filled hall before her: ranks upon ranks of monks, as evenly spaced and motionless as statues in an ancient tomb.

The drum ceased. The bell rang once more, and was silent. The transition from haste to stillness was as jarring as anything that had gone before. Such was the silence that when a voice finally spoke it was alien and incomprehensible. It was the red-robed monk who had let Zhu in. He was chanting. His pouched lids were as round as a beetle's wings; his cheeks sagged. It should have been a dull face. Instead its heaviness gathered upon itself: it had the potential of a boulder poised high above. Zhu, fascinated, barely breathed. After a moment the monk stopped chanting and other voices took it up, a ringing male murmur that filled even that massive hall. And then a board was struck, and the bell rang, and the monks and novices bolted to their feet and ran out of the hall as one, with Zhu stumbling behind.

The smell announced the next stop before she even saw it. Though a girl, Zhu was a peasant; she had no sensibilities to offend. Even so, the sight of monks and novices pissing and shitting in unison was shocking. Recoiling against the wall, she waited until the last of them had gone before relieving herself, then ran out looking for where they had gone.

The last gray robe was whisking through a doorway. Smell also announced this destination, but infinitely more pleasurably. *Food.* Single-minded, Zhu dashed inside—only to be grabbed by the collar and yanked back out again.

"Novice! Did you not hear the bell? You're late." The monk brandished a bamboo stick at Zhu, and her heart sank. In the long room beyond she could see the other monks and novices sitting on cushions in front of low individual tables. Another monk was setting out bowls. Her stomach panged. For a moment she thought she might not get to eat, and it was a feeling so dreadful it eclipsed even fear.

"You must be new. Take the punishment, or don't eat," the monk snapped. "Which will it be?"

Zhu stared at him. It was the stupidest question she had ever heard.

"Well?"

She held out her hands; the monk lashed them with the stick; she darted inside, panting, and threw herself down at an empty table beside the nearest novice. A bowl was laid before her. She lunged at it. It was the best food she had ever eaten; she thought she could never get enough. Chewy barley and sour mustard greens and radish stewed in sweet fermented bean paste: every bite was a revelation. No sooner had she finished than the serving monk poured water into her bowl. Following the other novices, Zhu gulped the water and wiped the bowl out with the hem of her robe. The monk came around again to take the bowls. The whole process of eating and cleaning had taken less time than it took to boil a pot of water for tea. Then the adult monks rose and stampeded away in their intense hurry to go somewhere and probably sit in silence again.

As she rose with the other novices, Zhu became aware of her stomach hurting in an unfamiliar way. It took her a few moments to understand what it was. *Full,* she thought, astonished. And for the first time since leaving Zhongli village—for the first time since her father had offered her up to the bandits and she had learned what nothingness really meant—she believed she could survive.

The novices, who ranged from small boys to grown men of nearly twenty, split into groups according to age. Zhu hurried up flight after flight of stone stairs behind the youngest novices. Her breath plumed against a crisp blue dawn. The mountain's tangled green slope climbed alongside them. The taste of it landed on Zhu's tongue: a rich, heady fizz of life and decay that was unlike anything she'd ever known.

From somewhere far beneath came a rhythmic wooden clacking, then the call of the bell. Now that there was light enough to see, Zhu saw the monastery was a series of terraces carved into the mountainside, each one jammed with green-roofed wooden buildings and courtyards and a maze of narrow paths between. Incense breathed out of dark recesses. In one recess she caught a glimpse of a pile of bright fruit surrounded by a crowd of white shapes. *More monks.* But even as the thought formed she felt a cold caress run over her shaved scalp.

Her heart hammered, and she was running before she realized it: upwards, away from that dark place. To her relief, a moment later the novices reached their destination on one of the very highest terraces. They stepped out of their sandals and went into a long airy room. The latticed windows had been flung open along one wall for a view of a neatly farmed valley beneath. Inside, about a dozen low tables were arranged on a dark wooden floor that had been polished by so many centuries of use that all Zhu could feel against her bare soles was liquid coolness.

She took an empty desk and felt her fright fading as she touched the curious things on it. A brush made of some kind of soft dark hair, and a white square of something like cloth. *Paper.* A sloping stone dish with a pool of water in the low end. A short black stick that left her fingers sooty. The other boys had already taken up their sticks and were grinding them in the dishes. Zhu copied them, and watched with growing delight as the pool in her dish became as dark as an eye. *Ink.* She wondered if she was the first person from Zhongli village to see these half-magical items the stories had spoken of.

Just then a monk swept in, smacking a bamboo stick into his hand. Split down the middle, the stick's two halves clacked so violently that Zhu jumped. It was the wrong move. The monk's eyes shot to her. "Well, well. Our new arrival," he said unpleasantly. "I hope you have more qualifications for being here than simply being as persistent as ants on a bone."

The monk stalked over to Zhu's desk. Zhu stared up at him in fear, her delight forgotten. Unlike the browned, dirt-encrusted Zhongli peasants, the monk's face was as pale and finely wrinkled as tofu skin. Every wrinkle was angled downwards by scorn and sourness, and his eyes glared at her out of dark hollows. He slapped an object down, making her jump a second time. "Read."

Zhu regarded the object with the looming, inchoate dread she recognized from nightmares. *A book.* Slowly, she opened it and gazed at the shapes running down the lined pages. Each shape was as unique as a leaf. And to Zhu, as comprehensible as leaves; she couldn't read a single one.

"Of course," said the monk scathingly. "A stinking, illiterate peasant, and somehow I'm expected to turn him into an educated monk! If the Abbot wanted miracles, he should have chosen a bodhisattva as his Novice Master—" He rapped Zhu's hand with the stick so she drew it back with a gasp, and prodded the book around until it faced the other way. "How different novice training is these days! When I was a novice we were trained by monks yelling orders at us day and night. We worked until we collapsed, then we were beaten until we got up again, and each day we had only one meal and three hours of sleep. We continued that way until we had no thought; no will; no self. We were only empty vessels, purely of the moment. *That* is the proper teaching of novices. What need does a bodhisattva, an enlightened one, have for worldly knowledge, as long as he can transmit the dharma? But this particular abbot—" His lips pursed. "He has different ideas. He insists on educating his monks. He wants them to be able to read and write, and use an abacus. As if our monastery were nothing more than some petty business concerned only with its rents and profits! But— regardless of how I feel, unfortunately the task of your education falls to me."

He regarded her with disgust. "I have no idea what he was

thinking to let you in. Look at the size of you! A cricket would be bigger. What year were you born?"

Zhu bowed low over her desk, ignoring the way the book's sweet smell made her stomach twinge with interest. "Year of the—" Her voice croaked with disuse. She cleared her throat and managed, "Year of the Pig."

"Eleven! When the usual age of admission is twelve." A new note of vindictiveness entered the monk's voice. "I suppose having received the Abbot's favor makes you think you're something special, Novice Zhu."

It would have been bad enough to be disliked for her own inadequacies. With a sinking feeling, Zhu realized it was worse: she was the personification of the Abbot's meddling in what the Novice Master clearly regarded as his own business. "No," she mumbled. She hoped he could see the truth of it. *Let me be normal.* Just let me survive.

"The correct formulation is: 'No, Prefect Fang,'" he snapped. "The Abbot may have let you in, but this is *my* domain. As Novice Master, it falls to me to decide whether or not you're meeting expectations. Rest assured that I'll give you no special considerations for being a year younger. So be prepared to keep up with the lessons and the labor, or save my time and leave now!"

Leave. Terror surged into her. How could she leave, when the only thing outside the monastery was the fate she had left behind? But at the same time she was painfully aware that she wasn't just a year younger than the youngest novices. *Chongba* was a year younger. She had been born in the year of the Rat, another year after that. Two years younger: Could she really keep up?

Her brother's face swam before her eyes, kingly with entitlement. *Useless girl.*

Some new hardness inside her answered: *I'll be better at being you than you ever were.*

Addressing the desk, she said urgently, "This unworthy novice will keep up!"

She could feel Prefect Fang's eyes burning into her shaved scalp. After a moment his stick came into view and jabbed her upright. He took her brush and swiftly wrote three characters descending from the top right-hand corner of her paper. "*Zhu Chongba*. Lucky double eight. They say there's truth in names, and you've certainly had luck enough! Although in my experience, lucky people tend to be the laziest." His lip curled. "Well, let's see if you can work. Learn your name and the first hundred characters of that primer, and I'll test you on them tomorrow." His sour look made Zhu shiver. She knew exactly what it meant. He would be watching her, waiting for her to fall behind or make a mistake. And for her, there would be no allowances.

I can't leave.

She looked down at the characters drying on the page. In all her life she'd never had luck, and she'd never been lazy. If she had to learn in order to survive, then she would learn. She picked up the brush and started writing. *Zhu Chongba.*

Zhu had never been so exhausted in her life. Unlike the pain of hunger, which at least waned into abstraction after a while, tiredness was apparently a torment that grew only more agonizing as time went on. Her mind ached from the relentless assault of newness and information. First she'd had to learn the song that taught the thousand characters of the reading primer she'd been given by Prefect Fang. After that had been an incomprehensible lesson with the Dharma Master, in which she'd had to memorize the opening of a sutra. Then there'd been an abacus lesson with a stooped monk from the monastery's business office. The only respite had been lunch. *Two meals a day.* It was such an abundance that Zhu could hardly believe it. But after lunch were even more lessons: poems, and the histories of past dynasties, and the names of places that were even farther away than their district seat of Haozhou, which was two full days' walk from Zhongli village and already the farthest place Zhu could imagine. By the end of the day's lessons she could understand Prefect Fang's point: apart from the sutras, she couldn't see why a monk needed to know any of it.

In the late afternoon and early evening the novices did chores. As Zhu struggled up the mountain under a creaking shoulder pole loaded with buckets of water from the river, she might have laughed if she hadn't been so tired. Here she was in this strange new world, and she was carrying water again. The effort of keeping all her learning in her head gave her a panicky, drowning feeling, but this: this she could do.

She had taken only another three steps when one of her buckets suddenly detached itself from her shoulder pole. The unbalanced weight of the other sent her smashing to her knees on the rocky path. For a moment she couldn't even be grateful that the buckets hadn't spilled, or fallen down the mountain; she could only hiss in pain. After a while the pain subsided to a throb and she examined the shoulder pole tiredly. The rope holding the left-hand bucket had snapped and unraveled into a puff of fiber, which meant there was no chance of just tying the bucket back on.

Another water-toting novice came up behind her while she was looking at the mess. "Ah, too bad," he said in a clear, pleasant voice. An older boy of perhaps thirteen or fourteen, to Zhu's starved eyes he seemed outlandishly robust: almost too tall and healthy to be real. His features were as harmonious as if they had been placed there by a sympathetic deity, rather than simply thrown down in a jumble from Heaven like everyone else Zhu had ever met. She stared at him as though he were another architectural marvel of this strange new world. He went on, "That pole probably hasn't been used since Novice Pan left. The rope must have rotted. You'll have to take it to Housekeeping to be mended—"

"Why?" Zhu asked. She glanced at the fiber she was holding, wondering if she'd missed something, but it was the same as it had been: unraveled hemp that would braid back into rope with only a few moments' effort.

He gave her an odd look. "Who else would be able to fix it?"

Zhu felt a sickening lurch, as of the world reorienting itself. She'd assumed that everyone could braid, because to her it was as natural as breathing. It was something she'd done her whole life. *But it was a female skill.* In a flash of insight so painful she knew it must be true, she realized: she couldn't do anything Chongba wouldn't have done. She didn't just have to hide her anomalous skills from the watching novice, but from the eyes of Heaven itself. If Heaven knew who had slunk into Chongba's life—

Her mind shied away from finishing the thought. *If I want to keep Chongba's life, I have to* be *him. In thoughts, in words, in actions—*

She dropped the rope, feeling ill with how close she had come to disaster, then untied the other bucket and picked up both buckets by the handles. She had to suppress a gasp. Without the shoulder pole, they seemed twice as heavy. She would have to come back for the pole—

But to her surprise the other novice picked up the pole and laid it over his shoulders alongside his own. "Come on," he said cheerfully. "Nothing for it but to keep going. Once we dump these buckets, I'll show you where Housekeeping is."

As they climbed, he said, "By the way, I'm Xu Da."

The handles of the buckets cut into Zhu's hands, and her back screamed protest. "I'm—"

"Zhu Chongba," he said comfortably. "The boy who waited for four days. Who doesn't know already? After the third day we were hoping they'd let you in. Nobody has managed even half as long before. You might be small, little brother, but you're as tough as a donkey."

It hadn't been toughness, Zhu thought, only desperation. She said, panting, "What happened to Novice Pan?"

"Ah." Xu Da looked rueful. "You might have noticed Prefect Fang doesn't have much time for people he thinks are stupid or useless. Novice Pan was doomed from day one. He was this sickly little kid, and after a couple of weeks Prefect Fang kicked him out." Sensing Zhu's concern, he added quickly, "You're nothing like him. You're already keeping up. You know, most boys can't carry water to save their lives when they first arrive. You should hear them complain: *This is women's work, why do we have to do this?* As if they hadn't noticed they're living in a monastery." He laughed.

Women's work. Zhu shot him a sharp glance, her insides stabbing in alarm, but his face was as tranquil as a statue of the Buddha: there was no suspicion in him at all.

After Housekeeping—where Zhu received a stroke across the calves for carelessness—Xu Da took her back to the dormitory. Noticing it properly for the first time, Zhu saw a long unadorned room with a row of simple pallets down each side, and on the far wall a two-foot-high golden statue with a thousand hands and a thousand eyes. Zhu stared at it, unsettled. Despite the anatomical impossibilities, she had never seen anything so lifelike. "Watching to keep us out of mischief," Xu Da said with a grin. The other boys were already folding their outer robes and placing them neatly at the foot of their pallets, then climbing in pairs under the plain gray blankets. When Xu Da saw Zhu looking around for an empty pallet, he said easily, "You can share with me. I was sharing with Novice Li, but the autumn ordinations were just the other day and now he's a monk."

Zhu hesitated, but only for a moment: the dormitory was freezing, and it wasn't even winter yet. She lay down next to Xu Da, facing away. An older novice went around and blew out the lamps. Lanterns in the internal corridor lit the dormitory's window-paper from behind, turning it into a long stripe of gold in the darkness. The other novices whispered and rustled around her. Zhu trembled with exhaustion, but she couldn't sleep before learning the characters Prefect Fang had set her. She mouthed the words of the primer song, carefully tracing the shape of each character onto the floorboards with her finger. *Heaven and earth, dark and yellow.* She kept dozing off and jerking back awake. It was torture, but if this was the price to pay—she could pay it. *I can do this. I can learn. I can survive.*

She was on the last line of four characters when the light coming through the window-paper dimmed and changed angle, as if a breeze had rushed through and disturbed the lantern flames. But the night was still. A prickle of fear raised chickenskin under her new clothes, although she couldn't say why. Then, projected against the illuminated window-paper, shadows appeared. People, gliding in succession down the corridor. Their hair hung long and tangled, and Zhu could hear their voices as they passed: a lonely, unintelligible murmur that was familiar even as it made her shudder.

In the days since leaving Zhongli, Zhu had all but convinced herself that the sight of her father and brother's ghosts had been nothing more than a nightmare born of shock and hunger. Now she saw that unearthly procession, and in an instant it was real again. Her fear surged. She thought desperately: *It's not what I think it is.* What did she know about monasteries? There would be some ordinary explanation. There *had* to be.

"Novice Xu," she said urgently. She was embarrassed by the quaver in her voice. "Big brother. Where are they going?"

"Who?" He was half-asleep, his body comfortingly warm against hers as she shivered.

"The people in the corridor."

He directed a sleepy glance at the window-paper. "Mmm. The night proctor? He's the only one out and about after curfew. He makes rounds all night."

Zhu's liver curled with dread. Even as Xu Da spoke, the procession continued. Their shadows were as clear on the windowpaper as trees against the sunset. *But he hadn't seen them.* She remembered the white-clad shapes she'd seen in that dark recess, clustered around the offerings. It had been dark in that space, as it was night now, and she knew from the stories that the spirit world's essence was yin: its creatures belonged to the dark and damp and moonlight. *I can see ghosts*, she thought in terror, and realized her body had clenched around itself so tightly that her muscles ached. How could she sleep now? But just as her fear peaked, the parade came to an end. The last ghost vanished, and the light stilled, and ordinary tiredness rushed back into her with a speed that made her sigh.

Her breath in Xu Da's ear roused him. He murmured with amusement, "Buddha preserve us, little brother. Prefect Fang got one thing right about you. You *stink*. Good thing it's bath day soon—"

Zhu was suddenly wide awake, ghosts forgotten. "Bath day?"

"You missed summer, we used to get one a week. Now we only get one a month until it gets warm again." He went on, dreamily, "Bath days are the best. No morning devotions. No chores, no lessons. The novices have to heat the bathwater, but even then we get to sit in the kitchen and drink tea all day long . . ."

Thinking of the communal latrine, Zhu had a terrible feeling about where this was headed. "Do we all take turns?"

"How long would that take, with four hundred monks? Only the Abbot gets to wash by himself. He goes first. Us novices go last. The water's mud by that time, but at least they let us stay in as long as we want."

Zhu saw an image of herself naked in front of several dozen male novices. She said adamantly, "I don't like baths."

A distinctly human figure entered the corridor and banged a split bamboo stick on the outside of the dormitory door. "Silence!"

As the night proctor strode away, Zhu stared into the darkness and felt sick. She'd thought that to be Chongba, it was enough to do what Chongba would have done. But now, belatedly, she remembered how the fortune teller had read Zhu Chongba's fate in his pulse. His fate had been in his body. And for everything she had left behind in Zhongli, she was still in her own body: the body that had received the nothing fate, and which now saw ghostly reminders of it all around her. The corridor light reflected faintly off the golden statue and its thousand watching eyes. How could she have had the temerity to think she could fool Heaven?

In her mind's eye she saw the three characters of her brother's name in Prefect Fang's slashing writing, with her own shaky version beneath. She hadn't written it, as Prefect Fang had, but only drawn it. An imitation, without anything in it of the real thing.

Bath day wasn't until the end of the week, which in a way was worse: it was like seeing that the road ahead had collapsed down the side of the mountain, but not being able to stop. As Zhu quickly discovered, there was no pause in monastery life. Lessons, chores, and more lessons, and each evening there were new characters to learn, and the previous day's to remember. Even the thought of sharing the night with ghosts wasn't enough to prevent her from falling asleep the moment she let herself succumb to exhaustion, and in what seemed like an instant it was morning devotions all over again. In its own peculiar way, life in the monastery was as unvarying as it had been in Zhongli village.

That morning she and Xu Da were knee deep in a sunken stone trough full of freezing water and dirty sheets: instead of lessons, it was the monastery's twice-monthly laundry day. Now and then another novice brought over a pan of slimy boiled soap beans and dumped it into the trough. Other novices rinsed and wrung and starched and ironed. The courtyard's ginkgo trees had turned yellow and dropped their fruit all over the flagstones, which added an unpleasant smell of baby vomit to the proceedings.

Zhu scrubbed, preoccupied. Even knowing her body anchored her to the nothing fate, she refused to accept the idea that she should simply give up and let Heaven return her to that fate. There *had* to be a way to keep going as Zhu Chongba—if not permanently, then at least for a day, a month, a year. But to her despair, the better she understood her new daily routines, the less opportunity she saw. In a monastery, every moment of every day was accounted for: there was nowhere to hide.

"If they wash *us* less in the cold weather, you'd think we could skip a few laundry days, too," Xu Da grumbled. Both their hands had turned bright red from the icy water, and ached fiercely. "Even spring ploughing is better than this."

"It's nearly lunchtime," Zhu said, momentarily diverted by the thought. Meals were still the bright spots of every day.

"Only someone raised in a famine could get excited by refectory food. And I've seen you looking at those soap beans. You can't eat them!"

"Why are you so sure?" Zhu said. "They're beans; maybe they're delicious." Now that she'd mastered the playful, brotherly tone of the novices' interactions, she found these exchanges pleasing. She couldn't remember ever talking *with* Chongba.

"They're *soap*," Xu Da said. "You'd burp bubbles. I guess it could be worse. This is just a regular laundry day. That time the Prince of Henan visited, we had to do the sheets *and* wash and starch all the monks' robes. You should have heard them rustle afterwards! It was like meditating in a forest." He added, "The rebels visit too, but they're just normal people; they aren't a bother." At Zhu's blank look, he said, "From the peasant rebellion. It's the biggest since before we were born. The Abbot hosts their leaders whenever they're in the area. He says that as long as the monastery stays on everyone's good side, we'll do fine for ourselves until it gets settled one way or the other."

Zhu thought it was a pity she couldn't get on Prefect Fang's good side. Her gloom rushed back in, heavier than ever. She asked miserably, "Big brother, are novices always expelled for making a mistake? Or are they sometimes just punished?"

"If Prefect Fang could get rid of every last novice, he probably would," Xu Da said matter-of-factly. "The only time he bothers with punishment is if you've really annoyed him, and he wants to see you suffer." Together they hauled out a sheet and slung it into the tub for the wringers. "He punished me once, when I was still new. We were fermenting the black bean harvest, and he made me stir the crocks. He made me so nervous that when he came to check on me, I knocked a whole crock onto him." He shook his head and laughed. "Do you know how bad fermenting beans smell? The other monks called him Fart Fang, and they refused to sit next to him for devotions or in the meditation hall until the next laundry day. He was *furious*."

There was a clacking in the distance: the proctor's advance warning for lunch.

"It was the Mid-Autumn Festival after that. Usually us novices climb the mountain to see the monastery all lit up with lanterns. But Prefect Fang made me clean the latrine instead. He said it was fitting that I be the stinky one. And it was ages until the next bath day, too." Xu Da climbed out of the trough and started drying himself off. "But why are you worrying? Even Prefect Fang can't kick anyone out without a good reason. You aren't planning on doing anything wrong, are you?" He grinned at Zhu as the bell rang, and went bounding up the steps towards the refectory. "Come on! We've worked hard enough that even I'm looking forward to brined vegetables."

Zhu trudged behind, thinking. Xu Da's story had dislodged an idea. Whatever the likelihood of success, just having an idea filled her with a stubborn hope that felt more authentic than any despair.

But for all that she told herself it would work, her heart was still pounding as hard as if she had run up every one of the monastery's staircases, with fear.

The other novices clearly found bath day as exciting as the New Year had been to them in their lay lives. In contrast, Zhu woke with a feeling of dreadful anticipation that persisted through the treats of lying abed until the sun rose; taking breakfast in the kitchen instead of the refectory; and endless cups of tea while they stoked the fires under the giant cauldrons of water for the bathhouse.

"Novice!" The kitchen's fire master threw a shoulder pole at her. "The Abbot must be nearly done. Take a couple of buckets of hot water to the bath to warm it for the department heads."

As Zhu caught the pole her sense of the world narrowed to a point of grim focus. *If this is the way, then it's up to me to do it. And I can. I have to.*

Absorbed in her thoughts, she startled when Xu Da came up and took one of her buckets. Probably he had seen her inwardness, but mistook it for exhaustion. "Let me help. You can help me on my turn."

"That just means we both have to make two easier trips, rather than one hard trip each," Zhu pointed out. Her voice sounded strange. "Wouldn't you rather get it over with in one go?"

"Where's the fun in suffering by yourself?" Xu Da said in his good-natured way. Surprised, Zhu realized he was probably her friend. She'd never had a friend before. But she wasn't sure suffering could be shared, even with one's friends. Watching her father and brother die, digging their graves, kneeling for four days in front of the monastery: all of them had been acts of exquisite aloneness. She knew that when it came down to it, you survived and died alone.

But perhaps there was still a comfort in having someone at your side while it happened.

"Took you long enough!" Prefect Fang said when Zhu and Xu Da came into the bathhouse. He and the two other department heads had already shucked their robes and were perched on the side of the sunken tub. Their bodies were as wrinkled as dried dates awaiting the soup; even their male parts seemed to have shrunk until they resembled the Buddha's own retracted organ. The steam swirling around them parted in the draft from the closing door, and Zhu flinched when she caught sight of what else occupied that damp, closed place. Ghosts lined the walls. They hung motionless, though the steam passing through their white-clad forms made them seem to shift and sway. Their blank eyes were fixed aimlessly on the middle distance. They paid no attention to Zhu or the naked monks. Zhu stared at them and forced herself to breathe. The ghosts' death-altered appearance was disturbing in some fundamental way that left her guts in knots, but they didn't seem—dangerous. *They're just a part of the place,* she told herself, feeling an involuntary tremor race through her. *No different from the steam.*

"What are you looking at?" Prefect Fang snapped, and all of a sudden Zhu remembered her purpose. Her pulse crashed back into her awareness. "Fill it quickly, and go!"

Xu Da emptied his bucket into the tub. Zhu made to do the same. Out of the corner of her eye she saw Xu Da's dawning horror, and his outstretched arm as he lunged towards her, but it was too late: she had already let it happen. The slippery bamboo floor snatched her sandals sideways from under her, her arms flailed, the heavy bucket leapt into the bath, and she was pulled in after.

For a moment she hung suspended in a bubble of warm silence. She had the urge to stay underwater, in that safe moment in which there was neither success nor failure. But she had already acted, and she was surprised to find that it created its own bravery: there was nothing else to do but continue, no matter how frightened she might be. Surfacing, she stood.

Xu Da and the three dried-up dates were looking at her with their mouths open. Zhu's robe rose around her like a floating lotus leaf. A corona of dirt worked its way out of it and spread relentlessly through the clean bathwater.

"Prefect Fang," said the Dharma Master repressively. "Why is your novice polluting our bath?"

Prefect Fang had gone so red that the grid of ordination scars on his scalp stood out stark white. He sprang into action with all the wrinkled flaps of his body flying, and in an instant had hauled Zhu out by the ear. She howled in pain.

He flung her across the room, right through the ghosts, and hurled the bucket at her. It smashed into her and knocked her over. "That's right," he said, trembling with rage. "*Kneel.*"

The touch of the ghosts' insubstantial forms was like being pierced by a thousand ice needles. Zhu hauled herself to her knees with a stifled whimper. Her skin stung from the ghosts; her head rang from hitting the floor. She watched dizzily as Prefect Fang struggled to decide what to do with her. And it wasn't just Prefect Fang watching. To her terror she could feel Heaven itself inspecting the shell of Zhu Chongba, as if sensing the presence of an irregularity within. Cold nothingness brushed the back of her neck, and despite the warmth of the bathhouse she trembled until her teeth chattered.

"*You little dog turd,*" Prefect Fang finally snarled. He snatched up the bucket and thrust it at Zhu's chest. "Hold that over your head until the evening bell, and for every time it drops I'll have you beaten one stroke with the heavy bamboo." His wrinkled chest pumped furiously. "As for proper respect for your elders, and care for your work: you can meditate on these principles when you're scrubbing yourself with cold well water. *Bath day is a privilege.* If I ever see, or even hear of you setting foot in the bathhouse ever again, I'll have you expelled."

He looked down at her with sadistic satisfaction. He knew exactly how much novices enjoyed bath day, and what he thought he was taking from her. And had she been any other novice, perhaps it would have been miserable: the never-ending grind of monastery life, with nothing at all to look forwards to.

Zhu shakily picked up the bucket. It was wooden, and heavy. She knew she would drop it hundreds of times before the evening bell rang. Hours of agony, and hundreds of beatings after that. It was such a terrible punishment that anyone else would have cried in fear and shame upon receiving it. But as Zhu raised the bucket overhead, her arms already trembling with effort, she felt her cold and fear burning away in the face of a relief so radiant that it felt like joy. She had done the impossible:

She had escaped her fate.

3

1347, SECOND MONTH

Zhu and Xu Da were perched astride the roof of the Dharma Hall, replacing the winter-damaged tiles. It was a dreamy place to be, suspended between the mackerel sky and a sea of glittering green roofs, their golden finials upcurling like waves. Past the tumble of courtyards, past even the valley, they could see a sliver of the shining Huai plain. All like things being connected, the shape of the clouds told them what that distant land looked like. There where the clouds resembled fish scales were lakes and rivers; there, where the clouds had the shape of shrubs, were the hills. And there beneath the slow-rising blooms of yellow dust: armies.

The sunshine was warm, and Xu Da had taken off his shirt and both robes to work half-naked in his trousers. At sixteen, the hard labor had already given him a man's body. Zhu said a little tartly, "You're asking to die, running around like that." Prefect Fang never hesitated to wield his bamboo on novices who violated the rules of dignified monkly attire. Twelve-year-old Zhu, who felt an existential chill whenever she was forced to acknowledge the fact of her boyish but undeniably not-male body, appreciated Prefect Fang's strictness more than anyone realized. "You think you're that good-looking everyone wants to see you?"

"Those girls did," Xu Da said with a smirk, meaning the village girls who had come, giggling, to make their offerings.

"Girls, always girls." Zhu rolled her eyes. Being younger and not yet hostage to the compulsions of puberty, she found Xu Da's obsession tedious. In her best imitation of the Dharma Master, she said, "Desire is the cause of all suffering."

"Are you trying to convince me you'd be happy joining those dried-up papayas who spend their lives in the meditation hall?" Xu Da gave her a knowing grin. "*They* don't desire. But you, I don't believe it for a moment. Maybe it's not girls yet, but anyone who remembers you coming to the monastery knows you know what it is to want."

Startled, Zhu remembered the desperate, animal need to survive that had driven her to claim Zhu Chongba's life. Even now she could feel it inside her. She had never before connected it to the desire that was the subject of the Dharma Master's lectures. For a moment she felt the burn of that old coal of resentment. It didn't seem fair that while others earned their suffering for pleasure, she should earn hers for nothing more than wanting to live.

Beneath them there was a sudden torrent of noise and light and color. Dozens of soldiers were streaming into the main courtyard, the standard-bearers lofting sky-blue pennants. The soldiers' armor shone, scattering light like water. Zhu had a flash of memory: that dark, sparkling river flowing over the dusty Zhongli hillside, a lifetime ago. The Abbot, distinctive in his red robe, had appeared on the steps of the Great Shrine Hall and was waiting with his hands clasped placidly before him.

"The Prince of Henan and his sons decided to drop by on their way home for summer," Xu Da said, coming over to sit by Zhu on the edge of the roof. Being older, he usually had the better monastery gossip. "Did you know the Hu can't campaign in the summer because they're cold-blooded, like snakes?" He used the term that most Nanren—the people of the south, the lowest of the Great Yuan's four castes—used to refer to their Mongol overlords. *Barbarians.*

"Don't snakes like warmth?" Zhu countered. "When was the last time you saw a snake in the snow?"

"Well, it's what the monks say."

The wind picked up the soldiers' capes, snapping them backwards over their gleaming shoulders. Their rows of round-cheeked faces stared ahead impassively. Compared to the soft monks, the Mongols seemed a breed apart. Not the horse-headed monsters Zhu had imagined long ago upon hearing her father's stories, or even the brutal conquerors of the accounts of Nanren scholars, but shining and inhuman like the offspring of dragons.

A flute note sounded. The Prince of Henan swept across the courtyard and up the steps of the Great Shrine Hall. The lush fur of his cape rippled and flexed like a live animal. A plume of white horsehair bucked at his helmet. He was trailed by three radiant youths. Bareheaded, their alien braids tossed in the wind. Two wore armor, and the third a gown of such gloriously shimmering magnolia purple that Zhu's first thought was that it was made of butterfly wings.

"That must be the Prince's heir, Lord Esen," Xu Da said, of the taller armored figure. "So the one in purple is Lord Wang, the younger son."

Princes and lords: people from the stories, made real. Representatives of the world beyond the monastery, which up until now Zhu had thought of as names on a map. *A world in which greatness exists,* she thought suddenly. When she had stolen Chongba's name and stepped into the discarded shell of his life, her only consideration had been the certainty that he would have survived. After securing that survival for herself, she had all but forgotten the fate Chongba was to have achieved with that life. *Greatness.* In the context of Chongba the word was still as nonsensical as when Zhu had heard it the first time in the light of the fortune-teller's candle. But now as she stared down at those majestic figures, the word "greatness" on her tongue, Zhu was surprised by a jolt of something that vanished the moment she recognized it: the queasy curiosity that people get when they stand in a high place and wonder what it would be like to jump.

Below, the Abbot gestured the Prince and his two sons into the Great Shrine Hall. The Abbot was all smiles until his eyes landed on their companion, the third youth. He recoiled in disgust, and said something in a carrying voice. Zhu and Xu Da watched with interest as an argument started between him and Lord Esen. After a moment the Prince, displeased, barked a command. Then he and his sons together with the Abbot swept into the dark maw of the hall. The doors swung shut. Their companion was left outside, his straight back facing the rows of watching soldiers. Standing there alone in a dazzling sea of pale stone, the sun blazing from his armor, he seemed as cold and remote as the moon. When he finally turned away from the hall—a proud, arrogant movement—Zhu gasped.

The warrior was a girl. Her face, as bright and delicate as a polished abalone shell, brought to life every description of beauty that Zhu had ever read in poetry. And yet—even as Zhu saw beauty, she felt the lack of something the eye wanted. There was no femininity in that lovely face at all. Instead there was only the hard, haughty superiority that was somehow unmistakably that of a young man. Zhu stared in confusion, trying to find something comprehensible in that visage that was neither one thing nor the other.

Beside her, Xu Da said in a tone of mixed fascination and revulsion, "The monks said Lord Esen owns a eunuch he treasures even more than his own brother. That must be him."

Zhu remembered those old stories, gilded with the patina of myth. Even more than warrior kings, the noble and traitorous eunuchs had seemed creatures of another age. It hadn't occurred to her that they might still exist. But now before her, she saw the flesh and blood of him. As she stared, a peculiar vibration started in her liver and spread outwards, as though she were a string sounding in response to its twin being plucked somewhere else in the room. She knew it as instinctually as one knows the sensation of heat, or pressure, or falling. It was the feeling of two like substances coming into contact.

And as soon as she knew it, she felt a cold disquiet. To

resonate in likeness to a eunuch, whose substance was neither male nor female—it was nothing less than a reminder from the world itself of what she tried so hard to deny: that she wasn't made of the same pure male substance as Zhu Chongba. She had a different substance. *A different fate.* She shivered.

"Can you even imagine?" Xu Da was saying. "I heard they don't even have *that thing* anymore." He clutched his own organ through his trousers as if to reassure himself that it was still there. "The Hu don't make many of them, not like our old dynasties used to. They hate the idea of mutilation. For them it's a punishment, one of the worst they ever give."

Monks found mutilation equally abhorrent. On days when the Great Shrine Hall was open to the public, its steps were always crowded with the excluded impure: beggars with faces eaten by disease; men with missing hands. Twisted children; women who bled. Like the women, the young eunuch's particular disqualification was hidden, but his face bore the indelible stamp of his shame.

"The Abbot may like to stay on everyone's good side," Xu Da said. "But I think he also likes reminding them that we have power, too. Even rebel leaders and Hu princes have to respect the monasteries, unless they want to come back in their next lives as ants."

Zhu gazed down at the eunuch's cold, beautiful face. Without knowing how she knew, she said, "I don't think he likes being the reminder very much."

A movement caught her eye. To her surprise, ghosts were flowing through the stationary ranks of the Mongol soldiers. Her hackles rose with unease. Since entering the monastery she had become more accustomed to ghosts—if not exactly *comfortable* around them—but ghosts were yin. They belonged to night and the monastery's dark places, not full daylight where yang was at its strongest. Seeing them out of place was disturbing. In the clear mountain sunshine their white-clad forms were translucent. Like water finding its lowest point, the ghosts moved smoothly across the courtyard, up the steps of the Great Shrine Hall, and drew around the young eunuch. He showed no sign of knowing they were there.

It was one of the eeriest things Zhu had ever seen. Her observations of the spirit world had taught her that hungry ghosts drifted aimlessly without interacting with the living, and only moved with intent if food was offered. They didn't *follow* people. She'd never seen so many ghosts all together in the same place. And still they came, until the eunuch was surrounded.

She watched him standing there for a long time, alone amongst that unseen crowd, his head held high.

1352, SEVENTH MONTH

"Why can I never get it right?" Xu Da said to Zhu. "Help!" Flushed and laughing, he was wrestling with a half-made lantern that looked more like an onion than the lotus flower it was supposed to be. Already twenty-one, he had matured into a strapping young man whose shaved head only highlighted the clean planes of his face. His ordination last autumn was still recent enough that Zhu found it odd to see him in a fully ordained monk's seven-panel robe instead of the simpler novice robes, his scalp marked with ordination scars. He and a few of the other young monks had invited themselves into the novice dormitory—ostensibly to help make the lotus lanterns that would be launched on the river to guide the spirits back to the underworld after their time on earth during Ghost Month. In reality, the young monks' visit had far more to do with the illicit wine that Zhu had made from windfall plums and which was being passed around with much guilty giggling.

After a while Xu Da gave up and leaned on Zhu's shoulder. Looking at her collection of finished lanterns, he said in mock despondency, "All yours look like flowers."

"I don't understand how you're still so bad at it, after all these years. How can you not get even a little bit better?" Zhu said fondly. She exchanged her cup of wine for his sad onion lantern and started rearranging its petals.

"It's not like anyone becomes a monk to fulfil some kind of artistic dream," Xu Da said.

"Does anyone become a monk because they have a dream about never-ending study and manual labor?"

"Prefect Fang, maybe. The joy he gets from manual labor—"

"From seeing *other* people do manual labor," Zhu corrected. She handed him back the fixed lantern. "I'm surprised he's not here right now, counting the number of lanterns we've made."

"Counting *us*, to make sure none of us have gone off to do anything scandalous with the nuns." Nuns stayed at the monastery during the autumn ordinations, all the major festivals, and for the whole seventh month of rituals and dharma assemblies for the spirits of the dead. They were housed in the guest quarters, which were made strictly off-limits to monks, and its boundary was patrolled by Prefect Fang with a diligence verging on the obsessive.

"Given how much he likes to think about us drinking and fornicating, I bet he's having more impure thoughts than all of us put together," Zhu said. In a rather un-Buddhist-like tone she added, "He'll give himself a heart attack."

"Ha! Prefect Fang has a death grip on life. He'll never die. He'll just get more and more dried up, and happily torment every generation of novices until the reincarnation of the Prince of Radiance." According to the Dharma Master, the reappearance of the Prince of Radiance—the material incarnation of light—would signal the beginning of a new era of peace and stability that would culminate in the descent from Heaven of the Buddha Who Is to Come.

"Better watch out for him, then," Zhu said. "Since if anyone's going to get into a scandal with the nuns, it's you."

"Why would this monk want a nun, those bony little fish?" Xu Da laughed. "This monk has all the girls he wants when he goes down to the villages." Sometimes out of habit he fell into the self-deprecating speech that monks used in the outside world. After his ordination he had been assigned to the business office with the job of collecting rents from the tenant villages, and these days spent the majority of his time outside the monastery. Zhu, who had shared a sleeping pallet with him for almost six years, had been surprised to find she missed him.

Reverting back to normal speech, Xu Da said cockily, "Anyway, I'm a full monk now, what can Prefect Fang do to me? It's only you novices who need to worry."

The door opened, prompting everyone to shove their cups up their sleeves, but it was only one of the other novices. "You done yet? Those who want should come down to the river; the Dharma Master's calling for the lanterns."

For most novices, Ghost Month was the most enjoyable time of the year. The monastery was awash in food from laypeople's offerings; the long midsummer days brought warmth into the frigid halls; and even solemn ceremonies such as the lantern launching gave novices the chance to play in the river the moment the monks headed back up to the monastery. It was different for Zhu, who could actually see the denizens of the spirit world. During Ghost Month the monastery *swarmed* with the dead. Ghosts loitered in every shady courtyard, under every tree, behind every statue. Their chill needled her until all she could think about was running outside to scour herself in sunshine, and the constant flickering in the corners of her eyes made her twitchy. The lantern launching ceremony wasn't compulsory, but in Zhu's first year of novicehood she had gone along out of interest. The sight of tens of thousands of blank-eyed ghosts streaming along the river had been enough to put her off for life—and that was even before she learned that the treat of post-ceremony playing in the water involved the loss of more clothes than she could safely countenance.

Somehow, Zhu thought with a sigh, she was always missing out on the fun parts of monastery life.

"Not joining?" one of the other novices asked, coming around to collect the lanterns.

Xu Da looked up with a smirk. "What, don't you know Novice Zhu is afraid of water? He *says* he washes, but I've had my doubts—" Leaping up, he wrestled Zhu to the ground and pretended to look behind her ears. "Aiya, I knew it! Filthier than a peasant."

As he lay on top of her, grinning, Zhu was reminded of her uncomfortable suspicion that Xu Da knew more about her than he let on. He'd always been remarkably prescient about herding the other novices out of the dormitory whenever she'd needed privacy.

Refusing to investigate the thought further, Zhu shoved at him. "You're squashing the lanterns, you clumsy ox!"

Xu Da rolled off, laughing, while the others watched tolerantly: they were all familiar with their fraternal squabbles. As he shepherded the novices out, he called over his shoulder, "At least Prefect Fang doesn't have to worry about *you* getting into trouble with the nuns. They'd get one whiff and run—"

"Run from *me*?" Zhu said, outraged. "We've *just seen* how bad you are with your hands. Any reasonable woman would overlook honest sweat for someone who can actually give satisfaction!"

Xu Da paused at the door and gave her a betrayed look.

Zhu said meanly, "Enjoy!"

Zhu scratched her flaky scalp as she finished the lanterns. Xu Da hadn't exactly been wrong: the summer months made her as sweaty as anyone else, and her bathhouse ban meant she had fewer opportunities to do anything about it. But now at least half the monks were down by the river, and those who weren't were probably at the Buddha Altar doing one last recitation for the spirits. It *was* a hot day. It might be nice to get clean for once.

Years ago Zhu had commandeered a small abandoned storeroom on one of the lower terraces for her infrequent scrubs. A single window, set high in the wall, looked out onto the adjacent courtyard at ankle level. When Zhu had first found the room the window-paper had been missing, but once she'd replaced it she had all the privacy she needed.

She carried the slopping washbasin to the storeroom, feeling a mild dislike at the sight of a few nuns climbing the stairs towards the guest quarters. As she stripped to wash, she was struck by the unpleasant thought that she probably bore more than a passing resemblance to those little bald women. Fully grown at sixteen, she'd turned out on the short side (for a man), and underneath her formless robes her body had changed shape and grown small breasts that she was forced to bind flat. A year ago her body had even started bleeding every month. She might be the novice monk Zhu Chongba, but her body kept the score of the years according to its own inviolable mechanism—an ever-present reminder of the fact that the person living that life wasn't who Heaven thought he was.

As she scrubbed, discomfited, she heard barking. It was the pack of dogs that roamed the monastery, their numbers always increasing because the precept against killing meant the monks couldn't get rid of them in the most effective way. Zhu wasn't sure if animals could actually *see* ghosts, but they could sense them: the dogs were always in a state of high excitement during Ghost Month, and occasionally during the rest of the year she would see a dog yipping cheerfully in the direction of a passing ghost. Outside, the pack came charging into the courtyard. There was a burst of enthusiastic baying; the sound of claws skittering across the flagstones; and then a dog burst through the paper window and landed directly on top of her.

Zhu howled and flailed. The dog did the same, and arrested its fall by scrabbling its claws over the wriggling body beneath it. Yelling with redoubled energy, Zhu threw the dog off, ran to the door and slammed it open, and when the dog lunged in her direction gave it a kick that sent it caroming out the door, still howling. She shut the door, breathing hard and crossly aware of smelling even worse than she had before: mud and fur and what was almost certainly dog piss.

And then the light dimmed, and she looked up to see Prefect

Fang crouched down and peering through the torn window, a look of incredulous outrage on his face.

Prefect Fang vanished. Zhu fumbled her clothes on with hands suddenly numb with cold, her breath and heartbeat roaring, and tied her outer robe just as Prefect Fang rounded the corner and wrenched the unlocked door open with such ferocity that it banged on its hinges like a thunderclap. As he dragged her outside by the ear, Zhu recognized the dreadful touch of the fate she had been running from, and felt fear swallow her whole. Her mind flew frantically. If she fled the monastery, she would have nothing but what was on her back. And without ordination scars or a full monk's robe to prove her monkhood, she would never be accepted into another monastery—and that was even if she survived the journey there—

Prefect Fang pulled her ear. Old monks had no fear of treating novices roughly; it never occurred to them that a boy might resist. He dragged Zhu along the corridor of storerooms, yanking on every door as they passed, a violent preoccupation swelling his features. When they reached the end of the corridor and there were no more doors, he pressed his face up against Zhu's and screamed, "Where is she?"

Zhu stared at him in confusion. "What? Who?" She pulled away and nearly fell when he let go, her ear exploding in pain.

"*The nun!* I know you were with one of the nuns!" Prefect Fang spat. "I saw her *naked*. You were in that storeroom with her! Shamelessly violating the precepts—engaging in sexual contact! Who was it, Novice Zhu? Believe me that I'll have the both of you expelled—"

All at once Zhu's fear was pierced by a wild upwelling that she recognized as the distant cousin to laughter. She could hardly believe it. Prefect Fang had seen what he had been so obsessed with seeing. He had seen Zhu's body, and thought it that of a nun. And yet—even with that luck, she was nauseatingly aware that she hadn't made it out of crisis. For if she denied the charge of violating the precepts, then who had the naked woman been?

"You won't answer?" Prefect Fang's eyes shone: the petty exercise of power was the only pleasure that dried-up body ever felt. "It doesn't matter. You'll never be ordained after this, Novice Zhu. When I tell the Abbot what you've done, you'll be *nothing*."

He grabbed her arm and began dragging her up the stairs in the direction of the upper terrace where the sacristy and Abbot's office were located. As she stumbled along beside him, Zhu gradually became aware of a gathering emotion she had last felt, in its true form, on that long-ago day she had knelt over her brother's body in Zhongli.

Anger.

That rising feeling was so visceral it would have shocked the monks more than any carnal desire. Monks were supposed to strive for nonattachment, but that had always been impossible for Zhu: she was more attached to life than any of them could have understood. Now, after everything she had suffered to live Zhu Chongba's life, it wasn't going to be some bitter, dried-up old novice master who held her down so the nothing fate could catch her. *You won't be the one to make me nothing.* Her determination was as clear and hard inside her as the sound of a bronze bell. *I refuse.*

A few uncaring ghosts hovered under the magnolia trees edging the stairways. Their white clothes and long hanging hair made alternating patches of light and shadow in the dusk. As Zhu followed Prefect Fang up one then another of the steep, narrow stairways, it suddenly occurred to her that, at that particular moment, Prefect Fang was the only one who knew about this incident. Her breath caught. Who would question it if he were to meet an accident? Elderly monks fell down the stairs all the time. Prefect Fang was much larger than she was. But she was young and strong. If he never had the chance to struggle—

But for all her anger, Zhu hesitated. She and the other novices broke the precepts all the time, but any reasonable person understood there was a difference between the minor sins like drinking and sexual contact, and murder.

She was still hesitating as they passed through a mid-level terrace where the scent of sun-ripened plums failed to mask a less pleasant odor. The latrine building had been decorated with bobbing lotus lanterns: clearly some novice hadn't cared too much about pleasing those sponsors who had paid handsomely to have their ancestors' names pasted on the lanterns so their spirits might receive merit. It wasn't the only unpraiseworthy behavior this particular courtyard had seen from a novice, either. Those plum trees were the origin of Zhu's homemade wine, and also where she hid her little cache. The latrine smelled bad enough that nobody ever felt inclined to linger and notice that a clutch of wine jars had replaced all the fallen plums.

The moment Zhu saw the trees, she realized what else she could do. Oh, it would break the precepts. But not *that* precept. Not quite.

She dug her heels in so hard she nearly yanked Prefect Fang over. "Let me go to the latrine."

Prefect Fang gave her an incredulous look. "Hold it."

"Not to piss," Zhu clarified. "Of course *you* wouldn't know. But after you've had, ah, *sexual contact* with a woman it can be beneficial to wash afterward—" She made a descriptive gesture over the relevant area. Then, putting on her most pious expression, she said accusingly, "You wouldn't want to offend the Abbot by hauling me in front of him when I'm *polluted*—"

Prefect Fang recoiled, dropped her arm as if it were red-hot, and scrubbed his hand on his robe. Zhu watched him with a feeling of bitter irony. If the thought of a woman's polluting excretions disturbed him that much, imagine if he knew what kind of body he really touched.

"Go clean yourself, you—you *filth*," Prefect Fang snarled. Underneath his performance of disgust and righteous outrage Zhu sensed a simmering prurience. As she went into the latrine, she thought coldly that it was better to be a flawed monk and desire honestly, like Xu Da. Denying desire only made yourself vulnerable to those who were smart enough to see what you couldn't even acknowledge to yourself.

4

Inside the latrine, Zhu stepped carefully across the excrement-dotted floor slats and gazed up at the ventilation gap between the roof and wall. It was even smaller than she remembered. Before she could doubt her course of action, she leapt. Her outstretched fingers caught the lip; her scrabbling sandals found purchase on the roughly plastered wall; and then she was up. If the effort hadn't left her breathless, she could have laughed: of all the grown novices, only she with her scrawny, non-male body was narrow-shouldered enough to fit through that gap. In another moment she had wriggled through and tumbled headfirst into the soft ground underneath the plum trees. She jumped up, and as quietly as she could, snapped a low branch off the nearest tree. Her heart raced. Would Prefect Fang hear? To her relief, the snap seemed to have been masked by sounds of merriment drifting from the other terraces. The monks who had opted out of the lantern-launching ceremony had finished their sutra recitations and were enjoying themselves. Zhu thought Prefect Fang would certainly disapprove of *that*.

She grabbed one of the wine jars from under the trees and, with the branch in her other hand, sprinted for the stairs. Too soon, she heard a furious shout: Prefect Fang had discovered her escape, and the chase was on. Focus erased all Zhu's higher thoughts. She was prey before the predator, and this was pure survival. Her lungs burned red-hot; her calves ached. The wheeze and whoosh and thud of her laboring body thundered in her ears. She ran with the urgency of knowing that her life depended on it. *I won't leave the monastery. I won't.*

The noise of pursuit faded, but it wasn't a reprieve. Prefect Fang knew she would be running to the Abbot's office to beg for mercy. He would be taking a different route to try to beat her there. And if they *had* been racing there, she didn't doubt he would win. Prefect Fang was slower, but he had been navigating the monastery's maze of courtyards for twice as long as Zhu had been alive. He knew every secret staircase and every shortcut. But Zhu didn't need to win the race to the Abbot's office. She just had to make it to one particular terrace before he did.

A final staircase, and Zhu flung herself onto the terrace with a gasp. An instant later she heard the slap of sandals coming up the staircase on the other side of the terrace. For all Zhu's lead earlier, now she barely had enough time to dash into the shadows at the top of those stairs. She braced herself and hefted her branch—and the instant Prefect Fang's egg-shaped bald head loomed out of the dimness below, swung.

The branch connected with a crack. Prefect Fang crumpled. Zhu's chest constricted in an agony of unknowing. Had she judged it right? She'd had to hit him hard; if he hadn't been completely felled he would have seen her, and known what she had done. That would be the worst possible outcome. But if she'd hit him too hard—

She crouched by his head, and was relieved to feel his breath against her hand. *Not dead.* She stared down at his slack, tofu-skin face and willed him to wake up. The first prickle of panic began in her palms. The longer it took for him to rouse, the higher the chance she would be caught here where she shouldn't be.

After an excruciating interval, Prefect Fang finally groaned. Zhu had never been so happy to hear from him in her life. Careful to stay out of sight, she helped him struggle into a sitting position.

"What happened?" he croaked. He touched his head uncertainly, as if he'd all but forgotten what had brought him running. Zhu saw his hand shaking in pain and confusion, and felt her determination flare bright and harsh inside her. It could work. It *would* work.

"Aiya, you could have hurt yourself," she said, lifting her voice into as high a woman's register as she could manage. Hopefully enough to prevent him from recognizing her. "Where were you going in such a hurry, esteemed monk? You fell. I don't think it's serious. Have this medicine, you'll feel better."

She offered him the jar from behind. He took it blindly and drank, coughing a little as the unfamiliar taste hit the back of his throat. "That's it," Zhu said encouragingly. "Nothing like it for a headache."

She left him drinking from the jar and slipped across the courtyard to the dormitory that flanked the terrace. The oily surface of the window-paper gleamed from within; voices laughed and murmured. Zhu's heart beat faster with anticipation. She took a deep breath, and shrieked as high and loudly as she could, *"Intruder!"*

She was already halfway down the stairs when the screaming started. The nuns, rushing out of the guest dormitory, shrilled accusations at such volume that Zhu could hear them as clearly as if she were still in the courtyard. A *monk*, fallen down with drunkenness! He violated their private space with the grossest lechery in his thoughts; he made a mockery of his oath and was a false follower of the dharma—

Bounding downstairs with a spring in her step, Zhu thought with satisfaction: *Now look who's broken the precepts.*

Zhu and Xu Da stood on the highest terrace and watched Prefect Fang emerge from the Abbot's office. Zhu saw an old man in a peasant's short robe, as different in appearance from their former novice master as a disheveled hungry ghost was from himself when he was alive. After Prefect Fang had been discovered drunk in the nuns' courtyard, the Abbotess had gone to the Abbot in a rage, and he had been immediately disrobed in disgrace. Prefect Fang stood there a moment, uncertain. Then he lowered his head and shuffled down the stairs towards the monastery gate.

He had been innocent, and Zhu had done that to him. She supposed it had been better than what she'd first considered. And it was certainly the outcome she had wanted. She examined her feelings and found pity, but not regret. *I'd do it again,* she thought ferociously, and felt a pulse of something like exhilaration race through her. *This is my life now, and I'll do whatever it takes to keep it.*

Beside her, Xu Da said quietly, "He found out, didn't he? That's why you went that far."

Zhu turned to him in horror. For an instant she had the terrible thought of having to do to Xu Da what she'd just done to Prefect Fang. But then she saw his face was as still as that of a graven bodhisattva—and, like those statues, full of compassion and understanding. Trembling with relief, she realized that deep down, she'd always known he knew. "How long—?"

Xu Da maintained his serious expression, but seemingly not without heroic effort. "Little brother. We shared a bed for *six years.* Maybe the other monks have no idea what a woman's body is like, but I do."

"You never said anything," Zhu said wonderingly. She felt a piercing nostalgia for all those times he must have protected her, while she had chosen not to realize.

Xu Da shrugged. "What difference does it make to me? You're my brother, whatever's under your clothes."

Zhu gazed up at that face that was more familiar than her own. When you became a monk, you were supposed to leave the idea of family behind. It was funny, then, that she had come *to* a monastery, and for the first time understood what it meant.

There was a cough behind them. It was one of the sacristy monks, the Abbot's personal assistants. He bowed slightly to

Xu Da and said, "Monk Xu, excuse the interruption." To Zhu he said sternly, "Novice Zhu, the Abbot sends for you."

"What?" Zhu was gripped by disbelief. "Why?" Of course Prefect Fang would have protested his innocence to the Abbot, and tried to cast whatever blame he could on Zhu. But what credence could be attributed to the allegations of a disgraced monk? The Abbot would never have taken it at face value. Feeling the first flutter of panic, Zhu reviewed her actions in the latrine and nuns' courtyard. She couldn't see the mistake. *It should have worked.* She corrected herself so vehemently that she thought she might actually believe it: *It* did *work. This is something else—*

"Surely it's not anything serious," Xu Da said hurriedly, seeing Zhu's expression. But he looked as sick as she felt. They both knew the truth: in all their years at the monastery, a novice had never had an audience with the Abbot that didn't end in expulsion.

Before they parted Xu Da gripped her arm in silent comradeship. Now as Zhu trudged down the steps, she did feel regret. *I made a mistake,* she thought bitterly. *I should have killed him.*

Zhu had never been in the sacristy before, let alone the Abbot's office. Her shaking feet sank into the patterned carpet; the writhing sheen of the rosewood side tables snatched her eye. Doors opened onto a view of the sacristy courtyard's crape myrtles, their slender stems flickering gold in the emanating lamplight. Seated at his desk, the Abbot seemed larger than Zhu's distant viewings of him at morning devotions had led her to believe, but at the same time smaller, too. For overlaid on her thousands of mundane memories was that elemental first sight of him standing over her like a judging King of Hell as she lay half-frozen before the monastery gate. It was in response to him that she had claimed Zhu Chongba's life for the very first time.

Now the weight of his power bore her down to the carpet, pressing her forehead into the thick pile.

"Ah, Novice Zhu." She heard him stand. "Why is it I've heard so much about you?"

Zhu had a vision of his hand poised coolly over her, as ready to strip Zhu Chongba's life from her as he had been to grant it. A jolt of pure refusal brought her head up, and she did what no novice ever dared do: she stared directly at the Abbot. The effort of even that small defiance was crushing. As their eyes met, she thought it would be impossible for him to miss the desire pouring from her. Her unmonkly attachment to life—her desire to survive.

"This business with Prefect Fang was unfortunate," the Abbot said, seemingly neither offended nor impressed by her boldness. "It burdens me in my old age to have to deal with such things. And the besmirching of your character that he offered upon departure, Novice Zhu! He had quite the sordid tale to share. What do you say to that?"

Zhu's heart, which had clenched the instant she heard Prefect Fang's name, opened in relief. If all the Abbot sought was a denial of Prefect Fang's accusations—

"Esteemed Abbot!" she cried, and bent back to the carpet. Her voice trembled with a sincerity of emotion, which in the absence of factual truth was all she could offer. "This unworthy novice swears upon the four relics that he has never done anything to deserve the imprecations of Prefect Fang. This undeserving one has always obeyed!"

She saw the Abbot's immaculately socked feet stroll around the desk, framed by the swaying gold hem of his robes. "Always? Are you not human, Novice Zhu? Or perhaps already enlightened?" He stopped in front of her, and she could feel his gaze on the top of her head. He went on, softly, "It's interesting. If evidence had not so clearly contradicted my feelings on the matter, I would have believed Prefect Fang never to have taken a drop of wine in his life."

There was knowingness in his voice. It shot a chill through her spleen. ". . . Esteemed Abbot?"

"You really threw him into it, didn't you?" Not waiting for a response, the Abbot nudged Zhu with his toe. "Sit up."

And Zhu, rising to her knees, saw with horror what the Abbot had in his hands.

Two wine jars. The one Zhu had left with Prefect Fang—and its identical twin, last seen amidst merriment in the novice dormitory. The Abbot considered the jars. "It's funny how novices break the precepts in exactly the same ways, generation to generation." For a moment he sounded amused. Then it was gone, and he said harshly, "I don't appreciate being made a puppet for another man's dirty work, Novice Zhu."

Proof she had broken the precepts, in the Abbot's hands. Gripped by dread, Zhu could barely understand how she had dared join the other novices in breaking the minor precepts, believing herself to be just like them. Believing she was actually Zhu Chongba. She thought, agonized: *Maybe this was always going to be when my fate caught me, no matter what I did.*

But even as the thought formed, she didn't—*couldn't*—believe it. "Esteemed Abbot!" she cried, flinging herself down again. "There's been a mistake—"

"Strange, that's what Prefect Fang said." In the Abbot, displeasure was elemental; it was nothing other than the promise of annihilation. In the pause that followed, Zhu listened to the empty sound of the trees in the courtyard and felt that emptiness creep into her, little by little, for all she fought and wept and raged against it.

Above her, the Abbot made a sound so unexpected that at first Zhu had no idea what it was. "Oh, get up!" he said, and when Zhu jerked a look at him she could only stare in disbelief: he was *laughing.* "I never liked Prefect Fang, that dried-up old papaya. He always bore me a grudge; he thought the most pious monk should have been made abbot." The Abbot raised one of the wine jars and, meeting her eyes over the lip, drank deeply. "Green plums, is it?"

The *Abbot*, violating the precepts—Zhu's mouth fell open.

The Abbot chuckled at her expression. "Ah, Novice Zhu. A pious man would make a poor abbot in these troubled times of ours. Do you think Wuhuang Monastery has survived this long in the midst of Nanren rebellion and Mongol retaliation solely due to the smiling regard of Heaven? No, indeed! I see what needs to be done to keep us safe, and I do it regardless of what a monk should or shouldn't do. Oh, I know I'll suffer for it in my next lives. But when I ask myself if future pain is worth it for this life I have now, I always find that it is."

He crouched and looked Zhu in the eye where she knelt. His drooping skin was held taut on the inside by a thrumming vibrance: the ferocious, irreligious joy of a man who has willingly cast aside any chance of nirvana for the sake of his attachment to life. And Zhu, staring at him in a daze, saw in him a reflection of herself.

"I remember you, you know. You were the one who waited outside the monastery. Four days without eating, in the cold! So I always knew you had a strong will. But what's unusual about you is that most strong-willed people never understand that will alone isn't enough to guarantee their survival. They don't realize that even more so than will, survival depends upon an understanding of people and power. Prefect Fang certainly didn't lack will! But it was *you* who realized that it was possible to turn a greater power against him, and who did so without hesitation.

"You think about how the world works, Novice Zhu, and that—that interests me."

He was looking at her as intently as anyone had ever looked at her. She shuddered under it, her fear as present as a raptor's shadow. Even as his interest seemed to offer a way out of expulsion, it felt dangerous beyond belief that someone should see something of *her*. The only part of Zhu Chongba that had ever been uniquely hers: the determination to live.

The Abbot said contemplatively, "Outside our walls, chaos and violence are increasing. As time goes on, it grows harder and harder for us to maintain our position between the rebels and the Mongols. Why do you think I'm so determined for my monks be educated? It isn't strength, but knowledge, that will be our best tool for surviving these difficult times ahead. Our task will be to secure our wealth and our position in the world. For that, I need monks who have the intellect and the desire to understand how the world works, and the disposition to manipulate it to our advantage. Monks who can do what needs to be done."

He stood and looked down at her. "Few monks have this kind of character. But you, Novice Zhu: you have potential. Why don't you come work for me until your ordination? I'll teach you everything you wouldn't learn from whichever pious monk I'll choose to replace Prefect Fang. Learn from me how the world really works." A knowing smile creased the Abbot's massive features. "If that's something you want."

Will alone isn't enough to guarantee survival. With the existential fear of her encounter with Prefect Fang still in her bones, Zhu didn't need to think twice about her answer.

This time she didn't grovel, and her voice didn't shake. Looking up at the Abbot, she cried out, "This undeserving one offers his gratitude for whatever knowledge the Esteemed Abbot deigns to bestow upon him. He promises to do whatever needs to be done!"

The Abbot laughed and went back to his desk. "Ah, Novice Zhu. Don't promise yet, before you know what that might be."

1354, NINTH MONTH

It was still dark, no later than the Tiger hour, when Zhu woke to a fumbling at the door of her small room in the sacristy. After a moment Xu Da came in and sat on the edge of her pallet.

"I can't believe they're letting you sleep the night before your ordination," he said severely. "Prefect Fang made us meditate all night."

Zhu sat up and laughed. "Well, Prefect Fang is gone. And why do you always act like your own ordination was *so long ago*? You're only twenty-three!" Technically Zhu was nineteen— still a year shy of ordination age—but as with most differences between herself and the Zhu Chongba who would have been twenty, she avoided thinking about it too much. More than two uneventful years since the incident with Prefect Fang, she still felt uneasy that any acknowledgment of difference, even within her own mind, might be enough to alert Heaven that not all was as it should be. After a moment Zhu's eyes adjusted and she made out Xu Da's straw hat and traveling shawl. "But are you going already? You weren't back for long."

His smile was a crescent in the dark. "Some business has come up. Prefect Wen is involved in the ordinations, so he asked me to handle it. Actually: Can I ask your opinion? One of the tenant villages is refusing to pay their rents. They said the rebels just came and took a tax to support the rebellion, so they're short. Should we insist on payment, or waive it?" Xu Da, like the rest of the monks, knew that Zhu's closeness to the Abbot made her almost as good a source of guidance about the monastery's interests as the Abbot himself.

"It can't actually have been the rebels," Zhu commented. "They've been engaged with the Great Yuan's forces since the start of the month. But probably something did happen: it's a good harvest year, so I don't see why they'd suddenly start pushing back against the rents. Maybe it was bandits pretending to be rebels." The word "bandits" tugged at her memory; she ignored it. "Offer to let them defer payment until next harvest. They should still have enough to plant in spring, if we don't overextend them now. Charge interest, but half the usual rate. You can't expect them to refuse a rebel army, but if they'd had a militia they could have done well enough against bandits. Charging interest should motivate them to put something together."

"They'd have to be braver than me to face bandits," Xu Da said wryly. "Poor fools. But that all makes sense. Thanks." He embraced her warmly before he rose to leave. "I'm sad to miss your ordination, though. Good luck! When we meet again, we'll both be monks."

When he had gone Zhu lit a candle from the hallway lantern and did her ablutions. Her room, usually reserved for an ordained monk holding the position of the Abbot's personal secretary, adjoined the Abbot's. She knocked lightly on his door and, hearing his reply, went in.

The Abbot was standing by the open doors to the terrace. "Novice Zhu," he greeted. "It's early yet. Couldn't sleep?"

"Monk Xu woke me before he left."

"Ah. It's a pity he couldn't be here for your big day."

It was growing light. Birds trilled, and an expansive autumn coolness breathed across the terrace, sharp with the silvery smell of dew on trees. Past the dark valley a line of clouds came in like a wave. In the far distance, a dark blotch marred the expanse of the plain. "Lord Esen is pushing deep into rebel territory this year," Zhu observed. It had been a few years since the aging Prince of Henan had passed command of his army to his eldest son. "Why's he so eager?"

The Abbot gazed pensively at the distant army. "I haven't told you this yet; I only just found out myself. I imagine the Great Yuan is reacting to the news that the Prince of Radiance has been found. By the rebels." He added, "The Red Turbans. That's what they're calling themselves now."

Zhu stared at him, shocked. The Prince of Radiance, the herald of the beginning of the new. His arrival meant a change was coming: something so monumental that it would leave the world transformed. All around the Abbot's room the candles bent under the influence of something even she couldn't see, and she shivered.

"He's only a child," the Abbot said. "But he was witnessed selecting the items belonging to his last incarnation, so his identity isn't in question. No wonder the Mongols are afraid. What else can his presence mean but the end of the Great Yuan? By all reports the Emperor's Mandate of Heaven shines no brighter than a drowning lamp flame, and that's from the last time he dared show it in public. He could have lost it entirely by now. But even if he no longer has the Mandate, he'll hardly give up power. He'll have ordered the Prince of Henan to do everything he can to put down the rebellion this year. And with the Red Turbans made bold by having the Prince of Radiance—the chaos outside will surely worsen before it improves." The strengthening dawn light lit his features powerfully from beneath. He was a man facing a difficult future not with despair, but the bullish confidence of someone who has met headfirst everything that came before, and survived. "Undoubtedly, chaos brings danger," the Abbot continued. "But there will be opportunities, too. After all, it's due to chaos that we're living through a moment in which even ordinary men can aspire to greatness. What are those Red Turban leaders other than ordinary? But they believe they can oppose princes and lords—and now for the first time in centuries, it's true."

Greatness. The word kindled Zhu's dried memories. Feelings rushed into her, hot and alive: the thrill and wonder of her first glimpse of greatness in the majestic figures of the Prince of Henan and his sons, tiny beneath her in the monastery's courtyard. And from an even older memory—a memory from a candlelit room in a village she tried hard to forget—her confusion and sadness upon hearing the word "greatness" for the first time, and knowing that it belonged to a world of emperors and kings and generals that she would never touch.

That was the world of greatness, out there on that distant plain. As Zhu gazed at it, she felt a pull in her middle. It was different from the feeling she'd had as a child of twelve—the abstract curiosity of what it would feel like to jump. This was the feeling of *having* jumped. After the jump, but before the fall: the moment the world gripped your body in preparation for bringing it back to where it belonged. It was the feel of a force that couldn't be overcome by will, that belonged to the world itself. *Fate,* Zhu thought abruptly. She had the unsettled feeling of encountering something beyond her abilities to interpret. It was a pull from a fate in the outside world, where greatness was made.

"How all you young monks chafe for adventure!" said the Abbot, noticing the intensity of her gaze. "Loath as I am to lose your assistance, I can probably give you a year or so of freedom. But I think we can find work more suited to your skills than what your brother Monk Xu does. What do you think: After your ordination, shall I make you Wuhuang Monastery's first emissary to the outside world?"

The pull became stronger; it was a leaching heaviness in her belly. Was it possible that in living as Zhu Chongba for so many years, in having subsumed her every difference until even Heaven believed they were a single person, her fate had changed? But even as the thought came, Zhu knew it was wrong. That heaviness was a promise of the inevitable—and what it stirred wasn't hope, but fear. She looked down from the height of the monastery into that faraway world where chaos and violence boiled under the tidy patterns of green and brown, and knew that as much as that world contained the promise of greatness, it contained the promise of nothingness.

"Esteemed Abbot, are you so willing to curse me with an interesting life?" she said with false lightness, hoping with all her might that Heaven wasn't listening. "I don't need adventure. If you're loath to let me go, why don't you keep me next to you in the sacristy, where I can be of most use?"

The Abbot smiled, pleased. "Ah, that's why you're my favorite, Novice Zhu. Don't fear that a life on this mountain will disappoint! Together we'll weather these changes and guide this monastery into the era of the Prince of Radiance, and afterward the pleasures of peace and prosperity will be ours to enjoy." He added, casually, "And when my time has passed, I'll make it such that you succeed me as the next abbot of Wuhuang Monastery."

Zhu caught her breath. That was a promise indeed. In her mind's eye, she saw the microcosm of the monastery: the administration monks strolling to the business office, the great

sandal-shuffling herd of meditation monks, the laughing novices in the valley's freshly turned fields. The rising green-tiled
roofs and the tilted mountain, all contained under the dome
of the golden sky. A small, safe world. It wasn't something she
wanted so much as it was an escape from what she feared. But
it was something she knew, and would have power over, and
would never have to leave.

She gave a last glance at the outside world. The white bolt
of the sun had risen slantwise to stand atop the tallest peak
of the distant southern mountains, masking the land beneath
in formless dazzle. As she turned away, the bright traces still
dancing in her eyes, she thought:

If you jump, you die.

The Hall of Guardian Kings' four immense statues glared down
at the line of kneeling novices. Behind them, the monks murmured the two hundred and fifty precepts of the monastic oath.
Zhu's sinuses throbbed from the fog of incense smoke that darkened the already dim hall, and her knees were exploding with
pain; they had been kneeling for hours. Choked sounds of a different kind of pain came along the line of novices toward her as
one after another was ordained.

Then the Abbot was in front of her, a special knowingness
in his expression for just the two of them. "Novice Zhu." He
laid cool, restraining hands on either side of her face as the
other monks placed the twelve incense cones upon her head.
Smoke cascaded around her face, its familiar fragrance mixed
with something new: the smell of her own seared flesh. The
pain was like being crowned with burning stars. A grid of light,
burned directly into her brain. As the pain went on it changed
and became transporting. She felt as if she were hovering in an
emptiness in the center of the world, her body's every quiver of
life coming to her from across some vast distance.

"Zhu Chongba, always the different one. You didn't even
scream." The Abbot regarded her with amusement as the monks

pulled her up, supporting her as her legs buckled. Her head glowed with agony. She was wearing only her short inner robe and trousers, and now the Abbot draped the seven-panel robe over her shoulders. It was heavier than the novice robes; the weight of it turned her into someone else. "Monk Zhu—"

"Esteemed Abbot!" They all jumped as a young monk burst in, sweating. As the Abbot turned an incredulous look upon him, the monk threw himself into a reverence and blurted hastily, "A thousand apologies. But—the general of the Prince of Henan's forces is come!"

The Abbot frowned. "What? Why were we not informed of this visit in advance? Where is he now?"

The young monk opened his mouth but a light, raspy voice said, "It's been a long time, Esteemed Abbot."

The light dimmed as the general stepped through the great doors of the Hall of Guardian Kings, and the monks gasped in horror. They recoiled from his defiling presence in fear and anger and disgust, for the Yuan's general was the eunuch Zhu had seen from the roof of the Dharma Hall all those years ago. He had been a youth then, probably younger than Zhu was now. Those years should have turned a youth into a man, but now Zhu had the impression of seeing an echo made flesh: someone as slight and beautiful as he had been all that time ago. Only his girl's face had lost its pure loveliness to become something more unsettling: a sharp, eerie beauty held in as high a tension as the finest tempered steel.

Instead of a normal soldier's leather armor, the general wore metal. His circular chest plate was a darkly glimmering mirror. On each side of his head his hair was braided into the thin loops of a Mongol warrior. As he came closer Zhu saw he was actually of Nanren blood. But that made sense: no Mongol would have borne the humiliation of such a punishment, nor permitted it upon his own.

"You trespass, General," the Abbot said, impolitic with shock. In this, his own domain, he was king—and the blatant offense to his power, in front of his gathered monks, made him hard. "Let me remind you that even the Princes of the Blood are beholden to our rules when they set foot upon these grounds. It is not permitted for you to enter this place."

"Ah, that rule. I'd forgotten," the eunuch general said as he approached. His face was so blank as to give the impression of someone with no inner life at all. "I apologize." He spoke Han'er, the northern language often used by the monastery's visitors, with a jarringly flat accent that Zhu had never heard before. *Mongolian.* Behind him the lamp flames sank, then sprang back in a flare of light, as the ghosts came slipping over the threshold. As he had remained the same, so had they. Zhu's skin crawled. If anything, the sight of their pale forms massing around him was even stranger than it had been the first time. In all the years since—with all the people she had met—she had still never seen anything like it.

As she stared at the eunuch standing there amidst his ghosts, she suddenly felt the half-forgotten twang of a string plucked deep within her. *Like connecting to like.* A searing awareness of her difference from the person she was supposed to be shot through her. But even as she recoiled in rejection of that connection, she felt understanding flowing through it. *Like knows like.* She remembered the eunuch's humiliation at the Abbot's hands those many years ago, and knew instinctively that his blankness concealed a sardonic feeling. He knew perfectly well how his presence distressed and insulted the monks. He was returning pain for pain; he had never forgotten.

The eunuch's gaze moved past the Abbot to the line of singed novices. "But I see I'm interrupting, so let me be brief. In light of recent concerning events, the Great Khan has commanded the empire's defenders to redouble their actions against its enemies. The Prince of Henan desires the monasteries' assurances that he has their support for his endeavor to restore stability to the south." He spoke so neutrally that Zhu thought she was the only one who heard the underlying savage emotion as he added, "I'm sure this monastery, being a loyal subject of the Yuan, will not hesitate to cooperate to the fullest."

Recent concerning events. The Red Turban rebels' discovery of the Prince of Radiance. The Great Yuan, feeling its Mandate of Heaven slipping, obviously feared enough for itself to take steps to remove any temptation for the monasteries to put their wealth and influence behind the Nanren rebels.

The eunuch glanced around the hall, taking in the finely wrought woodwork of the beams and pillars, the golden statues, and the porcelain censers. "How this monastery has prospered since I was here last. Golden halls and roofs tiled with jade! Indeed, Heaven has been smiling upon you." Returning his attention to the Abbot, he said, "The Prince of Henan bids me inform you that this monastery is to henceforth submit two-thirds of its annual revenue from its lands and all other sources directly to the provincial administrator for use in the Prince of Henan's effort against the rebels." He added, blandly, "Given that the aim of monks is to relinquish all earthly comforts, I'm sure this will be no hardship."

Two-thirds. Zhu saw the enormity of that figure hit the Abbot, and his dawning fury. It was a fury without politesse, and to Zhu's alarm she saw that the Abbot, who had always held knowledge as his greatest strength, had no idea that the eunuch bore him a grudge for that past humiliation. All he saw was that beautiful surface, as opaque as white jade.

She stepped forwards, the movement provoking an explosion of agony in her head and knees. Inside the agony was another, smaller pain: the throb of her connection to the eunuch. He turned to look at her, a faint furrow of perplexity marring the cool perfection of his face. *Like knows like,* she thought, disturbed. She said urgently, "Esteemed Abbot—"

But the Abbot didn't hear. Focused upon the Yuan general, he raised himself to his full height. He was a tall, heavy man, and in his anger he towered over the slight eunuch. "Two-thirds!" he thundered. He knew as well as Zhu did that it would leave them beggared. "That the Prince of Henan should send his creature to insult me so!"

"Do you refuse?" the eunuch said, with a terrible quickening of interest.

"Know well, General, that everything a monastery owns is in accordance with Heaven's will. To demand what is ours is to turn your face from the Buddha's blessing. With knowledge of the consequences, will you still proceed down this path?"

Zhu knew what the harsh triumph in the Abbot's voice meant. And why shouldn't the Abbot refuse? It was impossible to defeat a monastery's greatest defense: that any harm to it would be repaid to the perpetrator as suffering, in life after life.

But to the monks' horror, the eunuch just laughed. It was an awful sound, the profaning of all that was sacred. "Esteemed Abbot, are you trying to frighten me? No doubt that threat would have worked well enough on the Prince of Henan, or even my master Lord Esen. But why do you think it was me they sent?" A dark rasp came into his voice: a viciousness aimed at himself as much as at the Abbot. "Do you think someone such as I am has any fear of what suffering you could lay upon me, in this life or the next?"

And with that, Zhu saw his inner self as clearly as if his face were transparent ice. She saw the shame and fury seething underneath the blankness, and with a flash of terrible insight she knew the eunuch had never wanted the Abbot to yield. He had wanted the Abbot to refuse, so he could have the satisfaction of forcing him to feel his power. He had come desiring revenge.

The eunuch general called, "Come in."

Clinking and creaking, the dark river of his soldiers flowed into the hall. Their bodies overlapped those of the ghosts, dark replacing light. It was the outside world penetrating what had been a sanctuary, and Zhu gasped at the sudden agony of being *pulled*. In a blaze of pain she realized the inevitability of what was happening. The monastery was never to have been forever; she was always going to be expelled into that world of chaos and violence—of greatness and nothingness.

Nothingness. She had run from it for nine years, and she

wasn't going to stop now. *There's always a way out.* And the instant she thought it, she knew the way. If the outside world contained greatness as well as nothingness—then the only escape from one was to become the other. Zhu Chongba had been fated for greatness. If she had to be in the outside world, then while she was there she would be Zhu Chongba so completely and utterly that she would achieve his fate, and survive.

Desire is the cause of all suffering. All Zhu had ever desired was to live. Now she felt the pure strength of that desire inside her, as inseparable as her breath or qi, and knew she would suffer for it. She couldn't even begin to imagine the awful magnitude of the suffering that would be required to achieve greatness in that chaotic, violent world outside.

But the eunuch general wasn't the only one unafraid of suffering.

You may have ended this, but you haven't ended me, she thought fiercely at him, and felt the truth of it shining inside her so brightly that it seemed capable of igniting anything it touched. *Nobody will ever end me. I'll be so great that no one will be able to touch me, or come near me, for fear of becoming nothing.*

The eunuch showed no sign of having felt any of her thoughts. He turned his back on the monks and passed through the doors, the ceaseless flow of his incoming soldiers parting around him like a stream around a rock.

He said to them, "Burn it to the ground."

PART TWO

1354–1355

5

HUAI RIVER PLAINS, TENTH MONTH

Autumn mornings on the plains were cool and drab. Under its cap of dung smoke, the Prince of Henan's army encampment bubbled with activity. The eunuch general Ouyang and his second-in-command, Senior Commander Shao Ge, rode toward the infantry battalions. So vast was the camp that it would have made a long walk. Leaving the center where the army's leaders had their round felt gers, they passed the tents of the Semu foreigners who provided the army's expertise in engineering and siege weaponry, then the supply wagons and the herds of livestock, and only after that came to the periphery and the infantry: some sixty thousand conscripts and volunteers from the bottom of the Yuan's social order. These men, Nanren according to the official name of their caste, were the former subjects of the fallen native emperors of the south. The Mongols more often called them the Manji. *Barbarians.*

"Betraying the Great Yuan to join the rebels," Ouyang said as they rode. "He was a good general; I don't know why he did it. He must have known how it would end."

Until last week the newly named Red Turban rebels of the Huai plains had been led by General Ma, a seasoned Yuan general who had defected some years ago. Now he was dead. Ouyang, who had killed plenty of men in his career, found that the old general's face had stayed with him more than most. Ma's last expression had been a despairing realization of the inevitable. As much as Ouyang would have liked to flatter himself that he had been the inevitable, he suspected Ma had been thinking of something else.

"It was a good victory," Shao said in Han'er. Because they were the rare Nanren leaders in a Mongol army, Shao had taken to using Han'er when they were alone together. It was a familiarity Ouyang disliked. "I thought we'd have bad luck after you flattened that monastery, but it seems Heaven hasn't decided to make you eat bitterness quite yet. It must be saving that for later." He gave Ouyang a sly sideways smile.

Ouyang was reminded that he didn't just dislike Shao's familiarity, but Shao himself. Unfortunately, sometimes it was necessary to put up with what one disliked. It was something at which Ouyang was well practiced. Pointedly using Mongolian, he said, "It went easier than expected." Strangely easy, given how slow their headway against the Red Turbans had been in previous seasons. General Ma had been no slouch.

Shao looked resentful: he understood the rebuke. He said in Mongolian, "They'll be even less of a challenge without General Ma. We should be able to cross the Huai and take Anfeng before winter." Anfeng, a small earthen-walled city nestled in a crook of the Huai River, was the Red Turbans' base—though the rebels liked to call it a capital. "And once the Prince of Radiance is gone, that will be the end of that."

Ouyang grunted noncommittally. The Prince of Radiance had attracted popular support like no rebel leader before, but there had been rebellions before him and doubtless there would be rebellions after. Ouyang thought privately that there would be rebellions for as long as there were peasants. And if there was one thing the south had never lacked, it was peasants.

They came to where Commander Altan-Baatar's infantry battalion was quartered along the river on the camp's southern border. A drill was already under way. Subcommanders stood at the head of each thousand-man regiment, shouting the count. The action of thousands of feet upon the earth sent its top layer pluming up into hanging curtains of yellow dust. The Nanren soldiers, massed in their identical armor, wheeled through it like a murmuration of birds.

Altan rode over. "Greetings to the Yuan's finest general," he said, a jibe in his voice. He was bold enough to be disrespectful because he was kin to the Prince of Henan and the son of the wealthy military governor of Shanxi; because his sister was Empress; and because he was seventeen.

"Continue," said Ouyang, ignoring Altan's tone. The boy was only slightly less subtle than his elders in making known his belief that a general should have better qualifications of body and blood. But unlike those seasoned men, Altan was still eager to show off his skills to his superiors. He had a privileged youth's expectation of doing well, of being recognized and raised to his rightful place at the top of the world. Ouyang looked at the knot in Altan's throat, speckled with chicken-skin follicles through which the new beard protruded, and felt revulsion.

The men completed the drill. It had been serviceable; the other infantry battalions had done about as well.

"Inadequate. Again," Ouyang said.

How transparent Altan was. All those expectations laid bare without any idea that he might be hated for them. He watched the emotions race across the boy's face like clouds: surprise, disbelief, resentment. The resentment was particularly satisfying.

The subcommanders were watching them. Frowning self-consciously, Altan turned from Ouyang to relay the order.

The drill was performed once more.

"Again," Ouyang said. He cast his gaze over the men, deliberately passing over Altan's look of naked outrage. "And you may continue to do it, until correct."

"Perhaps if you would tell me exactly what you're looking for, General!" Altan's voice trembled in anger. Ouyang knew he believed himself betrayed. According to the unspoken compact between the Mongol elite, a young commander's efforts should have been rewarded.

Ouyang gave him a contemptuous look. He thought he had never been so young himself. "As this drill is too taxing for your present competence, perhaps we should try another." He glanced at the river. "Take your battalion across to the other side."

Altan stared. The river was at least half an arrow's-flight wide, as deep as a man's chest in the middle, and the day was frigid.

"What?"

"You heard well enough." He let the boy's anger ferment a moment longer, then added, "And have their hands tied before them, to test their balance."

After a long silence, Altan said rigidly, "There will be casualties."

"Less if they have been trained well. Proceed."

The boy's throat worked for a moment, then he yanked his horse around to the waiting subcommanders. Receiving the instructions, one or two of the men glanced to where Ouyang and Shao were watching. From the distance it was impossible to tell their expressions.

The exercise was cruel. Ouyang had intended it to be. Pressed forwards by their screaming subcommanders, cringing under the whips, the regiments waded into the river. Perhaps on a warmer day it would have been easier, but the men were cold and terrified. At the deepest point of the river more than a few were seized by panic, tripped, and sank. The better subcommanders, who had accompanied their men in, pulled these ones up and urged them on with words of encouragement. The worse ones yelled from the bank. Altan, his own horse chest-deep in the water, rode back and forth along the lines. His face shone with ire.

Ouyang and Shao rode across, keeping a safe distance from the turmoil. When all the men had joined them on the far bank, and the unfortunates fished out and revived, Ouyang said, "Too slow. Again."

Upon their return to the near bank: "And again."

The men's resistance peaked at the third crossing; having then grown exhausted, a certain mechanical compliance set in. Those with a tendency to panic had already panicked and been removed, and for the remainder, the terrifying novelty of immersion had become merely unpleasant. "Again."

At noon he called the exercise to a halt. Standing in front of his subcommanders, Altan regarded Ouyang furiously. Most of the subcommanders dripped with mud; a smaller number were dry. Ouyang gazed at the latter. "You," he said to a particularly smug Mongol. "Your regiment did poorly, and you lost a number of men. Why?"

The subcommander saluted. "General! The men are not used to these exercises. Fear makes them slow. The Manji are the problem. Manji are natural cowards. I regret that I have not yet had the opportunity to remedy them of this deficiency."

Ouyang made an encouraging noise.

"They're afraid of cold water and hard work," the subcommander elaborated.

Ouyang adopted a considering air. Then he said, "Subcommander, I noticed you remained on your horse the entire time."

"General!" the man said, puzzled.

"You criticize them of being afraid of cold water and hard work, yet I see no evidence of the opposite in your own actions. You managed to keep yourself remarkably dry while a number of your men drowned. Did you see them struggling and not think to bestir yourself to save them?" Despite his control, some of his natural feelings seeped out; he heard the coldness in his voice. "Was their worth as natural cowards too low?"

The subcommander opened his mouth, but Altan interrupted, "General, I only just promoted him. He is new to his position."

"Surely a promotion is on the basis of skills already possessed? If not, then for what, I wonder." Ouyang smiled at Altan: a blade slipping beneath armor. "No, I think he is not leadership material." He turned to Shao. "Replace him."

"You can't just replace my officers!" Altan almost shouted.

"But I can." Ouyang felt a surge of vicious pleasure. He knew it was petty in the way that people considered character-istic of eunuchs, but sometimes it was difficult not to indulge. "Pick up the dead. Do the necessary to ready your battalion. Be ready to ride out in two days at Lord Esen's order!"

He could hear Altan's muttered imprecations as he left, but there was nothing new in it. "Fuck eighteen generations of that bastard's dog ancestors! How dare he act like that, when he's nothing but a *thing*?"

The ger belonging to Lord Esen-Temur, the Prince of Henan's heir and leader of the Great Yuan's armies in the south, glowed at the center of the camp like a ship at night. Laughter emitted from within its round walls. Ouyang wouldn't have expected anything else: his master was gregarious by nature, always en-joying company more than the contents of his own thoughts. He nodded briefly to the guards and slipped under the doorflap.

Esen looked up from where he was lounging in the middle of a group of commanders. Tall and muscular, with a neat well-shaped mouth under his beard, he was so perfect an example of a Mongol warrior that he resembled the hagiographic por-traits of the great khans even more than the real men them-selves had. "About time!" he said, and waved an easy dismissal to the others.

"My lord?" Ouyang raised his eyebrows and sat. As usual his movement caused a rush of air that made the fire in the cen-tral hearth lean away from him. Long ago a physician had at-tributed it to Ouyang having a surfeit of dark, damp, female yin energy, although that was a diagnosis any fool could have made of a eunuch. "Had you sent a summons?" When he reached for the bag of fermented milk airag at Esen's side, the other passed it across, smiling.

"Summons are fit for a minion who addresses me by title. But I was expecting the pleasure of a friend's company."

The argument over informal address was an old one between them. During Ouyang's rise from slave to bodyguard to Esen's general and closest companion, Esen had pressed to change the language between them, and been resisted equally strongly by Ouyang on the grounds of what was proper. Esen had finally conceded defeat, but continued to use the matter for ammunition whenever possible.

"Expecting?" Ouyang said. "You could have been disappointed. I might have gone to refresh myself first, rather than rushing to brief you. Or we could have spoken tomorrow, which would have avoided my interruption of your gathering."

"I don't regret it; your company brings me three times the enjoyment."

"Should I expect three times the reward for providing it?"

"Anything," Esen said lazily. "I know you're so attached to your armor that you'd sleep in it if you could, but it stinks. I'll give you a new set."

Ouyang had a vain streak when it came to armor: the mirror plates he favored were uniquely recognizable, a bold declaration of his status as a feared general of the Yuan. He said tartly, "My apologies for offending my lord's delicate sensibilities. It seems you would have preferred I change."

"Ha! You'd just be wearing so many clothes that they'd probably do as well against arrows as actual armor. Have pity and take off your helmet; I feel hot just looking at you."

Ouyang made a face and took it off. It was true that when he wasn't in armor, he liked to layer. The easier reason was that he got cold easily, not having ancestors hailing from some miserable frozen steppe. The other reason he preferred not to think about.

Esen himself was newly scrubbed. His deep outdoors tan concealed his naturally ruddy, fair-skinned steppe complexion, but his chest, visible through the gap in his robe, gleamed ivory in the firelight. He sprawled comfortably on the cushions strewn over the rug-covered felt floor. Ouyang sat upright next to him, less comfortable. Armor was not compatible with sprawling; in any case, it was beneath his dignity.

"Heard you put fear of the ancestors into Altan this morning."

"He spoke to you?"

"He knows there's no point complaining to me, if there was anything to complain about. Was there?"

Ouyang smiled thinly, remembering Altan's anger. "The exercise served its purpose. There were a few deaths. Shanxi men. Will it cause problems for your father?"

"Don't worry about it. Pity I was busy; I'd have liked to have watched."

"It was tedious."

"Which part?"

"All of it. No, just the parts involving Altan. Most of it."

Laughing, Esen stretched for the bag of airag. The movement pulled his robe askew and Ouyang caught a brief flash of the shadow between his thighs. He felt his usual sick fascination at the sight. A perfect male body, lived in so casually—its owner never even having given a thought to its wholeness. His mind flinched from any comparison between it and his own mutilated shell.

Not noticing Ouyang's distraction, Esen poured them both drinks. "What of the other battalions?"

Ouyang gave his report. Over the years they had developed a format, which had evolved into something more like a ritual. He enjoyed the feeling of Esen's lazy, pleased attention on him; the familiar sight of him playing with the beads in his hair as he listened.

When he finished Esen said, "My thanks. How would I manage without you?"

"If you asked Altan's opinion: perfectly well."

Esen groaned. "I can't get rid of him; his father is too important."

"He's not stupid. You could probably train him up as a replacement general over the next ten years. Fifteen years."

"I couldn't bear it," Esen said theatrically. His smile happened mainly around his eyes; firelight shone on his barely parted lips. "Don't leave me."

"Who else would have me?"

"That's a promise; I'll keep you to it."

"Do I ever joke?"

"Ha! Nobody would ever accuse you of it." Then, as Ouyang rose to leave: "But won't you stay awhile longer to talk? I can't understand why you have to put that awful bare ger of yours so far away. How can you enjoy being alone all the time?"

Esen never could grasp why Ouyang might choose to keep himself apart, and why he lived with an austerity that bordered on monasticism. Most men who had risen so dramatically in station delighted in luxury, and Ouyang knew Esen would have gladly given him anything he wanted. But what did a eunuch soldier need other than weapons and armor? Ouyang thought of the abbot's scorn, Altan's curses. *Creature. Thing.* A tool that needed nothing, had no desires of its own.

Esen was giving him a hopeful look. Handsome, charming Esen, who was never refused. Ouyang's stomach twisted. But it was only the drink; he had never had a tolerance for strong wine. "It's late, my lord."

He suppressed a guilty feeling at Esen's disappointment. But they would be on the road tomorrow, and Esen was right that Ouyang's armor—and himself by extension—stank. After tonight there would be no further opportunities for bathing until Anfeng, and victory.

The drums sounded. As Ouyang stood at the head of the assembled army, Esen emerged from his ger in his ceremonial armor. His cape was silver fur, which flattered his browned skin. His beard had been trimmed so the column of his throat stood clear and smooth. He strode forwards like a groom to his wedding day, reddened by the dawn light. A warm propitious breeze, unusual for this time of year, carried with it the smells of metal and horses.

Ouyang waited, sixty thousand men at his back. His mirror armor had been polished until it blazed even under the lowering sky. The battlefield beacon that men looked to, or fled in terror.

As Esen drew close Ouyang sank to his knees. Esen's boots paused by his head. Ouyang cried out, his head bowed over that noble instep, "My lord! Give your praise to my lord, the son of the Prince of Henan!"

"Praise the son of the Prince of Henan!" the voices cried.

"My lord! Your army stands ready."

He felt Esen stand straighter, taking in the sight of the massed army. As Ouyang knelt the faint sounds of jingling and creaking washed over him. Even an army standing perfectly still makes a noise. He could see it in his mind's eye: the columns of men covering the plain; the tens of thousands of identical soldiers, receding into an indistinguishable billow of dark metal. A forest of pikes, and above them the endless rows of banners, the pure blue of a flame or the cloudless steppe sky, that heralded the might of the Mongols' empire of the Great Yuan.

"Stand, my general." Rising, Ouyang was lit by Esen's smile. "Your army pleases me. As it pleases me to reward you for it." Esen gestured to an aide. Gift in hand, his smile turned to a smirk. Private and pleased, teasing. He said, "As soon as I beheld her, I knew immediately to whom she was suited."

The gift was a black mare, her neck almost as thick as a stallion's. She swiveled her ears towards Ouyang and whickered the odd greeting that animals gave when meeting him for the first time. She was ugly and powerful and magnificent—and to a people for whom horses were the highest and most treasured good, a gift of kings. Ouyang regarded her with a pang of sadness. It was only ever Esen who thought Ouyang deserving of reward. Who refused to see what everyone else saw.

Their bare hands, exchanging the reins, brushed.

"Ride beside me, my general." Esen mounted his own horse and gazed out. In a ringing voice, he said, "Great army of the Yuan! Forces of the Prince of Henan! Move out!"

Ouyang called the order; it was picked up and repeated by each commander of ten thousand men, each subcommander of a thousand men, each leader of a hundred men. Their voices formed into a flocking and swooping chorus, an echoed song thrumming in a canyon. All at once the mighty army began to move. The light-swallowing columns flowed across the land; the metal crushed the grass and sent up a wave of earthen smell. And the restless banners flew above them: Lord Esen and General Ouyang, side by side at the head of the army of the Great Yuan on its march to the Red Turbans and Anfeng.

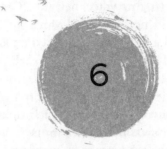

6

ANFENG, SOUTHERN HENAN, ELEVENTH MONTH

Anfeng, the capital of the Red Turban rebels, was a miserable place in the rain. The girl Ma Xiuying trudged umbrellaless through the mud in the direction of Prime Minister Liu's palace. It was a summons everyone had been waiting for: the Prime Minister was finally going to choose the Red Turbans' new general. Ma felt a sick wrench at the thought. Her father, General Ma, had led the rebels to so many victories over the Yuan's southern cities that everyone had come to regard him as infallible. And then, suddenly, he had not only lost, but been killed. Somehow, Ma thought bitterly, none of his trusted men had been there when he had needed them. She imagined her father coming face-to-face with the Prince of Henan's eunuch general and finding himself alone. *Betrayed.* She knew without needing to know that it had been the Prime Minister's doing. Ever since the discovery of the Prince of Radiance, Prime Minister Liu had changed. The Prince of Radiance's promise of victory over the Yuan had made him paranoid. The greater he dreamed his power would be, the more he saw aspirations to his power in everyone else. General Ma had disagreed with the Prime Minister two days before he left to face the Prince of Henan's forces. And now he was dead.

As Ma rounded the corner she caught sight of a familiar tall figure striding ahead in the drizzle. Hardly someone to buoy the spirits, but familiarity was good enough. "Guo Tianxu!" she called, picking up her skirts and running. "Let me walk with you."

"Walk yourself," her betrothed retorted, speeding up. Commander Guo was only twenty-two, but the constant action of his eyebrows swooping crossly over his nose had already worn three vertical lines between them like the word "river." Within Anfeng he was known as Little Guo, which he hated. His father, the Red Turban government's Right Minister, had the privilege of being the original Guo. "You're too slow."

"If you're that worried about being late for the Prime Minister, maybe you should have left earlier," Ma said, annoyed.

"Who's worried?" Little Guo stopped with bad grace. "I just can't stand walking with short people. And even if I were late, do you think the Prime Minister could start the meeting without me? Let him wait."

Ma glanced around hastily to see if anyone else had heard. "Are you crazy? You can't speak about the Prime Minister with that kind of disrespect."

"I'll say what I like. And don't *you* tell me what not to say." Perhaps because Ma had been given into the keeping of the Guo household too many years ago, her relationship to Little Guo was less like an engagement and more like the hostile interactions between siblings from different wives. Resuming a brisk pace, Little Guo said, "It's a pity about General Ma, but it's past time we had some new ideas on how to take this rebellion forward. This is my chance to put them into action."

Ma said slowly, "Are—you going to be the next general?" It made sense and it didn't. Little Guo was neither the most experienced nor most talented of the Red Turban commanders, and everyone but he knew it.

"Who else should it be? The Prime Minister has already promised it to my father." He rounded on Ma. "What, don't you think I'm capable?"

"It's not that. It's just that the Prime Minister has his own ideas about strategy. If you come in wanting to make a mark with all your own ideas—" Remembering her father, Ma felt sick again. "Don't be too ambitious, Guo Tianxu."

"The Prime Minister probably disagreed with your father's idea because he knew it wouldn't work. And it didn't! He knows good ideas when he hears them. And anyway, we have the Prince of Radiance now. As long as we show Heaven we're worthy of its Mandate, how can we lose?"

"We had the Prince of Radiance when my father was defeated," Ma said dully. She knew the presence of the Prince of Radiance on earth promised the beginning of a new era, perhaps even a better one. But if her father being killed was an indication of the kind of change that would be required to get them there, they should all be terrified.

A blare of sound surprised them. A crowd had formed in the middle of the street. Taut with interest, it compressed around a figure buoyed at shoulder height. Then the crowd exploded and the figure came surging forth: not on shoulders, but horseback. Incongruously, it had the shaved head and gray robes of a monk. The horse ricocheted down the street, barging into stalls and provoking a tirade of curses; the crowd's interest reached fever pitch; and then the horse dug in its feet and deposited its baggage into a mud puddle. The crowd screamed with laughter.

The horse, displeased, trotted towards Ma. She stuck her hand out and caught its bridle.

"Hey!" Little Guo shouted, striding over. "You useless turtle eggs!" Seeing their commander, the men lapsed into guilty silence. "You! Yes, you. Bring that—*person*—here."

The monk was fished from the puddle and placed, not roughly, in front of Little Guo. He was young and wiry, with a memorable face. Too broad on top and too sharp below, it resembled that of a cricket or praying mantis. "The Buddha's blessings upon Commander Guo," he said in a light voice, bowing.

"You," Little Guo said brusquely. "What's your purpose in Anfeng?"

"This monk is just a clouds and water monk." A wandering monk, not attached to any particular monastery or temple. "Just passing through. It's nice to see people again, after the countryside." The monk's eyes smiled. "Have you noticed that these days, the people in the countryside aren't really the kind you want to meet?"

"Do you take me for an idiot, to think you're a real monk?" Little Guo glanced at the horse. "Caught with your hands on Red Turban property. I guess that makes you a thief."

"If this monk had managed to get his hands involved, he'd probably have stayed in the saddle longer."

"So a *bad* thief, then."

"We were gambling," the monk said, the smile in his eyes intensifying. He spoke with the educated, self-conscious diction you'd expect from a monk—which only increased the likelihood that he wasn't. "This monk happened to win."

"Cheated, more like. Which makes you—oh, a thief."

"This monk thought he was just lucky," the monk said mournfully.

"Let me remind you what happens to thieves here." Little Guo jerked his head at Anfeng's earthen wall. "*That.*"

The monk took in the row of heads on spikes. His eyes widened. "Ah. But this monk really *is* a monk." Then he fell to his knees. Ma thought he was begging for his life, or perhaps crying, but then she heard the words. He was chanting.

"Oh, for—" said Little Guo, his face creasing in irritation. He reached for his sword, but before he could unsheathe it Ma dashed forwards and grabbed him by the elbow.

"He *is* a monk! Listen!"

Little Guo gave her a poisonous look and extricated his arm. "He's just farting through his mouth."

"Fart—it's the Heart Sutra!" Ma hissed. "How can you not know that? *Think*, Guo Tianxu. If the Prince of Radiance is a sign that we have Heaven's favor, how long do you think that will last if you go around executing monks?"

"*You* know the sutras and you're not a monk," Little Guo said sourly.

"Look at his robe! And do you think he branded his own head for the fun of it?" They stared at the chanting monk. His bowed head bore a grid of round scars, as though someone had laid a red-hot beaded placemat on it. His young face was lit with concentration and tension. For a moment Ma thought the tension was fear, until his dark eyes slid across and met hers. That look, fearless, jolted her. It was then that she recognized the tension for what it really was. It was certainty: the consuming, almost religious focus of someone who refuses to believe that the outcome will be anything other than what he desires.

Little Guo, observing the crowd's credulous expressions as they watched the monk, underwent a visible struggle: the desire to not lose face warring with concern for his future lives. "Fine," he said. Ma winced at his tone; Little Guo was the proverbial hardheaded person who wouldn't cry until he saw the coffin, and developed grudges when cornered. To the monk, he said, "You think this is a place for useless people? This is an army; everyone here fights. I hope your *monastic vows* don't prohibit it."

The monk stopped chanting. "And if they do?"

Little Guo regarded him for a moment, then strode to the nearest unit leader, grabbed his sword, and flung it at the monk. The monk, fumbling, promptly dropped it in the puddle. Little Guo said with bitter satisfaction, "If he insists on staying, put him in the vanguard!" and stomped off.

That was his revenge, of course. The vanguard, made up of the most worthless recruits, existed almost solely to absorb the rain of Mongol arrows that started any confrontation. It was certain death for the monk, and not even Heaven could blame Little Guo for *that*.

The crowd dispersed, leaving the monk scraping mud off his robes. Ma saw he was no taller than she was, and as thin as a bamboo stalk. It was strange to realize he was barely more than a boy; it didn't fit with what she'd seen in him.

"Esteemed monk," she said, handing him the reins, "maybe next time you should learn to ride before winning a horse."

The monk looked up. Ma felt a second jolt: his face was so purely sunny that she realized she must have been mistaken, before. There was no intensity there at all—it didn't even seem like he knew he'd avoided one death only to receive another.

"Is that an offer of assistance?" he asked, apparently delighted. "Or—but you *can* ride?" He assessed Ma's pancake-shaped face, then her big feet. "Oh! You're not a Nanren. You're one of those Semu nomads, of course you can."

Ma was surprised. Of course she was Semu: her father had been a general of the Yuan, and generals were either Mongol or from the Semu caste of steppe nomads and western peoples. In the whole Great Yuan there was only one Nanren general, and everyone knew who *that* was. So the monk was right, but he had seen it in a glance.

He was beaming at her. "This humble student's name is Zhu, esteemed lady teacher. Please give him your instruction!"

The sheer effrontery of it made her laugh. "Too bold! Aiya, so much trouble. Let me tell you something, Master Zhu. Just take your horse and leave. Don't you think you'll stay alive longer that way?" Shaking her head, she gave the horse a pat (it tried to bite her), and walked off.

Behind her, there was squawking: the monk getting dragged along by the horse. She felt a brief throb of pity. Whether in the Red Turban vanguard, or wandering the bandit-filled countryside, what chance did an innocent clouds and water monk have of survival? But then again—in the clash of rebels against empire that was all Ma had ever known, nobody's survival was ever guaranteed.

Ma stood at the back of the Prime Minister's throne room, cradling a teapot. Since Anfeng had never been a capital before the Red Turbans occupied it, it wasn't a real throne room—and it certainly wasn't in a real palace. When the rebels who would become the Red Turbans had taken Anfeng from the Yuan years ago, much of it had been burned, including its governor's residence. As a result Prime Minister Liu Futong ruled the movement from a large but dilapidated two-story wooden house with several courtyards. The throne room had originally been an ancestral shrine, and it still smelled of incense and dried tangerine peel. White mold bloomed on the dark walls. On the dais at the front of the room, the Prime Minister sat on the smaller of the two thrones. Above the frayed collar of his gown his white beard and darting eyes gave him the paranoid, vicious air of a winter ermine. Beside him sat the Prince of Radiance.

In comparison to the Prime Minister, the material incarnation of light and fire shone as brightly as a freshly minted coin in a beggar's hand. A small child of seven or eight, encased in a crisp ruby gown that seemed to glow from within, his presence was ageless. His gaze, reaching them from behind the many strings of jade beads hanging from his hat, was luminous; his smile as graceful and unbending as a statue's. Ma knew he was a real child; he breathed; but in the many months he had been with the Red Turbans, she had never so much as heard those beads click. That serene visage, unchanging but promising change, made her scalp swarm with ants. What did he think about as he sat there? Or did he not think at all, and was only empty: a conduit for the will of Heaven? She shuddered, and the lid on the teapot rattled.

The Red Turbans' senior leadership knelt before the thrones. In the front row, Right Minister Guo Zixing and Left Minister Chen Youliang held identical postures of respect, their bare heads pressed to the floor. The second row contained two of the Red Turbans' three young commanders: Little Guo and his fast friend Sun Meng. The third, Commander Wu, was absent: he had been saddled with the unenviable task of holding their gradually retreating front line against the eunuch general.

The only other absence was General Ma. For all Ma mourned, it was an abstract feeling. She had lived in the Guo household since she was fourteen, and before his death her father had only greeted her in passing as though they were strangers. By then she had already served her use to him: cementing the allegiance between himself and Right Minister Guo.

"Rise," said the Prime Minister, descending from the throne to the sand table they used for planning. He signaled to Ma to pour the tea. When the other Red Turban leaders joined him, he surveyed them with controlled fury. "It's past time for us to have our new general. Not someone who can only win petty skirmishes, but our true leader who will take us to our final victory over the Hu. And make no mistake: he will be someone who puts the Red Turbans' mission before his own ambitions. General Ma—" His mouth pinched shut, but Ma recoiled from his harsh look of intolerance. If she had ever had any doubt, that look erased it: the Prime Minister had seen her father's disagreement as disloyalty. And to punish it, he had been willing to risk everything the Red Turbans had accomplished.

The two ministers exchanged hostile glances. There was no love lost between Chen and Guo. Within the smothering atmosphere of paranoia and secrets that the Prime Minister cultivated, they were two ambitious men trying to hide their ambitions as they jockeyed for power. Guo was the longer follower of the Prime Minister, but now with his ally General Ma gone, his position was less secure than it had been.

Chen said, "Your Excellency, if this servant may make a humble suggestion: I think Commander Wu has the capacity." In his forties, Chen was some ten years younger than his rival. He had a small neat face with a deep vertical crease on each cheek that put one in mind of a tiger's striped face, as seen from far too close. Neither his scholar's black hat nor his gown offered any illusion that he had ever had such a gentle occupation. Before joining the Prime Minister he had been a warlord known for his brutality. It was he who had taken Anfeng, which was the reason so few of its original structures—and none of its original people—were left.

"Commander Wu is doing well and has proven loyal, but

he is not even twenty," Guo said. "How can such a young man command the forces of our entire movement? It would not be seemly." Like everyone else in the room, Guo knew that Commander Wu lived in Chen's pocket. "Your Excellency, Commander Guo is the natural choice. He has several more years' experience than Wu, and inspires devotion and enthusiasm in the men. You can have full confidence in his abilities against the Hu."

The Prime Minister directed his hard gaze at Little Guo. Apparently Little Guo had been right about the matter having been settled beforehand, since after a moment the Prime Minister said curtly, "Guo Tianxu. Are you the one who will lead us to our triumph over the Hu, where that traitor General Ma failed?"

Little Guo looked as satisfied as if it had been his own doing. He thumped his chest with his fist in a salute of acknowledgment. "I am!"

As Ma leaned between Chen and Little Guo to pour tea, she saw Chen's face flicker with an emotion even milder than disappointment. He hadn't expected to win. *Which means he's after something else.*

"Very well, General Guo," the Prime Minister said. "Then prove yourself worthy of the title. Take the rest of our forces to support Commander Wu in holding the line against the Yuan. Our strategy should be one of delay. Resist without sustaining too many casualties, then fall back. Our aim should be to ensure their campaigning season ends before they make it as far as Anfeng. Then we can retake ground over summer."

It was a conservative plan. Even the Prime Minister recognized that his sacrifice of General Ma had weakened their position, especially now that the Yuan were newly determined to press the attack.

"Agreed, Your Excellency," Right Minister Guo murmured.

Chen turned to Little Guo and said smoothly, "General, please provide us with your thoughts on the situation."

Ma saw Little Guo open his mouth. With dread, she realized

Chen's plan. Why engage seasoned and cunning Right Minister Guo, when you could attack the Guo faction's weakest link? Foolish, arrogant, ambitious Little Guo.

Gripped with horror about whatever was going to come out of Little Guo's mouth, Ma flicked the spout of the teapot at his hand. It might even have worked, had an iron grip not wrenched her wrist at the same time. The tea hit the table and Ma swallowed a cry of pain. Chen tightened his fingers around her wrist until tears sprang to her eyes. In a pleasant undertone, he said, "Dear Yingzi, if you scald your future husband every time he opens his mouth, how will we ever hear his worthy input?"

Right Minister Guo took advantage of the pause to say quickly, "Your Excellency, I suggest allowing General Guo the opportunity to review Commander Wu's situation reports. Then we can reconvene."

Chen said, "I'm sure General Guo already has an excellent grasp of the situation. I beg the Right Minister's indulgence to hear his thoughts." He released Ma without another glance. "General, please continue."

Little Guo swelled with pride; he loved the sound of his own voice. Ma could have cried. He had no sense at all. She had *told* him. How could he be so unaware of what had happened to her father—of how thin the line was in the Prime Minister's mind between a reasonable effort to succeed, and punishable ambition? Her wrist throbbed, and she saw Chen's smug look.

Little Guo said, "Why should we give men and territory to the Hu for nothing in return? And once they've come far enough to see Anfeng, will they really turn around and go home, even if the weather is too warm for their liking? Surely they'll cross the Huai in the hope they can take it quickly. Why should we let them set the terms of the engagement? Their next major obstacle will be the Yao River; we'll have the advantage if we challenge them there. Let's be bold enough to take the fight to them, and send them crawling back to their prince in defeat!"

"Indeed, why not be bold?" Chen purred. "If we trust enough

in our eventual triumph over the Hu, should we not also trust that Heaven will guide our *true* leader to victory in battle?"

"Guo Tianxu," said Right Minister Guo, looking constipated. "Perhaps a more conservative—"

"Conservative!" cried Little Guo, who disagreed with the wisdom that truth is rarely found in the loudest voice. "Will we be conservative until we die of a thousand cuts? For sure they have the larger army, but didn't Zhuge Liang defeat a hundred thousand with a force of only three thousand?"

And that was Little Guo in a nutshell: he had no shame comparing himself to the best strategist in all history.

A bucket put out under the leaking roof played a random tune as the water dripped in. After a moment the Prime Minister said darkly, "If that's your opinion, General Guo, then go forth and lead us into battle at the Yao River. Let the Prince of Radiance bless our worthy endeavors and bring us victory!"

The Prince of Radiance looked down on them with his benign smile. If he knew Heaven's will for the outcome of the forthcoming confrontation, he showed no sign. Ma felt clammy with anxiety. If Little Guo couldn't produce a victory, his difference of opinion would become a matter of loyalty. And for a Prime Minister for whom loyalty was everything, she knew there was no position more dangerous.

She glanced at Chen. The corners of his small mouth were turned up: an expression that conveyed all of the pleasure, but none of the warmth, of a smile.

Inside its walls, Anfeng's hills undulated smoothly under the sprawling camps of tents and shanties in which the Red Turban men lived. All that was left of the original city were ghosts and a handful of two-story mansions, their glowing upper windows rising up in the blue gloom like river ships at night. Zhu stood with her horse and breathed in deeply of the chill air and dung-fire smoke. She had made it to Anfeng, where she wanted to be.

But now that she was here, she could see with startling clarity the dangers ahead on this path she had chosen. The weight of the sword she carried was a reminder of the most pressing of these dangers. She had never held a sword before. She didn't have the first clue how to use one, and she couldn't even ride a horse like Xu Da could. She had learned so much in the monastery, but none of it seemed applicable to the problem of how to survive on a battlefield. The thought sent a fear-spiked anticipation through her, so concentrated and intense that it almost felt like pleasure. She thought: *There's always a way.*

Someone said, "You're the lucky monk."

Zhu, turning, saw a boy's face floating next to her in the dusk. Despite being weighed down by a nose as big as a temple stele, it had a calculating liveliness. The face was framed by loose hair. Since he was clearly old enough to tie it up like a man, Zhu figured it was an attempt to hide ears as large as his nose.

"Aren't you?" The boy gave her a charming smile.

Zhu said, amused, "This monk admits to being a monk. And you are—?"

"I've met fake monks. They know people will just give them food." As an afterthought: "Chang Yuchun."

"My young friend Chang Yuchun, let me give you some inside information: there really is very little free food," said Zhu, thinking of her long, hungry walk to Anfeng. She tipped her head so he could see her ordination scars. "This monk is willing to bet nobody's faked being a monk longer than three days."

Yuchun inspected the scars with prurient curiosity. "Well, lucky monk, you're gonna need that luck. Heard Little Guo loved you so much, he sent you to the vanguard." He gave Zhu an up-and-down look, noting the sword. "I'm guessing you have no idea how to use that thing. Not that it matters, 'cos you're just going to catch an arrow in the first five minutes."

"There actually *are* warrior monks," Zhu said. "I never

particularly wanted to be one until now. But, little brother, how well you seem to know Anfeng! Please give your valued advice to this monk."

Not missing a beat, Yuchun said, "Sell the horse."

"It's my best asset," Zhu protested. "It's my only asset."

"*If* you can ride." He gave her a scornful look. "You're a monk who can't ride, can't fight, and you don't want to sell your horse. Can you do *anything*?"

"This monk can pray. People do say it's occasionally useful." She headed down the street, leading the horse. "This way to the vanguard?"

"Watch it!" The boy steered her around a pothole. "Hey, lucky monk, here's my actual advice. Leave. You think a prayer can stop a Hu arrow?"

"Why do people keep saying *leave*? There's nothing for this monk out there." She spoke lightly, but at the thought of leaving Anfeng she felt a brush of cool nothingness, as fleeting as the touch of a hawk's shadow. Whatever the uncertainties and challenges of this path, rejecting greatness wasn't an option. Down that other path, there was only one ending.

"What exactly is it you think you'll get if you stay? Anyway, the vanguard's over there." Yuchun pointed to a sprawl of campfires in an open field. "But I'm going this way. See you round, lucky monk."

Zhu went on, enjoying her anticipation. She had gone only a small way when there was a flicker in her side vision. The horse snapped, quick as a snake.

"Turtle's anus!" Yuchun dodged the horse and accosted her. "Give it back!"

"What do you—" The purse, flung with some force, smacked into her chest. "Ow!"

"And why'd that hurt?" he shouted. "Because it's *full of fucking rocks*."

"Which is this monk's fault because—"

"Because I ended up with a *purse full of rocks*, while my own purse is somehow missing!"

Zhu couldn't help it: she laughed. Boys of that age took themselves so seriously. It went double for those who'd had to survive off their own wits, and thought the world their fool. Her laughter made Yuchun even angrier. "You fake! Monks don't laugh and they don't steal. I *knew* it."

"No, no." Zhu controlled her twitching mouth. "This monk really is a monk. Perhaps you need to meet a few more, before you know what we're really like." Locating his purse in her inner robe, she examined it. "Wah, little brother! This is impressive." In addition to the copper coins and now almost worthless paper currency, there were six silver taels. "How have you been tolerated so long, thieving in this quantity?"

"Think you're gonna live long enough to tell anyone about it?" Yuchun scowled. "Give it back."

"Are you going stab me?" Zhu asked with interest.

"I should! What if you tell everyone I'm a thief?"

"Everyone already knows you're a thief." For a moment Zhu stopped playing and let her deeper self show. Yuchun blinked uneasily and looked away. She said, "They didn't bother about a kid taking a couple of coins here and there. But you're not a kid any longer. One day soon you'll take something. Probably not even anything important. But that'll be what they kill you for, and then it will be your head on the wall."

There was a flash of fear on Yuchun's face, quickly masked. He snatched the purse back. "Speaking about my fate like you're a fortune-teller! Why would I believe a useless rice bucket like you? Save your concern for yourself. You're the one in the *vanguard*." His lip curling, he gave Zhu a calculating look. "But, monk, don't you think you need someone to show you around? You nearly broke a leg just walking down the street. Keep it up, think you'll even make it to the battlefield?"

"You offering?" Zhu said. She liked the boy's opportunism and defiant spirit, and even his ugly face: they reminded her of herself.

"It'll cost you the horse." He added, "I can collect after you're dead."

"That's the most generous offer this monk has had all day."
The street had grown dark; in the distance, the vanguard's
campfires beckoned. Zhu said, smiling, "Well, little brother.
Why don't you start by helping this monk find where he needs
to go?"

Zhu followed Yuchun through the cramped maze of tents and
campfires in the open field. Every few paces she had to step
around a pile of refuse or a circle of men gambling on crickets.
Her senses reeled from the reek and the noise. She remembered
how the monastery's hundreds of monks had made it seem
a city. This was a hundred times that. She had never seen so
many people in one place before.

The tent city suddenly opened onto a clearing. A raised platform had been erected in the middle of it. Lit by torches along
its edges, it floated forth in the darkness like a blazing ship
above the sea of men jostling beneath.

"What's happening?"

"Blessing ceremony," Yuchun said. "It'll start soon. Don't
you want the Prince of Radiance's blessing before you set off to
your certain death? You should push to the front."

Zhu, looking at the crowd upon which her future depended,
saw a motley assortment of sturdy young peasants in scavenged
armor and the movement's signature red head rags. In a land
where every opportunity for those of Nanren blood had been
closed off, a rebel movement attracted a higher caliber of person than it might have otherwise. But Zhu remembered the
Yuan's beautiful, cold-faced eunuch general, and his soldiers
flowing into the monastery in their identical dark armor, and
felt a chill.

The River of Heaven rose overhead, its immensity threatening to flatten them all to the skin of the earth. Drums beat so
loudly that Zhu felt like they were trying to squeeze her heart
into their rhythm. The crowd thickened, and men began to
howl and shout. And then finally a red-clad figure emerged onto

the stage. Its small size made it seem very far away, as though it were hovering somewhere between Heaven and earth. A child.

The Prince of Radiance came forwards. He wore a serene smile, his hands extended in beneficence. Overhead the wind thumped and rattled the flags against their poles. The men's shouts rose to a new pitch.

And then, suddenly, the child was holding a flame in his hand. Zhu's skin pimpled in surprise. The child hadn't gestured, or made any other movement. The flame had just *appeared*. A red flame, as eerily luminous as a blood moon. As the crowd roared, the flame grew. It ran up the Prince of Radiance's arms and across his shoulders and over the top of his head, until he stood before them shrouded in a deep red fire that instead of repelling the darkness, turned it as lush as sable.

Zhu stood rooted in awe. *The Mandate of Heaven.* Like everyone else, she knew the stories about the Emperor's divine light—the physical manifestation of the right to rule, granted to the Son of Heaven. The light of the Mongol rulers burned blue; that was why the Great Yuan's flag was the color it was. Clouds and water monks passing through the monastery had sometimes spoken of being in Dadu—the capital the Mongols called Khanbaliq—in the early days of the Emperor's rule, and seeing him summon a blue flame with a finger snap. Zhu herself had never intended to leave the monastery, and knew anyway that the Emperor no longer showed his power in public, so she had never thought she would see the Mandate in the flesh. But this was it. The red flame like the setting sun, the color of the vanished Song Dynasty emperors, the last who ruled before the barbarians came.

Suddenly, it made sense why the rebels had taken red as their color. Why they had named themselves for it. Zhu looked up at that glowing figure, and felt a tingle run through the top layer of her skin as if in response to the charged air before a storm. The Prince of Radiance heralded change. Her desire gripped her, as strong and hot as it had been when she was flung from the monastery. *This is where it starts.*

"Don't be too impressed," Yuchun yelled in her ear. "It's just a light; it doesn't do anything."

"Then why is everyone so excited?" Zhu shouted back. But even in the face of Yuchun's cynicism, she thought she could understand. The sight of Heaven's power filled her with a wild energy that felt like the wind at her back as she ran as fast as she could towards the future.

The front line of the crowd crushed forwards, their hands straining for the red light. "Touch the light, get the blessing. They all die anyway, though. I've seen it." A second figure strode onstage. "That's the Prime Minister."

As the Prime Minister approached, the Prince of Radiance extended his hand and sent flames arcing between them. The fire mantled on the Prime Minister's shoulders, and when he raised his arms it spilled down onto the crowd like liquid. He cried, "Witness the Mandate of Heaven that ran in the blood of our last emperors. The light that will extinguish the darkness of the Hu—the light of the new era of the Prince of Radiance!" and the men laughed and cried hysterically in response. They were young men; they didn't believe they could die. And as they stood there in that magical red light, for a moment it seemed impossible.

As Zhu watched the crowd rejoice, she found herself wondering. Presumably the Prince of Radiance's Mandate meant that the Great Yuan would *eventually* fall. But Zhu was a monk; she had read the dynastic histories. History twisted and turned like a snake. When you were in the moment, how could you tell which way it would turn next? There was nothing about the Mandate that promised the rebels this particular victory—or indeed any victory at all.

And alone of all that crowd, Zhu knew exactly what they faced. *Who* they faced. Through that strange quiver of connection to the Yuan's eunuch general, she had seen beneath that carved-jade mask to his shame and self-hate and anger. He had a wound for a heart, and that made him a more dangerous opponent than anyone here realized. He had just defeated the Red

Turbans' most experienced leader, and now he would be determined to do to the rebels what he had done to Wuhuang Monastery.

And that, Zhu thought grimly, would be inconvenient. In times like these the only path to greatness lay via an army, and the Red Turbans were the only army around. Without them, she would be nothing at all.

7

YAO RIVER

Zhu sat with the thief Yuchun at the small cooking fire in front of the tent she shared with the four other members of her squad. For once it wasn't raining, which made it the first dry day in two straight weeks. First it had rained the whole weeklong march from Anfeng to the Yao River, and then it had rained for another miserable week while they waited at the Yao for the Yuan to arrive. Now that the Yuan *had* finally arrived on the other side of the Yao, Zhu wished they were still waiting. Despite all her puzzling over the upcoming engagement, she had yet to come up with a solution that would address both parts of her problem: her own immediate survival in the vanguard, and the likely annihilation of the Red Turbans at the hands of the Yuan's eunuch general. Frustratingly, half measures were useless: to solve one part without the other would leave her either dead, or without an army and her path to greatness, which amounted to the same thing. There *had* to be a solution, but so far all her endless circling had yielded was a headache and a grim feeling of mounting dread.

Zhu stirred the bubbling pot of yellow beans on the fire. As the squad's newest member she had been put in charge of turning their meager rations into something edible. Yuchun, who wasn't a member of the Red Turbans and so didn't receive rations, rented the squad the (presumably stolen) cooking pot in return for a bowl of whatever was cooked in it. Smoke and starchy beans: it was the smell of a life she thought she'd escaped forever. "All we need is a lizard," she said, feeling ironic.

Yuchun gave her a look of disgust. "Ugh, why?"

"Ah, little brother, you must never have been very hungry. You're lucky."

"Luck, ha! I'm smart enough to avoid being in a situation where I'd have to eat a *lizard* to survive," Yuchun said. "Don't even tell me it tastes like chicken."

"How would this monk know?" Zhu pointed out. "There aren't any chickens in a famine, and monks are vegetarian."

"Pork is better," Yuchun said. "Don't tell my ancestors I said that, though; they're Hui." The Hui people's religious avoidance of pork made them an oddity in the pork-obsessed south. "You know, I think I could afford a pig or three. What do you think, lucky monk: When the Yuan kill you all tomorrow, should I take your horse to the coast and open a restaurant?"

"If that's your plan, you should be the one cooking," Zhu said. She tasted a bean and made a face. "You think we'll lose?"

"I hope you'll lose," Yuchun corrected. "The Yuan soldiers won't care about taking your crappy stuff, so that means I get it. The other way round isn't nearly as good."

"Is that so," Zhu said mildly. Despite the eager anticipation the Yuan's arrival had produced in nearly everyone else in the Red Turban camp, she had only become even more certain of the outcome that awaited them if she didn't intervene.

The Yao, running north–south, drained a large dammed lake system into the larger Huai River, which ran east–west. Together, the two rivers made a protective right angle across the northern and eastern approaches to Anfeng. A Tang-era stone arch bridge spanned the Yao directly downstream from the dam. Downstream from the bridge, the Yao spread and became a marshy delta where it joined the Huai. Since the Yao was too wide for an army to cross downstream, and the lake was upstream, the bridge was the Yuan's only way across. The Red Turbans had arrived first and taken control of their bridgehead, so they had the advantage. But looking now at that dusky far shore, Zhu saw the pale smoke from the Yuan's campfires standing up like lines of text on a tomb tablet. Somewhere out there was the eunuch general, perhaps looking back in her direction. And something told her that instead of anticipating the battle like the young Red Turbans, just like her he was feeling the cold certainty of how it would end in his favor.

"The beans will probably take another hour. Maybe you should keep an eye on them while this monk goes to pray," Zhu said, using her usual excuse to wander out of camp to find some privacy for personal functions. In her last years in the monastery she'd had a room of her own, and she'd hardly had to think about her physical differences. Now, forced to find ways of keeping those differences hidden, she hated both the bother and the reminder of the fate that awaited her should she not achieve greatness.

Yuchun took the stirring stick grudgingly. Despite his perpetual presence in the squad, he considered himself a visitor and resented being given menial tasks. "If some Hu is praying for his arrow to hit you, and you're praying equally hard for it not to, don't you think they'll cancel each other out?"

Zhu raised her eyebrows. "Then what happens?"

"You get hit by someone else's arrow," Yuchun said promptly.

"If that's the case, then this monk will pray not to get hit by *any* arrows. Or swords. Or spears." She paused. "What other ways are there to die in battle?"

"Ha, you think you can make a watertight argument to Heaven?" Yuchun said. "Can't pray away your fate, monk."

Zhu left, shaking off the darkness of Yuchun's comment. She was Zhu Chongba, and she was going to achieve greatness, and the only thing she had to concern herself with right now was making that happen. She headed out of camp, relieved herself, then followed the riverbank towards the dam and hiked up to the lake.

From the vertiginous slope on the other side of the lake, a field of giant bodhisattva statues, each three times a man's height, fixed her with their serene regard. Zhu thought uneasily: *Heaven is watching.* According to local legend, the statues had belonged to a long-ago temple that had slipped down the hillside and into the lake's depths, where it had become a home to foxes and other inhuman spirits. Zhu, who had never seen a non-human spirit, had always had doubts about their existence. But there was something about that dark, still surface that made the idea less implausible.

She sat cross-legged on the soggy ground and considered her problem yet again. The best solution would be one that prevented the two armies from meeting at all. Perhaps if she could destroy the bridge—but that was easier said than done. Nothing short of an earthquake could bring down a Tang stone bridge, and this one had already survived five centuries. What could she possibly do against it?

She gazed at the distant statues. For the first time she noticed they were leaning forwards, as if straining to impart some important message. Had they been that way yesterday? Even as she thought it, she became aware of something else new: a murmuring deep within the ground, so low it was more felt than heard, as if the bones of the earth were grinding together. And the moment she realized what that sound was, her circling mind fell quiet under the dreadful relief of having found the solution.

All these years she had given everything to avoid Heaven's notice, for fear of being found living Zhu Chongba's life. Feeling safe had meant feeling hidden, as if she were a crab inside a borrowed shell. But that had been in the small, orderly world of the monastery. Now she saw—terribly—that achieving greatness in the outside world was beyond any person's individual control. It would be impossible without Heaven's will behind it. To succeed, she needed to call on Heaven and have it respond not to her, but to *Zhu Chongba*: the person destined for greatness.

She could hardly breathe. To deliberately attract Heaven's

attention risked everything. She had lived as Zhu Chongba for so long, trying her best not to acknowledge their differences even to herself, but now she would have to *be* him. She would have to believe it so deeply that when Heaven looked, it would see only one person. One fate.

It would be the biggest gamble of her life. But if she wanted greatness—she was going to have to stand up and claim it.

Heaven being far away, certain equipment was needed to catch its attention. Following Yuchun's directions, Zhu led her horse to the far side of the camp where the more senior Red Turbans pitched their tents. In the end it was easy to find who she was looking for. Outside one tent an array of buckets had been set up so they dripped and dropped between themselves. To Zhu's surprise, a box set over one of the buckets sprang open and spat out a bead that went scudding down a wire onto a pile of other beads. It was a water clock. Although she had read about such devices, she had never seen one before: it seemed magical.

The clock's owner came outside and frowned at her. Jiao Yu, the Red Turbans' engineer, had a Confucian scholar's wispy beard and the belabored expression of someone who thought himself surrounded by fools. He said dourly, "Are you a real monk?"

"Why does everyone ask this monk that?"

"I suppose they assume monks took some kind of monastic oath against killing," Jiao said. "You're wearing a sword." He shouldered past.

"It's only that General Guo forced this monk to take it," Zhu said, following Jiao as he went to rummage through a donkey cart piled with scraps of wood and metal. "He said if this monk didn't, he'd put his head on the wall."

"Sounds like General Guo," Jiao grunted. "He's done stupider things than behead a monk. Like: bringing us here for a head-on confrontation with a Hu army that's twice the size and five times better."

"Everyone else seems to think we'll win tomorrow," Zhu observed.

"Everyone else is a white-eyed idiot," Jiao said succinctly. "Having the Mandate is all well and good, but when it comes to practical matters I'd rather place my trust in good generalship and a numerical advantage rather than the likelihood of a Heaven-sent miracle."

Zhu laughed. "A pity we don't have more practical thinkers in our ranks. Well, Engineer Jiao, if you're concerned about tomorrow, I have an offer for you. Don't you think your chances of survival would be better if you had a horse at hand? I presume you'll be here in camp while useless rice buckets such as myself are out on the front line, but if the Yuan prevail—" Zhu lifted her eyebrows. "You'll need an exit strategy."

Jiao's eyes sharpened. She'd read him correctly: he had no intention of being here tomorrow while it all came down around their ears. He glanced at the horse, then gave it a longer second look. "Where'd you find a Hu warhorse?"

"I'm sure it'll be equally happy heading into or away from battle," Zhu said. "I can't ride. But it seems to me that you're educated, and probably from a good family, so I'm sure you can. In return for it, though, I need you to make me something."

When he heard Zhu's specifications, he laughed darkly. "Just the kind of useless thing a monk would ask for. I can make it. But are you sure it's what you want? If I were you, I'd want a weapon."

"I already have a sword I can't use," Zhu said. She handed him the horse's reins. "But if there's one thing monks know how to do, it's to pray so that Heaven hears."

As she walked away, she heard Yuchun's smug voice in her head: *Can't pray away your fate.*

But maybe, she thought grimly, you could pray and claim another.

It was dark by the time Ouyang's men finished making camp. He collected Esen from his ger, and together they rode down to the bridgehead to survey their opponents. On the opposite bank the Red Turbans' campfires burned long lines across the hills like traces of wildfire. The light from both camps reflected off the clouds and silvered the tips of the rushing black water beneath the bridge.

"So this is what their new general likes," Esen said. "A direct confrontation. All or nothing." His mouth never moved much when he smiled, but tiny crescents appeared on either side. For some reason Ouyang always noticed them. "A man after my own heart."

"Don't insult yourself," said Ouyang, who had already received the intelligence on the person in question. "His main qualification is being the son of their so-called Right Minister. His name is Guo Tianxu; he's twenty-two; and by all accounts he's a raging fool."

"Ah well, in that case," Esen said, laughing. "But he has enough brains to have picked this spot for the engagement. It's a good position for them. By forcing us across the bridge, we'll lose our advantages of numbers and cavalry. We won't overwhelm them in a day, that's for sure."

"We'd win, even if we did it that way," Ouyang said. In front of them the bridge's pale stone arches seemed to float in the darkness, giving the illusion that it went on forever. Even a practically minded person like Ouyang could appreciate it as one of the greatest accomplishments of a native dynasty long ended. A slow crawl went up and down his spine. Perhaps his Nanren blood recognized the history of this place. He wondered if he had walked across it in a past life, or even built it with his own hands. It was tempting to think his past lives must have been better than this one, but he supposed that couldn't be true; he must have done something in them to have earned this life and fate.

"So you'll go ahead with the other way?"

"If my lord agrees." Thinking about the bridge had made Ouyang lose the last of his lukewarm enthusiasm for the kind of drawn-out engagement the rebels wanted. "The scouts found a firm section of riverbank about a dozen li downstream. It should be able handle a couple of battalions without turning into a bog."

The Red Turbans clearly considered the Yao uncrossable downstream. It was wide, and as deep as a man's height in the middle. But the rebels were Nanren; they came from sedentary stock. Had they Mongols amongst their number they would have known that any river was crossable with enough determination. Or sufficient lack of care for how many conscripts might be expended in the effort.

"Conditions aren't ideal," Esen said, referring to the rains that had made the river run high and fast. "How long will it take to get the flanking force across and into position?"

Ouyang considered. If not for the rain, he would have sent the force across at night. As it was—"I'll have them start crossing at first light, otherwise the casualties won't be worth it. They can be in place by the beginning of the Snake hour." Halfway between dawn and midday. "By then we'll already be underway with the engagement, but it won't have been going for too long."

"You know I don't mind a bit of hand-to-hand," Esen said. It was an understatement: he loved battle. His eyes crinkled. "We'll just play until the flanking force has finished crossing, then finish it. Ah, it's almost a shame it'll be done so quickly! We'd better enjoy every moment."

For all that Esen's features were as smooth and regular as a statue's, his passions ran too high for serenity. Ouyang always felt a twist to see him like this: bright with anticipated pleasure, the blood of his steppe warrior ancestors pumping through him. There was a touching pureness to it that Ouyang envied. He had never been able to inhabit a moment of pleasure as simply and purely as Esen did. Just knowing that it was transient—that any moment would be drained of its sweetness and vividness once it became memory—made it bittersweet to him even as it was happening.

Feeling a stab under his breastbone, he said, "Yes, my lord."

The commanders woke Zhu and the rest of the Red Turbans before dawn with the order to move into position at the bridgehead. The boy Yuchun had already vanished without a word of farewell, and Zhu assumed Jiao had done the same. For all the men's faith in the Prince of Radiance and his Mandate, the previous day's excitement had muted into anxious anticipation. In front of them the arch of the bridge rose up over the black water and fell away into darkness.

Zhu waited, the clouds of her breath trembling before her. The pale winter light crept into the sky above the high lake and drew back the darkness on the other side of the bridge. The far bridgehead appeared, and behind it row upon row of soldiers. With each moment of increasing light another row emerged behind the last. Back and back, until the whole shore was revealed, cloaked in identical lines of dark-armored men.

In front of that massive army, a figure waited on horseback. His armor swallowed the light, glimmering only on its sharp edges. His looped braids were like a moth's opened wings. And behind him the ghosts, standing between himself and his front line like an army of the dead. *The eunuch general.*

A vibration of connection pierced Zhu so sharply that she caught her breath from the pain of it. Then, reeling, she shoved the pain and connection from her in a surge of anger. She wasn't *like* him—not now, and not ever—because she was Zhu Chongba.

The other Red Turbans, who in previous engagements had always retreated from the Yuan to stay alive and fight another day, suddenly realized that they were about to enter a fight that would last until one side won. And in that instant of see-ing the Yuan army laid before them, they knew it wouldn't be them.

Zhu felt the moment their confidence broke. As a moan rip-pled through the men around her, she glanced up towards the lake, where the smiling, shadowed faces of the bodhisattva stat-ues looked down on the two armies. Then she walked through her side's lines and stepped onto the bridge.

There was a single truncated yawp from her unit captain. The chill of the stone rose through her straw sandals. She felt the heavy weight strapped to her back, and the tiny sharp pains in her lungs and nostrils as she inhaled the cold air. The silence felt fragile. Or perhaps it was she who was fragile, suspended in the pause. Every step was a test of her courage to be Zhu Chongba, and her desire for that great fate. *I want it,* she thought, and the force of her desire pumped her blood so strongly that it seemed a miracle her nose didn't bleed from it. The pressure grew, all but unbearable, crushing her fears and doubts smaller and hotter until they ignited into pure, burning belief. *I'm Zhu Chongba, and greatness is* my *fate.*

She reached the center of the bridge and sat down. Then she closed her eyes and began to chant.

Her clear voice rose out of her. The familiar words gath-ered into a panoply of echoes, until it sounded like a thousand monks chanting. As the layers built, she felt a strange shiver in the air that was like dread manifested outside the body. The hair rose on her arms.

She had called, and Heaven was listening.

She rose, and unslung the gong from across her back. She struck it, and the sound rang across the high lake. Were the statues leaning towards her to hear? "Praise the Prince of Ra-diance!" she cried, and struck the gong a second time. "May he reign ten thousand years!"

The third time she struck the gong, the Red Turbans sprang out of their stupor. They roared and stamped their feet as they had done for the Prince of Radiance himself, hard enough that the bridge shook with it and the gorge roared back in answer.

The eunuch general's only response was to raise his arm. Behind him, the Yuan archers drew their bows. Zhu saw it as if in a dream. Inside her there was only the perfect, blank brightness of belief and desire. *Desire is the cause of all suffering.* The greater the desire, the greater the suffering, and now she desired greatness itself. With all her will, she directed the thought to Heaven and the watching statues: *Whatever suffering it takes, I can bear it.*

As if in answer, the shiver in the air thickened. The Red Turbans fell silent, and the Yuan men swayed so their notched arrows trembled like a forest in a breeze.

And then the slope beneath the statues gave way. Loaded with heavy rain, destabilized by the vibrations of the Red Turbans' stamped and shouted praise, and released by Heaven in response to Zhu Chongba's call. With a long, soft roll of thunder, the trees, rocks, statues, and earth all slid into the lake just as that long-ago temple had done. The black water closed over all of it and stilled. And for a moment there was nothing.

The first person to notice gave a strangled shout. The scale was so enormous that it seemed to be happening slowly: the surface of the lake was lifting. A great black wave, seemingly stationary except for the fact that the sky above it was shrinking and losing its light as the water climbed between the narrow confines of the sheared cliff face and the steep hill on the other side. Its cold shadow fell over them, and Zhu heard its sound: a roar of pure elemental wrath that shook the ground as the wave overtopped the dam and crested, and broke.

For one frozen moment, as the water's roar obliterated every other sound in the world, Ouyang and the monk stared at each other. Ouyang felt a lancing pain—a vibration that pinned him in place, like a spear quivering in a corpse. *Horror,* he thought distantly. It was the pure, unfiltered horror of his realization of what the monk had done, and in an agony of humiliation he knew the monk saw every flicker of it in his face.

With a gasp he wrenched free of the feeling, turned his horse and *ran*.

On every side his men were fleeing for their lives, scrambling away from the riverbank as the great black wave thundered down from the lake. Ouyang and his horse struggled up the churned incline. At the top he turned back. Even having had some idea of what to expect, for a long time he could only stare dully. The destruction had been absolute. Where before there had been a bridge, now there was nothing but a rushing brown flow that came twice as high up the riverbank as it had before. Downstream, ten thousand of Ouyang's infantry and cavalry had either been in the middle of crossing that same river, or else marshaled on low ground waiting their turn. Now, without doubt, he knew they were dead.

Loathing, shame, and anger rushed through him as a series of escalating internal temperatures. The anger, when it finally came, was a relief. It was the cleanest and hottest of the emotions; it scoured him of everything else that might have lingered.

He was still staring at the river when Shao rode up. "General. The situation here is under control. Regarding the others—" His face was pale under his helmet. "There may yet be some survivors who reached the other side before the wave came."

"What can we do for them now, with the bridge gone?" Ouyang said harshly. "Better they drowned and took their horses and equipment with them, than the rebels finding them—"

The loss of ten thousand men in an instant was the worst defeat the Prince of Henan's army had had in a lifetime or more. Ouyang's mind jumped forwards to Esen's shock and disappointment, and the Prince of Henan's rage. But instead of producing trepidation, the exercise made Ouyang's own anger burn brighter. He had told the abbot of Wuhuang Monastery that his fate was so awful that nothing could make his future worse—and for all that this was his worst professional failure, and he knew he would be punished for it, what he had said was still true.

He made an involuntary noise, more snarl than laugh. As he swung his horse around he ground out, "I have to find Lord Esen. Gather the commanders, and issue the order for the retreat."

8

ANYANG, NORTHERN HENAN, TWELFTH MONTH

Ouyang rode silently at Esen's side as they approached the Prince of Henan's palace. In winter they would normally be out on campaign, and the countryside seemed strange under its layer of snow. Located in the far north of Henan Province, the Prince of Henan's appanage sprawled over the fertile flatlands around the ancient city of Anyang. Farms, garrisons, and military studs made a patchwork all the way to the mountains that marked the border between Henan and its western neighbor Shanxi. The appanage had been a gift to Esen's great-grandfather from one of the earliest khans of the Great Yuan. Despite suddenly being in possession of a palace, that old Mongol warrior had insisted on living in a traditional ger in the gardens. But at some point Esen's grandfather had moved inside, and since then the Mongols had lived in a manner almost indistinguishable from the sedentary Nanren they despised.

Their arrival at the gate was greeted by an explosion of activity. Palace servants rushed towards them with the pent-up vigor of a flock of loosed pigeons. Over their heads, Ouyang caught sight of a figure standing in the courtyard with his hands tucked fastidiously into his sleeves. A clot of stillness amidst the chaos, watching. As was his habit, the other had set himself apart: his fussy silk dress was as vivid as a persimmon on a snowy branch. Instead of Mongol braids, he wore a topknot.

His only concession to proper Mongol fashions was a sable cloak, and perhaps even that was only a concession to the cold.

As Ouyang and Esen dismounted and entered the courtyard, the Prince of Henan's second son gave his brother one of his slow, catlike smiles. Blood ran strange in the half-breeds. Despite his narrow Mongol eyes, Lord Wang Baoxiang had the slender face and long nose of the vanished aristocrats of Khinsai, the southern city once called imperial Lin'an. For of course the Prince of Henan's second son was not really his son, but his sister's child, sired by a man long dead and long forgotten except in the name carried by his son.

"Greetings, long-missed brother," Lord Wang said to Esen. As the lord straightened from his shallow genuflection, Ouyang saw his cat's smile had a satisfied edge. In a warrior culture that looked down upon scholars, a scholar naturally took pleasure in seeing defeated warriors coming home in disgrace. With a limp gesture that seemed calculated to annoy, Lord Wang produced a folded document from his sleeve and proffered it to Esen.

"Baoxiang," Esen said wearily. His face had thinned during the return journey. The defeat had been weighing on him, and Ouyang could tell he was dreading his upcoming encounter with the Prince of Henan—although perhaps not as much as Ouyang was. "You look well. What's this?"

His brother spoke lazily, although his eyes weren't lazy in the slightest. "An accounting."

"What?"

"An accounting of the men, equipment, and materiel lost by your beloved general on this campaign, and the cost borne by the estate for the same." Lord Wang gave Ouyang an unfriendly glance. Ever since childhood he had been jealous of the favored position Ouyang had in Esen's attention. "Your warmongering is becoming expensive, dear brother. With things the way they are, I'm not sure how much longer we can afford it. Have you considered spending more time on falconry?"

"How can you have an accounting already?" asked Esen, exasperated. Lord Wang was the provincial administrator, a role he had taken up a few years before. Everyone knew he had done it to spite the Prince of Henan, who despised everything associated with bureaucracy, but nobody could accuse Lord Wang of not having developed an interest in the minutiae of administration. "Even I haven't received a full report yet! Must you have your cursed bead-pushers everywhere?"

Lord Wang said coolly, "It does seem a number of them died crossing a river, downstream from a notably unstable dam, after weeks of heavy rain. I can't think what possessed them to try."

"If you weren't constantly passing off your men as my soldiers, they wouldn't have died!"

His brother gave him a disdainful look. "If losses of assets were only recorded when you returned home, they wouldn't be accurate enough to be useful. And if everyone knew who was responsible for the counting, wouldn't they bribe the counters? Before you even rode into battle, equipment would already be sold and profits in pockets. You might battle for the glory of our Great Yuan, but rest assured that your men prefer an income. This method is more efficient."

"Planting spies," Esen said. "In my army."

"Yes," said Lord Wang. "Once you've made your own accounting, make sure to bring any discrepancies to my attention." He paused, and for an instant Ouyang saw a crack appear in that sheen of satisfaction. "But before you do that, our father the Prince of Henan sends word that he will see us all in his study at the Monkey hour. Why, this will be the first time I've seen in him in months! I usually never have the pleasure. How glad I am indeed for your early return, brother."

He swept away, cloak rippling behind him.

When Ouyang entered the Prince of Henan's study he found Esen and Lord Wang already standing rigidly before their father as he glared down at them from his raised chair.

The Prince of Henan, Chaghan-Temur, was a squat, frog-cheeked old warrior whose beard and braids had already turned the iron gray of his name. In military power within the Great Yuan he was second only to the Grand Councilor, the commander of the capital's own armies. Chaghan had spent most of his life personally leading the fight against the rebellions of the south, and had as much warrior spirit as any steppe-born Mongol. Now even in his retirement he was strong in the saddle and hunted with the vigor of a man decades younger. For failures, weaklings, and Nanren, he had nothing but scorn.

The Prince of Henan's choleric eye fell upon Ouyang. His lips were colorless with anger. Bowing, Ouyang said tightly, "My respects, Esteemed Prince."

"So this is how a worthless creature repays the house that has done so much for him! Having lost me ten thousand men and the gains of an entire season, you dare come into my presence and *stand*? Get down, or I'll put my boot upon your head and put it down for you!"

Ouyang's heart was thumping harder than it ever did in battle. His palms sweated and his body flooded with the sick anticipation of a fight, even as his throat closed with the effort of control. He felt like he was choking with the pressure of it. After a moment's hesitation, he sank down and pressed his forehead against the floor. In the sixteen years he had served the house of the Prince of Henan, Ouyang had never forgotten what it had done for him; it was a memory that lay as close to him as his own mutilated skin. He remembered it with every beat of his heart.

"When my son came and asked me to make you his general, I let the foolish attachment of a youth sway me against my better judgment." Chaghan rose and came to stand over Ouyang. "General Ouyang, the last of that traitor Ouyang's bloodline. It mystifies me how my otherwise sensible son could have thought anything good or honorable could ever come from a eunuch! Someone who has been proven willing to do anything, no matter how shameful or cowardly, to preserve his own miserable life." For a moment the only sound in the room was the old man's harsh breathing. "But Esen was young when I made you. Perhaps he's forgotten the details. I haven't."

The blood pounded in Ouyang's head. It seemed that there was a flaring of light around him, a simultaneous bending of the lamp-flames that made the room sway as though he were in the grip of a deranging fever. He was almost glad to be kneeling and unable to fall.

"You remember, don't you? How your traitor father dared raise his sword in rebellion against our Great Yuan, and was taken to Khanbaliq where he was executed by the Great Khan's own hand. How after that, the Great Khan decreed that every Ouyang male to the ninth degree should be put to death, and the women and girls sold into slavery. Since your family was from Henan, it fell upon me to carry out the penalty. They brought you all to me. Boys with their hair still in bunches; old men with barely three breaths left in them. And every one of them went to his fate honorably. *Every one except you.* You, who was so afraid of death that you were willing to shame the memory of your ancestors even as the heads of your brothers and uncles and cousins lay on the ground beside you. Oh, how you wept and begged to be spared! And I—I was merciful. I let you live."

Chaghan put his boot under Ouyang's chin and tipped it up. Staring up into that hated face, Ouyang remembered Chaghan's mercy. A mercy of such cruelty that anyone else would have killed himself rather than bear it. But that was what Ouyang had chosen. Even as a boy, weeping in the blood of his family, he had known what kind of life his choice would bring. It was true that he had begged to be spared. But it hadn't been from fear of death. Ouyang was the last son of his family; he was the last who would ever bear its name. Defiled and shamed, he lived and breathed for a single purpose.

Revenge.

For sixteen years he had held that purpose tightly inside him, waiting for the right time. He had always thought it would be something he arrived at after long consideration. But now, as he knelt there at Chaghan's feet, he simply knew. *This is the moment it all starts.* And with the strange clarity that one has in dreams, he saw the rest of his life running out before him, following the purpose that was as fixed as the pattern of the stars. This was his journey to reclaim his honor, and anticipation of its end was simultaneously the sweetest and most terrible feeling he had ever had. The terrible part of it brought out a self-loathing so deep that it flung him out of himself, and for a moment he could only see what others saw of him: not a human but a contemptible shell, incapable of generating anything in the world except pain.

Chaghan dropped his foot, but Ouyang didn't bow his head. He matched Chaghan look for look. Chaghan said, low and dangerous, "My mercy is exhausted, General. To live in shame, and to bring shame upon your own ancestors, is one thing. But to have brought shame upon the Great Yuan is a different scale of failure entirely. For that, don't you think you should apologize with your life?"

Then another body was suddenly between them, snapping the tension with such force that Ouyang jerked as if slapped. Esen said, ragged and determined, "Since he is my general, it is *my* failure." He knelt. As he pressed his head to the floor at Chaghan's feet, the nape of his neck between his braids seemed so vulnerable as to invite a hand to be laid tenderly upon it. "Father, it is I who deserves punishment. *Punish me.*"

Chaghan said in controlled fury, "I indulged you, Esen, with your choice of general. So, yes, take responsibility. And what punishment is fitting? Shall I follow the example of our ancestors, and drive you from the clan to wander the steppe until you die alone in disgrace?"

Ouyang could feel Esen's tension. It was something that happened infrequently in Mongol culture, but it did happen: a family killing one of its own for some disgrace they had brought to the honor of the clan. To Ouyang, who had endured his entire life for the purpose of avenging his blood, it was a practice so alien as to be incomprehensible. He didn't know what he would do if Chaghan killed Esen.

And then the storm passed. They felt it even before Chaghan spoke again. In a softening tone he said, "Had you been anyone else, I would have done so. You cause me trouble as well as shame, Esen."

"Yes, Father," Esen said quickly, subdued.

"Then we can speak of what needs to happen to make right of this mess." Chaghan cast Ouyang an unpleasant glance. "You: go." For all that he had turned Ouyang's life upside down, had started Ouyang's future in motion, to him it had been nothing. He had no more idea of Ouyang's internal state than one did of a dog or a horse.

Ouyang left. His hands and feet were clammy, and he felt more drained than after a battle. The body became used to exercise, particular sounds and sensations, or even physical pain. But it was strange how shame was something you never became inured to: each time hurt just as much as the first.

Esen, still prostrated on the floor, heard Ouyang leave. The image lingered painfully in his mind: his proud general with his head bowed to the floor, his hands on either side white with pressure. Contrary to his father's assertions, Esen did remember. It was only that in his memory it had happened to someone else. Ouyang was so much a fixture in his life that he seemed devoid of any past other than the one he shared with Esen. It was only now that he was forced to see that memory truly, and acknowledge that Ouyang and that child were one and the same.

Above him, his father sighed. "Get up. What do we need in order to secure victory over the rebels next season?"

Esen stood. He should have kept his armor on. Ouyang had, clearly having wanted to have as much metal as possible between himself and the Prince of Henan's wrath. And perhaps even that hadn't helped. The thought of Ouyang's terrible empty expression gave Esen a feeling of deep injury, as though Ou-yang's shame were his own.

He said to his father, "Only fighting units were affected by the disaster. Our heavy cavalry is still intact. A third of the light cavalry was lost, but if it can be bolstered by at least a thousand more men and mounts, it can operate at reduced size. The three infantry battalions can be merged into two. It should be sufficient for victory against the Red Turbans next season."

"So: a thousand skilled and equipped cavalry men. And the commanders?"

"We lost three: two from the infantry, and one from the light cavalry."

Chaghan contemplated this, then directed an unpleasant look at Baoxiang. Esen had almost forgotten he was there. Now his brother said stiffly, "Don't request it of me, Father."

"You dare speak that way! I've been lenient with you for too long, letting you waste your time on useless things. It's past time you met your duty as a son of this family. I tell you now: when your brother's army rides again, you will join them as a battalion commander."

"No."

There was a dangerous silence. "No?"

Baoxiang sneered. "Apart from it being ridiculous that all one needs to lead is Mongol blood, I'm the *provincial admin-istrator*. I can't just leave. Or would you prefer that your es-tate, and this entire province, grind to a halt in the hands of the incompetent and corrupt? That would certainly get you the Great Khan's attention. Not to mention another defeat, since of course your men will have no horses to ride, nor grain for their families—"

"Enough!" Chaghan rounded on him. "Wang Baoxiang, son of this house! You would let your brother ride alone, while you count taxes in your office like a coward dog of a Manji? For all your brother's failure of a general is a neutered animal, at least he fights like a man! But you would refuse your most basic responsibilities?" He stood there, breathing heavily. "You disappoint me."

Baoxiang's lip curled. "When haven't I?"

For a moment Esen thought Chaghan would strike Baoxiang. Then he collected himself and bellowed loudly enough for the servants in the corridor outside to hear: "Summon Military Governor Bolud's son!"

Presently Altan came in, still in his armor. His expression brightened as he took in the tension in the room. "My respects to the esteemed Prince of Henan."

Chaghan viewed him dourly. "Altan, son of Bolud-Temur. Your father the Military Governor of Shanxi has long been united with us against these rebellions against our Great Yuan."

"It is so, Esteemed Prince."

"Given our recent losses, I would request of your father one thousand men suitable for the light cavalry, with all their mounts and equipment. I will ensure he receives all deserved credit before the Great Khan's court when we vanquish the rebels this upcoming season."

Altan bowed his head. "The men will be yours."

"My family thanks you. I am aware your father has no need of additional riches, but it pleases me to reward your personal service with a token of our esteem. A gift of lands from my own estate. I bequeath to you all the lands and households lying between Anyang and the northern river, to do with as you please." That these lands were part of those supporting Baoxiang's residence was a fact that escaped nobody.

Altan's face transformed with surprise and satisfaction. "The Prince of Henan is most generous."

"You may leave." Chaghan's voice soured. "All of you."

Esen, Altan, and Baoxiang left in bitter silence. Esen was halfway down the steps of his father's residence before he realized Altan and Baoxiang were no longer beside him. Glancing behind, he saw Baoxiang looking with revulsion at Altan's hand on his arm. He made as if to throw it off, but Altan, grinning, applied his greater strength to keep it there.

"Cousin Baobao, won't you let me thank you for this princely gift?" His voice dwelt mockingly on the Han'er nursery name. Continuing with relish, he said, "But how strange to think you'd prefer to give up your land than do a man's duty. You might even have to sell your books to pay the servants! I thought that prospect might have been enough to overcome your reluctance, but I see not. So is it true, then, you've forgotten how to draw a bow? Or did your mother never teach you properly, she was too busy being whore to a Manji—"

Another man would have fought him for the insult. Even Esen, whose mother hadn't been insulted, found himself opening his mouth to deliver a rebuke. But Baoxiang just wrenched his arm free, gave Altan and Esen a shared look of loathing, and stalked away.

Esen left it several days—enough for tempers to cool—before going in search of his brother. Located in an outer wing of the palace, Baoxiang's residence doubled as the provincial administration office. A long line of peasants waited outside for hearings on their various complaints. Inside, minor officials, almost all of them Semu, walked purposefully across the cobbled courtyards with their brass and silver seals swinging from their belts.

Servants directed him to a distant studio. It was a room perfectly to his brother's taste, which was to say not to Esen's at all. Landscapes, some from his brother's hand, covered the walls. The desk was smothered in a billow of drying calligraphy, some of it in their own Mongolian script and the rest in the unnecessarily complicated native characters that Esen had never bothered to learn.

His brother sat in the center of the room with a pair of Manji merchants. The table between them was scattered with the detritus of a fruitful conversation: cups, seed husks, crumbs.

They were speaking the soft language of the coast, which Esen didn't understand. When they saw him they broke off politely. "Our respects, my lord Esen," they said in Han'er. Bowing, they stood and made their excuses.

Esen watched them go. "Why are you wasting your time with merchants?" he said in Mongolian. "Surely one of your officials can haggle on your behalf."

Baoxiang raised his thick straight eyebrows. The delicate skin under his eyes looked bruised. Although the studio was warm, he was wearing multiple layers: bright metallic cloth underneath, gleaming against a rich plum outer. The color gave his complexion an artificial warmth. "And this is why you know nothing about your own supporters, save that they come when you call. Do you still think of the Zhang family as no more than salt smugglers? Their general is quite competent. Only recently he took another large tract of farmland from anarchic elements. So now the Zhangs control not only salt and silk, canalways and sea lanes, but increasingly grain—all on behalf of the Great Yuan." He fluttered a hand at the room's handsome yellow-lacquered furniture. "Even that chair you sit on is from Yangzhou, brother. Any power with such comprehensive reach should be understood. Perhaps especially if they're on our side."

Esen shrugged. "There's grain in Shanxi, salt in Goryeo. And by all accounts Zhang Shicheng is a useless rice bucket who spends his days eating bread and sugar, and his nights with Yangzhou prostitutes."

"Well, that's true. Which would be relevant if he was the one making the decisions. But I hear Madam Zhang is quite the force to be reckoned with."

"A woman!" Esen said, thinking it a nice story, and shook his head.

Servants cleared the table and brought food. Despite the Prince of Henan's punishment, there was no sign of it yet in Baoxiang's circumstances. There was a freshwater fish soup, savory with mushrooms and ham; wheat buns and jeweled millet; more vegetable side dishes than Esen could count; and rosy red strips of brined, smoked lamb in the style of eastern Henan. Esen took a piece with his fingers before the plate had even been set down. His brother laughed, slightly unkindly. "Nobody is fighting you for the right to eat, you glutton." Baoxiang always ate with chopsticks, swooping for morsels with an extravagant flourish that brought to mind the mating of swallows.

Eyeing the artworks as they ate, Esen said, "Brother, if you spent half as much time on swordplay as you do on books and calligraphy, you would be competent enough. Why must you persist in this war with our father? Can't you just try to give him the things he understands?"

He got a cutting look in return. "You mean the things *you* understand? If you had ever bestirred yourself to learn characters, you would know there are things of use in books."

"He is not deliberately set against you! As long as you show him enough respect to try in good faith, he will accept you."

"Is that so?"

"It is!"

"Then more fool you to think it. No amount of practice, no matter how much I *try*, is going to bring me up to your level, my dear perfect brother. In our father's eyes, I'll always be the failure. But, strangely, despite being a *coward of a Manji*, I still prefer failure on my own terms."

"Brother—"

"You know it's true," Baoxiang hissed. "The only thing I could do to make myself less like the son he wants is to take a beautiful male lover, and have the entire palace know he takes me nightly."

Esen winced. Though not unheard of amongst the Manji, there was little worse for a Mongol's reputation. He said uneasily, "At your age most men are already married—"

"Has water leaked into your brain? I have no interest in men. Certainly less than you, keeping the company of those hero-worshipping warriors of yours for months on end. Men you've trained personally, shaped to your *requirements*. You'd only have to ask and they'd willingly debase themselves for you." Baoxiang's voice was cruel. "Or don't you even have to ask? Ah, you still don't have any sons. Have you been so busy 'doing battle' that your wives have forgotten what you look like? And oh, that general of yours *is* beautiful. Are you sure your love for him is only that of a fellow soldier? Never have I seen you fling yourself to your knees quicker than when our father was set on flaying him—"

"Enough!" Esen shouted. He regretted it immediately; it was just his brother's usual game-playing. He could feel a headache coming on. "Your anger is at our father, not me."

Baoxiang gave him a brittle smile. "Is it?"

As he stormed off, he heard his brother laughing.

Ouyang strode into the provincial administration office in search of Lord Wang, his fist clenched around a bundle of ledgers. He was immediately assailed by the bureaucratic reek of ink, moldy paper, and lamp oil. The place was a claustrophobic maze of bookshelves and desks, and no matter how many dark little nooks he passed there was always yet another hunched official presiding over his pile of paper. Ouyang hated everything about the place. Over the past years under Lord Wang, the office had expanded its authority and multiplied officials like rabbits. Now nothing was possible without at least three seals being applied, abacuses consulted as though they were I Ching tiles, and entries made in ledgers. Every ruined horse and lost bow was owed its explanation, and getting a replacement was a process arduous enough to make a hardened warrior weep. And when you had lost ten thousand men and half as many horses and every piece of equipment they had been carrying, it didn't bear thinking about.

For all that Lord Wang was the provincial administrator and a lord, his desk was no larger than those of his officials. Ouyang stood in front of it and waited to be acknowledged. Lord Wang dipped his brush in ink and ignored him. Even here in his office the lord's gestures were as artificial as a dancing girl's. A performance. Ouyang recognized it, because he performed too. He had a small body and a woman's face, but he wore armor and lowered his voice and carried himself brusquely, and although people saw his difference, they responded to his performance and his position. But Lord Wang's performance flaunted his difference. He invited stares and disdain. *As if he likes being hurt.*

Lord Wang finally looked up. "General."

Ouyang made the least reverence that could be considered acceptable and handed Lord Wang the ledgers. Seeing all his losses laid out on paper had been confronting. With a surge of anger he thought of the rebel monk. By causing his loss, and his shaming by Chaghan, the monk had triggered the start of his journey towards his purpose. He couldn't find it in himself to be grateful. It felt like a violation. A theft of something he hadn't been ready to give up. Not innocence, exactly, but the limbo in which he could still fool himself that other futures were possible.

To Ouyang's surprise Lord Wang put the ledgers aside and went back to writing. "You may go."

Since Ouyang knew Lord Wang's character, he had prepared himself for a confrontation. In contrast to the Prince of Henan's efforts, it was only slightly annoying to be belittled by Lord Wang. By this point there was even a ritual quality to their interactions, as if they were acting roles in a play they were both obliged to be in. But no doubt Lord Wang's own punishment was weighing on him.

Just as he bowed and turned to leave, Lord Wang said, "All those years of yearning, and you finally get Esen kneeling for you. Did it feel good?"

There it was. It was like he couldn't resist. For all Ouyang understood the jealousy behind it, he still had the sick, stripped feeling of having something private and barely acknowledged to himself flung out into the cold air to wither. Lord Wang, who relished his own pain, had always known how to wound others.

When Ouyang didn't respond, Lord Wang said with a bitter

kind of understanding, "My brother's an easy person to love. The world loves him, and he loves the world, because everything in it has always gone right for him."

Ouyang thought of Esen, generous and pure-hearted and fearless, and knew what Lord Wang said was true. Esen had never been betrayed or hurt or shamed for what he was—and that was why they loved him. He and Lord Wang, both in their own different ways. They understood each other through that connection, two low and broken people looking up to someone they could never be or have: noble, perfect Esen.

"He was born at the right time. A warrior in a warrior's world," Lord Wang said. "You and I, General, we were born too late. Three hundred years before now, perhaps we would have been respected for what we are. You as a Manji. Myself as someone who thinks that civilization is something to be cherished, not just fodder for conquest and destruction. But in our own society's eyes, we're nothing." Bureaucracy hummed around them, unceasing. "You and Esen are two unlike things. Don't fool yourself that he can ever understand you."

Ouyang could have laughed. He had always known that Esen, like everything else one might desire in life, was out of his reach. He said bitterly, "And you understand me?"

Lord Wang said, "I know what it's like to be humiliated."

It was a quality of jealousy that you could only feel it for people who were like you. Ouyang could no more be jealous of Esen than he could be of the sun. But Ouyang and Lord Wang were alike. For a moment they stood there in bitter acknowledgment of it, feeling that likeness ringing through the space between them. The one reviled for not being a man, the other for not acting like one.

Ouyang made his way out of Lord Wang's office through the maze of desks, feeling raw.

"—the invitation to the Spring Hunt has come? We'll have them out of our hair for a while—"

The two Semu officials broke off and bowed as Ouyang passed, but he had heard enough. The Spring Hunt. The Great Khan's annual hunting retreat, held high up on the Shanxi plateau in a place called Hichetu, was the most prestigious invitation of the calendar. Hundreds of the Great Yuan's most notable members gathered for hunting, games, and entertainment. It was the one of the few opportunities for provincial nobles, like the Prince of Henan, to build connections with members of the Khanbaliq imperial court. Ouyang had attended once when he was twenty, when he had been the commander of Esen's personal guards. But the next year the Prince of Henan had retired from campaigning, and since then Esen and Ouyang had always been in the south during the Spring Hunt. This would be the first time in seven years that Esen would be available to accompany the Prince of Henan to Hichetu. And it was all because of Ouyang's defeat.

All at once Ouyang knew, deeply and unpleasantly, that none of it was a coincidence. His defeat by the monk, his shaming at Chaghan's hands. All of it had been nothing more than the mechanistic motion of the stars as they brought him this opportunity: the path to his fate. And once he stepped upon it, there would be no turning back.

It was an opportunity he wanted, and at the same time it was the very last thing he wanted: it was a future too horrible to bear. But even as he prevaricated and agonized, and shrank from the thought of it, he knew it wasn't a matter of choice. It was his fate, the thing no man can ever refuse.

9

ANFENG, THE NEW YEAR, 1355

Zhu knelt before the Prime Minister. In light of the surprising events at Yao River, she had been granted a special audience with the Red Turban leaders. Outside the weather had been brightening daily with the approach of the New Year, but the Prime Minister's throne room was still as dank as the cave from which the bear has departed. The red candles smoked and bled.

"A victory ordained by Heaven itself!" the Prime Minister crowed. "The eunuch general has more audacity than any of us realized. If not for Heaven's intervention, his ploy to cross downstream would have succeeded. We would have been annihilated! But in this miracle, what clearer proof could we have that the Mongols have lost their Mandate to rule?"

It *had* been a miracle, but not quite the same one Zhu had planned and prayed for. When she had come up with the idea of causing the landslide, all she had intended was to destroy the bridge so that she and the Red Turbans might be spared annihilation. But instead of that, Heaven had given her a victory that neither she nor anyone else had known was possible. She had stood up as Zhu Chongba and claimed greatness, and Heaven had validated it. In the blink of an eye, ten thousand of the eunuch general's men had become nothing. She shivered with awe, and with her feverish desire for something she had never thought she would desire. Her fate.

"The monk must be rewarded," the Prime Minister said. "Now that Guo Tianxu is general, there is a vacancy at the commander level. Let the monk fill it."

"Your Excellency wants to make—the *monk* a commander?" said Right Minister Guo. Zhu peered at him from her prostration, and saw him frowning. "I understand he has done us a service, but surely—"

"We don't owe that monk anything!" Little Guo burst in, indignantly. "He might have prayed, but it was my decision to face the Yuan at Yao River. If Heaven decreed we should win, doesn't it make it *my* victory?"

"Guo Tianxu," his father said repressively. His eyes flicked to the Prime Minister. He knew perfectly well that if Zhu hadn't won Yao River, Little Guo would be facing the Prime Minister's wrath.

Zhu wasn't alone in her bystanding. Left Minister Chen was watching the two Guos, and there was nothing passive about his attention. Like a naked weapon, it promised violence. Chen, feeling her gaze on him, looked over; their eyes met. His regard had neither warmth nor hostility. Only the vertical creases on his cheeks deepened, which could have meant anything at all.

The Prime Minister said coldly to Little Guo, "*That monk's* intercession was the necessary condition for every part of your success."

"Your Excellency," Right Minister Guo interjected. "It's not that it wasn't an achievement, but—"

"Regardless of why anything happened, he didn't even fight!" said Little Guo. "*He can't even hold a sword*. How can a commander not have any military experience? Why not put him here in the throne room, attending the Prince of Radiance? Isn't that more fitting for a monk?"

Chen cleared his throat. In a tone of eminent reasonableness, he said, "If I'm not mistaken, neither the Prime Minister nor the Right Minister had any experience of war before becoming leaders. They achieved success on the basis of their natural talents. Why should the monk need experience when they did not?"

In the gleam in Chen's eye, Zhu saw what her role was to be: the wedge for him to drive between the Prime Minister and Right Minister Guo. She had known that advancing within the Red Turbans would mean choosing between Chen and the Guos in their struggle under the Prime Minister. Now a side had chosen her. But, she thought, it was the side she would have chosen anyway.

Little Guo gave Zhu a poisonous look. "Any kind of fool can stumble into success once or twice. If his natural talent is praying, and we believe it works, then why not ask him to take Lu for us?"

Lu, a walled city not far south of Anfeng, was one of the strongest in the area. In all the decades of unrest, it alone of the Yuan's cities in the region had never fallen once to the rebels. Zhu's stomach clenched at a sudden ominous feeling.

Chen regarded Zhu with the look of someone who was perfectly happy to gamble, since it was with someone else's money. "A decade of Red Turban actions have failed to take that particular city, General Guo."

"So it's a good test. If he can pray his way to victory: make him a commander. And if he fails—well, then we'll know exactly how much use he is."

Internally cursing Little Guo, Zhu pressed her forehead back to the throne room's cracked tiles. "Although this unworthy monk is nothing but a speck of dust, he will gladly lend his meager talents to serving Your Excellency's will. With Heaven's backing, we will bring about the fall of the Hu and see the Prince of Radiance in his rightful place upon the throne of our own empire!"

"The monk speaks well," the Prime Minister said, mollified. "Let him go, to return with fortune and the Buddha's blessing." He rose and left, followed by his two ministers: one annoyed, and the other with a cool look of contemplation that masked who knew what.

Zhu, rising, found Little Guo in her way. His face was ugly with satisfaction. "You're even more of a lard-hearted idiot than I thought if you think you can *pray* your way to taking a walled city. Why don't you just run away and leave war to the people who know how to do it?"

He was so tall that Zhu strained to look up at him. She gave him her best imitation of the Dharma Master's tranquil smile. "The Buddha taught: *begin in hopelessness*. Only when we surrender to the hopelessness of the current moment can suffering begin to dissolve—"

"The Prime Minister might love you now," Little Guo said viciously. "But you're going to fail. And when you do, don't you think he'll rather have you killed as a false monk than believe Heaven willed a failure?"

She said, hardening, "Heaven doesn't will *my* failure."

When Ma came into the room that had once been the Guo mansion's library, she found Commander Sun Meng saying placatingly to Little Guo, "Does it really matter who's getting credit for the victory? The Prime Minister's happy, and it's put Chen Youliang back in his place. You know he was hoping you'd fail so he could challenge your father."

The two young men were sitting on the floor at a low table, eating the dinner Ma had brought them earlier: tofu simmered with ham and chestnuts, sliced soaked lotus root, and millet. They were surrounded by shelves stacked with paper-wrapped cabbages. Only Ma, who as a general's daughter had received more than the usual education, missed the books. The cabbages gave the unheated room a damp vegetal smell, like a field after a winter rain.

Seeing Ma there, Sun patted the space next to him. "Yingzi, have you eaten? There's some left." Sun was as slight as Little Guo was tall, and as good-tempered as his friend was sour. He had a lively, pretty face topped with a shock of wavy, reddish hair that was always escaping his topknot. Despite his boyish looks, he was in fact the best by far of the Red Turbans' three young leaders.

As Ma smiled and sat, Sun said, "So how do you like our victory?"

"I think you were incredibly lucky, whatever the cause." Borrowing Sun's bowl and spoon, Ma reached for the tofu. "And I think water has leaked into your brains if you think this has put Chen Youliang in his place. Guo Tianxu, did you really challenge that monk to go take the city of Lu? Haven't you learned by now that whenever you show your resentment, you're giving Chen Youliang something to use against you?"

"You dare criticize?" Little Guo's face reddened. He snatched the clay pot from under Ma's hand and emptied the tofu into his own bowl. "What do you know, Ma Xiuying? You thought I couldn't win at the Yao. Well, I did. And if I'd followed the Prime Minister's plan, we'd still be out on that plain losing a hundred men a day, with nothing to look forward to but that little eunuch bitch coming for us over the Huai. And this is the respect my victory gets?"

"It's not about respect," Ma said crossly. "I'm just saying that with Chen Youliang watching, you should take more care—"

"With everyone watching, *you* should learn not to criticize—"

Sun inserted himself between them. "I did ask for her opinion, Xu'er. Aiya, you two are such a bad match. Can't you have a single conversation without fighting?"

"You want a woman's useless opinions, *you* listen to them." Glaring at them, Little Guo drained his cup and stood. "I'm leaving first." He didn't bother shutting the door behind him.

Sun looked after him and sighed. "I'll talk to him later. Come on, Yingzi: see me out." He draped his arm about Ma's shoulders in a friendly way as they walked. It was one of Little Guo's quirks that despite his petty nature, her friendship with Sun didn't bother him at all. It was like he couldn't fathom the possibility of a woman finding Sun's effeminate looks more attractive than his own. Ma thought wryly: and yet even in that, he was blind. If it had been a matter of choosing one over the other, of course she would have picked the flower boy with his cheeks as round and smooth as a girl's. But of course: she hadn't had a choice.

She asked, "Do you think what happened was really because of that monk?"

"I have no idea. All I know is that we needed a miracle, and we got one."

To walk onto a bridge between two armies: it was an action that was hard to comprehend. Which was easier to believe: that the monk was a naïve fool with an extraordinary amount of luck, or an enlightened bodhisattva with no concern at all for his own skin? Ma remembered his sharp glance at their first meeting, and thought: *Not a fool.* But she wasn't sure the other was correct either.

"What are you worrying about now?" asked Sun, who could tell her moods. "We have the Mandate of Heaven and our best victory in years. The Yuan will be rebuilding until next autumn, so we'll have six months to take back ground and build a strong position." He gave her a gentle squeeze. "This is the moment everything changes, Yingzi. You'll see! In ten years when the Prince of Radiance sits on the throne of our own empire, we'll look back at this moment and smile."

The flickering late winter sunshine had dried Anfeng's mud. Zhu sauntered through the cold shade between the market stalls. It was more crowded than usual—almost lively. Since the resounding defeat of the Yuan at Yao River, the city had an air of renewed enthusiasm. Hope, one might think.

"Hey, granny!"

Well, less hope for some. Zhu, observing the unfolding human drama, felt a stirring of unease: the memory of something witnessed so long ago that it might as well have been in a past life.

"Hey, I said: hey, granny!" The group of men pressed around an old woman sitting behind her pile of vegetables. "You're gonna give us a few of these for keeping the troublemakers away, aren't you? Anfeng is a pretty dangerous place to be! You better thank us well for our support—"

"*Support,* you rotten turtle eggs?" Someone elbowed their way in, furious; Zhu was surprised to see it was the Semu girl who'd saved her from Little Guo. General Ma's daughter. To the old woman's downturned head, the girl instructed: "Don't give them anything."

"You can shut up," said the men's leader.

"You dare talk to me like that! Don't you know who I am?"

After a pause one of them observed, "Isn't it Little Guo's woman?"

The leader gave the girl a closer examination, smirking. "That half-empty vinegar bottle who calls himself a general? Think I give a fuck?"

The girl Ma refused to give ground. Glaring, she said, "Get lost!"

"Or what?" As his men descended on the old woman's vegetables, the leader grabbed the girl and flung her easily into the street. She cried out as she landed on her hands and knees. The leader laughed. "Roll back to your mother's cunt, bitch."

After the men had gone Zhu went over and crouched next to Ma. "So, that went well."

She got an angry look in return. Even with that expression, the girl was striking. The smooth golden tone of her skin was only more luminous in contrast to a small dark mole high on her forehead. Her hair fell as straight and shining as black clouds. Perhaps her looks missed the Nanren standards of classic beauty, but in her face there was such a depth of raw and innocent emotion that Zhu's eye was drawn as if to the scene of an accident.

"What should I have done? Ignored it?" Ma said, scowling. She dabbed her bleeding palms with her skirt.

"You're upset," Zhu observed.

Ma looked up fiercely. "Yes, I'm upset! Oh, I know, it happens all the time. She's used to it. *Everyone's* used to it. It's just—"

"It hurts." Zhu felt a sense of wonder at the girl's empathy. If Zhu had ever had such a soft part of herself, capable of tenderness based on nothing more than a shared humanity, she wasn't sure it was still there.

"Of course."

"Of course?" Zhu said, amused. "Don't assume. Hardly anyone's like that." She bounced up and bought a cup of soy milk from the neighboring stall, and gave it to Ma.

Ma accepted it with a skeptical look. "I thought you were a clouds and water monk without two coins to rub together."

"This monk has nothing but what the generosity of others has blessed him with," Zhu said piously. She did actually have more than two coins, since she had traded the gong back to Jiao (who had come back after the victory) in return for the horse and a few strings of copper cash. It made sense to turn a profit—it was the gong that could summon Heaven, after all.

Zhu saw Ma examining her from under her eyelashes as she drank the milk. It was a vexed look, as if she were convinced there was something else happening under Zhu's monkly naïveté, but she couldn't tell what it was. Still, she was the first person in the Red Turbans who'd even seen that much. Zhu supposed that if General Ma had been as competent as everyone said, it made sense that his daughter was smarter than most of the Red Turbans' actual leadership. Curious to know the girl better, Zhu said, "The horse."

"What?"

"This monk's horse. You remember it. Since General Guo has given this monk the modest next task of conquering a city, this monk was thinking he might prefer to ride the horse for the fighting part. It might make his survival less dependent on miracles." She gave Ma an inviting look. "Know any riding tutors?"

"This again? Why are you so sure I can ride?"

"Your name is *horse,* isn't it?" Zhu said playfully. "Names don't lie."

"Oh, please!" The girl was scornful. "On that principle, every drunkard named Wang would be king. And you'd be—" She stopped.

"Red?" teased Zhu. "Like a—Red Turban?"

"That's a different kind of a red! What's the rest of your name, anyway?"

When Zhu told her, she shook her head and laughed in exasperation. "Red *and* lucky double eight? Your parents must have been happy to have you."

Images of a childhood—not Zhu Chongba's—shuttered across Zhu's mind like flashes seen through torn window-paper. But she was Zhu Chongba, and just as much as his fate was now hers, so was his past. She said, "Ah, it's true: despite never having shown much promise, this monk's parents always believed he'd achieve great things." She waggled her eyebrows. "And now look! Here he is: an educated monk instead of a peasant. What more could farmers ask for?"

Zhu thought she'd spoken lightly, but when Ma gave her a searching look she wondered what inadvertent truth might have shown on her face. But the girl said only, "Nice to meet you, Master Zhu the Extremely Lucky."

"Aiya, so formal! This monk had better call you Teacher Ma, since you'll be giving him lessons."

"Who's giving lessons!"

"Or if you're not giving lessons, should this monk call you big sister Ying?"

"Oh, too bold!" Ma exclaimed. Shooting Zhu a perspicacious glance, she said, "And who's older than who, exactly? If you're a monk, you have to be at *least* twenty."

Zhu grinned: it was true that Ma herself couldn't be more than seventeen. "So Teacher Ma it is, if you can't bear this monk calling you anything else."

"*That's* your argument?"

Zhu arranged her face in her best expectant look. The girl

stared, seemingly torn between outrage and exasperation, then sighed. "All right! One lesson. *One.*"

"This monk is a fast learner. But the horse—who knows?" Zhu said, feeling lighthearted at her success. She liked the idea of seeing Ma's snapping eyes again, and of teasing her with more naïve-monk performance. "Maybe you can give him extra lessons separately, if it's this monk that's too much of a headache for you."

"Yes, you're the headache! Now get lost."

But when Zhu glanced back, she saw Ma was smiling.

Zhu looked down at Anfeng from her high-up perch on the temple steps and watched the colorful New Year traffic flowing through the narrow streets as thickly as rivers and dragons. The temple in Anfeng's eastern quarter had been a filthy ruin when Zhu had come across it. Knowing an opportunity when she saw one, she had immediately moved in. With her came the two hundred raw recruits that Little Guo had grudgingly given her for the purpose of taking Lu. The sight of all those tents cluttering the temple grounds made her feel as if she had an army of her own. But if it was an army, it was still far too small. Zhu was worried about Lu. The more she learned about the city, the more she understood what an impossible challenge Little Guo had given her. Who could take a stone-walled city with two hundred men?

But now as she saw a powerful black-clad figure making its way up the steps towards her, she thought: *Here comes a chance.*

"Greetings, Master Zhu," said Left Minister Chen. An ironic smile played on his mouth. His presence engulfed Zhu like the shadow of a mountain.

Zhu felt a ripple of excitement that was partly an awareness of danger, and partly the thrill of subterfuge. She knew instinctively that Chen, the most cunning and ambitious of the Red Turban leaders, would one day be even more of a challenge for her than Little Guo. But for the moment, when he still had no idea of her desires, she had the advantage. She bowed, even lower than was expected of a young monk receiving an important guest. "Minister! This unworthy monk is too lacking to receive your esteemed person at this humble temple." Her hands folded beneath her downcast eyes, she let her sleeves tremble. No doubt Chen would flatter himself to think it was a stolen insight into her character, rather than a gift she'd let him have.

"Humble? For once there's some truth to that word," Chen said, making a show of surveying the crumbling structure and its hodgepodge of tents. His real attention hadn't moved: Zhu felt it on her, as sharp as an awl. "At least you've cleaned out the stray dogs."

"Whatever other tasks this monk may have been entrusted with, his first duty is to the Buddha and his earthly envoys. This monk only regrets that he has too few resources to refurbish the temple and make it a fitting place for worship."

Chen's dark eyes bored into her, hard to read. "A commendable attitude, Master Zhu. Your prayers certainly won the day at the Yao River. But I wonder whether such a feat can be replicated against Lu. You'll find a city a more difficult challenge."

"Anything is possible with the Buddha's blessing," Zhu murmured. "We can only have faith."

Chen gave her one of his small smiles. "Indeed. Ah, how refreshing it is to find a young person with such faith in our purpose. If only General Guo would follow your example." The ironic expression was back. She thought he hadn't fully bought her naïve monk routine, although neither had he dismissed it—yet. Watching her closely, he said, "Don't you think even an endeavor of faith can be made more certain with the addition of men and equipment, Master Zhu?"

This was her chance. She widened her eyes in her best imitation of perplexity. ". . . Minister?"

"I suppose you'll have little enough chance, whatever I do," Chen mused. "But I find myself moved to improve your odds. I've instructed Commander Wu to give you five hundred men before your departure. How many will you have then, seven hundred or so?" His laugh was like a slab of meat hitting the butcher's block. "Seven hundred men against a city! I wouldn't try it myself. But let me do what I can for you afterwards: if you do manage to win Lu, I'll convince the Prime Minister to let you keep whatever you've taken from it. Then you'll have enough funds for your new temple." His black eyes glittered. "Or for whatever else you'd like to do."

Seven hundred men was better than nothing, though they both knew it was a far cry from the minimum needed for a reasonable chance at success. And even if she did succeed, the price would be becoming Chen's playing piece in the pitched battle between himself and the Guos. But there was no point worrying about that yet. *One problem at a time.*

Chen was waiting for her answer, though he knew perfectly well there was only one answer she could give. She bowed three times: humble, grateful. "This unworthy monk thanks the Minister for his generous assistance! Even though this monk is lacking in the skills of warfare and leadership, he will do his best to bring honor and success to the Red Turbans—"

Chen's teeth gleamed like those of a predator that would devour you without even spitting out the bones. The first fireworks of the New Year bloomed in the darkening sky behind him. "Then use the skill you do have, Master Zhu, and pray well."

At first watch Ma slipped out of the front gate of the Guo mansion. She was only discreet out of habit: during the two weeks between the New Year and the Lantern Festival, everyone in Anfeng could be found wandering around at all hours enjoying the novel sight of the city's streets packed with food stalls and drinking tents, acrobats and musicians and cricket fights, face readers and fish-ball makers.

She found the monk Zhu waiting outside with his horse, a triangular straw travel hat tilted down over his face. All she could see under the hat's shadow were his narrow lips, curved in a smile. The dramatic effect lasted until the instant he saw her and burst out cackling. Slapping his hand over his mouth he said, muffled, "Is that . . . a disguise?"

"What? No. Shut up." For ease of riding Ma had put on a man's short robe, trousers tied at the knee, and boots. "Should I have put on trousers under my skirt?"

"Why not? It's not like anyone's going to think you're a man."

Ma glared at him. It was true, though, that male clothing did nothing to hide her feminine shape. With her sturdy thighs and rounded hips, nobody was ever going to compose a poem comparing her to a slender willow, or a gracefully bending blade of grass.

The monk was looking down. "Your feet are even bigger than this monk's. Look." He compared them.

"You—you!" It was *rude*.

"Don't worry, this monk doesn't like bound feet. Women should be able to run a bit during a rebellion," he explained.

"Who cares what you like! You're a monk!"

He laughed as they walked towards the western gate. "It's not like monks never see women. People were always coming into the monastery with offerings. Sometimes girls who wanted to learn more about the dharma would stay for scripture study with novices who were particularly . . . advanced. If you know what I mean." The hat tilted; she saw a flash of teeth and, shockingly, a dimple. "Do you? Know."

"I'm sure I don't," she said witheringly. "And if that was how the monks of Wuhuang Monastery carried on, no wonder that eunuch could burn it down without any bad karma."

"You've been checking up on this monk!" he said in delight. "Wuhuang was a good place. I learned a lot there." His tone turned rueful, touched with genuine sorrow. "After the Prince of Radiance appeared and the Great Yuan tried to curtail the monasteries' power, our abbot refused. He always was stubborn."

"Clever people know when to give in," Ma said bitterly, thinking of Little Guo.

Together they passed under the earthen battlements of Anfeng's western gate. On the other side was a denuded pasture, lumpy in the moonlight, and beyond that the sparkling black loop of the Huai. Glancing around, the monk gave a theatrical shudder. "Ah, it's so dark! Doesn't it scare you to think that this is exactly the kind of place ghosts will come when the New Year drums drive them out of the city?"

"If we're accosted by hungry ghosts, I'll take the horse and leave them to eat you," Ma said, unimpressed.

"Ah, so it's this monk who should be scared," he said, laughing.

"Just get on the horse!"

"Like—?" He clambered astride. "Ha! That wasn't so—"

Ma slapped the horse on the rump. It bolted; the monk, separating in midair from his hat, came down like a sack of river gravel. When she went over he was lying flat on his back grinning up at her. "Honestly, this monk can't ride."

After an hour of instruction, Ma still didn't know if that had been true or not. If he really was a beginner, he hadn't been exaggerating about being a quick learner. Watching him in a relaxed canter, his robes dark under the moonlight and face obscured by the hat, she found herself thinking that he didn't look much like a monk at all.

He pulled up and dismounted, smiling. "Just think how much quicker this monk would have made it to Anfeng if he had been able to ride."

"You think we were missing you?" Ma scoffed.

"Do you think miracles happen without prayers?" he said, grinning. "It's useful to have a monk around."

Miracle. Ma felt a realization trying to surface. It was related to the feeling she'd had the last time they met: a suspicion that his joking smile hid more than it revealed. She remembered the strange jolt she'd felt when she'd seen him kneeling before Little Guo on his first day in Anfeng. How, just for an instant, he'd seemed like someone who knew exactly what he was gambling, and why.

And then she knew. Her breath caught. "That landslide at Yao River wasn't Heaven's work. *You* did it. You knew you'd be killed if that battle went ahead. You made everyone shout at the top of their lungs, knowing it would trigger a landslide, burst the dam, and destroy the bridge." She said accusingly: "Prayers had nothing to do with it!"

She'd surprised him. After a startled pause he said, "Trust me, this monk prayed."

"For *your* life, maybe. Not for the victory that the Prime Minister's giving you credit for!"

"What kind of monk would pray for the deaths of ten thousand men?" he said, and she thought at least that was true. "That would be a violation of the precepts. This monk didn't know the Yuan were sending across a flanking force. It was Heaven's decision to give us what we needed to win."

"I suppose it doesn't matter how," she said uneasily. "You survived once, and got a victory out of it. But now you're heading off to Lu, and the Prime Minister thinks you can pray your way to another victory. But you can't, can you?"

"You don't believe it was because of this monk's prayers that Left Minister Chen gave him another five hundred men?" His voice lightened and gained a teasing edge. "This monk is touched by your concern, Teacher Ma, but the situation isn't as bad as you think. This monk may yet win."

He was as slippery as a catfish; she couldn't tell if he believed it or not. "Better hope they can fight better than you do! And don't you see Chen Youliang is just using you to undermine the Guo faction?"

"It's true that General Guo doesn't inspire others to wish him success," he said wryly.

For all Ma was more than familiar with Little Guo's flaws, the criticism struck a nerve. She snapped, "You're bold enough to think you can play in the Left Minister's games?" She remembered Chen's fingers grinding her bones together. "His patronage never ends well for anyone but himself. Surely you can see that."

His eyes went to her wrist, where she'd touched it without realizing. "Laypeople have this idea of monasteries as serene places where no one wants anything but nirvana. But I can tell you, some monks who called themselves pious were as vicious and self-interested as Chen Youliang."

It startled her to hear him say *I*. It was like reaching for someone's cheek in the dark, but finding instead the intimate wetness of their open mouth. She said, unsettled, "Then you do know. If you join his side, you'll regret it."

"Is that the lesson you think I learned?" His eyelids lowered, and for a moment the cricket-face under the hat was shadowed with something she felt herself curling away from. Then he said, "Anyway, monks don't take sides. Left Minister Chen can think what he likes, but this monk serves only the Buddha and his earthly envoy, the Prince of Radiance."

Looking at him, she saw the eunuch general's ten thousand dead men. "Sometimes that might look a lot like serving yourself."

His eyes flicked up, as sharp as a hook. But after a moment he just said, "Teacher Ma: since this monk is leaving soon for Lu, do you have any sage guidance?"

Her answer was interrupted by red fire blooming above Anfeng. Shimmering threads of light fell in the shape of a jellyfish. "Is that a firework? I've never seen one like that."

"Jiao Yu's work. He does have quite a talent for fire-powder." After a moment of observation the monk added, "It's exactly the same color as the Mandate."

Or the color of temple candles, Ma thought, watching the light bleed into the sky. The color of piety and prayers to the ancestors. Of her dead father. Suddenly she felt a violent surge of frustration about everything: the Yuan, the rebellion, the selfishness of old men as they competed for power. At Heaven itself, for its opaque signs that could seemingly point in any direction you wanted. "How little lives are worth in this war," she said bitterly. "Theirs and ours, both."

He said after a moment, "You have a lot of feelings in you, Ma Xiuying."

"Don't mistake it for caring about *your* life or death, monk." But it was too late: she already cared. *All it took was for him to ask for help.* She said reluctantly, "You know my father used to be one of the Yuan's generals. Towards the end of that time he got to know the man who became Lu's governor. A Semu, like my family. That man wasn't very popular in Dadu, because late in life he married a Nanren girl out of love, and people used that against him. But my father had a lot of respect for his talents. Later, when my father joined the Red Turbans, he always refused to attack Lu: he said with that man as governor, it was too strong. But he died not more than a month ago. The Yuan will be sending a replacement from Dadu. Who knows what he'll be like? But if you can get there before him—you could have a chance." She amended, "Part of a chance."

She didn't know if she had scared Zhu or given him hope. After a mulling silence he said, "That's useful. You've taught this monk well tonight, Teacher Ma." He remounted and said in a completely normal voice, as though they hadn't been discussing his inevitable death, "But why are we out here when the fireworks are so much better up close? Come on. It'll be quicker with both of us riding."

He took her hand and swung her up in front of him. The strength and sureness of his grip surprised her. She'd thought monks spent all day sitting with their eyes closed. Striving for unimpressed, she said, "I'm the one who can ride. Shouldn't I have the reins?"

From within the circle of his arms she *felt* him laugh. "This monk can't ride? Since you only offered the one lesson, this monk thought he was qualified."

"*Qualified* to fall off the first time someone shoots at you!" She leaned forwards and snapped her fingers next to the horse's ear. It piked left in surprise, and Zhu went tumbling off the back.

By the time Ma collected the horse and brought it around, he had caught his breath and was pretending to admire the stars. "Well. Maybe this monk could do with another lesson."

Ma snorted. "One lesson already makes you better than most people here who have a horse." She pulled him up behind; he was lighter than she'd expected.

He said, smiling, "If we go faster than a walk and you don't want me falling off, I'm going to have to hold on somehow." But he held her with just his fingertips, chaste. For some reason she was too aware of that light pressure, and the warmth of his body against hers.

She would probably never see him again. She felt a surprising stab at the thought. Not quite pity.

Six days after the Lantern Festival in the middle of the first month, the boy thief Chang Yuchun found himself on the march with Monk Zhu's seven hundred men through the lake-dotted plain between Anfeng and the walled city of Lu. Spirits were low, although someone (probably Zhu himself) had started spreading a story from the ancient Three Kingdoms period, in which General Zhang Liao of Wei's eight hundred cavalry had defeated the entire army of the kingdom of Wu, numbering no less than two hundred thousand men, just outside of Lu. Yuchun, who had never been told stories in his childhood, refused to believe it as a matter of principle.

They had already broken for the day at the afternoon's Monkey hour, and were making camp. Yuchun lounged next to the tent of the newest addition to Zhu's force, and asked with genuine curiosity, "So, at what point do you think you're going to regret leaving Commander Sun's force for an incompetent monk's suicide mission?"

Jiao Yu was holding a length of metal about a foot long. One bulbous end tapered to a narrow mouth at the other. As Yuchun watched with interest, he touched a flaming stick to a hole in the bulbous end and took aim at a tree about twenty paces distant. A moment later there was an astonishing retort that left them both choking in a cloud of smoke. Yuchun said, reeling, "Was something supposed to happen to the tree?"

"He's not incompetent," Jiao said evenly. He banged the weapon on the ground until a handful of tiny metal balls and pottery pieces fell out the open end, then peered inside muttering to himself.

"It's not too late to run. If I were you, I'd be seriously considering it. I'm just saying." Yuchun picked up one of the metal balls. It seemed too small to cause any kind of damage. "What *is* that?"

"A hand cannon." Jiao took the ball away from Yuchun. "The monk asked me to think about fire-powder weapons. The problem is reliability—"

Yuchun looked at the completely intact tree. "You could reliably hit someone over the head with it, I guess. And how is he not incompetent? He can't even swing a sword. Do you think he's going to be able to take a city without fighting?"

"*To win a hundred victories in a hundred battles is not the pinnacle of skill. To subdue the enemy without fighting is the pinnacle of skill.*"

"Skills, victories, what?" said Yuchun, struggling with the classical language.

"That monk knows exactly what he wants. The night before the battle at Yao River, he asked me to make that gong for him. I made it, he used it, and he won," Jiao said. "I've met his type before. They either go far or die early. And either way, they have a tendency to make collateral damage of normal people." He raised his eyebrows at Yuchun. "Are you special, little brother? Because if you're not, I'd watch out."

"I—" Yuchun started, then broke off as he saw movement. "What—"

"Bandits!" came the howl.

The camp dissolved into chaos. As the hundreds-strong pack of mounted hillmen, Yuan deserters, and former peasants descended upon them, Zhu's men grabbed their weapons and defended themselves in the manner of every man for himself. Yuchun, who had always prided himself on avoiding the violent parts of the rebellion, found himself abruptly in the middle of a battle. Forgetting Jiao, half-blind in panic, he stumbled through the chaos with his arms uselessly shielding his head.

When he nearly ran into a horse, he looked up at a familiar triangular silhouette. Under his hat Monk Zhu had the frozen look of someone helpless to prevent a past terror from happening again. It was the first time Yuchun had seen him anything less than composed. Yuchun stared up at him, the man leading them who was a *Buddhist monk*, and felt a disembodied stab of intense clarity: *I'm going to die.*

A bandit sheared past and Yuchun ducked, but when he came up there was an even taller one in his face. He stumbled backwards—but instead of coming after him, the tall bandit stopped in his tracks at the sight of Monk Zhu.

"Stop!" the bandit yelled, flinging up a commanding hand. "Stop!"

The fighting tailed off into the last clash of steel and the rising mutters of men denied. Nobody was screaming, and the few men on the ground rose slowly to their feet clutching shallow wounds. Strange as it seemed, only a few heartbeats had passed. The Red Turbans and bandits glared at each other, their blood roused.

The tall bandit's eyes were fixed on Monk Zhu. Under his rags his solid body seemed made for violence. Even his hair had been cut short in a violence against his ancestors. His sword quivered in his hand. To Monk Zhu he said with calm intensity, "Get off that horse."

After a moment Monk Zhu dismounted. Standing there, unarmed and unarmored, he seemed pathetically small. Out of all the Red Turbans, Yuchun was the one with the longest-standing bet against the monk's survival. Now, faced with his winning hand, he felt a peculiar hollowness. He could see it already: the monk's shaven head hitting the ground; the bright arc of blood across his face. That was how it always ended.

The tall bandit lunged at Monk Zhu. Yuchun, who had closed his eyes at the last moment, opened them and stared in astonishment at two bodies locked not in violence, but a ferocious embrace. Monk Zhu's face was shining with joy as he reached up and took the back of the tall bandit's head into the palm of his hand, a possessive gesture that aligned strangely with their relative sizes. *"Big brother."*

"See?"

Yuchun jumped; it was Jiao. Watching the monk and the bandit, Jiao went on, "He didn't need to fight to win. Don't underestimate him because he's a monk. What someone *is* means nothing about what kind of person they are. Truth is in actions. And if we consider actions: that monk killed ten thousand men in an instant. So what does that make him?"

Before Yuchun could find his voice, Jiao answered himself: "Someone to be careful of."

10

ANYANG, FIRST MONTH

This is the moment it all starts, Ouyang told himself as he left his rooms in the quiet outer wing of Esen's residence. A storm was rising outside, and the lamps did little to banish the dimness along the corridor. The cold black smell of coming rain penetrated the window-paper.

"General," the servants cried as Ouyang came into Esen's private quarters. "Lord Esen is out on the training field, but given the weather he will no doubt return soon. May it please you to wait!" and they withdrew in a patter. Ouyang sat, and stood, and sat again. He wanted Esen to come, and it was the last thing he wanted.

Some of that turmoil must have shown on his face, because when Esen came in he gave Ouyang a shocked look and exclaimed, "What news?" He waved dismissal to the servants who had run back into the room to extract him from his armor, and started undoing it himself. His color was high from exercise, and stray hairs from his braids lay damp against his neck. Ouyang could smell the soapy suede of his armor, mixed with metal and the mild odor of his warm male body: a combination as intimate as the inside of a tent.

"Nothing of importance, my lord. A minor query." Seeing Esen struggling with the lacing under his arm, Ouyang stepped forwards to work the knot. It was only after he'd started that he realized what he was doing.

Esen laughed in surprise. "That a general of the Yuan would lower himself so."

"Haven't I done this many times?"

"That was a long time ago. You were just a child."

Sixteen years ago. More than half their lifetimes. "So were you." He put Esen's armor on the side table and took the fresh clothes from the clothes tree while Esen finished undressing. He came behind Esen to settle the garment on his shoulders. When his hands touched Esen's shoulders, the familiarity of that old gesture stunned him. After leaving behind his time as an attendant slave, Ouyang had only served Esen once again during his whole long rise from guard to commander to general. He remembered that time in flashes: Esen's surprise as he looked down to see his armor and flesh laid open by the spear. How in the physician's ger, Esen's blood had coated Ouyang's hands as he struggled to strip the ruined armor off, not trusting anyone else to do it. He remembered his desperate urge to ease Esen's pain, as intense as if it were his own body bleeding. And even then, in the moment that their bodies had been joined in a kinship of suffering, a smaller part of Ouyang had remembered his fate.

He smoothed the fabric across Esen's shoulders and stepped away.

Esen was quiet a moment, as if the weight of memories had stilled him, too. Then he shook himself and said, "Eat with me, my general. I need the company."

As the servants came in with the midday meal a blow of wind slammed the latticework in the corridor outside, immediately followed by hammering rain. Ouyang heard women's shrieking from elsewhere in the residence, the sound eerily disembodied and snatched by the wind. Opposite him at the round table, Esen ate with an uncharacteristic drained look. For all he was a lord, in Anyang he always exuded an air of being out of place: a wild plant taken off the steppe and put in a pot for the pleasure of others. All of a sudden he burst out, "How I hate their games and demands!"

Ouyang dipped a piece of jellied pork cheek in black vinegar and said neutrally, "Your wives?"

"Oh, Ouyang. Women are terrible! The *politics*." He groaned. "Consider yourself lucky you'll never have to suffer this kind of torment."

Esen never meant to hurt, and Ouyang had always taken care to pretend matter-of-fact acceptance about his exclusion from family life. Why should he blame Esen for not reading his mind to see the anger and pain there? But the truth was: he did blame Esen. Blamed him even more than he would a stranger, because it hurt more that someone so beloved should not see the truth of him. And he blamed and hated himself, for hiding that truth.

He said with distaste, "I did run into Lady Borte earlier today. She sends her greetings, and asks when she might have the privilege of hosting you again." In Ouyang's opinion all four of Esen's wives lacked in appearance and personality, and the presence of any of them made his skin crawl. He hated their unmoving faces beneath their thick white makeup, their tiny steps that made them take forever to get from one place to another, and their stupid column hats that towered above their heads further than Ouyang's hand could have reached. Even their smell was repulsive: a decayed flower scent that clung to Esen for hours after his visits. Ouyang, who knew Esen better than anyone, couldn't fathom what he found attractive about them. The thought of Esen fucking one of them gave him the same visceral horror as the idea of an interspecies mating.

"If only one of them would bear a son, that would put them in order," Esen complained. "But at the moment all of them think they have a chance to be on top. It's a nightmare. When I'm here they treat me like nothing but a breeding stallion." He added indignantly, "They don't even serve me tea first!"

Esen's inability to throw sons was the subject of concern and amusement from the servants; his wives were concerned but certainly not amused; and lately Esen himself had been considering adoption, although he admitted to Ouyang that the suggestion had sent the Prince of Henan (who regretted Lord Wang) into an apoplexy.

Even with the screens drawn the force of the storm was enough to make the lamp flames bob even more wildly than Ouyang's presence caused. It was the kind of storm that the Nanren believed boded ill for the future of the Great Yuan. But for all that Ouyang was a general of the Yuan, he didn't fight for the empire. His efforts had only ever been for Esen. He suddenly felt a deep longing to be back on campaign. Campaign was his and Esen's world, where the only things that mattered were the pride of carrying oneself honorably in battle, and the love and trust between warriors. The only place where Ouyang was ever happy.

But what bearing did happiness have on how one should live one's life? He said painfully, "My lord, the matter on which I came—I heard the invitation to the Spring Hunt had come. Will you attend this year?"

Esen grimaced. "I'd rather not, but my father has already conveyed his expectation that I accompany him."

"You should. When the Prince of Henan is gone, you'll inherit his titles. It's important for the court and the Great Khan to know you as more than just your father's son. This year is your opportunity to impress them."

"I suppose you're right," Esen said, without enthusiasm. "But the thought of being apart from you for so long seems strange to me. As it is, I feel I've hardly seen you since coming back. Since—" He had the grace to stop before saying: that moment with the Prince of Henan.

Ouyang realized his hand was clenched around his chopsticks. He laid them down and said, "If that's the case—my lord, why not ask the Prince of Henan if I can come with you to the Spring Hunt?"

Esen looked up with delight. "Really? I will, gladly. The only reason I haven't already is because I thought you'd never come. I know how much you hate smiling and making conversation."

"I suppose I should take my own advice. If the Great Khan knows your name, perhaps he should also know mine."

"This pleases me. Truly." Esen attacked the steamed ginseng chicken with renewed vigor, smiling.

The residence's doors banged and slammed as if by angry ghosts, and Ouyang felt his ancestors' eyes upon him as he ate with the son of his family's murderer, the person he held dearest in all the world.

Ouyang and Shao's overcoats flapped in the wind as they made their way through the palace grounds. The storm had transformed spring back into winter, and the fallen blossoms in the courtyards had turned brown. Ouyang felt grim: he always suffered in the cold. "I'll be accompanying the Prince of Henan, Lord Esen, and Lord Wang to the Great Khan's Spring Hunt. That will be the beginning of it. I need you to make everything ready in my absence."

"So the time has come. Can you do it?" The cool look Shao gave him was all wrong, coming from inferior to superior, but Ouyang cared not a shred for whether Shao liked him or not, or was disgusted by him or not—only that he did what was needed.

Before he could answer they rounded a corner and saw Lord Wang striding briskly in their direction across the courtyard.

"Greetings, Lord Wang." Ouyang and Shao made their reverences in unison.

"General," said the lord, inclining his head fractionally. "A fortuitous meeting. Last night's rain has flooded and destroyed a number of villages. Send me two battalions of men immediately to rebuild the roads and drainages." He swept past.

"My lord." Ouyang bowed in acknowledgment and continued on his way, a remembered pang of sympathy muting his usual annoyance at the lord.

Hurrying after Ouyang, Shao said, "Will you really have our soldiers delay their preparations to dig ditches?"

"Would you rather his enmity for the entire off-season? I have no desire to fill in five pages of paperwork for every extra arrow I need." Ouyang shook his head impatiently. "Let him take the battalions; we have time enough."

"You take his disrespect too easily. You're a general, and he's a man who won't even take up a man's role. Why do you still let him demean you like a servant?"

Ouyang thought that Lord Wang had more respect for him than Shao did. He said, "Why should I care how Lord Wang treats me? He's only like that because he knows he's unimportant. Even his own father hates and scorns him."

"And Lord Esen?"

"Esen doesn't hate anyone," Ouyang said, feeling a flash of familiar pain. "But he should. That adoption was a fool's mistake. Chaghan should have known. Roots are ineradicable. How could Lord Wang have ever brought pride to Chaghan's line? He has his father's blood."

"Our blood," said Shao.

Blood. His father's blood in his veins. His ancestors' blood. Hearing it said out loud shocked him as much as a nearby lightning strike. "Never let anyone hear you say that," he bit out. "When I'm away, you'll be in command. Your loyalty is to the Great Yuan; that is all that must ever be seen. Do you understand?"

"Yes, General," said Shao, and tapped his fist to his chest in acknowledgment. But there was an unrepentant smirk beneath the gesture. Something about it made Ouyang shudder: the ghostly touch of blood and betrayal and fate.

11

OUTSIDE LU, SECOND MONTH

Zhu sat beside Xu Da at their campfire as the men set up camp, and catalogued all the changes in that familiar handsome face. His cheekbones stood out more sharply, and there was a new shadow in his eyes. His grown-out hair puffed around his head like the fur of a Tibetan temple dog. Out of his gray robes, which were the only clothes Zhu had ever seen him in, he seemed like a different person. A dangerous, unknown person. *A bandit.*

Xu Da said quietly, "Look at us now. A praiseworthy pair of monks, aren't we?" The shadow in his eyes was in his voice, too. He had always been the most laughing, good-natured monk, but now she saw his recent experiences had wounded him. "I didn't mean to, you know. Break my vows."

It was startling coming from him, he who had never been particularly devout. He had first slept with a girl when he was thirteen, and had never felt a pang of conscience about the many women afterwards, as far as Zhu could tell.

As if he knew what she was thinking, he said, "Not that vow. That one doesn't mean anything. I didn't mean to kill." The shadows on his face gathered inwards: regret, bitterness. "At first."

Water hissed from the green logs in the fire. Zhu watched the bubbles gathering on the cut ends, like the froth on a dead man's mouth, and had a strange twinned memory of bandits killing her father, as if seen simultaneously from the perspectives of two different people: a boy, and a girl. She wondered if, even now, her father was one of those unmourned ghosts drifting just outside the circle of their firelight.

Xu Da said, "After I found out about the monastery I stayed in one of the tenant villages. I let them keep their rents, since who was I going to take it back to? So they tolerated me for a while. But then bandits came. They knew the monastery's protection was gone. When they came to the house I was in, they laughed when they saw me. A monk! Harmless, right? But when one grabbed me, I hit him. There was a rock behind him, and when he fell it smashed his head in." He fell silent for a moment. "I wanted to live, so I took a life. And after I joined the bandits, and they started to follow me—I took more lives. Deliberately. Even though I knew that I'd be reborn into suffering, life after life."

Zhu looked at his lowered face, burnished and hollowed by the firelight. She thought of praying on the bridge, and Heaven answering her prayer by killing ten thousand men. She hadn't prayed for those deaths, but they had been because of her, and she had welcomed them. She had broken her vow, too, because she had desired.

She slung her arm around Xu Da's broad shoulders and pulled him against her. His muscles twitched under his skin like a distressed horse. With her other hand she turned his face towards her, so close that their foreheads touched, and told him fiercely, "All that means is we have to make this life count."

He stared at her. She saw the moment the relief kindled in him, of having found her again to follow. The shadows on his face were already breaking apart. Through the cracks she saw the boy in him again. He said, wonderingly, "Who did you become, when we were apart?"

She smiled. "The person I was always supposed to be." And as long as she kept being that person in the eyes of Heaven, and even in her own mind, she could keep this precious new feeling: of fate drawing her ever onwards, into the future. *Into life.* "And one day, I'll be great."

The fire crackled, steaming the day's moisture from her robe and Xu Da's stained shirt and trousers. He said, "Remember how I always said you wouldn't become one of those dried-up papayas in the meditation hall? Even as a child, you had the strongest desire of anyone I'd ever met." His cheek moved against her hand as he spoke, their unselfconscious intimacy springing back like a vine. "From anyone else, I'd think they were just blowing up the cow skin. What does that even mean: to *be great*? But from you—I believe it."

People said that a single day without a dear friend could feel like three autumns. For the first time since the destruction of the monastery, Zhu let herself feel how long the months without him had been, and the relief she felt at their reunion. Pulling back and looking at him warmly, she said, "I'll need your help for it, big brother. Right now, I'm heading for a challenge. I have to take Lu."

"Lu? The *city*?" Xu Da stared at her. "And your leaders gave you how many men to do it with—not even a thousand? *It has a wall.*"

"I said a challenge, didn't I? Unsurprisingly, one of those leaders would love to see me fail. But I think an assault could still work, if Lu is leaderless." She filled him in on what Ma had said. "The population will probably panic and surrender without even trying to test us. But before we do anything, we should go and find out exactly what we're dealing with."

Xu Da gave her a narrow glance. The shadows were sloughing away, a hint of his old liveliness creeping back into his expression.

"We should go inside," Zhu clarified, cheered by the sight.

"I know what you meant! Ah, Zhu Chongba, you haven't changed a bit. Don't you know what cities do to people they think are thieves? How do you think they'll greet a rebel and a bandit?"

"I know exactly what they do to thieves; Anfeng tried to do it to me," Zhu said. "But from that I can say: as long as you can make the case that you're something *other* than a thief—"

She drew a handful of long, whippy sticks from the pile of firewood beside them, intending to weave a basket, then paused as the back of her neck prickled. It felt ominously like Heaven watching. After a moment the feeling subsided, and Zhu started weaving with lingering unease. She was Zhu Chongba, but if she used skills he could never have had—

The more I do things he couldn't or wouldn't have done, the more risk I run of losing the great fate.

Her hands tightened on the weaving. *I have to be him. I am him.* "Big brother—"

He was watching the nimble movements of her hands, fascinated. *Seeing me doing women's work.* Forcing away a chill, she said as brightly as she could, "Can you find me a couple of rats?"

"Purpose of your visit," said the Lu guard, half-bored and half-suspicious. Above them the Lu walls stretched the height of a six-story pagoda: smooth pale gray stone, so cleanly fitted together that they resembled the limestone cliffs above Wuhuang Monastery.

"Pest exterminators," said Xu Da, who could manage a better peasant mumble than Zhu. He made the more convincing-looking exterminator, too: big and burly, and as dirty as a bandit. In an unplanned degree of verisimilitude, he was bleeding from a rat bite on his hand.

"Uh-huh," said the guard, leaning in to inspect the trap Zhu held up, and startling when he came eye to eye with one of the rats. "If you're exterminating them, why're you carrying them around alive like that? You should let them go. *Outside* the city."

"Let them go?" said Xu Da. "Why'd we do that? We sell them. In the countryside."

"Sell—?"

"You know. To eat."

Giving them a look of disgust, the guard waved them through.

"Ugh. Go on, go on. Be out by nightfall, and stay out of the way of the procession—"

"Procession—?" Zhu said, almost crashing into Xu Da's back as he came to a sudden halt. "Oh. *That* procession."

In front of them a richly carved and lacquered wooden palanquin was being borne along in a flow of servants. Swaying hawberry-red tassels edged its domed roof, and the latticed windows were shut tightly with curtains.

"The new governor, arrived from Dadu just this morning," said an onlooker to Zhu's question.

Zhu exchanged a tight look of annoyance with Xu Da as they moved with the crowd in the wake of the palanquin. Having missed her part-of-a-chance by a matter of hours seemed worse than having missed it by days. Xu Da murmured as they walked, "We'll have to do it while he's settling in. It will only get harder the longer we wait."

An under-resourced assault on a walled city had been a bad enough idea before, but now it seemed as clearly suicidal as Little Guo had thought it would be. *At least we found out before we tried.*

They were approaching the governor's residence. Zhu and Xu Da might have been raised in the region's richest monastery, but the sight of that palace-like compound widened even their eyes. Above the whitewashed outer wall Zhu could see the main building was at least thirty columns wide, each column carved and painted and thicker around than Zhu's arms could have reached. The other buildings were almost as large, arranged around courtyards planted with towering camphor and parasol trees. Glimpsed above the foliage, mountain-shaped roofs bore turquoise tiles so thickly glazed that they broke the light like water. Gold-painted carp finials leaped into the streaky spring sky.

Zhu and Xu Da pushed through the crowd and saw the palanquin halt at the gate of the residence in front of the greeting party that had emerged from within. It was a group of the expected old advisers, and a woman in white mourning. The dead governor's Nanren wife. The spring breeze lifted the gauzy outer robe away from her dress so it fluttered like cherry petals. Her pale face bore a dislocating intensity. Even without being able to see such details from a distance, the tension in her carriage made it impossible to believe she wasn't trembling.

Governor Tolochu emerged from the palanquin. A stern-looking Semu man of middle years, he viewed the small party with his hands clasped behind his back and a dissatisfied look. To the woman he said, "Lady Rui, I presume. What are you still doing here?"

The tension in that gauze-wrapped form was like a primed cannon before the explosion. There was an edge in Lady Rui's voice as she said, "I pay my respects to the esteemed Governor. This unworthy woman was promised to be allowed to stay here in this residence, after my husband's death."

Governor Tolochu scoffed. "Promised? Who can make such a promise?"

"There is no place for me in Khanbaliq—"

"There is no place for you here, either! Are you a woman without shame, that you would be a burden upon my house?" The Governor was obviously the kind of person who received as much spiritual contentment from berating others as a cold man does from a bowl of soup. "No, I think not. To Khanbaliq or elsewhere, it matters little to me; I have no responsibility for my predecessor's debts and belongings. I cannot even fathom what he was thinking: to bring his wife with him to his post! He must have been a self-indulgent man. I will have much to correct of his work here."

Zhu watched Lady Rui's hard downturned face as Governor Tolochu's tirade beat upon her. If anything, she seemed to become even harder. Zhu had the impression that she was clenching her fists inside her sleeves. When the Governor finished he glared at Lady Rui for another moment, then swept past and into the residence. As soon as he had gone, Lady Rui straightened. She was not a beautiful woman, but the look on her face drew Zhu's attention like a wound: inwards and dreadful.

Xu Da said, frowning, "A hard man. It won't take long for him to assume control and put the militia in order. Perhaps if we do it tonight—"

Zhu's eyes were still on the Nanren woman. She didn't know what it was, but there was *something*—

Then she *did* know, even as she had no idea how she knew, given the absence of anything as obvious as a rounded belly. A dozen little observations, all coming together into a single conclusion. With a sick lurch, she realized it was something the person she was supposed to be would never have noticed. But she couldn't unsee it: the explosive potential that could end a woman, and that for a widow spelled a fate of hardship and misery.

In seeing what she shouldn't have seen, Zhu glimpsed a terrible opportunity. Every instinct screamed in alarm, and she recoiled from the idea with disgust. And yet with a wall and a strong governor now standing between her seven hundred men and success, it was the only opportunity she could see.

Governor Tolochu's servants streamed into the compound, laboring under boxes and furniture—a procession that had seemed endless on the city streets, but that was now rapidly diminishing. As Zhu watched them enter the gate, her thoughts raced. Her heart thudded a nauseating counterpoint. She knew instinctively that by doing this, she would be increasing her risk for a catastrophic future. But it was risk for the sake of a better chance of success in the here and now. For her *only* chance of success.

Risk is only risk. It doesn't make it a certainty. Not if I never do anything like it again—

She interrupted Xu Da, "Not tonight. Wait until tomorrow, then do it."

"Do—*me?*" His eyes widened. "Where will you be?"

"I have to speak to Lady Rui. Quick: let the rats out, make a distraction for the crowd so I can join those servants. *Now*, before they're all inside!"

Xu Da grabbed her arm as she lunged towards the procession, his voice rising in panic. "*Wait*. What are you doing? Get inside, then what? Lady Rui will be in the women's quarters, surrounded by maids—you won't have a chance of getting near her, let alone talking to her!"

Zhu said grimly, "*You* wouldn't. I will."

Lady Rui was sitting in front of the bronze mirror with a shaded, saturnine expression. The front of her dress lay open, baring the green veins branching across the downwards slope of her breasts. When she saw Zhu enter from behind, she glanced up; their eyes met in the metal, blurred as if through a veil. "I have no need of you at the moment. Leave me." She spoke with the unhesitating forcefulness of someone used to commanding servants.

Zhu drifted forwards. The air around her was thick and sweet, like an orchard on the hottest day of spring. It was the smell of a woman's inner sanctum, as alien to Zhu as a foreign country. Wide skirts swished around her legs, and the scarf over her head fluttered. Women's clothes gave her new dimensions, as if she were moving through space as someone else. The stolen disguise had done its job: nobody had looked at her twice as she passed through the compound and into the women's quarters. But with every moment her feeling of suffocating wrongness mounted. A violent litany repeated inside her head: *This isn't me.*

Lady Rui's inwards look sharpened. "You—! I said leave!" When Zhu still approached, she turned and delivered an openhanded slap across Zhu's face. "Are you deaf, worthless dog?"

Zhu turned her face to avoid the worst of the impact. The scarf slithered to the ground. She felt a burst of relief to have it gone. Her shaved head with its ordination scars, the one thing that set her apart from all those others who wore women's clothing, was the indelible mark of her true identity: her monk self. *That's right*, she thought, as she swung to face Lady Rui. *See who I really am.*

At the sight of Zhu's shaved head, Lady Rui gasped and snatched her clothes around herself. Before she could scream, Zhu clapped her hand over the woman's mouth. "Shh."

Lady Rui's flailing arm encountered a teapot on the side table, and smashed it hard into the side of Zhu's head.

Zhu staggered, blinded by a starburst of pain, and felt a gush of warm liquid drench her neck. She recovered just in time to catch Lady Rui's arm as she plunged the remaining piece of teapot towards Zhu like a knife. Zhu squeezed Lady Rui's wrist until she dropped the improvised weapon. Her eyes flashed mutely at Zhu from behind the silencing hand.

"Good!" Zhu said, her head swimming. "I knew you had spirit." But it had been the very opposite of good. The pain of the blow had been cold, like the touch of a familiar shadow: the nothingness that belonged to a woman's body. Just thinking of it sent a spike of panic through Zhu. She released Lady Rui and tore at her blouse and skirts in a paroxysm of dread.

Lady Rui watched her. Her first fear had been replaced by the brittle scorn of someone who had seen a grimmer future than any Zhu might represent. As Zhu stepped out of the ruins of the women's clothing and straightened her crushed robes, Lady Rui said with some hostility, "Unless you stole that robe too, I assume you must be a monk. But do tell me, esteemed one, what business requires you to go to such lengths to seek an audience. Or is it that you simply want to eat someone else's tofu? I had thought monks eschewed the carnal pleasures—" Her mouth twisted. "But then again: men are men."

She sees a monk, not a woman. Zhu could have gasped with thankfulness. She was still Zhu Chongba, and for all she had deviated from his path: it had only been for a moment.

"Greetings to Lady Rui," she said, wincing at the throb in her skull. "Normally this monk would beg forgiveness for the disrespect, but you've taken your revenge quite well. Rest assured that this monk intends no ill will—he comes bearing only a message."

"A message? From who?" Lady Rui's expression hardened.

"Ah. The Red Turbans. They even have the monasteries on their side now?" The bitter look was back. "But none of that has anything to do with me. That's all the new Governor's problem."

"Perhaps Governor Tolochu's problems aren't yours, but forgive me, Lady Rui: I can't help noticing that he seems to be something of a problem for you," Zhu said. "You're a young widow expecting a child, and he plans to send you back to your birth family to whom you'll be nothing but a shame and burden. It can't be what you want. Will you simply accept it?"

Though it had been Lady Rui's intensity that had aroused Zhu's interest in the first place, the strength of her reaction was still impressive. Her cherry petal face darkened with anger and humiliation, and she looked as if she were perfectly willing to risk her future lives by slapping a monk. "What business is it of yours, that you dare comment? And even if I didn't *want* it, what else is there?" Zhu opened her mouth, but Lady Rui cut her off viciously. "No. Who are you, a *monk*, to come and speak of my situation, as if you can understand the first thing about what women can and can't do?"

A memory leaped up, involuntarily: the hot coal of resentful submission a girl had felt, a long time ago. Zhu *did* understand, and the fact that she did sent a frisson of danger down her spine. She answered carefully, "Sometimes it takes people outside the situation to help us see clearly. Lady Rui: What if this monk can provide you with another option, one that's to both our benefits? Governor Tolochu is nothing but a Dadu bureaucrat. He has no particular knowledge of this city which qualifies him to govern. And so why let him, when there's one better qualified—one who already knows the mechanisms and office, and the characters of the men to be commanded?"

Lady Rui said, frowning, "Who?"

"You," said Zhu.

The peppery smell of chrysanthemums swirled up from the censer on the table between them. After a moment Lady Rui said flatly, "Are you mad?"

"Why not?" Not having anything concrete to offer, all Zhu

could do was open her eyes and let Lady Rui see her the depth of her sincerity. *I understand.* Even more than the act of wearing women's clothing, the acknowledgment of that girl's past was a moment of such terrifying vulnerability that she felt like she'd pulled open her skin to show her organs beneath. "Why is that so preposterous? Take power for yourself. Call upon the men who still have loyalty to your husband. Pledge Lu to the Red Turbans, and with our support even the Yuan won't be able to take it from you."

"You *are* mad," she said, but Zhu caught a flicker of puzzlement. "Women can't govern. The Son of Heaven rules the empire, as men govern cities, and fathers head the family. That's the pattern of the world. Who dares break it by putting a substance in a place contrary to its nature? It's in men's nature to take risks and lead. Not women's."

"Do you really believe that? Are you weaker than Governor Tolochu, simply by virtue of your substance? This monk doesn't think so. Aren't you risking your life right now to bear and raise a child? A woman gambles all of herself, body and future, when she marries. That's more courageous than any risk a bureaucrat takes when it concerns only his face, or his wealth." Zhu's own mother had made that gamble, so many years ago. She had died of it. Now the only person in the world who knew where she was buried was someone who was no longer a daughter, but who remembered, unwillingly, a little of what it was like to be female.

"You think I'm capable of governing *because* I'm a woman?" Lady Rui asked incredulously.

"If this monk knows equally little about Governor Tolochu or you, why wouldn't he choose you? A pregnant woman has more at stake than any man. She knows what it's like to fear, and suffer." Zhu dropped her monk speech and said, raw and urgent, "I might not know you, but I know what you want."

I recognize it.

The woman was silent.

"Let me help you." Zhu picked up the half teapot from the

ground, and pressed it into Lady Rui's pale, limp hand. "Let me give you the means to survive."

Lady Rui fingers tightened around the handle. Blood gleamed on the jagged edge: Zhu's blood. "What about the Governor?"

"If you're ready to step up—"

Lady Rui said suddenly, "Kill him." Her eyes flicked open and stabbed Zhu. Zhu all but reeled back at the violence of it. Unleashed, this delicate woman in her white gauze had all the subtlety of a crashing trebuchet.

Zhu's headache tripled. She remembered Xu Da's face: *I didn't mean to kill. At first.* "Actually, what I meant was—"

"You said I have the desire to survive? Well, you're right: I do." Lady Rui's jaw was tight with the same intensity Zhu had glimpsed earlier: a compressed rage that had as its heart the female desire to survive all that sought to make her nothing. "And since you're so determined to believe I can take a risk, believe that this is the risk I'm taking." She swiveled back to her position in front of the mirror. *"Kill him.* After that, we'll talk." Her eyes, hooded, stared coldly at Zhu from the metal. "Don't come into my rooms again."

"Come in," Governor Tolochu called from inside his office. Zhu, bearing a fish-oil lamp in one hand and a document for his seal in the other, stepped over the raised threshold and into the room. She felt a peculiar internal judder that was neither trepidation nor anticipation. Her hands sweated. For all that this was the right way, the culmination of the opportunity that had been presented to her in the form of Lady Rui, Zhu was unnaturally aware of her intent. The twelve ordination scars on the crown of her head burned. A reminder of her monastic oath, the first precept of which was: *Abstain from killing any living thing.*

Tolochu looked up as Zhu came in. His lavishly appointed office was lined with bookshelves. A perimeter of candles cast their familiar vegetable-wax smell into the room, reminding Zhu of kneeling before the monastery's altars. A shiver radiated along her shoulders. She wondered if it was the sorrowing glance of the bodhisattvas at what she was about to do.

"A monk?" Tolochu said, taking the document. "I haven't seen you before. Did my predecessor fear for his future lives so badly that he felt the need for constant guidance?" Taking up his seal, he suddenly jolted with disgust. "What—"

His fingers came away from his gown slick with oil. He shot a murderous look at Zhu. "You incompetent—!"

"Forgive me, Governor," Zhu said. "It seems the lamp leaked." The bodhisattvas were boring a hole in the back of her head, or perhaps it was only Lady Rui's headache. As Tolochu gaped in astonishment at her unservile tone, Zhu came forwards and with a single stroke swept the candles from their ledge so they fell to the ground in a burning rain.

One might have expected a sound, but in that first moment there was none. The silent wave of fire swept across the oil-soaked floor and snatched the hem of Tolochu's gown. In another instant he was a human candle. The sheet of fire spread to the edges of the room and sent its fingers into the books on the shelves. And then it did have a sound. It was a whisper that deepened into a throaty roar like the wind through pines, except this was a vertical wind. As it blew the dark smoke roiled ever faster upwards, curling upon itself as it met the ceiling so that above there was nothing but descending blackness.

Zhu watched, transfixed. For a moment she forgot all about Tolochu, and her broken vow, and the greatness and suffering that lay ahead. All she could see was the speed and power of the fire's destruction. The monastery had burned, but not like this: terrifying and present, almost alive. It was only when the heat grew oppressive that she realized she had been there too long. She turned to go.

There was movement in the corner of her eye. She twisted, too late, as a blazing figure slammed into her and bore them both to the ground. Zhu struggled as Governor Tolochu loomed over her, his face a cracked black mask with red bubbling through from within. His hair was a pillar of flame, melting the fat from his scalp so that it ran down his cheeks like tears. His teeth seemed to have elongated, standing out stark white in that lipless mouth that was open and soundlessly screaming. But there was still strength in his hands as they closed around her throat.

Zhu fought like a cat, but she couldn't break his hold. Thrashing, choking, her flailing hand found something on the floor that branded her even as she grasped it, and with the strength of desperation she thrust it straight into Tolochu's face.

He reared up, a writing brush sticking from his eye. Then he lunged back at her, and they rolled thrashing across the floor. They rolled again as Tolochu continued his hitching, silent screaming. This time Zhu landed on top. Some animal part of her knew what to do. She leaned forwards and pressed her forearm against his throat, feeling it slip on blood and fluid. Tolochu jerked under her. She kept pressing, coughing and retching from smoke. Beneath her, Tolochu's mouth opened and closed like a fish. Then, finally, it stopped.

Zhu staggered off the corpse and towards the doorway. Every breath seemed to sear her from the inside, and she had the terrifying thought that she was crisping and curling around it like a piece of grilled meat. The room was a furnace of bright flame and that ever-lowering ceiling of smoke. She fell to her knees and crawled, then threw herself outside.

She lay gasping on the cold stone, looking up at the black sky. *The Buddha said: live life like your head is on fire.* If she'd had the strength, she would have laughed and shuddered at the same time. She and Tolochu had been on fire: they had felt the fragile nature of their own lives. But instead of being lifted into enlightenment, they had fallen. The pressure of their mortality had driven every human thought from them but the determination to survive. And Zhu, who had nurtured that desire since childhood, had been the stronger and taken Tolochu's life.

She had felt his life ebbing under her hands and the moment it stopped. She had killed ten thousand Yuan soldiers, but this was different. She had *wanted* it. She remembered Xu Da's grief at his own acts. *There is no redemption for murder.*

The world was revolving, and she felt herself tipping slowly into the center of it. She was falling, but instead of into nothingness she was falling into smoke with flames licking far, far beneath.

Zhu coughed herself awake. In addition to a pounding headache, a body comprised solely of aches and pains, and lungs full of black phlegm: she was in jail. A cold, damp, dark, underground jail with ghosts in every corner. But while it wasn't her favorite kind of place, the important thing was that she was still alive. With the vividness of a nightmare, she suddenly remembered the hot collapsing feel of Tolochu's flesh as she pressed on his throat. *I killed him, so I could live.* When she'd imagined the act beforehand, she had thought she would get a grim satisfaction from it—that despite everything else, at least it proved she was capable of doing what she needed to do.

Now she knew: she *was* capable. But there was no satisfaction in it, only a lingering sick feeling.

After a length of time in which one could have drunk five or six pots of tea, an upper door clanged. A light footfall descended. Presently Lady Rui appeared in front of Zhu's cell and observed her through the bars. Zhu, coughing, was disturbed to see a powerful inwardness about her: something new and evasive. Lady Rui said coolly, "You nearly burnt down the entire residence. That certainly would have had people thinking it was an accident. As it is, it would have looked better if you had died with him."

Zhu rasped, "*Monk.* Not assassin." She wondered where the conversation was heading. "You got what you wanted, didn't you?"

"Indeed," said the other. Her face was as seamless as an egg.

"So then we have an agreement."

"That I become governor, and pledge this city's loyalty to the Red Turbans?"

"That's the one," Zhu agreed. Every word from her crushed throat was an agony. No doubt Governor Tolochu's spirit would be pleased by the thought of his murderer having been branded with a necklace of his fingerprints.

Lady Rui drifted closer, one white hand settling on the lock. Her floating gauze made her seem as insubstantial as the ghosts lingering in the empty cells. "It happened just the way you said. I issued my commands to those who had been loyal to my husband, and the men followed me. Now I have a walled city to call my own. I have my own militia. And it makes me think— perhaps I don't even need the support of either the Yuan or the Red Turbans." Her composure seemed the embodiment of the underground chill. "You've opened my eyes, esteemed monk. There are so many more options open to me than I thought."

In other circumstances, Zhu might have admired her flowering. She said, "And you think if you leave me here, you'll have even more options."

"Indeed," she said. "In one respect, I suppose it's a pity. I do admit to some curiosity about you. You saw something in me that I didn't know myself. I find it strange. What kind of man bothers to see potential in a woman, and encourages her despite her own doubts? At first I thought it was because you were a monk. But such a strange monk, coming to me in women's clothes. It made me wonder—" She paused, then went on, "Is that why you helped me? Because you're a woman, too."

Zhu's heart slammed hard once, then seemed to stop. "*I'm not*," she said violently. It came tearing out of her abused throat before she even knew what she was saying, like blood from a wound. In a burst of clarity, she saw what loomed in front of her for the transgression of having understood a woman's pain: to be stood up in front of Heaven, so her name and great fate could be stripped from her.

No, she thought with increasing fury. Lady Rui didn't have that power over her. She was only speculating; she didn't know. And while Lady Rui might have options, Zhu hadn't exhausted all her options yet either. Her heart resumed beating, murderously alive.

"My name is Zhu Chongba, of the Red Turbans," Zhu said with icy control. "And rest assured that the only reason I helped you is because it gets me closer to what I want."

As they glared at each other, there came a sudden clanging from upstairs, and raised voices. A guard charged down the stairs calling, "Lady Rui, the city is under attack!"

At that, Lady Rui's facade shattered and she looked at Zhu in raw surprise. Then, mastering herself, she said, "I see. You didn't trust me either. Friends of yours?"

"Better to let them be your friends, too, don't you think?" Zhu said. Her relief was sharp-edged, as vicious as revenge. "Unless this is the moment you want to put your newfound control to the test. Would you like to try, and see who has the better command of their men?"

It was still mostly a bluff. Even Zhu's steel determination couldn't change the fact of seven hundred men against a city. But she let Lady Rui look into her eyes, and see her belief in her own future greatness there—and even before Lady Rui drew the key from her sleeve, Zhu knew she had won.

Lady Rui unlocked the door with a vinegary expression. "It seems I still have something to learn. Go, Master Zhu, and tell your men to come inside, in peace." There was something about the way she said *Master Zhu* that gave Zhu the unpleasant feeling she was being returned a similar female understanding to the one she had extended to Lady Rui earlier. "We have a deal. The Red Turbans will protect Lu, and I'll give you everything you need. I give you my word."

Zhu stepped from the cell. "Rule well with the Buddha's blessings, my lady," she said. As she turned from Lady Rui, she was alarmed to feel, for the first time in her life, a strange, muted pang of sisterhood. Disquieted, she shoved it into that same deep place she kept the pain of her battered body, and ran up the stairs towards the door that led out to Lu. *My city. My success.* She had tempted fate by using tools that Zhu Chongba might not have had, and broken her monastic oath by taking a human life with her own two hands—but despite how those actions had felt, and whatever future suffering they would bring, they must have been the right choices. *Because in the end, I got what I wanted.*

The thought jolted her to a stop on the dark staircase. She heard an echo of Xu Da's voice: *What does that even mean: to be great?* Even before joining the Red Turbans she had known she needed power. She had known that greatness needed an army behind it. But the idea of greatness itself had been abstract, as if she were pursuing something she would only recognize once she had it. But now, in a flash of insight, she knew exactly what had been threatened by this encounter with Lady Rui. What she had killed for.

Hesitantly, Zhu extended her closed right hand. The darkness should have made the gesture foolish, but instead it felt grave and real. She summoned her memory of the Prince of Radiance's red flame hovering in his cupped palm. And then she *believed*. She believed in what she wanted so hard that she could *see* what it would look like. The acid taste of power filled her mouth. *The power of the divine right to rule.* She took a breath and opened her hand.

And her belief was so strong that for the first moment she thought she *did* see that red flame, exactly as she had imagined. It was only a heartbeat later that she realized:

There was nothing.

The bottom fell out of Zhu's stomach, and she felt as sick as she had ever felt. She couldn't even tell herself it had been a joke. She had *believed* it: that she would have the Mandate, because it was her fate. But she didn't have it. Did that mean that killing Governor Tolochu was only the beginning of what she was going to have to do to get what she wanted? Or—had she already done too much that wasn't what Zhu Chongba would have done, and lost her chance at that fate entirely?

No. She pushed that thought away in violent refusal. It wasn't that she didn't have it; it was only that she didn't have it *yet.* Putting all her determination behind the thought, she told herself: *As long as I keep moving towards my great fate, and keep doing what I need to do, one day I'll have it.*

Somewhere in her head, Lady Rui murmured: *The Son of Heaven rules the empire—*

When Zhu clenched her fist she felt her nails bite into her palm. Then she shouldered open the heavy dungeon door, and stepped out into the blinding sunlight of the walled city of Lu.

Ma Xiuying, standing atop Anfeng's crumbling battlements, saw them arrive from Lu: a strange admixture of Red Turbans, bandits, and two thousand orderly, well-equipped city soldiers marching in their leather armor. Behind them came the wagons piled high with grain, salt, and bolts of silk. And riding on his bad-tempered Mongol horse at the head of the procession was Monk Zhu himself. An unprepossessing little figure in robes instead of armor. From Ma's elevated perspective his circular straw hat made him look like a lopped stump. It was hard to believe that someone like that had done the impossible. But even as she thought it, Ma remembered him saying *I*. It hadn't been the speech of a monk detached from earthly concerns, but that of someone keenly aware of his own interests. *Someone with ambition.*

Monk Zhu and his procession came through the gate to the stage that had been set up to receive them. The Prince of Radiance and the Prime Minister sat on thrones that gleamed dully under the cloudy sky. The other Red Turban leaders waited at the foot of the stage. Even from a distance Ma could recognize Little Guo's humiliated, disbelieving posture. He and his father had bet against Chen—and somehow, because of the monk, they had lost. The monk in question dismounted and knelt before the stage. Ma saw the thin brown stem of his neck under the tilted hat. It disoriented her: that someone who seemed incapable of failure could be housed in that small, vulnerable body.

Left Minister Chen moved to Zhu's side. "Your Excellency, your faith in the monk has brought upon us a thousand fortunes. And this is only the beginning of what Heaven has promised us. From this point on our victories will be increasingly numerous until the descent of the blessed Buddha himself."

The Prime Minister, who had been gazing devotedly at the kneeling monk, leapt to his feet. "Indeed! Our highest praises upon this monk, who brought the light of the Prince of Radiance into the city of Lu, and who gives us the faith and strength to defeat the darkness that remains before us. Praise upon the monk! Praise the new commander of the Red Turban battalions!"

Zhu rose and cried, "Praise the Prime Minister and the Prince of Radiance! May they rule ten thousand years!" The power of his light voice shocked Ma to her core. It rang across dusty Anfeng like a bell, and in response the men threw themselves to their knees and performed their reverences to the Prime Minister, and shouted aloud their loyalty to him and the sacred mission of the Red Turbans.

On the stage, high above those men standing and kneeling and standing again like breaking waves, the Prince of Radiance watched from behind his strings of jade beads. From the angle of his hat, Ma could tell he was watching Monk Zhu. When Zhu finished his prostrations and glanced up at the stage, Ma saw the Prince of Radiance's head jerk backwards. The strings of his hat swayed.

"May the leaders of the Red Turbans rule for ten thousand years!" cried the crowd with such force that Ma felt the vibrations in her chest, and faint tremors in the great wall beneath her feet.

The Prince of Radiance raised his small head to the sky. The crowd hushed at the sight. With his head thrown back, the beads around his face had parted, and they saw he was smiling.

As he stood there the crimson color of his gown intensified, as though a single ray of sunshine had penetrated the clouds and was touching him alone. And then the light escaped his boundaries; it surrounded him in a dark, shimmering aura. No drowning lamp flame as of the Mongol emperors, but a consuming fire that filled the whole space between Heaven and earth with its eerie red light.

The Prince of Radiance said something that Ma couldn't hear. The crowd picked it up, repeating it until the murmuration built into a cry that raised the hair on Ma's arms: *The radiance of our restored empire will shine for ten thousand years.*

The world was drenched in red, so intense that it seemed more akin to darkness than light. For a moment Ma felt so oppressed she couldn't breathe. Shouldn't radiance be brighter? For all that red was the color of fortune, of prosperity—she couldn't shake the image of their new era awash in blood.

Two days later Ma picked her way through the throng of men, horses, and tents in the grounds of the ruined temple and went inside. She had expected it to be just as busy inside, but the main hall was empty. There was only an unpainted wooden statue at the back, sitting serenely amidst the shafts of light piercing the disintegrating roof. At its feet a pot of ash and grains held a few smoldering incense sticks.

Ma had just seated herself on a fallen beam when Monk Zhu came in. She glimpsed a roofless annex through the doorway behind him. A simple split-bamboo pallet was laid out under a tree that had grown up through the broken paving stones.

"Your prayers won't be heard that way. Incense?" He offered her a handful of sticks.

Instead of taking one, she searched his face. He bore her scrutiny tolerantly. He was still wearing the same shabby robes. His expression was the same too: mild interest. But how much of that was performance?

"How did you do it? Unseat the Yuan's governor and put a *woman* in his place?"

He smiled. "I didn't do much of anything. I just saw what she wanted." He was still using *I*. Something about the cool closeness of the temple made it seem profound, like a promise of the future.

"You recognized it because you want something too. No one else knows, do they?"

"Knows what?" His face flickered, and for one irrational moment she felt afraid.

She said, less certain, "You didn't accidentally stumble into Anfeng. You *came* here."

His tension released, and he laughed. "Came here deliberately?" He sat down beside her. "Aiya, why would I do that? Anfeng was hardly welcoming to this clouds and water monk. Don't you remember how your own betrothed nearly chopped off my head the moment he saw me?"

More performance, she thought, and just like that she was certain again. "Don't pretend! You came here, and even from the beginning you wanted command within the Red Turbans, didn't you?" Out loud, it sounded preposterous. Monks weren't supposed to want things. They weren't supposed to have *ambition*. And yet—

After a moment Zhu said, "You know what else no one knows?"

"What?"

His eyes smiled at her. Ordinary eyes in an unhandsome face; it was strange how they captured her. He said, "That you're smarter than all of them put together. You're right. I did come."

Hearing that preposterous statement from his mouth, having it proved real, was more disconcerting than validating. "But why the Red Turbans? If you wanted to lead, you could have easily become a bandit like your monk friend. Why take the one in a million chance of success at Lu?"

"What are bandits but rabble?" he said softly. "Why would I want to be their leader?"

Looking at him through the dimness, Ma felt a chill. "Then what *do* you want?"

She couldn't understand how someone could want anything so much that he would face the impossible for it. It wasn't that he thought himself infallible, she thought. That would take stupidity, and for all he pretended naïveté, he wasn't stupid. It was almost as if his desire were so fundamental to him that the thought of letting it go was more dreadful than any risk to pursue it. Ma found it unsettling. If your desire was the most important thing in the world, what wouldn't you do to achieve it?

He was silent. She thought he might not answer, but then he said simply, "My fate."

She hadn't expected that. She frowned. "What's the point of wanting your fate? It'll happen whether you want it to or not."

His gaze had gone to the wooden statue at the back of the temple. Seen in profile, the contour of his cheekbone gleamed in the imperfect dark, statue-like. But under the stillness there was a churn Ma couldn't make sense of. Doubt? It made no more sense to doubt the inevitability of fate than it did to doubt the color of the sky. At length he said, "I don't think you've ever really wanted, Ma Xiuying."

The truth of that took her aback. But if everything in your life was as preordained as your fate, what point was there in wanting? Ma's father had given her to the Guo family; she would marry Little Guo; she would bear his children; and one day she would give her daughters to other men. That was how it would go. It was the pattern of the world. She said rather sharply, "I thought monks teach that desire is the cause of all suffering."

"It is," he said. "But you know what's worse than suffering? Not suffering, because you're not even alive to feel it." An incoming draft stirred the air, blurring the thin lines of incense smoke. His eyes flicked to her, and she startled. *He sees me*, she thought, and the peculiar intensity of it made her feel like she was being seen for the very first time. As if spilling some hard-won secret into the closeness between them, he said, low,

"Learn to want something for yourself, Ma Xiuying. Not what someone says you should want. Not what you think you should want. Don't go through life thinking only of duty. When all we have are these brief spans between our nonexistences, why not make the most of the life you're living now? The price is worth it."

She stared at him, the hairs on her arms prickling. For a moment she saw that long scroll of the world's time, each of her lives no brighter or longer than a firefly's flash in the darkness. She knew instinctively that he hadn't been performing—it was something he believed. But in the same instant she saw that raw truth of him, she realized that that was all it was: something that was true for *him*. A man could want anything the world offered and still have a chance, no matter how small, of achieving it. For all he had acknowledged her as a being capable of desire, he hadn't seen her reality: that she was a woman, trapped within the narrow confines of a woman's life, and everything that could be wanted was all equally impossible.

She rose to leave. "Maybe *your* suffering is worth whatever it is you want to achieve," she said bitterly. "But mine wouldn't be."

12

HICHETU, SHANXI, THIRD MONTH

The sight of Hichetu's wide open plains, where the wind rolled the grass west in endless waves of green and yellow, never failed to bring a deep ancestral yearning into Esen's heart. The Great Khan's hunting camp, though, was to a steppe nomad camp as a city is to a village. Instead of felt, the gers were of finest woven lambswool; at their doors carpets were unrolled beneath flickering satin awnings. Roaming from carpet to carpet was everyone of note in the Great Yuan. Ministers and generals; Princes of the Blood and imperial princesses; provincial governors and hostage princes from the vassal states. And everywhere the thousands of servants, maids, chefs, doctors, guards, grooms, huntsmasters, priests, and entertainers required to tend their masters. The guests drank grape wine and airag, ate meat prepared in the exotic fashions of the western khanates, and used the finest Jingdezhen porcelain. Their horses and herds ate the grass down until it was as bare as a monk's head, scattered all about with the jeweled gers glittering in the steady plateau sun.

In the center of them stood the Great Khan's ger. Its immaculate white silk walls had been embroidered with such a density of gold thread that they crinkled as the wind blew. Inside, the Great Khan sat on a raised platform. Esen, prostrated on the carpet in a row with his father and brother, cried out with them, "Ten thousand years to the Great Khan, ten thousand years!"

The Great Khan, the tenth emperor of the Great Yuan, said, "Rise."

Esen had fought his whole life for the abstract concept of Great Yuan. Now, being in the presence of its very embodiment, he was overcome with an intoxicating feeling of purpose. He sat up on his heels and dared take his first look at the Son of Heaven. The Great Khan wore a gown the color of a gold tael; dragons ghosted within like the clouds in a clear soup. His face was surprisingly ordinary: round and fleshy, with red cheeks and heavy eyelids. There was a lassitude in that face that surprised Esen and made him uneasy. Even though he had known better, some part of him had always believed the Great Khans were still warriors.

"We bestow our greetings upon the Prince of Henan," the Great Khan said. "We hope your journey here was smooth, and that your family and herds remain in good health."

"It has been a long year since this unworthy one last paid you his respects, Great Khan," Chaghan replied. "We are grateful for the opportunity to enjoy your hospitality, before returning to executing your will against the rebels."

The Great Khan's gaze wandered over Baoxiang and landed on Esen. "We have heard much of the son of yours who leads your army. Had you brought him before, we would have gladly recognized him. Is this he?"

Esen's body flooded with anticipation. He performed another prostration. "This unworthy servant pays his respects to the Great Khan. I am Esen-Temur, first son of the Prince of Henan. I would be honored to present my account of the situation against the rebels in the south."

"Mmm," said the Great Khan. As Esen rose from his prostration, his anticipation turned to confusion: the Great Khan had already lost interest. "The Grand Councilor will have received your reports."

Esen had spent the last two days preparing for this encounter. He had braced himself for castigation, and hoped for at least some praise. He knew how critical his campaigns against the rebels were to the security of the Great Yuan. Now, blindsided by this most blatant disinterest, he said uncertainly, ". . . Great Khan?"

"Great Khan." An official stepped from behind the throne. Unlike the Great Khan, whose bearing disappointed, the Grand Councilor spoke with all the composure and authority one expected from the supreme commander of the Yuan's military. He regarded the three of them with an inscrutable expression. "Indeed I have been kept well informed about the accomplishments of the Prince of Henan's forces. This past year has once again seen them achieve magnificent victories against the Great Yuan's enemies in the south. A crushing defeat of the entire Red Turban movement is at hand. Great Khan, please reward them!"

The Grand Councilor's elision of his defeat left Esen thankful and, at the same time, disturbed. It seemed an important matter to be glossed over. He didn't like the idea that his successes and failures, so hard-earned in the field, might be nothing more than weapons for the court's internecine battles.

The Great Khan smiled vaguely down at Chaghan. "The Prince of Henan has always been the Great Yuan's most loyal subject, and deserving of our highest praise," he said. "He shall be rewarded. But now, Prince: go forth and eat and drink, and let me see your sons in competition tomorrow. It brings us pleasure to see the future of the Great Yuan out on the field."

As they rose and backed away from the throne, Esen thought wretchedly of his shattered expectations for the meeting. The Great Khan was supposed to be the personification of the culture and empire that Esen cherished and made his life's work to protect. To discover that the Great Khan was no more than a—

But he couldn't even make himself even think it.

As they stepped outside, they collided with the next group of nobles waiting to give their greetings to the Great Khan.

"Why, Chaghan!" said Military Governor Bolud-Temur of Shanxi in a boisterous voice. "Good to see you looking well. I trust your family and herds are in fine health." At his side, Altan bestowed upon them his customary look of pimply satisfaction. Unlike the rather austere Prince of Henan, the Military Governor of Shanxi was a man who took pleasure in excess. His ostentatiously embroidered riding costume, styled with a pleated skirt in the current fashion of the imperial court, was such a violent shade of aquamarine that Esen was surprised he hadn't attracted every winged insect within five li. Already the father of the Empress, Bolud somehow managed to carry himself in the manner of someone expecting even higher imperial favors.

"I must say: what a surprise it was to receive your request for extra troops," Bolud went on. "I wouldn't have imagined such a defeat was even possible against those peasants. What do they even fight with, spades? Good thing you had me to bail you out, eh? Anyway, this must be your first son, Esen-Temur. It's been so long since I've seen you here, Esen, I can't help but think of you as still a boy. Well, I'm sure you've learned a lesson or two from recent events. If *I* had a general who lost ten thousand men in a single night, I'd have him wrapped in carpet and thrown in the river. Though I did run across him just before, and I see why you haven't. By Heaven, he's a pretty one! You should sell him as a woman and get three times the price as for a failed general—" He guffawed. "And here's Wang Baoxiang! I couldn't believe it when Altan told me you still aren't leading a battalion. At your age! And every year you refuse to play here in the competitions. Surely it's not because you can't draw a bow, but—"

Archery was the Mongols' birthright; there wasn't a man or woman who could call themselves Mongol if they couldn't draw a bow. As Bolud glanced pointedly at Baoxiang's smooth hands, Esen found his blood boiling on his brother's behalf. Not for the first time, he regretted their dependence upon Bolud.

Baoxiang said, far more politely than Esen expected, "Perhaps this year I'll break my habit and play, Esteemed Military Governor. I'm sure it will please my father."

"Well, good!" said Bolud heartily, as if he hadn't insulted everyone present in nearly a single breath. "I look forward to your performance."

Baoxiang bowed, but Esen saw his calculating eyes tracking the Shanxi nobles all the way into the Great Khan's ger.

Much to Ouyang's displeasure, the Great Khan's competitions lasted from sunup to sundown of the lengthening spring days. Men—and even some women—contested in every feat of skill under the sun. Archery and horse racing, trick riding and goat pulling and cow-skin blowing, falconry and polo and knife throwing and every type of armed and unarmed combat from all the lands of the four khanates. Both he and Esen, who were accustomed to spending their energies on productive warfare, found it bizarre. In Hichetu it was the performances that were praised, not the outcomes; often a loser with a flashier style was feted.

"What did you expect, that merit is the basis for advancement in court?" Lord Wang had said acerbically when Esen pointed it out, and strolled away under his parasol with a drink in his hand.

Ouyang, standing in the middle of the competition field with the harsh plateau sun pounding on his helmet, thought that for once Lord Wang had the more enviable activity. At the field's perimeter court nobles lounged in silk pavilions and laughingly laid bets, and were attended by flocks of servants bringing around all manner of snacks that were far too peculiar for Ouyang's tastes: sweet and spicy dried squid cooked with almonds; rice-stuffed fried red dates in osmanthus syrup; salty yak-butter tea; baskets of alarming-looking tropical fruits from the far south. He felt sweaty and irritated. He had been competing in sword-fighting bouts all morning, and every single one of them had gone the same way. Opponents, assuming they were facing someone with the strength of a stripling boy (or worse: a girl), charged in and received their correction. Ouyang's style was neither graceful nor artistic, which displeased the crowd. It was, however, extremely effective.

"General Zhang Shide of Yangzhou to contest the next match against General Ouyang of Henan!" a herald bellowed, and Ouyang's next opponent came towards him across the grass. He saw a Nanren whose handsomeness seemed unrelated to his particular features, which were undistinguished. A square hairline and strong brow; the rest already careworn. But there was deeply felt emotion in the way the shadows fell beneath his eyes and around the corners of his mouth. A thousand future expressions waiting to form.

"But can this really be the first time we meet?" Ouyang asked, speaking Han'er. The Zhang family, whose mercantile empire controlled the coast and the Grand Canal that supplied Khanbaliq with its salt and grain, was of such importance to the Great Yuan that Ouyang had a long familiarity with General Zhang's name and personality. It was odd to realize the knowledge had no basis in real connection.

For a bare instant General Zhang's eyes flicked behind Ouyang in something like surprise, then the look was gone as he gave a warm smile of greeting. "It's strange, isn't it? This feeling that we already know each other. When I heard you would be here in Liulin"—he used the Han'er name for Hichetu—"I looked forward to this meeting as with an old friend." He threw an ironic look at the audience. "Though I didn't *quite* have these circumstances in mind."

"Never underestimate Mongols' taste for competition," Ouyang said. "Give two men a piece of meat each, and they'll compete to see who can finish first."

"And do you share that taste?" Zhang said, with amusement.

Ouyang smiled slightly. "To be sure I don't enjoy losing."

"That's hardly exclusive to Mongols. When the Emperor asked me to compete, do you know I felt it beneath my station?

I considered throwing one of the matches, to be let off earlier. But unfortunately my pride refused to let me lose. So now here we both are. The mighty defenders of the Yuan, about to chase each other around at midday for the entertainment of the masses."

They made their genuflections to the imperial pavilion and turned to face each other. Ouyang said, "Maybe it's a good thing: if we only know a little of each other now, we're sure to know each other very well afterwards."

"We could have done the same over a nice meal."

"By seeing who could finish first?"

Zhang laughed. "Ah, you have the name and face of one of us, but I see you really are a Mongol. Apart from a love of competitive meat eating, your accent in Han'er gives you away. Shall we?"

Although only of medium build, Zhang was larger than Ouyang and had the advantage of experience. In his first attack he revealed a style that was warm and passionate; it had all the sensitivity and artistry that Ouyang's lacked. The crowd cheered, finally getting the show that Ouyang had denied them.

Parrying Ouyang's counterattack, Zhang said, "Are you really that desperate to win and go up against the Third Prince?"

"The Third Prince?" The sole royal prince to have survived childhood, the Third Prince was the son of the Great Khan's favorite and most powerful concubine. Already nineteen, he still showed no sign of having come into the power of the Mandate of Heaven that was the requirement to be appointed crown prince. Since it was vanishingly rare for princes to acquire the Mandate in adulthood, most Mongol nobles believed that a more suitable prince would be born one day to inherit the Mandate and the throne.

"You didn't pay attention to the other bouts? He'll play the victor of this one, in the final. Though I have to say, his skills are what you'd expect of someone who's never allowed to lose."

"An easy victory, then," Ouyang said, as they broke apart to regroup.

Zhang, who had lost the athleticism of his prime, was panting a little. "Maybe so, but surely the winner ought to be worried about his career. Do you care that much about the prizes?"

Ouyang's future contained more to worry about than his career. Even now he was preternaturally conscious of the imperial pavilion beckoning to him like the edge of a cliff. He knew it wasn't the right time to poke this particular wound. But for all that, he knew he still would.

Pretending lightness, he said, "Does that mean you're giving up?"

"Not at all," Zhang said, grinning. "I'm happy to step up against the Third Prince. No harm in him knowing my face. I'll just throw the match when I'm there. Gracefully, of course. A young man likes to have his skills flattered."

"A young man should know honestly how his skills compare to others," Ouyang scoffed.

"Have you really made it so far in your career without the need for flattery?"

"With sufficient competence, there's no need of flattery." *If only the whole world worked that way.*

"Aiya, it's a good thing you ended up in the military. You and I are simple men. Politics would be the end of us—" Just as he was finishing, Ouyang saw an opening in his defense and lunged, and sent the other general flying.

"I see you don't flatter my skills," Zhang said ruefully from the ground.

Ouyang pulled him up. "You know how well your talents are! You don't need my flattery."

Zhang brushed himself off. Ouyang saw he was considering whether or not to deliver advice. But in the end all he said was, "Good luck, General," and left the field with a parting smile.

"The Third Prince!" the herald called, as a handsomely broad-faced young Mongol strode onto the field. The beads in his braids were lapis and silver, to match his earrings and armor.

"General Ouyang," greeted the Third Prince. Despite being on the very cusp of adulthood, and having a well-developed warrior's build much like Esen's, there was a poorly masked vulnerability in his bearing that made Ouyang think of someone much younger. The Third Prince examined Ouyang with perverse interest, as if excited by his own repulsion at meeting something new and unnatural. "Would you like to rest a moment before our match?"

Ouyang prickled beneath the examination. He made a point of not lowering his gaze, so that when the Third Prince's assessment came up to his face the young man startled. Ouyang knew that surprise: it was that of someone who had forgotten that Ouyang's face concealed a man, with a man's thoughts and experience. "Your Highness. It is an honor for this unworthy servant to compete against you. Please, let us continue."

The Third Prince lifted his sword. He might have resembled Esen physically, but his form was nothing like: it was as pretty as it was useless. "Then let's begin."

Ouyang struck. One quick, irritable blow, as he would give a fly. The Third Prince slammed into the dirt. Even as he lay sprawled, Ouyang had already forgotten him. The Third Prince meant nothing, either as a threat or an opportunity, just as this victory was nothing but an opportunity he should know better than to take. A mysterious sensation was building inside him. His heart pounded from the strength of it; the pain of it drove him to action. *I want to see the face of my fate.* The crowd rumbled.

"The victor shall approach the Great Khan!"

Ouyang approached the imperial pavilion and knelt. He felt stretched thin around that terrible, unknowable feeling. Perhaps it was his whole life, condensed into a single emotion. He bowed his forehead to the worn grass three times. Then, finally, he looked up at the Great Khan. He beheld that golden figure on the throne, and the world stopped. There, not twenty paces distant, was the one who had killed his father. The one who had ordered the Prince of Henan to slaughter every Ouyang male to the ninth degree, and ended the Ouyang bloodline forever. Ouyang stared at that ordinary face and saw his fate, and felt that opaque emotion swell until there was nothing else left inside him. The Great Khan was his fate and his end. The thought of that end brought a burst of relief. After everything, that would be the moment when it would all stop.

Black spots crept across his vision. He came back to himself, gasping; in all that time, he hadn't breathed. He was shaking. What did the Great Khan think of him, trembling down there? Did he look at him and feel his fate, as Ouyang felt his?

Ouyang had no idea how he would be able to speak, but he did. "Ten thousand years to the Great Khan!"

There was a long silence from above. Far longer than Ouyang would have expected, until it disturbed. The crowd murmured.

"Rise," the Great Khan said. When Ouyang pushed back onto his heels he was unsettled to find the Great Khan staring fixedly at some point behind him. For a moment Ouyang was possessed by the mad idea that if he whipped around fast enough he might actually *see* something: the miasma of his emotions, casting a withering shadow upon the grass. Seemingly addressing himself to whatever it was that held him transfixed, the Great Khan said distantly, "We would know this general's honorable name."

Ouyang found he was no longer shaking, as if he had entered the last stages of death by exposure. "Great Khan, this unworthy servant's family name is Ouyang."

The Great Khan startled and looked at Ouyang for the first time. "An Ouyang from Henan?" His hand clenched on the armrest of his chair, and weak blue flame spurted from between his fingers. It seemed completely involuntary. Was he only remembering, or was it something else that disturbed him? All of a sudden Ouyang had the terrible feeling that there was something at play that was outside the grasp of his understanding. That somehow, he had made an awful mistake—

But then the Great Khan shook himself free of whatever haunted him. He said forcefully, "This general's skills are exceptional. You bring the highest honor to your master the Prince of Henan. Please continue to serve him loyally and well." He gestured to a servant. "Reward him!"

The servants came out with boxes borne on richly embroidered cushions. Wealth equivalent to the spoils of a successful campaign. Two, even.

The whiplash from impending disaster to success left Ouyang euphoric. As he touched his forehead to the grass, behind his eyes he already saw the next time they would meet. "The Great Khan is generous. Ten thousand years to the Great Khan! Ten thousand years!"

He could still feel the Great Khan looking at him as he backed away.

The day's competitions yielded to the evening's entertainments. The feasting and drinking had begun several hours ago, and the air was greased with the aroma of stone-roasted lamb. Hundreds of tables had been laid out on the grass, the pearl-inlaid table ornaments twinkling in the light of tiny lamps. Above, silk canopies bellied in the night wind, their undersides catching the glow of the huge lanterns set on tripods throughout the space. Ouyang sat next to General Zhang, several empty ewers of wine between them, watching the line of dignitaries bearing gifts up to the raised table where the Great Khan sat with the Empress, the Third Prince, and the Grand Councilor.

Zhang observed, "One of the courts of hell must be reserved for this kind of boredom." He looked effortlessly masculine in a gown of decadent Pingjiang brocade, but as the night had worn on his elegant topknot had started to come loose.

"Just drink more." Ouyang poured him another cup. The drunker he got, the more startled he became by the sound of his own distant voice speaking Han'er. It was like having a series of realizations that there was someone inside his body who spoke and thought a different language.

"You Mongols drink more than I could have ever believed."

Ouyang scoffed. "This is nothing. All the next week will be drinking too; you had better be prepared."

"I can only prepare to endure," Zhang said sadly. Ouyang wondered if his own cheeks had the same hectic flush as Zhang's. Compared to Mongols, Nanren were notoriously bad at holding their wine. Zhang glanced at the throne and said, "Was it hard for you to meet the Emperor?"

Ouyang was so well numbed he didn't even have to repress a flinch. "Why? Because of my sorry origins?" He downed his drink and waited for Zhang to pour him another. "That's all past history. I never think of it."

Zhang regarded him. The unstable lantern light made a more impressive show of his golden hair clasp than it did the gold beads in the Great Khan's own hair, and cast deep shadows into the noble creases of his brow. What was that expression? Ouyang might be drunk, but he knew from experience that he could be all but passed out and still keep his blank facade intact. Now, though, he had the unpeeled feeling that Zhang could tell, in some very specific way, that he was lying. But perhaps Zhang decided to take pity on him, because in the end all he said was, "And the Third Prince? You're not worried he'll remember you badly?"

Ouyang relaxed; this was safer territory. "Let him remember. I don't care."

"Not just you, but the Prince of Henan and your Lord Esen. What of when they want to advance out of the regions, to the Dadu court?"

The unfamiliar Han'er name for Khanbaliq gave Ouyang a discombobulated feeling, as if he and Zhang were denizens of different worlds who had chanced upon each other in the uncanny space between. "Esen would never thrive at court," he said, feeling a prophetic sadness.

"Clearly neither would you. And what if you meet the Third Prince again next year?"

Another set of nobles approached the throne, performed their reverences, and presented their gifts. Ouyang's whole body felt hot from the wine. Despite Esen's constant urging, he usually moderated his intake. Tonight, however, he was gripped by the awareness of what tomorrow would bring. He thought muzzily: *I should suffer.*

"This is the first time I've been at one of these things in seven years," he said. "We're always on campaign in spring. I don't plan for it to happen again."

"Ever? Surely one day you'll crush the rebels. Finish your war."

"Do you believe that? That one day we'll be out of a job, because of peace?" Ouyang could imagine the death of the Great Khan, but he couldn't imagine the end of an empire. Neither could he truly imagine its return to stability. Imagination was, after all, powered by one's investment in the outcome.

"*You* could put yourself out of work," Zhang said. "But what's peace for merchants? Since the driving force of commerce is only to expand itself, the job of its general is never done. I'll be serving my master's ambition until I'm dead."

"Your brother's?"

"Ah, I had thought you knew us so well. Don't you trust the reports you receive of my brother? *He* has no ambition. Come visit us one day and you'll see. But to say we have no ambition would also be wrong."

"Ah," Ouyang said slowly. "Madam Zhang."

Zhang smiled. "Do you not believe a woman can head an enterprise?"

Esen often imputed a competence to his wives that Ouyang had never witnessed, and didn't actually believe existed. Whole men were biased when it came to women, although they always insisted that what they saw was objective fact. Ouyang said diplomatically, "You're too modest. You downplay your own contributions."

"Not at all. I'm a general like you. You carry out the orders of your master Lord Esen; I carry out the orders of mine. I know my own talents within my realm, but I also know I have little vision when it comes to commerce. It's her ambition we serve, and it's by her decision that our loyalty lies with you. Those who underestimate her tend to regret it."

There was a particular tone in Zhang's voice when he spoke of Madam Zhang, but deciphering it seemed like too much effort. Ouyang poured them both drinks instead. "Then our partnership is sound: within the broader Great Yuan, may your commercial endeavors succeed."

Zhang raised his cup. For an instant his eyes slid past Ouyang, finding interest in the empty space between the tables. This time Ouyang knew that look. It was the same distant look the Great Khan had worn, and as soon as Ouyang recognized it he was gripped by the cold, acute horror of being watched from behind. All the hairs on his neck stood up. For all that he *knew* there was nothing there, he still shuddered with the urge to turn and fight.

And then the light changed, and the dread ebbed away. From across the table Zhang was smiling at him. "Cheers."

They drank, watching Military Governor Bolud of Shanxi approaching the Great Khan's table. He was followed by his sons. Altan, being the youngest, came last.

"Seems that boy wants to make a good impression," said Zhang, referring to the great cloaked box borne alongside Altan by four servants.

"Better that he had focused such efforts into pleasing his general," said Ouyang. He was aware of betraying a rather ungeneral-like annoyance with an inferior, but found it hard to care. "I can't stand him. Unfortunately the Prince of Henan believes we need Bolud's support to successfully put down the Red Turbans. But all Bolud provides is numbers! Numbers can always be found elsewhere, can't they?"

"And with the Empress out of favor, Bolud is no longer a big fish," Zhang said consideringly.

In front of the high table Altan gestured to his servants, and the cover was whisked off the box. Even in that rowdy space of drunk people, the reveal of its contents produced a sudden intake of breath and silence.

The box was a cage, containing a very fine hunting cheetah. One of the rarest and most coveted gifts, its procurement must have taken great pains, over a very long period of time. Its cost was inestimable.

It was dead.

The Great Khan recoiled. With a thunderous brow he rose and bellowed, "What is the meaning of this insult?"

Everyone present knew the insult: a dead animal wished nothing but the same for the Great Khan. It was the grossest treason.

Altan, who had been staring at the cage with his mouth hanging open and his face gone gray, fell to his knees and began crying his innocence. His father and brothers threw themselves down beside him and began shouting over the top of each other. The Great Khan towered over them, glaring with lethal rage.

Zhang said, "I didn't expect that."

Ouyang found himself laughing. Even to himself it sounded hysterical. A distant part of him, the part that never let go despite how much he drank, realized he had just received an unexpected gift. Out loud he said, "Ah, that bastard has my respect."

"What?"

"I'm not the only one who dislikes Altan."

The Great Khan shouted again, "Who is responsible for this?"

Bolud, having groveled forwards until his head was nearly upon the Great Khan's instep, cried, "Forgive me, Great Khan! I had no part in this. I have no knowledge of it!"

"How can the fault of the son not also be the fault of the father!"

Suddenly the Empress rose, her red and gold ornaments glittering and swaying. Of all the Great Khan's women she was the only one who wore the traditional Mongolian hat. Its long column rose up under the lantern-light and cast dancing shadows as she trembled. She cried, "Great Khan! This useless woman begs your forgiveness for my father. Please believe that he had nothing to do with this. The boy is at fault. Please let your punishment be for him alone!"

Kneeling and shivering at the Great Khan's feet, Altan seemed small and pathetic: a boy, abandoned by his family.

The Third Prince was watching the Empress with a small smile. Of course he had no fondness for the woman who could bear a Heaven-favored son to displace him.

Seeing the Third Prince's look, Zhang said, "Him?"

Ouyang leaned his head back against his chair. His pleasure at the usefulness of what had just happened was muddled with a terrible sadness. The canopied space shone and vibrated around him. A world he wasn't part of, but was just passing through on his way to his dark fate. He said, "No."

"Take him!" the Great Khan roared, and two bodyguards sprang forwards and hauled Altan up by the elbows. "For the gravest insult to the Son of Heaven, we sentence you to exile!"

Altan was dragged away, limp with shock.

Across the twinkling tables Ouyang saw Lord Wang watching with satisfaction, his catlike eyes sleepy with amusement.

"This," Chaghan said. "This is your doing, Wang Baoxiang!"

Even inside their father's ger Esen could hear the uproar of people bustling from ger to ger to discuss the night's events. As Esen had crossed the camp he had seen that Bolud's household had already packed up and disappeared: all that was left were the flattened circles in the grass.

Chaghan was standing over Baoxiang, the lanterns swinging as if blown by the force of his anger. The Prince was only the same height as his adopted son, but from his breadth and the bristling of his beard and braids he appeared much larger.

Esen winced as Baoxiang looked their father insolently in the eye. Just like Chaghan, Esen had known instantly who had been the cause of the Shanxi contingent's downfall. At least Baoxiang had responded to insult, as a man should. On the other hand, it had been a dishonorable attack: a coward's response. Esen felt a familiar surge of frustration. Why couldn't Baoxiang just be easier, and do what was expected of him? Esen might be suited to his occupation, but it wasn't as if he had never struggled or made personal sacrifices to fulfil his father's expectations. It was what a son *did*. But Baoxiang refused. He was selfish and difficult, and to Esen impossible to understand.

Baoxiang said, "Do you even have reason to think it was me, Father?"

"Tell me it wasn't."

Baoxiang smirked. Under the bravado, though, there was something bruised-looking.

"You selfish egg! How dare you put your own petty revenge over the concerns of everyone in this family! If Bolud finds out—"

"You should be thanking me! If you bothered to think for a moment, maybe you'd realize that now Bolud has lost favor in court, you finally have the chance to step up!"

"Thanking you! How can you say with that shameless face that you did this for *us*? Without Bolud's support everything we've fought for will be lost! Our house will be ruined! Do you spit on the graves of your ancestors so easily?"

"*You don't need Bolud,*" Baoxiang shouted. "Haven't I done everything to help you break free of your dependence? Stop thinking that you need that buffoon, and have the courage to take power for yourself! Do you think it will come to you if you wait?"

"You helped me?" Chaghan's voice could have melted sword steel.

Baoxiang gave a brittle laugh. "Ah. Surprise. You have no idea what I've been doing for you this entire time. You don't even care enough to know! Don't you realize that I'm the only reason you still have an estate? Without the roads and irrigation and tax collections, do you think you'd even have the funds to continue serving the Great Khan? Your only value to him lies in your army, and *you wouldn't even have an army*.

SHE WHO BECAME THE SUN 209

You'd be nothing but a washed-up provincial whose lands are being swallowed on one side by the rebels, and Bolud on the other!"

Esen felt a pang of embarrassment on Baoxiang's behalf. Didn't he see how badly it reflected on himself to try to equate the work that Esen and Ouyang did, and that Chaghan had done before them, with the paperwork that occupied Baoxiang's days?

Chaghan spat, "Listen to you. *Irrigation.* We're Mongols! We don't *farm.* We don't dig ditches. Our armies are the Great Khan's arm in the south, and as long as the Great Yuan exists our family will defend it with honor and glory."

"Do you actually believe the idiocy that comes out of your mouth?" Baoxiang sneered. "Perhaps I didn't speak plainly enough. Without me Henan would have fallen already, whether or not you have Bolud's support. Rebellions promise their followers everything we fail to give. So if your peasants are starving, your soldiers unpaid, don't think they'd be loyal to you, or the Mongols, or the Great Yuan. They'd join without a second thought. The only reason they don't is because *I* govern and tax and administer. I pay their salaries and rescue their families from disaster. *I am the Yuan.* I uphold it more than you can ever do with the brute force of your swords. But in your hearts, don't you still think of me as worthless?"

"How dare you even imply that the Great Yuan could fall!"

"All empires fall. And if ours does, what will happen to *you,* Father, as a Mongol?"

"And you? Which side will you be on? Are you a Manji or a Mongol? I spent my breath raising you as one of us, but you would turn around to join your bastard father's people?"

Baoxiang reeled back. "My bastard father?" he hissed. "The father of my blood? Your words betray you, *Chaghan.* You never raised me as one of you. You never accepted me for who I am; you never even saw everything I did for you, all because I'm not like my brother!"

"You Manji piece of scum, with the blood of dogs! Coward

and weakling. Nobody wants you. *I* don't want you." Chaghan strode across the room and backhanded Baoxiang across the face. Baoxiang fell. After a moment he slowly rose to his knees, touching the corner of his mouth. Chaghan snatched his sword from its stand and unsheathed it.

Esen's warrior instinct realized Chaghan's intent. For all his frustrations with Baoxiang, he couldn't conceive of his maddening, impossible, pigheaded brother being erased. "Father!" he shouted.

Chaghan ignored him. Gripped by such a fury that the naked blade trembled in the lamplight, he said to Baoxiang, "I'll cut your traitor head off. The death of a true Mongol is too good for you."

Baoxiang looked up from the floor. Blood ran from his mouth; his face was contorted with hate. "Then do it. Do it!"

Chaghan snarled. The blade flashed. But it didn't descend: Esen had flung himself across the ger and caught his father's wrist.

"You dare!" Chaghan said, wrenching at Esen's grasp.

"Father!" Esen said again, applying as much strength as he dared. He knew the moment he let go, Baoxiang was dead. He could have howled with frustration. Even in resisting death, Baoxiang was causing trouble. "I beg you, spare him." His father's wrist bones creaked under his grip, until with a gasp Chaghan dropped the sword.

Snatching his hand back, Chaghan's look of pure fury skimmed over Esen and landed with finality on Baoxiang. For a moment he seemed unable to speak. Then he said with an ominous, throttled quietness, "Curse the day I took you in. You bastard Manji from eighteen generations of cursed ancestors. Never come into my sight again!"

It wasn't until he was long gone that Baoxiang unclenched his fists. His deliberateness belied by a slight tremor, he took a handkerchief from his sleeve and dabbed his mouth. When he finished he looked up and gave Esen a bitter smile.

Esen found himself without anything to say. Up until this

moment he had truly believed that if Baoxiang would just *try*, he could still be the son Chaghan wanted. But now he knew it had always been impossible.

As if reading his mind, Baoxiang said simply, "See?"

The gers shone silver in the moonlight. The smoke from their apexes wended upwards like celestial rivers. Ouyang made his way through camp to where the Prince of Henan's mounts were tied on long tethers to an overhead line stretched between two tall anchor poles. A single figure stood midway along the line with the large shadows of horses clustered near him.

Esen didn't look around as Ouyang came up. He was stroking the nose of his favorite horse, a tall chestnut that looked black in the moonlight. The horse pricked his ears in recognition, not quite in Ouyang's direction. Not at Ouyang himself, he thought uneasily, but at whatever it was that trailed unseen behind him. His own mare was tethered a few horses down the line. When she noticed Ouyang she dragged her tether along the line, bunching up all the intervening tethers into a tangle the grooms would be cursing him for in the morning, and nudged him with her nose.

Esen's shoulders were tight with misery. It was easy to tell what kind of encounter he and Lord Wang had just had with Chaghan. As he looked at Esen's noble profile, for a moment all Ouyang wanted to do was ease his unhappiness. Ouyang felt his own pain at seeing Esen hurting, and tried to imagine it multiplied by a hundred, a thousand, ten thousand. He couldn't. He thought: *I'm still drunk.*

He said, "Your father and Lord Wang. How was it?"

Esen sighed. His brashness had gone out of him. It made Ouyang think of that moment when you went to a fire in the morning, and instead of embers found only cold gray stones. It filled him with sorrow. "So you know. Of course you do. Does everyone?"

"Not know, but suspect it. Would they be wrong?"

Esen turned away. Looking at Ouyang's mare, he said, "What did you name her?"

"I haven't." Ouyang rubbed the mare's nose. "Would it make a difference to how well she serves me?"

Esen laughed sadly. "You don't find that too cold?"

"Do you name your sword? Men get too attached to their horses. We're at war; they're going to die sooner rather than later."

"I see you think so highly of my gift," Esen said wryly.

Despite his preoccupations, Ouyang smiled. "She's been a fine gift. I think more highly of the giver."

"It's normal for people to get attached to horses. To other people." Esen sighed again. "Not you. You always push everyone away. What do you find in it, the loneliness? I couldn't bear it." The warm scent of animals rose up around them. After a long moment, Esen said, "Father would have killed him, had I not been there."

Ouyang knew it was true, just as he knew there was no possible world in which Esen could have let it happen. The thought pierced him with a feeling that mingled sweetness, longing, and pain.

"I didn't believe it," Esen said. "Before. I thought—I thought maybe they just had their differences. I thought they could be reconciled."

That was the pureness that Ouyang wanted to protect forever. Esen's large heart, and his simple, trusting belief in everyone. He made himself say, "You need to be careful of Wang Baoxiang."

Esen stiffened. "Even you, you think the same of him?"

"He just destroyed the Empress's brother. For what, a few insults? Those few households your father took from him? It makes you wonder what else he's capable of." Ouyang had the painful thought that Esen was like a pet that would look up at its owner with love and trust, and try to lick and wag its tail, even as its neck was wrung. He said, aching, "You trust too much. I admire you for it. That you prefer to draw people closer, rather than push them away. But it'll get you hurt. Would you take an injured fox to your breast and not expect a bite? The worst injury you can do to a man is shame him. He can never forget it. And Wang Baoxiang has been shamed."

Esen said, "Baoxiang is my brother!"

Ouyang kept scratching slowly at the lumps of shedding winter coat on his horse's neck.

Esen said again, more quietly, "He's my brother."

They stood for a long time in the moonlight without talking, their shadows stretching out across the sea of silver grass.

The day of the hunt dawned warm and bright. Pale yellow clouds streaked the sky like banners. Attendants on foot went ahead through the tall grass, beating drums to flush out the game. The nobles followed. The sight of hundreds of mounted men and women covering the plain in all the colors of a field of flowers was one of the empire's great spectacles. It should have been enough to lift anyone's mood, but Ouyang's was irredeemably grim. His hangover felt like justice. At the same time, the situation felt unreal. After so long, it hardly seemed like the moment had come.

Esen rode up with an expression of forced cheer. His favorite bird, a female golden eagle with taloned feet as large as Ouyang's fists, was perched on his pommel. Esen stroked its back absently. It was dearer to him than any of his human daughters, and Ouyang thought it was the only living being Esen missed from the palace while they were on campaign. "Why so dour, my general? Today we ride for pleasure. Isn't that a rarity enough that we should enjoy it?" His servants had been careless with his braids; they were already unraveling, strands flying away in the breeze. Ouyang could tell he was determined to avoid thinking about the conflict between the Prince of Henan and Lord Wang, and mostly succeeding. Esen had always been good at compartmentalization. It was a talent Ouyang seemed to have lost. After a lifetime of keeping the parts of himself separate, now they all bled into each other in an unstaunchable hemorrhage.

The Great Khan's personal party was some distance ahead, heading for the rocky hills where tigers could be found. Ouyang could just make out the Great Khan, resplendent in snow leopard fur. Chaghan, benefiting from Bolud's absence, rode at his side. As befitted the occasion, the Prince of Henan wore the kind of extravagant courtly attire he usually disdained, and was riding a magnificent young horse. Unlike the sturdy Mongolian horses that were trained to tolerate the wolf, bear, and tiger hunts that Mongols made sport of, Chaghan's new mount was one of the prized western breeds known as dragon horses for their speed and beauty. Delicate and temperamental, it was a poor choice for a hunt, but Ouyang understood Chaghan's reasoning: it had been part of the Great Khan's reward for their efforts against the rebels. It paid to flatter the taste of one's sovereign.

The hills were dry and folded. Paths twisted along the edges of crevasses and ran underneath cliff faces. Hunched crab-claw trees clung in the cracks of house-sized boulders, beribboned here and there with the good-luck prayers of hunting parties from years past. The large mass of the hunting party gradually thinned as pairs and groups broke off to pursue their preferred game. Ouyang, who had his own specific game in mind, said, "My lord, I saw an ibex; I'll go this way."

It was the first time he had ever lied to Esen.

"Are you sure?" Esen said, surprised. "I didn't see it. But if you're sure, let's catch it quickly. Then we can rejoin the Great Khan for the tiger hunt."

Ouyang shook his head. "Don't waste your time with me. Better you join the Great Khan and let him see your skills." He managed a wry smile. "Those others are only used to shooting at stationary targets, so I'm sure you'll do well. I'll meet you at the peak when we break for lunch."

He urged his mare away before Esen could argue. As soon

as he was out of sight he stopped and let the reins slacken. The small gesture felt fraught with anticipation: as of the moment between hurling an insult at an opponent and waiting for his response. He had no doubt that fate would respond. Fate made the pattern of the world, and Ouyang was nothing more than a thread joining a beginning and an end.

For a moment his mare stood there. Then her ears pricked in that familiar look of recognition, and she began moving steadily along the trail towards the higher ground that his game preferred. *As if led.* Ouyang's skin crawled at the thought of what unseen guides she might be following. The way was silent except for his mare's hooves on the hard ground, and the song of orioles. The smell of warmed rock and dirt rose up around him, cut through with sharper pine and juniper. He felt like he was in two places at once, but only tenuously in both. Here—as free and alone as he ever was—and also in the future, already seeing what would happen.

As he gained height the trees thinned further. He dropped his mare to a walk and scanned his surroundings. He saw without surprise that it was the perfect location for finding a wolf. And then as he caught sight of a familiar cerise gown just off a lower branch of the path, a perfect target for every predator in the area, he mentally added: *Or where a wolf can find you.* Lord Wang was sitting reading on a rock overlooking the view, his horse tethered beside him. From his absorbed air Ouyang guessed he had been there awhile: he must have abandoned the hunt early and come here for some solitude.

A shiver passed through the landscape. It was an absence: the orioles had stopped singing. Ouyang's mare shivered too, her ears swiveling, though she was too well trained to make a sound. It was exactly what Ouyang had been looking for, but it only swamped him in bitterness. It was all perfect: everything he needed, dished up on a plate. It was perfect because his fate was inescapable, and it would happen no matter what he thought or felt or did.

Lord Wang, oblivious, was still reading below. Ouyang felt a perverse curiosity to see how long it would take for the lord to notice the danger he was in. *If he even does notice.*

In the end it was Lord Wang's horse that noticed. It broke its tether, squealing, and clattered down the path. Lord Wang looked up with a start, then bolted to his feet. Slinking bodies flowed over the stony ground like cloud shadows, emerging from behind the rocks and out of the gullies, pouring down the path after Lord Wang's horse. *Wolves.*

One wolf broke from the pack and came pacing towards Lord Wang on long legs. Its movements were slow and deliberate: a predator confident of its success. Lord Wang made an aborted gesture, and Ouyang saw horror flash across his face as he realized his bow had been tied to his saddle. A quick look behind him showed him what Ouyang already knew: there was nowhere to retreat to. The beautiful view he had chosen had him trapped.

"Try it, then!" Lord Wang shouted at the wolf. His voice had jumped an octave with fear. "You think I can't take you?" Despite his grim mood, Ouyang nearly laughed as Lord Wang threw his book at the wolf. The wolf dodged it nimbly and advanced, tail low and shoulder muscles rippling. Ouyang unslung his bow.

The wolf sprang: a hurtling, thrashing blur that slammed into the dirt just short of Lord Wang's feet, Ouyang's arrow buried in its side.

Lord Wang looked up sharply. His drained face was brittle and vicious with humiliation. "General Ouyang. You couldn't have done that earlier?"

"Shouldn't my lord be grateful I didn't just stand back and watch it happen?" Ouyang said, feeling reckless with fatalism. He dismounted and came down the slope to where Lord Wang was. He ignored the lord and gathered up the surprisingly heavy corpse, then struggled back and slung it over his mare's withers. She flattened her ears and showed the whites of her eyes, but in the brave way of the best Mongolian horses she held still as he vaulted back into the saddle.

Ouyang extended his hand to Lord Wang. "Why don't I take you back to the Prince, my lord? You can take one of the spare mounts from his train."

"Don't you think my father would rather I be taken by wolves than see me?" Lord Wang spat. Ouyang could see he was weighing up the many hours it would take to walk back, versus the humiliation of everyone knowing he had been rescued by his brother's eunuch.

Ouyang waited, and felt not a shred of surprise when the lord finally said, "*Fine.*" He ignored Ouyang's hand and sprang up behind. "What are you waiting for? Let's get this over and done with."

The Great Khan's party had taken their lunch on a bald, round-topped peak that gave a superior view of the wrinkled hills and the grasslands beyond. By the time Ouyang and Lord Wang arrived, having traveled slowly due to riding double, everyone was already preparing to leave. Ouyang could see Chaghan, easily visible in purple, reining in his dancing, banner-tailed dragon horse as he conversed in a group of mounted nobles. Ouyang guided his mare carefully as they ascended the last stretch. The ground dropped off steeply around the peak and along the edges of the paths, and he had been a general long enough to have lost more than one man to similar terrain.

The Prince of Henan's grooms and attendants were clustered on sloping ground some distance from the nobles. As Ouyang and Lord Wang rode up the spare mounts stamped and blew at the scent of the dead wolf. The grooms might not be bold enough to look directly at a general, let alone give him a glare, but Ouyang knew they were cursing him: it would be their lives, too, if a horse went off the edge.

"You," Lord Wang said to the nearest groom, dismounting with all the poise of someone who hadn't nearly been eaten by a wolf. "Bring me one of those spares."

The groom froze. His expression was that of someone

offered a choice of death by beating, or death by steaming. "Lord Wang—" he faltered.

Lord Wang said impatiently, "Well?"

"My lord," the groom said, cringing. "This unworthy servant offers his most humble apologies. But . . . it isn't possible."

"What?"

"On the explicit orders of the Prince of Henan," the unfortunate man whispered.

"The Prince of Henan . . . *ordered* . . . that I not be allowed a mount?" Lord Wang's voice rose. "And what else will I shortly find I'm not allowed to have? Will I have to beg him for food, for firewood?"

The groom saw something over Lord Wang's shoulder and looked like his dearest wish was to roll up like a pangolin. Chaghan was bearing down on them with a dark face: a purple thundercloud promising a storm. As he neared them his high-strung horse caught the scent of wolf and shied. Chaghan curbed it rather too sharply and glared down at Lord Wang.

Lord Wang met his eyes, pale and defiant. "So am I to find out by happenstance, from the *servants*, that my own father has disowned me?"

Chaghan said coldly, "Your father? I thought I made it clear that you've lost any right you had to use that name. Would that my sister had died before getting you! Get out of my sight. Get out!"

Chaghan's horse rolled its eyes and threw its beautiful head from side to side. Chaghan was a master horseman, and under normal circumstances could have controlled even the rawest horse despite its growing distress from the smell of the wolf. But he was distracted, and in no mood to be patient. Surprised and annoyed, he dragged at the horse's head. "Rotten son of a turtle—"

The grooms and attendants scattered. Ouyang alone moved towards the pair. His planned movement felt like a choreographed dance, but one that he was only watching. His mare passed Chaghan, not quite a collision, and the dead wolf's fur brushed the neck of Chaghan's horse. Its nostrils already filled with the scent of predator, this touch was too much for the poor animal. It gave a tremendous leap, landing badly on its delicate legs and crumpling onto its shoulder with a scream. Miraculously, Chaghan managed to throw himself clear so as not to be crushed. He hit the ground rolling. For a moment it seemed as if that would be all—and then the slope snatched him. His limbs beat out a flailing tattoo as he rolled, faster and faster, and then he plunged over the edge and was gone.

"Father!" Lord Wang's voice was shrill with horror as he threw himself lengthwise into the dirt at the edge, heedless of his silks. Ouyang, craning his neck for a better view, saw with surprise that Chaghan hadn't actually fallen. Somehow the Prince had caught a ledge with one hand, and was straining upward for Lord Wang's hand with the other. It should have been concerning, but Ouyang was as coldly certain as he'd been when he released his arrow at the wolf. Events were unfolding as ordained by fate; there was only one way they could go.

He saw the two reaching hands grasp. The cords in Lord Wang's neck stood out with effort as he shouted, "General, help!"

Even as Ouyang dismounted, someone screamed. It could have been Lord Wang, but more likely it was Chaghan. There was a soft thump, no louder than peaches falling in the orchard. Ouyang went in a leisurely way to where Lord Wang lay stricken, his hand still outstretched, and looked down. Far below, Chaghan's purple silks were splashed out like a lone jacaranda blooming in the dust. *Dead*, Ouyang thought. *Dead like my brothers, my cousins, my uncles. Dead like the Ouyang line.*

He waited for the expected feeling of relief. But to his alarm, it didn't come. He had thought this partial revenge would have at least lessened the pain that drove him. It should have made the shame worth it. Instead of relief there was only a growing disappointment so heavy that the weight of it threatened to tear through the bottom of his stomach. As he stood there looking down at the ruined body of the Prince of Henan, Ouyang realized he had always believed revenge would *change* something. It was only in having done it that he understood that what had been lost was still lost forever; that nothing he could do would ever erase the shame of his own existence. Looking ahead to the future, all he could see was grief.

The sound of an approaching rider came to them: at first a casual gait, then sensing something amiss, gaining speed across the rocky ground.

Esen pulled up and threw himself from his horse. His gaze was on Lord Wang; his expression was of tragedy already known.

Ouyang, intercepting him, grabbed his arm. It was something he had never done before. "Esen, don't."

Esen turned to Ouyang with the vacant look of someone not quite registering an obstruction, and pulled away. He strode to the edge and stood transfixed as he looked down at his father's body. After a long moment he wrenched his gaze to his brother. Lord Wang had pushed himself up to his knees, his face white with shock. One of his sleeves, disarrayed, bared his reddened hand.

As he looked at his brother kneeling beside him in the dust, Esen's face changed: under the realization of what had happened, it slowly became a mixture of anguish and hate.

13

ANFENG, SUMMER

Following Monk Zhu's return with the riches and loyalty of Lu, Chang Yuchun noticed that things were changing in Anfeng. On the surface, the changes were what anyone would expect from a monk: he refurbished the temple, had the roof fixed, and filled it with new statues of the Prince of Radiance and the Buddha Who Is to Come. But at the same time the temple acquired a white-sand training ground and barracks to house the monk's men. The chaotic jumble of tents disappeared, and a foundry and armory and stables took their place. Volunteer peasants flooding in from the countryside were housed and included in the drills that started happening on the training ground under the supervision of the monk's bandit friend, Xu Da. As they marched back and forth through the temple grounds in their matching armor, with new well-made equipment, all of a sudden Monk Zhu's bandits and Red Turbans and Lu men no longer looked like a random assortment of people. They looked like an army. And somehow Yuchun himself had become a member of it.

Membership, which brought with it such perks as food and lodging and a lack of people wishing him dead, came with its own caveats. First among them was the monk dragging Yuchun out of bed every morning at the godforsaken Rabbit hour so that some old swordsmaster could drill both of them in the basics of how to fight. "I need a sparring partner," Zhu had explained cheerfully. "You're about my level, in that you know absolutely nothing. Anyway! You'll like it; learning new skills is fun." Suffering through the drills, Yuchun thought it a blatant lie— until, much to his surprise, it became true. The old swords- master taught well, and Yuchun, receiving the first praise and attention of his short life, found that he craved it; he had never been so eager to please.

After training, Monk Zhu rushed off: in addition to organiz- ing his fledgling army and running mock campaigns around the nearby countryside, he was always being called to the Prime Minister's palace to officiate various ceremonies involv- ing the Prince of Radiance, or say a blessing, or chant a sutra for someone who had died. Somehow Monk Zhu stayed cheer- ful despite this impossible schedule. During one morning ses- sion when the bags under Zhu's eyes seemed particularly large, Yuchun said, thinking he was just stating a basic fact, "You wouldn't be so busy if you didn't have to run to the palace every time the Prime Minister wants to hear a sutra. Don't you think it's too much, him expecting you to be a monk as well as a com- mander? Those are two jobs!"

Seeing the monk's expression, Yuchun suddenly realized he had made a mistake. Zhu said, deceptively mild, "Never, *ever* criticize the Prime Minister. We serve him without question."

Yuchun had spent the rest of the day kneeling in the mid- dle of the training ground as punishment. For just saying the *truth*, he thought bitterly. Even more embarrassing was that afterwards everyone else in Zhu's force seemed to know what he'd done wrong. The fucking monk had made him into an *ex- ample.* He'd thought that would be the end of their morning sessions, but the next morning Zhu had dragged him out of bed as usual, and then again the next day, and by the third day it had seemed easier for Yuchun to let his sullenness go. By then he had grasped that Zhu usually had his reasons.

And perhaps the monk had realized it actually was impos- sible to do everything himself, because towards the end of the month he turned up to training and said, "I have things to do, so you'll have to learn by yourself for a bit. Now that you know the basics, I've found you a new master. I think he'll be good for you."

Seeing the person in question, Yuchun howled, "What's he gonna teach me? He's a *monk*!" Honestly, two monks were already more than any army needed, and now there were three. He had a brief, terrible vision of himself chanting sutras.

"Different kind of monk," said Zhu, grinning. "I think you'll enjoy his teaching. Let me know."

Who knew there were different kinds of monks? Apparently this one was from some famed martial monastery; Yuchun had never heard of it. Old Master Li beat Yuchun mercilessly with spears and staves and his rock-hard old man hands, until after a while a few others joined and thankfully diverted his attention. United in pain, they ran laps around Anfeng's walls and carried each other on their backs and jumped endlessly up and down the temple steps. They sparred until they were covered in bruises and their calluses bled.

Now and then Zhu still found time to drop by and spar with one or another of them in the morning. "I need to keep my hand in," he said, grinning—and then, looking up ruefully from where Yuchun had put him in the dirt, "I'd worry that I was going backwards, but I think it's that you're getting so much better." He bounced up and dashed off to his next appointment, calling over his shoulder, "Keep up the good work, little brother! One day very soon, we'll be doing this for real—"

Then Old Master Li came out again and made them work until half of them threw up, and Yuchun thought he honestly might die before he even made it into battle. That whole summer was misery upon misery, and it was only in hindsight that he realized their bodies had hardened, and their minds become those of warriors.

"Master Zhu." It was Chen, hailing Zhu as she made her way along the corridor toward the Prime Minister's throne room.

Despite the heat, the Left Minister wore his usual scholar's hat and gown. His black sleeves, pendulous with embroidery, swayed beneath his folded hands as he gave Zhu a look that had every appearance of casual interest.

Zhu, who knew that Chen's interest was rarely casual, said mildly, "This monk's greetings to the honorable Left Minister Chen."

"I happened past the temple this morning. How surprising to see how much it's changed! For a monk, you seem to be managing all your resources quite well. You pick up things quickly, don't you?" He spoke carelessly, as though he were only saying what had come to mind then and there.

Zhu wasn't fooled. A prickle crept down her spine: the feeling of being watched by a predator. She said carefully, "This unworthy monk has no particular intelligence, Minister. His only praiseworthy attribute is a willingness to work as hard as he can to fulfil the wishes of the Prime Minister and the Prince of Radiance."

"Praiseworthy indeed." Unlike other men, Chen rarely gestured as he spoke. The stillness gave him a monumental quality, drawing attention as powerfully as the largest mountain in a landscape. "If only our movement should have a hundred such monks at our disposal. From which monastery did you come?"

"Wuhuang Monastery, Minister."

"Ah, Wuhuang? Shame about it." Chen's expression didn't change, but underneath it there seemed a redoubling of his interest. "Did you know I knew your abbot back in the day? I liked him. A surprisingly pragmatic man, for a monk. Whatever was required to keep his monastery high and dry, he would do it. And he always did it well, from what I hear, until that mistake at the end."

I see what needs to be done, and I do it. Had the Abbot ever killed? Zhu remembered herself at sixteen, so eager to be like him. Now she supposed she was. She had murdered a man with her bare hands in the pursuit of her desire. As she looked up at Chen's smiling tiger face, she recognized pragmatism taken to its natural endpoint: the person who climbed according to his desire, with no regard to what he did to get there. Zhu was surprised to feel, instead of sympathetic attraction, a tinge of repulsion. Was this who she would become in pursuit of her greatness?

For some reason Zhu found herself thinking of the girl Ma, stepping in to prevent a cruelty that Zhu had only watched unfold. An act of kindness that had been met by violence, and in the end hadn't made any difference at all. It had been the very opposite of pragmatism. The memory gave her an odd pang. The gesture had been pointless, but somehow beautiful: in it had been Ma's tender hope for the world as it should be, not the one that existed. Or the world that self-serving pragmatists like Chen or Zhu might make.

Zhu bowed her head and tried her best to project humility. "This monk never had such potential so as to receive the Abbot's personal attention. But even the lowest monk at Wuhuang can be said to have learned from his mistakes."

"No doubt. It must have been painful, learning that true wisdom lies in obedience." Chen's gaze flayed layers from her. Just then they heard voices approaching, and the pressure of Chen's regard retracted, like the tiger choosing—for the moment—to sheathe its claws. "Do let me know if you have any other needs in equipping your men, Master Zhu. But now come, and let us hear from the Prime Minister."

Zhu bowed and let Chen precede her into the throne room. His massive bulk moved lightly, clad in that black gown so heavy with its own thickness that it barely moved around him: the stillness of power.

"We have to take Jiankang next," Little Guo insisted.

On his throne, Prime Minister Liu wore an irritable look. With the full heat of summer upon them, the inside of the throne room was thick and soporific.

Although at least it wasn't facing the eunuch general, Zhu would have preferred a more gentle test of her new force. Jiankang, downstream on the Yangzi River, was the main gateway to the eastern seaboard and the most powerful city in the south. Since the time of the kingdom of Wu eighteen hundred years ago it had known a dozen different names under the kings and emperors who had made it their capital. Even under the Mongols, the city's industries had thrived. So rich and powerful had it grown that the city's governor had grown bold enough to style himself the Duke of Wu. The Great Yuan's officials dared not chastise him, for fear of losing him entirely.

Chen's dark eyes rested thoughtfully on Little Guo. "Jiankang? Ambitious."

"Shouldn't we be?" Little Guo's eyes blazed. "Strong or not, it's only four hundred li away! How can we keep swallowing our pride by letting it continue on under the Yuan? Whoever occupies Jiankang is the true challenger to the Yuan. It's rich, it's strategically located, and it has the throne of the ancient kings of Wu. *I* would be happy with that."

"*You* would be happy with that," the Prime Minister echoed. Zhu heard his sour, poisonous tone and shivered a little, despite the heat of the day.

Right Minister Guo said carefully, "Your Excellency, Jiankang would be a significant asset."

"The kingdom of Wu is ancient history," the Prime Minister said impatiently. "If we take Bianliang, we can put the Prince of Radiance on the throne of the line that bore the Song Dynasty's Mandate of Heaven. The northern throne of our last native emperors before the Hu came. Now *that* will be a challenge to the Yuan." He glared around the room.

The Song Dynasty's old northern throne is still ancient history, Zhu thought, just as impatiently. Bianliang, the Song emperors' double-walled capital on the Yellow River and once the largest and most breathtakingly beautiful city in the world, had fallen two hundred years ago to Jurchen invaders—the barbarians that themselves fell to the Mongols. Apart from the modest Yuan settlement that now nestled within its inner wall, the rest of Bianliang was nothing but ruin-dotted wasteland. Old men like the Prime Minister still held the idea of that ancient city in their hearts, as though the ancestral memory of its humiliation was entwined with their identity as Nanren. They were obsessed with restoring what had been lost. But Zhu, who had lost her past many times over, had no such nostalgia. It seemed obvious that the best thing to do was to put the Prince of Radiance on a throne—any throne—in an actually useful city. *Why insist on chasing the shadow of something lost, when you could make something new and even greater?*

As if echoing her thoughts, Little Guo said with open frustration, "What good does a symbolic victory do? If we pose a challenge, the Yuan will answer. We should do it for a good reason."

The Prime Minister's creased face tightened.

"Your Excellency," Chen murmured. In the stultifying warmth, his massive stillness felt smothering. "If this unworthy official can offer his opinion, General Guo's plan to take Jiankang has merit. Jiankang may be strong and well resourced, but it lacks a wall: it can be taken quickly, if the attack is sufficiently well organized. That should leave time for General Guo to also take Bianliang before the Prince of Henan's forces mobilize in autumn." Chen gave Little Guo a look of cool consideration. "Do you think that is within your capacity, General Guo?"

Little Guo lifted his chin. "Of course."

Right Minister Guo regarded Chen unfavorably: even in his relief at having the situation resolved in Little Guo's favor, he apparently thought Chen had overstepped his authority.

The Prime Minister's sour expression hadn't evaporated either. He said in ill temper: "Then act quickly, General Guo. Win me both Jiankang and Bianliang before the Hu come south again." They all heard, unspoken: *or else.*

Zhu left with the others, feeling concerned. Her force was still far too small, and a rate of casualties that Commander Sun wouldn't blink at could wipe her force out entirely. And even apart from that, it was obvious that Chen was planning something against the Guo faction. But what?

Ahead of her in the corridor she heard Little Guo crowing to Sun, "Finally! That old turtle egg sees reason, even if you have to beat it out of him. Ah, the Duke of Wu—it has it nice ring to it—"

"Even better would be the King of Wu," Commander Sun laughed. "It would suit you, your forehead is as big as a king's already—"

That was Chen's mountainous black shape strolling behind the two young commanders, and there was something about the set of his shoulders that made Zhu think he was laughing.

The evening's candles were nearly burnt down. Ma was in her room reading one of the diaries she had recently found cached under the floorboards of the Guo mansion's study. She wondered if the home's original owner had thought the Red Turbans would eventually leave and he might be able to return, or if he had just been unable to bear the thought of them destroyed.

"Ma Xiuying." It was Little Guo, letting himself in as though he owned the place.

As Ma turned the page she could feel the imprint of the diarist's words on her fingertips. The last physical traces of someone long dead. Ma murmured to herself, "I hope he had descendants to remember him."

"What? I can never understand what you're talking about." Little Guo threw himself on the bed. He hadn't even taken off his shoes. "Can't you greet me properly?"

Ma sighed. "Yes, Guo Tianxu?"

"Get me some water. I want to wash."

When she came back with the basin he sat up and unselfconsciously stripped off his robe and inner shirt. *As though I were no more than a maid, and he a king.* She had mostly succeeded in putting her strange last conversation with Monk Zhu out of mind, but all of a sudden it came roaring back, as unwelcome as ever. She remembered Monk Zhu looking into her with those sharp black eyes, and speaking to her not only as if she were a person capable of desire, but as someone who *should* desire. In her whole life she'd never heard anything so pointless. *This is the life I have,* she reminded herself. *This is what it looks like.*

But instead of her usual feeling of acceptance, what came was sadness. It was self-pity, but for some reason it seemed like grief. She felt like crying. *This is what it will be, for this life and every life thereafter.*

Little Guo hadn't noticed a thing. As he scrubbed he said with high spirits, "We'll be marching on Jiankang next! It's about time. What better location for our capital? I'm sick of this moldy old city; it's too poor for our ambitions." His eyes flashed under his impatient eyebrows. "But Jiankang won't do as a name. It needs something new. Something fitting for a new line of emperors. Heaven-something. Capital-something."

"Jiankang?" said Ma, startled out of her despondency. "I thought the Prime Minister wanted Bianliang as our new capital." With a sinking heart she realized she had made a mistake by missing that afternoon's meeting. *Not that my previous efforts to save Little Guo from himself have ever made any difference.*

"I'll take it after," Little Guo said dismissively. "Even Chen Youliang agreed—"

"Why would he support you?" Ma's body flooded with alarm. There was no altruism in Chen, nor even a commitment to mutual goals: he always went in the direction that served his own purpose.

"He knows sense when he hears it," Little Guo retorted.

"Or he wants you to lose! Don't be a stupid melon: Which is more likely, that Chen Youliang supports your success or waits for your mistake?"

"What mistake? Are you always thinking so little of me

that my defeats seem inevitable?" Little Guo's voice rose. "Such disrespect, Ma Xiuying!"

As she looked at his handsome face, flushed with indignation, she suddenly felt pity. Those who didn't know him might think him powerful-looking, but to Ma he seemed as brittle as a nephrite vase. How few people there were with the willingness to treat him tenderly, that he might not break. "That wasn't what I meant."

"Whatever." Little Guo flung the washcloth into the basin, slopping water on her dress. "Stop giving your opinions on things that don't concern you. Understand your place, and *stay in it*." He shot Ma a vengeful look, as though she were an irritant he couldn't wait to get rid of, then grabbed his clothes and stalked out.

Ma was coming out of the Prime Minister's living quarters with a tray when someone came around the corner. She dodged left; the person dodged right; they collided with a smack and a scream. When she saw the source of the scream, a jolt of raw feeling ran through her from head to toe. The monk, crouching, was looking up at her; somehow he had caught the tray on its way down. The cups rattled. A single cake teetered, then plopped to the ground.

"Did you make these?" Monk Zhu straightened and nudged the quivering casualty with his toe. "The Prime Minister's favorites! Worried about something?"

"Who says I'm worried?" Ma said repressively. Zhu had been busy since his return from Lu; all she had seen of him since their uncomfortable conversation had been glimpses of his small behatted figure running across town from one appointment to another. Now, meeting him again, she was disturbed by a frisson of strange new awareness. For whatever reason, he had gifted her with some truth of himself, and she couldn't unsee it: the unnatural, frightening immensity of his desire. She didn't understand or trust it, but knowing it was there filled her with the fascination of a moth for a flame. She couldn't look away.

Zhu laughed. "Who would bother with these fiddly things for no good reason? It's obvious you're trying to put the Prime Minister in a good mood." All at once the performance slipped off his face. He was a short man, so they were looking eye to eye; it gave the moment a shocking intimacy, as though something of his inner self was touching something of hers. He said gravely, "You're working so hard to help Little Guo. Does he even know?"

How was it he saw her as someone who acted of her own volition, when to everyone else she was just an object performing its function? It filled her with a sudden rage. She was grieving her life as she never had before, and it was all this monk's fault for having conjured the impossible fantasy of a world in which she was free to desire.

She snatched the tray from him, though it lacked the violence to be truly gratifying. "As if you know how much effort it takes, either!"

In the instant before performance swept back in, she thought she saw understanding in his small dark cicada face. It couldn't have been real—it was absurd to think a man could feel for a woman—but somehow it was enough to dissolve her anger in a tide of pain. It hurt so much she gasped with it. *Stop doing this to me*, she thought, anguished, as she turned and fled. *Don't make me want to want.*

She'd made it halfway down the corridor when someone hauled her around a corner. To her relief it was only Sun Meng, a half-serious glint in his eye. "Pretty cozy with that monk, sis. But remember, he's on Chen Youliang's side."

"He's not like Chen Youliang," Ma said reflexively.

Sun gave her a sideways look. "Do you think? But whatever he's like, he wouldn't be anything without the Left Minister. Bear it in mind." He helped himself to a cake and said indistinctly, "I think he likes you."

"What! Don't be an idiot." Ma flushed as her memory served

her that tingling fascination of knowing that Zhu desired. Against her will, he had given her this new sense with which to experience the world—an awareness of desire—and her inability to repress it filled her with shame and despair. "He's a *monk*."

"Not a normal monk, that's for sure," Sun said, chewing energetically. "I saw him training the other day. He fights like a man; who's to say he doesn't think like one? Ah well. Don't worry; I won't tell Little Guo."

"I haven't done anything for Guo Tianxu to think badly of me!"

"Ah, Yingzi, calm down. I'm just teasing." Sun laughed and slung his arm around her shoulders. "He isn't the jealous type. Look at me with my hands all over you. He's never cared, has he?"

"Only because you're so pretty he thinks of you as a sister," Ma retorted, raw.

"What! You mean I wasted all that blood trying to make him my sworn brother?" Sun's fake-mournful face vanished as fast as it came. "Hey, Yingzi, you know sworn brothers share *everything*? Once you're married—" He wiggled his eyebrows.

"Who's getting married!" What a non sequitur.

"What, the bride doesn't know? Little Guo told me you'll be married after we take Jiankang. The mourning period for General Ma will be done by then. I thought you must have talked about it last night."

"No," Ma said. A dreadful heaviness rushed into her bones. "Last night I was trying to give him advice." She couldn't imagine how she could survive under that weight for the rest of her life. She tried to tell herself she would get used to it; that it was only the shock of moving from one phase to the next. But now, facing the reality of it, it seemed more than anything like a kind of death.

"What's with the black face black mouth?" Sun said with surprise. "Are you worried about giving him a son? You're good at everything else, you'll have one straight off. He'd treat you well if you could even manage a couple; you know it suits a general to have lots of sons."

How casually he laid it out, the purpose of her life in the eyes of others. Sun's fey prettiness sometimes tricked Ma into thinking that he understood her better than Little Guo. But despite his looks he was just as much a man as Little Guo, and all men were the same.

Except Monk Zhu, a traitorous part of herself whispered. But it was as pointless as the rest of her thoughts.

She followed Sun outside and sat with him on a bench next to a stump in the middle of the courtyard. A single remaining branch had sprouted a few leaves. The last gasp of a dying tree, or new life? Ma didn't know.

She said, "Big brother."

"Mm?"

"I have a bad feeling about Jiankang. Can't you get Little Guo to change his mind?"

Sun snorted. "In which life could that happen? Even I don't have that power. But aren't you worrying too much lately?"

"I don't trust Chen Youliang."

"Who does? You'd have better luck putting your finger in a snapping turtle's mouth. But I actually agree with Little Guo on this one. The victory at Yao River has given us this extra-long summer season. This is our chance, so we should spend our efforts on a strategic target. Jiankang makes sense."

None of them ever *listened*. "Chen Youliang wants you to fail!"

Sun looked startled by her vehemence. "So then we just have to succeed, don't we? He wanted us to fail at Yao River, and look how that turned out." He flicked Ma's forehead, affectionate. "Don't worry. Everything will be fine."

Apparently hoping to change their minds was as pointless as wanting something different for the course of her life. Ma stared up at the blue box of Heaven framed by the four dark wooden wings of the Guo mansion, and tried to tell herself that she was worried about nothing. But she couldn't shake the feeling that they were all walking down a long nighttime road, the others chatting cheerfully, and somehow she was the only one who could see the hungry eyes in the dark all around them, waiting.

Anfeng rang with the sounds of departure. Thousands of torches in the streets made it almost as clear as day, and in a few more hours the bonfires would be lit. As Zhu stepped over the raised threshold of the Guo mansion's front gate, she remembered how Anfeng had looked the night before they went to Yao River: capped by an eerie dome of red light that spanned wall to wall, as of a city consumed by fire.

Despite the warming days, the inside of the Guo mansion breathed out the cool fragrance of smoky southern tea. Walls, floors, and ceilings of dark wood swallowed the light of the hallway lanterns. Zhu looked around curiously as she walked; being a member of Chen's faction, it was her first time in the Guo mansion. Empty rooms branched off the hallway. In what had once been a scholar's study, she saw two ghosts hanging in the filtered light coming through the window-paper, their still forms no more substantial than the dust motes. Had they been killed when Chen took Anfeng, or were they even older than that? Their vacant gazes were fixed on nothing in particular. She wondered if they were aware of time passing in this strange gap between their lives, or if to them it was nothing more than a long, restless sleep.

Zhu left the hallway and came out into an internal courtyard, wrapped above by a shadowy upper balcony. A wavering square of light showed halfway along. At the sight of it Zhu felt a tug of an unidentifiable emotion. She was already late for Little Guo's meeting, but before she could think about it she was slipping up the creaking stairs and into Ma's room.

Ma was sitting cross-legged on the floor, her head bent down in concentration, in the center of a constellation of small rectangular pieces of leather. It took Zhu a moment to realize the object in Ma's lap was Little Guo's armor, divested of all its lamellae. Ma had laid the lamellae out in the same positions they had occupied on the armor, which gave Zhu the disturbing impression of seeing a disassembled body laid out for study. As she watched from the doorway, Ma took up the book beside her, read a page with a sorrowing expression, then ripped it out and sewed it neatly onto the naked armor. After that she took up a handful of lamellae and sewed them one by one over the paper-reinforced backing. She held the armor with as much care as a lover's familiar body. Zhu marveled at it. Ma wasn't arrow-proofing Little Guo's armor out of duty, but a genuine desire to protect him from hurt. How could anyone go around in such a state of openness that a part of herself would attach to others with love and care, regardless of how much she liked them or they deserved it? Zhu couldn't understand it at all.

Ma glanced up and jumped. "Master Zhu?"

"General Guo called the commanders over to discuss the order of departure tomorrow," Zhu said, which explained why she was in the Guo mansion, although not why she was in Ma's room. Zhu was uncertain about that herself. She came in, noting how the room was unfurnished except for a simple bed. Nobody lived in any style in Anfeng, but it was plain even for that: as though Ma had no higher status in the Guo household than a servant. A mountain of string-tied flaxen boxes occupied one corner. "Wah, is that all food for Guo Tianxu?" Zhu exclaimed. "He doesn't need home cooking every night! Don't you think it's too much?"

Ma frowned and said pointedly, "It suits a general to be well fed. What's there to be proud of in a leader who's as skinny and ugly as a black-boned chicken?"

"Ah, it's true," Zhu said, laughing. "This monk grew up in a famine, and despite his years of fervent prayers on the topic, it seems he'll never get any bigger. Or handsomer, for that matter. But we work with what we've got." She squatted next to Ma and handed her the next lamella. "So I hear you'll be getting married after Jiankang. I can't help but think I should offer my condolences." She kept her tone light, but the idea that

Ma might never find anything to want for herself made her strangely angry.

Ma's hands clenched on Little Guo's armor. Her hair curtained over her downturned face, concealing her expression. At length she said, "Master Zhu. Aren't you worried?"

Zhu had a lot of worries. "About what?"

"Jiankang. Chen Youliang convinced the Prime Minister to support the attack. But it was Little Guo's idea. Doesn't that seem strange?" When Ma looked up her luminous face was wretched with anguish. It was so pure that Zhu felt an unexpected pang of the particular combination of awe and pity that one gets from seeing fragile pear blossoms in the rain.

She asked, "Shouldn't you mention this to Commander Sun?"

"He doesn't listen! None of them listen—"

Little Guo and Sun Meng didn't listen, but somehow Zhu had given Ma reason to think she would. Zhu felt a sudden shiver of unease. She thought unwillingly, *Zhu Chongba would never have understood.*

After a moment she said, "Maybe Chen Youliang is planning something against Little Guo. He probably is, though I don't know any specifics. He hasn't asked me to do anything. But you know this doesn't mean anything. How can you know I'm telling the truth? And even if it's true that I don't know anything, it doesn't mean he won't *do* anything. He may not trust me. Or he may not need me."

Ma said with sudden fierceness, "And if I ask you to help?"

Zhu gazed at her. How desperate did she have to be to ask? For a moment Zhu was overwhelmed by a wash of tenderness. She said honestly, "This is what I like about you, Ma Xiuying. That you open your heart, even though it means you'll get hurt. There aren't many people like that." It was a rare character to start with, and how many of those born with it made it any distance? Perhaps only those with someone to protect them. Someone ruthless, who knew how to survive.

To Zhu's surprise, Ma grabbed her hand. The immediacy

of skin against skin shocked her into a sudden, exaggerated awareness of the thin boundary between herself and the outside world. Unlike Xu Da, who'd been as familiar to the village girls around the monastery as a stray dog, Zhu had never held hands with a woman. She had never ached for it or dreamed about it like the other novices. She had only ever wanted one thing, and that desire had been so enormous as to take up all the space inside her. Now a foreign tremor raced up her arm: the quiver of another's heartbeat in her own body.

Ma said, "Master Zhu: please."

The thought of seeing Ma's spark crushed by Little Guo or Chen or anyone else was irrationally troubling. Zhu realized she wanted to keep that fierce empathy in the world. Not because she understood it, but because she didn't, and for that reason it seemed precious. *Something worth protecting.* The idea swelled, not quite enough to push aside Zhu's knowledge of the reality: that in a fight against Chen, there was no way Little Guo would win.

She hadn't answered quickly enough. Flushing with embarrassment, Ma yanked her hand free. "Forget it! Forget I asked. Just go."

Zhu flexed her hand, feeling the ghost of that touch. She said quietly, "I don't like Little Guo. And he would be a fool to trust me."

Ma's head fell, the curtains of her hair swinging shut. Her shoulders shook slightly, and with a spurt of anger Zhu realized she was crying for a person who had never spared her a thought in his entire life.

"Ma Xiuying," she said. It felt pulled out of her. "I don't know if I'll be able to do anything, and even if I can, I don't know how it will turn out. But I'll try."

It wasn't a promise, and Ma must have known that. But after a beat she said, low and heartfelt, "Thank you."

Perhaps, Zhu thought as she left, Ma had thanked her just for listening. She remembered how she had told Ma to learn how to want. It seemed Ma had learned the opposite. Even though she denied it even to herself, at some point since that conversation Ma had realized that she *didn't* want the life she was being forced into.

Zhu felt a stab of uncharacteristic pity. *Not-wanting is a desire too; it yields suffering just as much as wanting.*

14

SOUTHEASTERN HENAN, SUMMER

"What's wrong? You're brooding."

Zhu glanced at Xu Da as he rejoined her at the head of the column; he had been riding up and down its length all morning, keeping everyone moving in an orderly manner despite the excitement of their first real outing. That morning the entire Red Turban force had left Lu and started their eastwards trek across the flat plain towards Jiankang. The region's thousand lakes sparkled all around them under the roasting sun. That was the reason Mongols never fought in summer: neither they nor their horses could tolerate the southern heat. The Red Turbans, who were Nanren by blood and mainly infantry, trudged on. The columns belonging to Little Guo and the other commanders stretched ahead. The dust they kicked up gave the sky an opalescent sheen like the inside of an abalone shell.

"You can tell?" Zhu said, giving him a wry smile. It was good to have him by her side again, and even all this time after their reunion she still felt a twinge, like a stretched muscle releasing, whenever she saw him.

"Of course I can. I've known you all your life," Xu Da said comfortably. "I know at least three-quarters of your secrets."

That made Zhu laugh. "More than anyone, that's for sure." Sobering, she said, "This could get messy."

"Wall or no wall: a city this size, we're bound to take casualties."

"That too." She had been chewing over the situation since Lu. "Big brother, what do you think Left Minister Chen has in mind for Little Guo?"

"Are you sure there's anything? Little Guo is perfectly capable of screwing it up by himself. It doesn't need a plot."

"Chen Youliang likes control." That powerful, still presence filled her mind. "I don't think he'd leave it to chance. He'd want to use his power; to know that whatever happened was his own doing."

"But wouldn't we already know if he was planning for something to happen during this campaign?"

The dust made it seem like the plain went on endlessly in all directions, even though Zhu knew its southern border was the Huangshan mountains. She remembered looking at them from the monastery and marveling at how far away they were. The world was shrinking, coming within reach. She said, "He doesn't fully trust me yet. He could have given instructions to Commander Wu."

"To turn on Little Guo? Sun Meng would retaliate, and you know how strong he is. Chen Youliang wouldn't risk losing Commander Wu's whole force for that."

"No. He would have a plan for Sun Meng, too." Zhu brooded again. Like Yao River, it was one of those situations where she would have to wait in the hope that more information would eventually present itself. She knew that if Chen gave her orders against Little Guo, refusing to carry them out would be tantamount to taking a position on the losing side. That wasn't something she was willing to do. But on the off chance she was only indirectly involved, then perhaps she could act in Ma's favor. She found herself hoping the latter was the case. She sighed. "I suppose we'll just have to keep our eyes open."

"I'd have thought you'd be the last to cry about Little Guo meeting his fate. Why can't we just stand back and let it happen?"

Zhu admitted with some reluctance, "I told Ma Xiuying I'd look out for him."

"Who? Not—Little Guo's woman?" Then, grasping it, Xu Da put his full powers of innuendo into his eyebrows. "Buddha preserve me, little brother, I never thought I'd see it. But do you—*like* her?"

"She's a good person," Zhu said defensively. She thought of the girl's broad, beautiful face with her phoenix eyes full of care and sorrow. For Little Guo, of all people. The new protective feeling inside her was as tender as a bruise. Even as her pragmatic side warned her of its inevitability, she didn't like the idea of seeing Ma hurt, or of being miserable without even allowing herself to admit that she was miserable.

"So now you're going to save Little Guo from himself." Xu Da laughed. "And here I thought I was the only one who got manipulated by pretty girls. Even *I* don't go for the married ones."

Zhu gave him a withering look. "She's not married yet."

They stayed watchful as they crossed the Yangzi River and approached Jiankang. But in the end there was nothing. Little Guo led a wasteful, brutal assault that produced far too many casualties on the Red Turban side: a wave of flesh breaking against Jiankang's defenders. On a high-walled city like Lu, it would have been futile. But against unfortified Jiankang, Little Guo's assault began to have an effect. The slow and hard-won influx of Red Turbans was gradually matched by an outflow of fleeing citizens, and by the Horse hour of the tenth day, Jiankang had fallen.

Beautiful as they were, the palace grounds of the Duke of Wu (now deceased) were wreathed in smoke like the rest of the city. Not the everyday stink of burning clam shells and fruit pits, but the smell of the ancient Jiankang mansions: their lacquered furniture and grand staircases turned to nothing but ash. Floating in the haze above, the afternoon sun glowed like a red lotus.

In the middle of the palace's parade ground a line of women stood in their undyed underclothes. The Duke of Wu's wives and daughters and maids. Zhu and the other commanders waited to the side, watching Little Guo parade along the line. The red light gave his brow and aquiline nose a heroic glow. His smile carried the bone-deep satisfaction of someone who has achieved, against all the ill will of his doubters, what he had always known himself capable of.

Raking one shivering woman with an assessing glance, Little Guo pronounced, "Slave." To the next, "Concubine." Zhu saw him look at the next with even greater appreciation, taking her arm to see the fine texture of its skin and lifting her lowered face to see its shape. "Concubine."

Sun called out teasingly, "Are all of those for you? Don't you think Ma Xiuying will be enough?"

"Maybe one woman is enough for *you*." Little Guo smirked. "I'll have that girl, and a few concubines as well. A man of my status can't have none."

As he moved down the row the women trembled with their arms wrapped around themselves. With their tangling hair and white clothes Zhu could have mistaken them for ghosts. All save one. She stood tall, arms by her sides, unashamed of the revealed shape of her body. Her hands were hidden in her sleeves. She watched Little Guo with such bladed intensity that he startled a little as he came to her. "Slave."

She smiled at that, a wild and bitter smile. And the moment Zhu saw it, loaded with the woman's hatred of Little Guo and everything he represented, she understood instantly what she planned to do. As the woman flashed towards Little Guo, her knife arrowing towards his neck, Zhu was already flinging herself shoulder-first into Little Guo. He stumbled, crying out, and the knife skittered off his armor. The woman screamed with frustration and tried to stab Zhu, and then Xu Da was between them, wrenching the woman's arm so the knife fell ringing to the stones.

Zhu picked herself up. She felt oddly shaken. Even after the fact, the other commanders were still flailing in disbelief that a threat had come from a woman—and a barely dressed one, at that. But in the instant Zhu had looked at that woman and grasped her intent, she had *understood* her. More than that: for just a moment she had shared the woman's urge to see the surprise on Little Guo's face as the knife sank into him. To enjoy his disbelief at an inglorious death, when he had always believed the future held nothing but the best for him.

Zhu felt a spasm of cold dread. She couldn't fool herself that it was a reaction Zhu Chongba would have had. Worse than that was the realization that these moments seemed to be happening more and more frequently, the more she lived in the world outside the monastery. It had happened with Lady Rui, with Ma, and now this woman. There was something ominous about it, as though each time it happened she lost some fraction of her capacity to be Zhu Chongba. Her dread intensified as she remembered her empty hand outstretched in the darkness of Lady Rui's dungeon. *How much can I lose, before I can't be him at all?*

Little Guo recovered from his shock and rounded on Zhu, his embarrassment already turned to anger. "You—!" He gave her a hateful look, then shouldered her aside and snatched the woman from Xu Da. "Bitch! Do you want to die?" He slapped her face so hard that her head snapped sideways. "Bitch!" He struck her until she fell, then kicked her where she lay. Zhu, involuntarily remembering the long-ago sight of someone kicked to death, felt her stomach flip.

Sun hurriedly stepped in. He had forced a smile, but his eyes were strained. "Aiya, is this the behavior of the next Duke of Wu? General Guo, why are you lowering yourself by dirtying your hands like this? Let someone else take care of this trash."

Little Guo stared at him. Sun looked like he was holding his breath. Zhu realized she was holding her breath too. Then after a long moment, Little Guo grimaced and said, "Duke! Didn't you say I should be king?"

"King of Wu, then!" Sun cried, making a valiant effort. "Nobody would deny it to you. Come, this is your achievement of achievements, the Prime Minister will be beside himself. This is *the* city of the south, and now it's yours. Let the Hu come for us now! We'll show them—" Chattering all the while, he drew Little Guo away.

"A good outcome?" Xu Da asked wryly, coming up. "But was this it—Chen Youliang's plot against Little Guo?"

Zhu watched the woman heaving for breath on the ground, Little Guo's bootprint on her white dress. "I don't think so. I think she was just really angry."

"Little Guo tends to have that effect on people. And I suppose it isn't Chen Youliang's style. Where's the spectacle in a literal backstabbing?"

"Then it's still coming." Zhu sighed. "Well, let Little Guo enjoy his moment."

"He's definitely enjoying it," Xu Da said. "As we were coming in I heard him telling Sun Meng he wants to rename the city. He wants something more suited to a capital, like Yingtian." *Responding to Heaven.*

Zhu raised her eyebrows. "Yingtian? Who knew he had enough learning to come up with something good like that? But it's ambitious. The Prime Minister won't like it. I think he wanted naming rights."

"Why should he care what it's called?"

Zhu shook her head instinctively. "Names matter." She knew better than any of the Red Turbans how names could create their own reality in the eyes of either man or Heaven. And with that thought, she felt the dark beginnings of a realization about what Chen had planned for Little Guo.

"Finally!" Xu Da exclaimed as Anfeng's familiar earthen walls came into view. Their return journey had taken longer due to late summer's oppressive humidity, and they were all thoroughly sick of travel. The thought of their victorious homecoming was a balm to everyone's spirits. Even now a greeting party was emerging from the southern gate; it flew towards them under the fluttering scarlet banners of the Prince of Radiance.

The moment Zhu saw them, her shadowy half realization became as crisp as ink on a page. The action she and Xu Da had been looking out for had already happened. Chen hadn't even needed her; there was never anything she could have done to stop him. Even as she urged her horse down the length of her column, Xu Da half a length behind, she knew it was too late. She thought with genuine regret, *I'm sorry, Ma Xiuying.*

Ahead the banners had halted at the head of the leading column. Little Guo said in a loud displeased voice, "What's this?"

Zhu and Xu Da came up and flung themselves from their horses, and saw what he saw. Xu Da said, disturbed, "Aren't they the men we left at Jiankang?"

"You dare disregard your general's command?" Little Guo demanded. "Who ordered your return? Speak!"

Sun arrived at a gallop and dismounted, then stopped short at Zhu's side in confusion.

It was a man named Yi Jinkai who addressed Little Guo from the greeting party. Even including his wispy moustache, his was the kind of unmemorable face that nobody would think twice about. Zhu certainly hadn't, in the weeks since they had left him in charge of Jiankang. But now Yi was radiating power. *Borrowed* power: it was the vicarious pleasure of carrying out another's will. Of course Chen hadn't needed her, Zhu thought with detached clarity. Her loyalties were too new; why would Chen ask her, when others would so gladly do his bidding?

Now Yi said peremptorily, "General Guo, the Prime Minister summons you to an audience."

"You—!" Sun exclaimed in outrage.

Little Guo glared at Yi. This wasn't the fawning homecoming he had expected. Confusion, disappointment, and anger warred on his face, and Zhu wasn't surprised when the anger won. "*Fine,*" he said. "You've conveyed your message. Tell the Prime Minister I'll give him his audience when we reach Anfeng."

Yi took hold of Little Guo's horse. "The Prime Minister has ordered us to escort you."

Sun lunged forwards with a snarl. He stopped abruptly, Yi's blade at his throat. Behind Yi, the other members of the greeting party had drawn their swords.

Yi repeated, "Prime Minister's orders."

They remounted and departed, flanking Little Guo like a prisoner. Little Guo sat stiffly, his low brows drawn into a bitter mask. He was probably worrying that he would find his father dead—weeks dead. He would be wondering whether it had been an accident or an open assassination, and whether his father had suffered. Perhaps—though Zhu doubted it—he was even realizing that the girl Ma Xiuying had spoken truly about the danger Chen posed.

Sun was cursing Yi: "That motherfucker. Fuck eighteen generations of his ancestors!"

As Zhu watched the party diminishing towards Anfeng, she was reminded of Prefect Fang's last moments in the monastery. But Prefect Fang had known the fate awaiting him. Little Guo thought the danger had already happened; he didn't realize it was yet to come.

"Commander Sun," she said, remounting. "Come on. Quickly."

Sun gave her a vicious, accusatory look. But he didn't realize, either, what was happening.

As Zhu saw the future the rest of them had yet to grasp, she felt something unfamiliar. With astonishment she identified it as the feeling of someone else's sorrow, but within her own breast, as though it had come from her own heart. The pain of someone else's suffering.

Ma Xiuying, she thought.

Anfeng was as empty as an abandoned plague village. It was the middle of the day, so there weren't even any ghosts. Their horses' hooves clattered; the ground had dried as hard as stone during their absence. As they rode Zhu became aware of a growing energy. More a vibration than a sound, she felt it in her guts as a primal unease.

They came into the center of the city and saw the scene before them. High above the silent crowd a stage had been erected as if for a performance. The crimson banners flew. The Prince of Radiance sat on his throne under a parasol edged with silk threads that shimmered in the wind like a fall of blood. The Prime Minister paced in front of him. Beneath the stage, kneeling in the dust, was Little Guo. His hair and armor were still neat. Even though Zhu knew better, for a moment even she had the impression he was being honored.

The Prime Minister stopped pacing, and the containment of his agitation was even more awful: the quiver of a hornets' nest, or a snake about to strike. He looked down at Little Guo and said in a dreadful voice, "Tell me why you took Jiankang, Guo Tianxu!"

Little Guo sounded completely bewildered. "We all agreed that Jiankang made the most—"

"I'll tell you why!" The Prime Minister's voice carried clearly to where Zhu, Xu Da, and Sun sat on their horses. The crowd rippled. "Jiankang, the place where kings and emperors sit, isn't it? Oh, how you said that so many times. Guo Tianxu: I know your intentions! Did you really think you could take that city for yourself, ride back here, and tell me you didn't sit on that throne and call yourself king?"

"No, I—"

"Don't pretend you were ever a loyal subject of the Prince of Radiance," the Prime Minister spat. "You always had your own ambitions. You would betray the will of Heaven for your own selfish purposes!"

A large, black-clad figure was standing next to Yi at the foot of the stage. Even from this distance, Zhu could tell Chen was smiling. Of course Little Guo had been enough of a fool to announce his desires loudly, and Yi had reported them back to Chen. And who within the Red Turbans had more experience than Chen in stoking the Prime Minister's paranoia?

"No," Little Guo said, alarmed. His voice was that of someone who was only gradually realizing the seriousness of his situation. "That's not what I—"

"You dared take that city and call it Yingtian? You dared ask Heaven for the right to rule? When the Prince of Radiance is our ruler, and he alone possesses the Mandate of Heaven?" Leant down over the edge of the stage, the Prime Minister's face was reddened and distorted with fury. "*Traitor.* Oh, I know everything. You planned all along to come back here to kill the both of us, so you could have that throne for yourself. You traitor and usurper!"

Finally understanding, Little Guo cried out in horror, "Your Excellency!"

The Prime Minister hissed, "*Now* you call me that. When you've been sneering and plotting behind our backs all this time!"

There was a commotion: Right Minister Guo was forcing his way through the crowd. His robes were disarrayed; his doughy face had solidified in shock. He shouted, "Your Excellency, stop! This servant begs you!"

The Prime Minister rounded on him. "Ah, the father of the traitor appears. You would do well to remember that under the old rules, a traitor's family was executed to the ninth degree. Is that what you want, Guo Zixing?" He stared down at the other old man as though willing him to let him make it a reality. "If not, you should be on your knees and giving me thanks for sparing you."

Right Minister Guo threw himself towards his son. But he was caught and held. Despite the futility of it, the old man kept struggling. He cried, "Your Excellency, I beg for your mercy!"

Little Guo had apparently believed that his father's arrival might resolve the misunderstanding. Now, obviously panicking, he shouted, "Your Excellency, I can keep Jiankang for you—"

"Jiankang can go to the wolves! Who cares about Jiankang? The rightful seat of the Prince of Radiance and our restored Song Dynasty is Bianliang. Jiankang is nothing. You were only ever a pretender, Guo Tianxu. You only sat on a pretend throne."

Right Minister Guo, wrestling himself free with the supernatural strength of a parent seeing his child in danger, threw himself flat into the dirt beneath the Prime Minister. "Your Excellency, forgive him! Forgive us! Excellency!"

Zhu could imagine the maniacal glitter in the Prime Minister's eyes as he looked down at the groveling minister. Then he stepped back. "In the name of the Prince of Radiance, the traitor and pretender Guo Tianxu is sentenced to death."

High above on his throne, the Prince of Radiance's graceful smile never faltered. Reflected off the underside of his parasol, his light spilled over the stage and down onto the figures below, until they were drowned in an incarnadine sea. In that moment his child-self seemed to have been subsumed entirely. He was inhuman: the emanation of the dark radiance that was the will of Heaven.

On hearing his sentence, Little Guo bolted to his feet and ran. He made it a few steps before he was felled and dragged back to the stage, bleeding from a cut on his brow. "Father!" he cried, in fear and incomprehension. But instead of giving reassurance, Right Minister Guo seemed frozen with horror. He stared blankly as the Prime Minister beckoned from the stage and the men came forwards with the horses. They had been waiting there all along. *This was always Little Guo's fate*, Zhu thought. *There was never any escape.*

From the beginning she had been aware of Ma Xiuying's presence. Now she saw her in the crowd. There was space all around her, as though her association with the traitor had been enough for people to pull back from her. Her face was waxy with shock. For all Ma had feared the worst, Zhu saw she had never had any idea of what it would be like if it came true. Feeling a pang of that strange new tenderness, Zhu thought: *She's never seen life taken with intent.* For all the inevitability of it, for some reason Zhu found herself sorrowing for the loss of Ma's innocence.

Little Guo shouted and resisted as the men tied him to the five horses and then stood by. The Prime Minister, watching with the gleeful satisfaction of a paranoiac seeing the world made right, saw that they were ready. He raised his arm and let it drop. The whips cracked.

Zhu, watching Ma with an alien ache in her heart, saw the girl turn away at the critical moment. There was nobody to comfort her. She simply folded over onto herself in the middle of that empty bubble in the crowd, crying. Zhu felt a strong protective urge rise up in her at the sight. With alarm she realized it was a new desire, already rooted alongside that other desire that defined everything she was and did. It felt as dangerous as an arrowhead lodged in her body, as though at any moment it might work its way in deeper and cause some fatal injury.

The Prime Minister looked out over the crowd, his thin body vibrating. Left Minister Chen, smiling, ascended the stairs and stepped onto the stage. Bowing deeply to the Prime Minister, he said, "Your Excellency, well done."

Ma, bursting into the temple, found Zhu sitting on his pallet in his reroofed annex, reading. On an ordinary day she would have considered it a private moment. He looked introspective and, when she came flying in, startled. She must look terrifying enough: hair loose like a ghost; face pale; her dress stained and torn. She was being improper. She didn't care.

"I asked you to protect him!"

Zhu closed his book. Ma belatedly noticed he was only in his undershirt and trousers. He said, sounding uncharacteristically tired, "Maybe I could have, had Chen Youliang chosen another way." The candles next to his pallet made faint popping sounds as dust and tiny insects entered the flames. "I suppose he thought it was too risky to take Right Minister Guo on directly. So he used the Prime Minister's paranoia as his weapon. Didn't you tell Little Guo yourself to never say anything against the Prime Minister? But he called Jiankang his own. In the end, that was all Chen Youliang needed."

"Did you know this was going to happen?" Her rising voice broke. "You're on Chen Youliang's side; you must have known!"

"I didn't know," he said.

"You expect me to believe that?"

"Believe what you like." Zhu gave a wearied shrug. "Does Chen Youliang trust me? Not entirely, I think. But either way, he didn't need me. He already had Yi Jinkai in place."

She was crying then. Harsh, hiccuping sobs. She felt like she'd been crying for days. "Why do we have to play these awful games? What *for*?"

For a moment the changing candlelight made him seem to waver, as if his small body were only a container for something more terrible. "What does anyone want but to be on top, untouchable?"

"I don't want it!"

"No," he said. His black eyes were sad. "You don't. But others do, and it's for their sake that this game will continue until it's over. Who's next between Chen Youliang and the top? Right Minister Guo. So Chen Youliang's next move will be against him." After a brief silence he added gravely, "You should think about yourself, Ma Xiuying. If Chen Youliang destroys the Guo household, he'll find you a useful reward for the commander who pleased him best."

Perhaps she would have been horrified if it were a surprise. But even as Ma heard the words, she knew: it was just another part of the pattern of a woman's life. It still hurt, but instead of fresh pain it was the same unbearable heaviness she had felt upon learning of her impending marriage to Little Guo. For all that she had suffered watching Little Guo's death, it had changed exactly nothing.

His expression was solemn, as if he knew what she was

thinking. "Will you let that happen, or can you finally let yourself want something different?"

"I can't!" Her own shriek startled her. "Who do you think I am, to think I can make anything happen in my own life? I'm a *woman*. My life was in my father's hands, then it was in Little Guo's, and now it's in someone else's. Stop speaking as if I could want anything different! It's impossible—" How could it seem like he understood, when he couldn't understand *this*? To her mortification a sob burst out.

After a moment he said, "I know you don't want that life. A different one isn't impossible."

"Then how!" she cried.

"Join me."

She managed to glare. "Join your side? You mean *Chen Youliang's* side."

"Not his side," he said steadily. "My side."

It took her a moment to realize what he meant. When she did, the betrayal hit her as hard as a slap. "Join you," she ground out. "*Marry* you." She saw a vision of that awful pattern, as rigid as a coffin: marriage, children, duty. What room was there in it for her own desire? She'd thought Zhu was different—she had *wanted* to believe it—but he was just the same as the rest. Little Guo's death had simply given him an opportunity to take something he wanted. Sickened, she heard Sun Meng: *He looks at you like a man.* The cruelty of it took her breath away. Zhu desired, and he had spoken to her as if it was something she could do too, but he had never meant any of it.

And oh, at that moment she did want. She wanted to *hurt* him.

He caught her look of fury. But instead of triggering an outburst of the usual masculine rage, to her bewilderment his expression only softened. "Yes. Marry me. But not like it would have been with Little Guo. I want to listen to you, Ma Xiuying. You have something I don't: you feel for others, even the ones you don't like." A flash of self-castigation, almost too fast to see. "People who play this game will do whatever's needed to get themselves to the top, regardless of others. All my life I've believed I have to be like that to get what I want. And I *do* want my fate. I want it more than anything. But what kind of world will we have if everyone in it is like Chen Youliang? A world of terror and cruelty? I don't want that either, not if there's another way. But I can't see that other way by myself. So join me, Ma Xiuying. *Show* me."

Her anger was punctured by his unexpected honesty. *Or what seems like honesty.* With a flash of pain she realized she *wanted* to believe it. She wanted to believe he was different; that he was the kind of man who saw his own flaws, and who needed her as much as she needed him. "You want me to believe you're different," she said, and to her shame her voice cracked. "That you can give me something different. But how can I trust that? I *can't.*"

To her surprise a wrenching look passed over Zhu's face. Vulnerability and a shadow of fear, something she had never seen in him before, and it unmoored her more than anything else that had passed between them. "I can see how it would be hard to trust," he said. His voice had that odd inflection of understanding in it again, and Ma had absolutely no idea what it meant.

He set aside the book and rose, and started to untie his shirt. It was so bizarre that Ma found herself watching with a floating feeling that seemed half paralysis and half acceptance, as if she were a dreamer borne along by the strangeness of the dream. It was only when Zhu's bare shoulders slid into view that she came back to life with a jolt of embarrassment. She jerked her face away. It was hardly the first male skin she'd seen, but for some reason her face was burning. She heard his clothes fall.

Then his cool fingers were on her face, turning it back. He said, "Look."

Their bodies were so close, the clothed and the unclothed, and with that same sense of dreamlike acceptance Ma saw in the other her own reflection as seen waveringly in a bowl of water.

Zhu watched her look. Her face had a flayed vulnerability, something so raw and terrible that Ma flinched to see it. It made her think of someone baring a mortal wound they dared not look at themselves, for fear of the reality of it undoing them in an instant.

Zhu spoke calmly, but beneath the surface Ma sensed a shivering horror. "Ma Xiuying. Do you see something you want?"

I'm a woman, Ma had cried to Zhu in despair. Now, as she looked at the person standing before her in a body like her own, she saw someone who seemed neither male nor female, but another substance entirely: something wholly and powerfully of its own kind. The promise of difference, made real. With a sensation of vertiginous terror, Ma felt the rigid pattern of her future falling away, until all that was left was the blankness of pure possibility.

She took Zhu's small, calloused hand and felt its warmth flow into her until the hollow space of her chest blazed with everything she'd never let herself feel. She was yielding to it, being consumed by it, and it was the most beautiful and frightening thing she'd ever felt. She *wanted*. She wanted everything Zhu was offering with that promise of difference. Freedom, and desire, and her life to make her own. And if the price of all of that was suffering, why did it matter when she would suffer no matter what she chose?

She said, "Yes."

15

ANYANG, SUMMER

Anyang was still and gray on their return from Hichetu. The long corridors lay empty; the courtyards were bare. Walking through those echoing spaces gave Esen the feeling of being the only person left in the world. Even Ouyang lingered too far behind for comfort: a shadow that had somehow become detached. Esen came to his father's residence and stood at the entrance to the courtyard, and saw them there. All the households of his family, his wives and daughters, the officials and servants all arrayed in white, bowing silently in unison. As he walked through them their ceaseless waves of motion were like a thousand snow orchids opening and closing. Their mourning clothes sighed. He wanted to scream for them to stop, to leave, that this was not their place and this was not his; that his father was not dead. But he didn't. He couldn't. He ascended the steps of his father's residence and turned to face them, and as he did so a single voice rose up, "All praise the Prince of Henan!"

"Praise upon the Prince of Henan!"

And as Esen stood there he knew that it was all different; it would never be the same again.

The following long, hot days were full of the ceremonies. Dressed in his hempen mourning robe, Esen entered the cool halls of the family temple. Its dark wood smelled of ash and incense. Statues loomed deep within. He had the sudden eerie vision of someone doing this for him in the future. His children, then his grandchildren doing this for his children. His ancestral line with its accumulating dead: always more who were dead than were ever alive at any moment, to mourn them.

He knelt in front of the Buddha and laid his hands on the gilded box of sutras. He tried to keep his father in mind as he prayed. Warrior, true Mongol, the Great Khan's most loyal. But the temple's stale smell distracted him. He couldn't fix his mind to the prayers, couldn't seem to inhabit them properly to give them meaning. In his mouth they were empty words that did nothing for his father's spirit as it waited in that dark underground for its reincarnation.

Behind him, a door opened. A shadow cut through the cast square of light. Esen could feel his brother's presence like a brand. That shining insincerity; the empty performance. An insult rendered with his very being. As the days passed after Baoxiang had dropped Chaghan to his death, the emotions Esen felt towards his brother had sharpened. Now he thought it was perhaps the only thing that made sense right now: that clarity of hate.

He said sharply to the temple attendant, "I said nobody was to enter."

The attendant said, hesitating, "Lord—I mean, Esteemed Prince, it's—"

"I know who it is! Escort him out."

He tried to concentrate on the ritual prostrations, on the crinkle of the foil sutras as they were unrolled, but his awareness stayed with the servant's whisper, the withdrawal of the shadow and the dimming brightness as the doors closed. His prayers were worse than empty. Useless, ruined words, nothing better than the facile speech of traitors who moved their mouths while holding nothing in their hearts.

He stood abruptly, casting the sutras to the floor. A sacrilegious clatter that broke the head monk's recitations. He could feel the attendants' shock like an external pressure, all of them willing him to submit to the rituals, to finish.

"This isn't a true remembrance of my father," he said. "These *words.*" His heart pounded; he could feel the truth of it rushing within him as furiously as his blood. "I'll remember and honor him the way he would have wanted. The way he deserves."

He strode to the doors and flung them open, stepping out into the diffuse brightness of the hot pearl sky. The empty courtyard echoed with the memory of those hundreds of people in white. But today there was only the one figure there. From a distance Wang Baoxiang's elaborate white drapery and drained face had all the humanity of a piece of carved jade.

Ouyang came from where he'd been waiting, and Esen managed to wrench his eyes away from his brother. As much as Baoxiang's presence was agonizing, Ouyang's was comforting: it was all the order and rightness in the world.

Esen felt his inner turmoil slow. He said, "I wish you'd been able to come in with me. I shouldn't have had to do it alone."

A shadow crossed Ouyang's face. There was a peculiar distance in his voice as he said, "It's a son's role to honor his father and ancestors. Your father's spirit needs only your devotions."

"Let me make an offering on your behalf."

"You're confusing your own opinion of me for your father's. I don't think his spirit particularly wants to hear from me."

"He thought highly of you," Esen said stubbornly. "My father didn't suffer fools. Would he have allowed you as my choice of general if he didn't believe in your capabilities? The reputation of the armies of Henan would be nothing if not for you. Of course he wants your respect." Then he realized, "My father was a warrior. If we want to honor him and bring merit to his spirit—it won't be via some temple."

Ouyang raised his eyebrows.

"We'll win the war. You and me together, my general. Our armies of Henan will restore the strength of the Great Yuan; it will be the longest rule this land between the four oceans has ever known. Our house will be remembered forever as defenders of empire. Is that not the best honor my father could possibly ask for?"

The corner of Ouyang's mouth moved, more brittle than a

smile. The shadow across his face was too transparent to mask pain. Esen thought: *He mourns too.*

Ouyang said, "The thing your father wanted most in this world was always your success, and the pride you bring to the ancestral line."

Esen thought of his father, and for the first time felt something bright amidst the pain. Not enough to supersede the pain yet, but the seed of something that could grow. *I am the Prince of Henan, the defender of the Great Yuan, as my father and my father's father were before me.* It was a purpose and a destiny, ringing inside him as clearly as the high note of a qin. Esen saw Ouyang's face, and knew he felt it as strongly as Esen did. It warmed him to know that despite everything, he would always have Ouyang.

Ouyang's arrow thunked into the target. After his betrayal in Hichetu, his plan had been to keep his distance from Esen. Esen's grief and anger were unbearable: they gave Ouyang a gnawing pain that was like having sharkskin rubbed over every tender place of his body. What he hadn't counted on was Esen's new desire to keep Ouyang closer to his side than when Ouyang had been his slave. It was understandable; he supposed he should have anticipated it. *He has been orphaned. He curses his brother's name. All he has now is me—*

His next arrow flew wide.

Beside him, Esen loosed his own arrow. "To take Jiankang, only to abandon it—" His arrow met the target neatly. Despite being busy in the role of Prince of Henan, he had adopted the new habit of playing archery in the mornings before taking to his desk—which invariably meant Ouyang had to accompany him.

"Internal struggles," Ouyang said, collecting himself. His next arrow landed a finger-width from Esen's. "According to the intelligence, they have two factions fighting for control of the movement. The newest reports suggest Liu Futong may have put their young General Guo to death. We should have confirmation in a few days."

"Ha! When we aren't around to kill their generals, they feel the need to do it themselves?"

Tall cypresses cast their scented blue shadows across the manicured garden in which they were playing. In adjoining gardens, ponds blushed with lotuses. Purple wisteria poured over the crisscrossing walkways and down the stone walls on the perimeter. The rising warmth of the day had already quieted the birdsong, and even the bees seemed indolent. Despite their minimal exertion they were both sweating. Esen, because he was constitutionally unsuited to the heat; and Ouyang, because he was wearing too many layers. He felt throttled. In normal circumstances the rhythmic motions of archery would have been soothing, but now they only wound him tighter.

A servant came by with perspiring cups of cold barley tea and fragrant cold towels for the face and hands. Ouyang drank gratefully and pressed a towel against the back of his neck. "My lord, we could consider advancing our departure date a few weeks, to engage them before they resolve their infighting. We may as well take advantage of their distraction."

"Can you?"

"Logistically, yes. It only requires extra funds—" Ouyang left unsaid whose permission was needed for the release of such funds. Since Hichetu, Lord Wang had kept mostly to his own office and apartments and was rarely seen. Ouyang had only run into him once in the courtyards, whereupon Lord Wang had given him a penetrating, bitter look that drew him up and pinned him for inspection. The thought of that look gave him a pang of disquiet.

Esen's lips thinned. "Start your arrangements. I'll make sure you get the funds. Do you have any idea where the rebels will strike next?"

Ouyang felt a stab. Never had he experienced so many different kinds of pain, the one layered over the other. Even as the pain of his first betrayal hadn't healed, he already felt the painful anticipation of the next. Oh, he knew well enough where the rebels would go next. Having eschewed the strategic target of Jiankang, they would be looking for a symbolic victory. And if their goal was to cast doubt upon the Great Yuan's right to rule, they would aim to retake an ancient capital located in the center of Henan—in the very heart of the empire. They would want the last throne of the last great dynasty that ruled before the barbarians came.

Any Nanren would know. And for all that the Mongols had made him theirs, Ouyang was a Nanren. He thought: *Bianliang.*

Out loud, he said, "No, my lord."

"No matter," Esen said. "Wherever they pick, I hardly think we're in danger of losing." He raised his bow again and drew. "Although this time: no river crossings."

It felt like a lifetime ago that the rebel monk had called a tower of water down upon them and drowned ten thousand of Ouyang's men. That had been the start of it all. He had been shamed and forced to kneel; he had looked his fate in the eye; he had betrayed and killed. And now there was nothing left for him but pain. He felt a surge of hatred towards the monk. Perhaps his fate was fixed, but it was that cursed monk who had made it happen *now*; who had set it all in motion. Without him, how much longer might Ouyang have had with Esen? He was stabbed by a yearning of such intensity that his breath ran out of him. The easy pleasure of companionship on campaign; the pure sweetness of fighting side by side: it all belonged to the past, when Ouyang had still deserved Esen's trust.

As if reading his mind, Esen said in frustration, "I don't know how I'm going to bear it, having to stay here. Just because I'm the Prince now, and I don't have an heir yet." His arrow thunked into the center of the target. Ouyang was ordinarily the better of them at stationary archery, but since Hichetu a new aggressiveness had entered Esen's bearing. On the range and practice field, at least, it impressed.

"If anything were to happen to you—" Ouyang said.

"I know," Esen said, bitter. "The bloodline would end with me. Ah, how I curse those women of mine! Can they not at least perform their one use?"

They walked over to retrieve their arrows. Esen's were buried so deeply that he had to use his knife to cut them free. He said harshly, "Win for me, Ouyang. For my father."

Ouyang watched him stab at the wood. Dark emotions sat unnaturally on Esen's classically smooth features. The sight made Ouyang feel that he had broken something beautiful and perfect. Chaghan's death had been unavoidable: it had been written into the fate of the world from the moment Chaghan had killed Ouyang's family. In that respect, killing Chaghan hadn't been a sin.

But breaking Esen felt like one.

Esen sat at his father's desk, hating it. As per tradition, after his assumption of the title he and his wives and their households had all moved into Chaghan's residence. Perhaps someone else would have enjoyed the closeness of memory, but Esen found memories invariably unpleasant: they waylaid him unexpectedly, like slaps to the face. The only consolation was that he had been able to force his own residence upon Ouyang. Ouyang's insistence on living in isolation, beneath his station, had always mystified Esen and caused him some resentment. It seemed unfair that the person closest to his heart should persist in *choosing* loneliness and in so doing make Esen feel it too. But there was always something untouchable about Ouyang. He was always moving away, even as Esen wanted to hold him closer.

The door opened, and a Semu official came in ahead of a servant bearing a stack of papers. Officials all looked much the same to Esen, but the man's unsettling ice-pale eyes were distinctive. His mood soured instantly: it was his brother's secretary.

The Semu came forwards boldly and made his reverence.

Indicating the pile of papers, he said, "This unworthy official begs to trouble the esteemed Prince of Henan for his seal upon the following—"

Esen clamped down on his irritation and took his father's seal out of its paulownia box. The stamping face bled cinnabar ink. The sight of it filled Esen with despair. He couldn't countenance a lifetime of sitting down, stamping documents. He took the topmost paper, then paused. It was entirely in native characters. In a growing fury he snatched the pile from the servant and saw the same was true for all of them. Esen had always been proud of his capabilities. But unlike his brother, or even his father, he had no literacy in anything but Mongolian. It had never mattered before. Now his inadequacy sent a hot burst of shame through him. Turning on the Semu, he said sharply, "Why do you write in this useless language?"

His brother's secretary dared raise an eyebrow. "Esteemed Prince, your father—"

Behind the impertinence Esen saw his brother's supercilious face, and he felt a flash of pure rage. "You dare speak back!" he snapped. "Get down!"

The man hesitated, then sank down and placed his head on the floor. The bright sleeves and skirts of his dress splashed around him on the dark floorboards. He was wearing purple, and for a stunned moment all Esen could see was his father, after the fall.

His brother's secretary murmured, not entirely repentantly, "This unworthy servant begs the Prince's forgiveness."

Esen crumpled the paper in his fist. "Can a mere official be so bold just because he has my dog of a brother behind him? Do you take me for his puppet, that I would sign anything he hands me even if I can't read it? This is the Great Yuan. *We* are the Great Yuan, and our language is Mongolian. Change it!"

"Esteemed Prince, there are not enough—" His brother's secretary broke off into a satisfying yelp as Esen came around his desk in a rage, and kicked him. "Ah, Prince! Mercy—"

Esen shouted, "Tell my brother! Tell him I don't care if he

has to replace you and every one of his cursed minions to find ones that can work in Mongolian. *Tell him.*" He let the crumpled documents drop on him. His brother's secretary flinched, gathered his skirts, and scuttled away.

Esen stood there, breathing fast. *Baoxiang would make a fool of me in my own household.* The thought was inescapable. He felt himself revolving around it, each time winding tighter the mechanism of rage and hate. Since returning to Anyang he had done his best to pretend to himself that his brother no longer existed. He had hoped that erasing Wang Baoxiang from his thoughts would somehow erase the pain of betrayal and loss. But, Esen thought viciously, that hadn't worked.

He snapped at the nearest servant, "Summon Lord Wang!"

It was more than an hour before Baoxiang was announced. His fine-boned Manji features seemed more prominent, and there were shadows under his eyes. Under his familiar brittle smirk there was something as pale and secretive as a mushroom. He stood in his usual place in front of their father's desk. Esen, seated in their father's position behind it, felt unpleasantly disoriented.

He said harshly, "You made me wait."

"My most humble apologies, *Esteemed Prince.* I hear my secretary caused you offense." Baoxiang was wearing a plain-looking gown of driftwood gray, but when he bowed the silver threads in it caught the lamplight and sparkled like the hidden veins in a rock. "I take responsibility for the matter. I will have him beaten twenty times with the light bamboo."

It was all a performance; it was all surface. In a flash of anger, Esen saw his brother wasn't sorry at all. "And the other matter, of the language?"

Baoxiang said smoothly, "If the Prince commands it, I will have it changed."

His smoothness made Esen want to hurt—to twist until some jagged sincerity might be produced. "Then change it. And another matter, Lord Wang. You may be aware that I recently commanded General Ouyang to advance his departure dates for the next campaign to the south. I understand this will require additional funds from your office. I would have you provide them at your earliest convenience."

Baoxiang's cat-eyes narrowed. "The timing is not ideal."

"You speak as though I were making a request."

"I have a number of large projects under way that will be impacted if funds are withdrawn at this critical moment."

"What large projects?" Esen said scornfully. "More roads? Ditch-digging?" He felt a surly thrill of pleasure at the thought of crushing what his brother cared about. Returning pain for pain. "Which is more important, a road or this war? I don't care where you take it from, just make the funds available."

Baoxiang sneered. "Are you really so keen to undo all my efforts and run this estate into the ground for a single effort against the rebels?" Behind him on the wall, the horsetail death banners fluttered: one each for their great-grandfather, grandfather, and Chaghan. "Have you ever thought about what will happen if you don't win, brother? Will you go in shame to the court to tell them you have not the resources to continue your defense of the Great Yuan? The only reason they care about us is our ability to maintain an army. Will you throw away that ability for a chance of glory?"

"A chance—!" Esen said incredulously. "You can't think we'd lose."

"Oh, and last season you didn't lose ten thousand men? It could happen again, Esen! Or are you fool enough to believe the future will match your dream of it, with no consideration of the reality of the situation? If so, you're worse than our father."

Esen slammed back his chair. "You dare speak of him to me!"

"Why?" said Baoxiang, advancing. His voice rose. "Why can't I speak of our father? Do tell, is it something you think I did?"

The words flew out of Esen. "You know what you did!"

"Do I?" Baoxiang's face remained a cold mask of disdain, but his chest rose and fell rapidly. "Why don't you clear it up between the two of us, and say exactly what you think." He leaned over the desk and demanded, "*Say it.*"

"Why should I say it?" Esen shouted. His heart thumped as hard as if he were riding into battle. A cold sweat had sprung out all over his body. "Isn't it upon you to beg for forgiveness?"

Baoxiang laughed. It could have been a snarl. "Forgiveness. Would you ever forgive me? Should I kneel and take your punishment willingly, and beg and grovel for more, just to hear you spurn me? Why should I?"

"Just admit—"

"I don't admit anything! I don't need to! *You've already made up your mind.*" Baoxiang grabbed the desk and held on as if it were a slipping deck at sea; his pale fingers whitened further with the pressure. His narrow eyes blazed with such intensity that Esen felt it like a physical blow. "You can't reason with fools who refuse to see reason. Our father was a fool, and you're an even bigger fool than he was, Esen! No matter what I say, no matter what I do, both of you would think the worst of me. You slander me with ill thoughts I've never had—no, not even when he had me on my knees, and was cursing my very existence. You think I murdered him!"

Pressure rose in Esen; he felt his entire being throbbing with it. "Shut your mouth."

"And do what, vanish? Be silent forever? Oh, you'd love to be rid of me, wouldn't you, so you never have to see my face again. What a pity *our father* decided on a formal adoption, and only the Great Khan himself can strip a noble of his titles." His voice rose mockingly. "So what are you going to do about me, *brother*?"

Esen slammed his hands against the desk with such ferocity that it dealt a blow to Baoxiang and sent him stumbling. He straightened and glared at Esen with a pure fury that matched Esen's own. That look, raw with the sincerity that Esen had sought, split them with the finality of a falling axe blade.

Esen heard ugliness in his voice: it was his father's voice. "He was right about you. You're worthless. Worse than that: a curse. Rue the day this house took you in! Even if I have not the authority of the Great Khan, then at least my ancestors should witness the truth of my words in disowning your name. Get out!"

Two bright spots stood on Baoxiang's colorless cheeks. His body trembled inside his stiff robes; his fists were clenched. He looked at Esen for a long moment, his lip curled, then without saying anything further he left.

"General?" One of the servants was calling through the door, wanting to assist Ouyang with his bath.

"Wait," he said sharply, getting out and pulling on his inner garments. This act of self-sufficiency provoked a confused silence; the servants had yet to become accustomed to the peculiarities of a eunuch master. They had been left behind after Esen's move, the result of Esen's insistence that Ouyang maintain a staff commensurate with the status of the residence. The generosity had proven awkward, as several of them had been known to Ouyang during his own slave days, and he'd had to dismiss them.

Emerging from the bathroom and consenting to having his hair combed, he said, "Take down the mirrors in the bathroom."

"Yes, General."

He stared ahead as the servant worked. Around them, the faded floor was marked with dark rectangles where the furniture had been, like a house where the owner has died and the relatives have taken away all the things. It was unpleasant occupying a space that had been someone else's for so long. He was forever catching traces of a vanished presence: the oil Esen favored for his goatskin bridles; the particular mix of soap and fragrances his servants used on his clothes.

Outside a servant announced, "The Prince of Henan."

Ouyang looked up, surprised, as Esen entered. He visited Esen's rooms, not the other way around.

Surveying the empty territory, Esen laughed. There was a slur in his voice; he had been drinking. "I gave you so much space, you can live like a lord, and here you still are living like some penniless soldier. Why don't you ever need anything? I would give it to you."

"I don't doubt your generosity, my prince. But I have few needs." Guiding Esen to the table, Ouyang caught the eye of one of the hovering servants and gestured for wine. Esen was usually a cheerful drunk, but now it seemed that alcohol had loosened every restraint upon his misery: it billowed from him, unstable and dangerous. Ouyang wished he'd had time to prepare. Without his usual multiple layers to protect him, his hair hanging loose over his shoulders, he felt uncomfortably vulnerable. Too close to the surface; too open to Esen's sorrow.

Esen sat quietly at the table as they waited for the wine to be warmed. He still wore the white mourning overgarment in the evenings. Ouyang could see a glimpse of rich color through the splayed split in the skirts, like a wound. The smell of wine drifted off him, layered with the flowery smell of women. Esen must have come to him directly from one of his wives. It was already the second watch; he had probably been eating and drinking with her since the afternoon. The thought gave Ouyang a feeling of curdled distaste.

"Give me that." Esen took the wine from the servants and dismissed them. Not trusting him, Ouyang took the wine away and poured it for both of them. Esen took the offered cup and stared down into it, shaking his head slowly. The jade beads in his hair clicked. After a long while he said, "Everyone warned me. You warned me. But somehow . . . I never thought it would happen like this." Disbelief in his voice. "My own *brother.*"

Ouyang pressed his feelings down until they were packed as tightly as a cake of tea. "He's not your brother. He doesn't have your father's blood."

"What difference does that make? My father took him in, I thought of him as a brother, we were raised together. I never thought of him as less, even if he wasn't a warrior. We had our differences, but—" He seemed sunk in memory for a minute, then exhaled with a shudder.

Destroying what someone else cherished never brought back what you yourself had lost. All it did was spread grief like a contagion. As he watched Esen, Ouyang felt their pain mingling. There seemed to be no beginning or end to it, as if it were all they could ever be. He said, "There are people who say that grief will hurt as much as it's worth. And there is nothing worth more than a father."

"How long must it continue?"

Ouyang remembered once believing that grief must have an end, as all other emotions did. Between them on the table the lamp flame swayed and sank, as though his ballooning grief were a cloud capable of extinguishing everything it touched. He said, "I don't know."

Esen groaned. "Ah, how much easier life must be without family. Clean. None of these worries, concerns, encumbrances." Intoxicated, Esen was over-enunciating. Ouyang, staring at him in pain, saw anew the reminder of what he had always known: that Esen had forgotten that Ouyang had come from a family; that once he had been a son, a brother, too. "Better I should be like you, loving only my sword, none of this—*this*—" Esen gulped the wine.

A corona of tiny insects surrounded the dying lamp flame, their bodies giving off the singed smell of summer nights. Esen was absorbed in his cup, neither noticing nor caring that Ouyang had yet to join him in the drinking. The night watchman passed by outside.

Ouyang poured a refill, but when he handed it over Esen grabbed his arm and said with slurred vehemence, "*You*. You're the one I trust, when I can't even trust my own brother."

The touch sent a jolt through Ouyang's hard-won control. The warmth and pressure of Esen's hand was tempered by nothing but the single thin layer of his inner shirt. Feeling him tense, Esen shook his head and said irritably, "Why must you be so wedded to formality? Haven't we been through enough to-gether to be familiar?"

Ouyang was abruptly aware of Esen's physicality, how solid and purely masculine he was. Even tired and drunk, his cha-risma was powerful. His fingers slackened around Ouyang's wrist. Ouyang could have broken free in an instant. He didn't. He looked at Esen's familiar face, lined unfamiliarly with the pain he himself had put there. He saw the smoothness where the beard of Esen's upper lip failed to meet his beard below, his strong neck with its fluttering heartbeat. The generous and well-shaped lips. The flesh-and-bloodedness of his body, so much larger than Ouyang's own. Even in his grief and drunk-enness, everything about him seemed like the embodiment of some ideal. Handsome, strong, honorable. Ouyang was faintly aware of a vibration, a distant tickle: the night watch calling the time. He couldn't look away.

Esen said fiercely, drunkenly, "Baoxiang would never put himself on the line for me, or anyone else. But you, you'd do anything for me, wouldn't you?"

Inside, Ouyang recoiled from the image: Esen's mastery, and his own debasement. As if he were nothing more than a dog panting at Esen's feet for approval and affection. *Not a man, but a thing.* And yet—Esen was staring at him with a bold in-tensity that was uncouth in its raw interest, and Ouyang didn't turn away. Without altering his gaze, Esen slowly reached up and brushed the hair back from Ouyang's face. He felt the strange, slow drag of calloused fingertips from brow to cheek. He didn't lean into it, just let it happen. Esen's hand on his arm, the other hovering next to him in an uncompleted embrace. The air be-tween them seemed to have thickened into a pressure that kept him where he was. The closeness of Esen's body disturbed a willingness within him that he found deeply unsettling. He knew his face was as blank as always, but distantly he was aware that his breathing had shallowed, his pulse racing as though in exertion or fear.

Esen's voice took on a note Ouyang had never heard before, low and roughened with potential, as he said, "You really are as beautiful as a woman."

Later, Ouyang thought Esen wouldn't even have noticed: the moment his stillness of anticipation flicked into the stillness of shame, as quickly as capping a candle. His blood ran cold; his body burned. It was the feeling of a blade slid gently into his heart. He pulled away. Esen stayed leaning forwards for a moment, then slowly leaned back and raised his cup again.

Ouyang poured himself a cup with shaking hands and downed it. His compressed emotions had exploded into a swarm of stinging hornets. He had betrayed Esen, but now Esen betrayed *him*. It was incomprehensible how despite everything they had been through together, Esen could still think Ouyang might be *flattered* by that comparison. How could he be so completely ignorant of the shame that was the core of Ouyang's being? Burning with an emotion that seemed to contain the agonies of both love and hate, Ouyang thought furiously: *He chooses not to know.*

Across from him, Esen's gaze was already blurred. It was as though nothing had happened. Ouyang realized bitterly that for Esen, perhaps it hadn't. He owned everything he laid his eyes on, and that included Ouyang. He had merely reached for something beautiful, confusing it for another of his precious things, and when the object of this mild desire slipped away he didn't even remember it had been in his grasp at all.

"So you did it," Shao remarked, meaning Chaghan. They were sitting in Ouyang's private apartments. Ouyang saw Shao taking in the way the few tables and chairs hung moored in the empty space like boats in a lake. There was something about Shao that always seemed grasping and dishonorable. Ouyang hated that it was Shao who knew his private concerns, and used them towards his own low ends.

"Yes," Ouyang said bitterly. "Had you doubted I would?"

Shao shrugged as if to convey that his doubts were his own business.

"The Prince of Henan has ordered us to advance our departure," Ouyang said. The scramble of inked paper on the table between them held the accounting of their army: the men and equipment and gargantuan resources required to get them where they needed to go. "Now that the funds have been released, let us coordinate the logistics swiftly."

"What of Altan's replacement? We have to make a decision about that battalion. Jurgaghan"—a young Mongol from the family of Esen's third wife—"is expecting the position."

In Ouyang's opinion there was no functional difference between Jurgaghan and Altan; they and all their peers were entitled young men who had never had a disappointment in their lives. "Give it to Zhao Man."

They spoke quietly, since window-paper did little to keep voices contained. It did however keep the heat in, and the closed windows made the room stuffy. Shao fanned himself with a round paper fan that seemed to have been borrowed from a woman. A pair of mandarin ducks, boasting of love and marriage, winked at Ouyang from the back. Ouyang supposed even Shao must have a wife. He had never asked.

"You don't think the Prince will resist having another Nanren in command?"

"Leave the Prince to me," Ouyang said. He felt a dull rushing pressure: that unstoppable current bearing him towards his ending.

Shao arched his eyebrows in a way that made Ouyang's blood boil, but he said only, "And where will the rebels be heading this season?"

"Don't you know?" Ouyang said. "Guess."

Shao gave him a dark inscrutable look. "Bianliang."

"Exactly." Ouyang returned a humorless smile.

"The question is: Will you tell the Mongols that?"

Ouyang said harshly, "You know what I want."

"Ah, the fate nobody else would want." Cruelty surfaced in

Shao's voice. The gusts from his fan felt like a series of unwanted touches that Ouyang was rapidly beginning to find intolerable. "I hope you're strong enough for it."

Ouyang entertained a brief fantasy of seizing the fan and crushing it. "Your concern for my suffering is touching. But if our fates are fixed, then my strength is irrelevant. Blame Heaven; blame my ancestors; blame myself in my past lives. I have no escaping it." Unwilling to bare himself further to Shao of all people, he said abruptly, "Prepare the armament orders, and tell the logistics and communication commanders to come see me."

Shao tucked the fan into his belt, rose and saluted. There was something crawlingly unpleasant about his expression: it lingered between amusement and contempt. "Yes, General."

Ouyang had no choice but to let it pass. They needed each other, and even if he had to endure slights along the way: when they reached their goal, none of it would matter again.

16

ANFENG, EIGHTH MONTH

Neither Ma nor anyone else in Anfeng dared mourn Little Guo by wearing white. The only thing to remember him by was the ancestral tablet that Zhu had put up in the temple at Ma's request, and even that was hidden behind the names of all the other deceased. Little Guo's men had been given over to the newly appointed Commander Yi. Sun Meng was the only commander left on Right Minister Guo's side, and Ma hadn't seen either of them in public since Little Guo's death.

It was obvious Chen was just waiting to make his final move to destroy the Guo faction, and the only people to survive would be those unequivocally on Chen's side. Then there would be no one to rein Chen in but a paranoid and malleable Prime Minister. And unlike Prime Minister Liu, Chen's interest in defeating the Yuan wouldn't be for the sake of the Nanren people who had placed their faith in the Red Turbans and the Prince of Radiance, but for creating his own world of terror and cruelty.

The thought should have filled Ma with dread. Most of the time it did. But that evening, as she came down the temple steps in her red wedding dress and veil, she found her worries washed away by a new lightness. She'd spent her whole life anticipating marriage as a duty, never dreaming for a moment that it could be an escape. But someone impossible had given her something that shouldn't exist. Her veil tinged the world red, and for once the color reminded her of good fortune instead of blood. Through her veil she marveled at the small red-gowned figure leading her down the steps by the scarf tied between them. She had no idea what her future held—only that in this life, it could be different.

Zhu reached the throng of well-wishers at the bottom of the steps, then suddenly came to a halt and bowed. Ma, struggling to make out details through the veil, came up beside her and stopped just as abruptly.

"Master Zhu," Chen greeted, approaching through the crowd. On all sides bodies bent towards him like stalks under the wind. "Or I suppose it must be Commander Zhu, since you're married now. I barely recognize you out of those gray robes! Congratulations."

Smiling, he handed his gift to Zhu. "And I see your bride is the beautiful Ma Xiuying." Even with her veil as protection, Ma shrank from the piercing regard of his tiger eyes. He said to her politely, "I'd wondered if it would be Commander Sun's turn to have hot tea poured on him, since he's a good-looking young man. But I knew you were a smart girl. Good choice."

He turned back to Zhu. "The Prime Minister sends his congratulations. He thinks well of you, Commander Zhu. He often mentions his wish that the other commanders' forces emulate your men's discipline and humility. Commander Yi, for instance, has inherited a force which is particularly lacking, due to his predecessor's faults." Chen's tone was relaxed, but his attention on Zhu reminded Ma of a collector's pin poised over an insect. He said, "Your second-in-command, the tall one with the short hair. Was he a monk too?"

If Zhu was as concerned as Ma, she hid it well. "Minister, Second Commander Xu was also an ordained monk of Wuhuang Monastery."

"Perfect," Chen said. "Why don't you second him to Commander Yi for the next month? That should be enough time for him to have a positive influence. Teach a few sutras and the virtues of humility. What do you think?"

Ma's dread swept back in, erasing every trace of the lightness she'd felt moments before. By taking Zhu's best friend hostage, Chen was making very sure she had no choice but to support whatever he was planning against the Guo faction.

There was no chance Zhu hadn't realized that, but she only bowed. The black scholar-style hat she had worn for the wedding matched Chen's perfectly, so that together they resembled a classic image of master and disciple. "This unworthy commander is honored to oblige. If the Minister is so generous as to allow it, this servant will send him around after the wedding banquet this evening."

Chen smiled, the vertical creases in his cheeks deepening until they looked like knife cuts. "Of course."

Zhu and Ma's new home as a married couple was a plain room in the barracks, though Zhu saw it had been haphazardly decorated with red streamers that looked like they had been part of a military banner in a past life. Daylight flickered through the gaps in the rough wooden walls, giving the place the secret feel of a children's hiding spot in a bamboo forest.

Ma took off her veil. Her dangling hairpin decorations chimed softly against each other as she sat next to Zhu on the bed. Zhu noticed she positioned herself further than a woman might sit from another woman, but closer than she would to a man. As if instead of being like Zhu Chongba, Zhu belonged in the same category as the eunuch general: neither one thing nor the other. The thought sent a judder of uneasiness through her. She had known that exposing her secret to Ma had increased, by some unknown amount, her risk of being recognized as the wrong owner of that great fate. It was the unknown part that worried her most. *A risk is only a risk*, she reminded herself. If it'd been a certainty, she would never have done it. She tried not to think about that ominous feeling of momentum that had troubled her after Jiankang. *Risks can be managed.*

She forced herself out of that line of thinking and into a

cheerful demeanor. "Well, thanks to Chen Youliang, this isn't quite the romantic mood I'd always dreamed of for my wedding."

Ma hit her on the arm. The stiff white makeup didn't suit her; Zhu missed her bare-faced liveliness. "What are you talking about! Monks don't dream about their weddings."

"You're right," Zhu said, mock-thoughtfully. "Look at Xu Da. I'm sure it's never even occurred to him to wait for marriage— he goes right ahead and does it."

A wedge of unpowdered skin along Ma's hairline went scarlet. "You and he—?"

It took Zhu a moment to realize what she was asking. "Buddha preserve us!" She felt a moment of true horror. "With women! *Not with me.*"

"I didn't mean the business of rain and clouds," Ma said crossly, although of course she had. "But he must know."

"Well, I never *told* him," Zhu said, ignoring the taboo feeling of saying it out loud. "But he knows more about me than anyone. He's my brother." At the flash of guilt in Ma's eyes, she added, "It's not because of you that Chen Youliang is taking him hostage. You might have come from the Guo household, but Chen Youliang won't think that's enough to tip my loyalties over. He's just taking precautions. He's a smart man, and he doesn't want any surprises when it comes to the crunch."

Ma's face was very still under her makeup. "Loyalties. You would have helped him anyway?"

Zhu remembered Ma's attachment to Sun. She said gently, "I know how you feel, Ma Xiuying. I don't like Chen Youliang any more than you do." But the cold, pragmatic side of her saw the strength of his position.

Groups of men tromped by outside, their shadows falling through the gaps in the wall and onto the swept dirt floor. From next door came burbling sounds, and the intense porky odor of boiling offal. Ma suddenly said, low and desperate, "Don't do it. Don't help him. Pledge your allegiance to Right Minister

Guo and Sun Meng; get them to act before you have to give up
Xu Da—"

Ma's hope was like seeing the world through the irides-
cent wing of an insect: a glowing, soft-edged version of itself in
which the arc of history could still trend towards kindness and
decency. Ma always felt so *much,* and with such a foolish, beautiful intensity, that witnessing her emotions made Zhu's own
internal landscape seem as barren as a cracked lake bed. Regretfully, Zhu shook her head. "Think. Even if I had time, how
many men do I have? Nowhere near enough. Sun Meng might
have more than either of the other commanders individually,
but against them together—"

Tears welled up in Ma's eyes. No doubt she was remembering Little Guo's death, and imagining the same for Sun Meng.
But then she startled Zhu by saying savagely, "No, *you* think.
If you take Chen Youliang's side and help him put down Right
Minister Guo and his supporters, you'll be setting your own
men against other Red Turbans. Do you think your force will
come through the same, after that? It's one thing to kill a Yuan
soldier, but it's something different to kill another rebel. Have
you thought about that?" Her tears didn't fall.

Zhu paused. Chen's eventual victory over the Guos was so
obvious that she hadn't ever felt like she was *choosing* his side,
but was just taking the only available path. And because it was
the only path, she had always thought of its unpleasant repercussions as something she would have to manage as well as
possible when the time came. It had never occurred to her that
they might be unmanageable. She frowned. "Better to have
men with damaged morale than no men at all."

"They follow you because you built them up—because you
earned their trust and loyalty. But force them to turn on their
own, and you'll lose all that! They'll see you for what you are.
Not their leader, but someone who's using them. And when
that happens, they'll *only* be following you out of self-interest.
Then how long do you think it will be before Chen Youliang

takes them away? All he'll have to do is make them an offer."
Ma said bitterly, "Just like he did to Little Guo."

Disconcerted, Zhu remembered Commander Yi's gleeful assumption of power. Nobody, not even Zhu herself, had noticed Yi's monstrous self-interest. But Chen had. "I—"

Ma cried, "*Listen.* Isn't this why you wanted me, so I could tell you what you don't see? If you don't want to be witness to a world of nothing but cruelty and suspicion and paranoia, then *find another way.*"

Zhu closed her mouth. The monks had taught that empathy and compassion were gentle emotions, but Ma's cracked wedding makeup reminded her more than anything of the harsh, unyielding faces of the monastery's all-seeing Guardian Kings. The sight of Ma's judgment caused a wrenching contraction in the pit of her stomach. The feeling pulled her out of joint: she was pierced by the keenest sense of pity she had ever felt, simultaneously suffused with tenderness and aching with some mysterious longing. She stared at Ma's crumpled, defiant face, and the ache intensified until she thought she might have to press her fist into her chest to relieve the pain of it.

As long as I want to find it, there's always another way. Hadn't she found ways to succeed at Yao River and Lu, when they were much harder problems? Already the cooking smell from next door was giving her an idea so uncanny it raised the hair on the back of her neck out of disbelief that she could dare try it. But at the same time it felt *right.* Since she had become Zhu Chongba, there had been an aspect of the world that only she could see—and for that same length of time, she had thought it nothing more than an oddity. Realizing now that it was knowledge she could *use* was as pleasing as picking up a leaf and discovering that it was perfectly symmetrical. It felt like fate.

She shuffled along the lumpy bed and pressed her red-robed knee gently against Ma's. "I can't help Sun Meng directly. What I *can* do is stay out of it in a way that won't raise Chen Youliang's suspicions. But even then—you have to know that Sun Meng still has next to no chance of success."

Ma gave her a fierce look that barely had any gratitude in it, as though she had merely bullied Zhu into an act of basic decency that had nothing to do with Ma's personal desires. "At least he'll have *some* chance."

Zhu's insides twisted at the thought that Ma was going to be disappointed by what Zhu considered decent. She said in warning, "It might give a better outcome, but Yingzi: there are no kind solutions to cruel situations."

A cold, wet draft blew into the temple, bringing with it incongruous laughter: despite the rain, Zhu's men were already gathering in anticipation of the wedding banquet. Inside, Zhu knelt in the red glow from the massive columnar candles. The burning wicks had tunneled deep within the candles so their flames projected dancing shapes on the insides of their red wax shells, like the sun viewed through closed eyelids. At Zhu's request the cooks had already brought the pots and baskets of wedding food into the temple, ostensibly to keep them out of the rain until the festivities started. Zhu had since moved a careful selection of dishes to the front of the temple and left them uncovered before a field of unlit incense sticks.

Now she took one incense stick and lit it from a candle, then pressed it to the other sticks one by one. When they were alight, Zhu blew them out so their smoldering tips sent up thin streamers of smoke. Then she backed away and waited.

It was the memory of someone who no longer existed. Zhu remembered standing in her family's sprung-open wooden house, her father's dried blood under her feet, looking at the two melon seeds on the ancestral shrine. The last food left in the world. She remembered how desperately she had wondered if what the villagers said was true: that if you ate the ghost offerings, you would sicken and die. In the end she hadn't eaten—but only from fear. She hadn't known, then, what it looked like to see the hungry ghosts come for their food. But the person she was now, Zhu Chongba, knew. She thought of the countless times she had passed the offerings in the monastery—piles of fruit, bowls of cooked grain—and seen ghosts bent over, feeding. The monks had always thrown that food out afterwards. They might not have known about ghosts in quite the same way Zhu knew, but they knew.

There was a murmur that could have been nothing but a gust of wind in the rain. Then the streams of incense smoke all bent to the side, and the hidden candle flames leaned over inside their columns until the wax glowed hot and sweated red droplets. An icy breeze flowed in the open door, and with it came the ghosts. A stream of the unremembered, their chalk-white faces fixed towards the front. Their unbound hair and tattered clothes hung still despite their motion. Even as accustomed to ghosts as she was, Zhu shuddered. She wondered what it must be like for the eunuch general to live his entire life in their company. Perhaps he'd never even felt the world unmediated by their chill.

The ghosts lowered their heads over the offerings like feasting animals. Their rising murmur resembled distant bees. As Zhu watched them, she had the sense of what had become ordinary regaining its magical strangeness. Her heart thrilled. *She could see the spirit world.* She could see the hidden reality, the part of the world that made sense of all the other parts, and it was something only she could do. She was using the spirit world, as others did the physical world, to serve her desire. She glowed with the realization that the strange fact about herself was a power that made her stronger—better. More capable of achieving what she wanted.

Warm with satisfaction, she barely noticed the discomfort in her knees. It would normally take hours of kneeling before pain forced her to get up and move. But perhaps this time she twitched without realizing it. Or perhaps she simply breathed.

The ghosts snapped around, faster than any human could

have. Their murmur shut off so suddenly that Zhu reeled at the silence. Their inhuman faces turned to her, they *looked* at her, and the touch of their terrible black eyes exploded her delight and satisfaction with a shock that felt like being grabbed around the throat by ice-cold hands. Horrified, Zhu remembered the ominous momentum that had started in Lu. The feeling that some mysterious pressure was building with every divergence she made from Zhu Chongba's path, and it would only keep growing until something happened to release it. *To return the world to the way it's supposed to be.* All of a sudden she was trembling uncontrollably where she knelt.

The ghosts, their eyes still on her, began murmuring again. At first Zhu thought it was only their normal unintelligible ghost murmur, then she realized they were *speaking*. She recoiled and clapped her hands over her ears, but flesh was no barrier to the sound issuing from those dead throats:

Who are you?

The ghosts' voices rose; sharpened. Zhu had become ice, and the terrible sound of their accusation was the gong note that would shatter her into pieces. The ghosts knew she wasn't the person she was supposed to be—who the world thought she was. Her belief that she *was* Zhu Chongba had always been her armor, but those words peeled her open. They stripped her down to the raw quick of herself, to the person she couldn't ever be, and laid her exposed beneath Heaven.

Who are you? She would be hearing it in her dreams. There was a blinding pressure in her skull. The ghosts moved towards her, and perhaps it was only because Zhu was between them and the door, but suddenly the sight of their motionless hair and faceless faces was unbearable. She heard herself make an awful rasping sound. Whatever risks she had accumulated by acting differently from Zhu Chongba, this mistake had stupidly—foolishly—multiplied them by some astronomical amount. Risks piled upon risks, until her path to success was as narrow as a needle.

Stumbling to her feet, she fled.

Monk—*Commander*—Zhu had put on a fairly decent wedding banquet, Chang Yuchun thought, surveying the lantern-bedecked tents that were keeping the rain off the men beneath. Zhu's entire force was there. Yuchun supposed if he were marrying someone as beautiful as Ma Xiuying, he might feel like spreading the good fortune around too. But despite the meat and lanterns and dancing, it didn't feel much like a celebration. Word had spread that Second Commander Xu was being sent away as a hostage, which was the most recent in a series of signs that something deeply unfortunate was about to happen. Anfeng felt as dangerous as a steamer with the lid sealed shut. Fortunately in addition to the food, Zhu had provided an endless supply of wine to soothe their nerves. Yuchun and the others drank themselves insensible under the gently watchful gazes of Zhu and Ma Xiuying from the dais above them, and all the while the rain sheeted endlessly off the awnings and drew curtains across the moon.

The next day everyone was hungover and surly. Without Second Commander Xu their routines were all awry, and for some reason Zhu hadn't appointed anyone to replace him. Even the next day Zhu left them to their own devices. Normally they would have welcomed the holiday, but their hangovers were strangely persistent. They sat around nursing their headaches and complaining about the rain, which was well on its way to turning Anfeng back into a mud pit. A few men developed a short cough, which Yuchun presumed was simply the cold having gotten into them.

His first indication that something was wrong was when he woke in the middle of the night to an unpleasant twisting in his stomach. Stepping on his roommates in his haste, he made it outside just in time to vomit. But instead of feeling better, he was overcome by the violent urge to take a shit. Afterwards, gasping, he felt as limp as an overcooked noodle. As he wobbled back into the barracks he nearly collided with someone else running out to the latrine. A permeating smell of sickness rose up from the room. He felt like he should be more concerned about this turn of events, but it took every last bit of his strength to find his pallet again. He collapsed onto it and passed out.

When he came to, someone was squatting next to his head with a ladle of water. Zhu. The foul stench of the room nearly made him gag. After the water Zhu fed him a few spoonfuls of salty gruel, then patted his hand and moved on. Time passed. He was vaguely conscious of men groaning around him; the imprisoning tangle of his sweat-soaked blanket; and then finally a ferocious thirst that drove him outside on his hands and knees. To his surprise it was daylight. Someone had helpfully placed a clean bucket of water just outside the door. He drank, choking with haste and weakness, then sank panting against the doorframe. He felt—well, not *better*, but awake, which was an objective improvement of some kind. After a while he drank some more and looked around. Under the midday sun the street was completely deserted. Flags fluttered overhead. Not the familiar flag of their rebellion, but a cluster of five uncanny banners: green, red, yellow, black, and white, each bearing a red-painted warding talisman at its center. Yuchun gazed at them for a long time, his brain churning, until the meaning dawned.

Plague.

Yuchun turned out to be one of the first stricken, and the first to recover. He didn't know whether it was because he was younger and fitter than average, or whether his ancestors had finally decided to look out for him. Having started in a fairly contained way, the mysterious plague caught fire: it tore through Zhu's force, felling everyone in its path. The illness—which according to Jiao Yu was caused by an overabundance of yin in the major organs—started with a cough, progressed to vomiting and uncontrollable shitting, then finally a ferocious fever that melted the fat from a man's body in the space of days.

After that, it was a matter of luck as to whether the patient's gravely diminished yang vital force began replenishing itself, or whether he was one of the unfortunates whose imbalance worsened even further until their qi ceased to circulate, and they died.

Commander Yi, fearing a spread of the plague to his own men, sent Second Commander Xu back in a panic. The Prime Minister ordered Zhu's entire temple quarter quarantined. Gates were built and chained shut, and a number of Yi's men stood reluctantly on guard with their thumbs dug into the qi points in their palms in the hope of staving off infection. The gates were opened only to let food in. Even the dead were forced to remain inside, and had to be buried in shameful mass graves.

Perhaps one in ten men, including Commander Zhu, were fortunate enough to never get sick at all. (Yuchun thought they must be the ones with an overabundance of yang, but when he'd posited this theory to Jiao, the engineer had snorted and pointed out that Zhu's plucked-chicken physique was hardly that of someone with *too much* masculine energy.) Zhu, wearing the guilty expression of someone who knew he hadn't done anything to deserve his good health, directed the efforts of the other survivors in cooking and cleaning. For two weeks he even went around personally comforting and tending the victims. Then one day he vanished: his wife Ma had fallen ill. After that Second Commander Xu took over. He had shaved his head before his secondment to Yi's command, apparently in the hope that a blatantly religious appearance might offer protection against "accidents." His bare scalp, combined with plague-hollowed cheeks, made Yuchun think uncomfortably about the stories of hungry ghosts that roamed the countryside in search of people's livers.

From inside the plague fence it seemed that elsewhere in Anfeng life went on as usual. Every now and then Yuchun saw the other commanders' forces going about their training, and heard the drumming of the Prime Minister's ever-more-frequent ceremonies in praise of the Prince of Radiance. But he'd been around long enough to know that what he saw—an Anfeng that was calm, orderly, and obedient—was only the surface.

Zhu sat at Ma's bedside. Her helplessness in the face of Ma's suffering made her feel wretched with guilt. In the mornings the girl slept; in the afternoons and all through the night she thrashed with fever, screaming about ghosts. There was nothing Zhu could do other than offer her water and gruel, and replace the sweat-soaked sheets. Sometimes during Zhu's ministrations Ma roused and flailed at Zhu, a terrible fear in her eyes. That fear stabbed Zhu's insides: it was fear for *Zhu*, that she might get sick from touching Ma. This whole situation was Zhu's fault: it had never occurred to her that the illness might spread beyond those who had eaten the ghost offerings. Out of carelessness she had unleashed far more than she had sought, and Ma was her victim. But even in the depths of her sickness, Ma cared about Zhu's suffering.

Her heart aching, Zhu trapped Ma's frantic hand and squeezed it with all the reassurance she could muster. She had a lot of worries, but dying from ghostly contact wasn't one of them. "Don't worry, Yingzi," she said darkly. "The ghosts won't catch me. I can see them coming."

Perhaps the ghosts wouldn't catch her, but dead men haunted Zhu's dreams. Even apart from the horrific outcome of having been noticed by the ghosts, Zhu wasn't sure this had been the better way. Nearly as many of her men had died as would have if she had backed Chen in the coup. She supposed at least they had died with clean hands, which was good for their next lives. The only person's hands covered in blood were Zhu's own. And the coup hadn't even happened yet. She dreaded the thought that her men might recover, and the quarantine be lifted, before Guo and Sun even made their move. What if she had wrought all this for nothing?

Her entire life Zhu had considered herself strong enough to

bear any suffering. The suffering she had pictured, though, had always been something of her own body: hunger, or physical pain. But as she sat there with Ma's hand burning in her own, she recognized the possibility of a kind of suffering she had never imagined. *To lose the ones I love.* Even a glimpse of it felt like having her guts dragged out. Xu Da had recovered, but what if Ma's life was another consequence of Zhu's mistake?

Zhu wrestled with herself. Her stomach shrank as she felt the resurgence of her oldest fear: that if she prayed, Heaven would hear her voice and know it was the wrong one.

With all her might, she seized that fear and pushed it down. *I'm Zhu Chongba.*

She knelt and prayed to Heaven and her ancestors more fervently than she had in a long time. When she finally got up she was surprised and gratified to find that Ma's forehead was already cooler. Her heart flew with relief. *She won't die—*

And even as Zhu stood there with her hand on Ma's forehead, she heard a familiar roar in the distance: the sound of battle.

Guo and Sun's coup attempt lasted a day, put down nearly as quickly as it had started. The city was still smoking when Chen's men opened the plague gates and issued the summons. Zhu, taking in the scale of the destruction as they walked through the streets, thought that Guo and Sun had come surprisingly close to success. But of course a loss by any margin was still a loss. Everywhere blood was mixed into Anfeng's yellow mud. Whole sections of the city lay blackened. Since Anfeng was a wooden city, some men might have hesitated at the idea of setting Sun's barricades alight. But Chen was not that sort of concerned person.

In the center of the city the corpses had been piled high at the foot of the platform. This time both the Prime Minister and the Prince of Radiance were absent. This was Chen's show. The remaining Red Turbans, including Zhu and her men, gathered silently beneath. Zhu noticed that although Yi's force was there, Yi himself was nowhere to be seen. Presumably someone had killed him. She hoped Little Guo's spirit appreciated the gesture.

After a sufficient amount of time for contemplation of the corpses, Chen's men brought out the surviving leaders of the uprising. Zhu saw Sun, Right Minister Guo, and three of Sun's captains. They had been dressed in white, with the blood already showing through. Sun was missing an eye and his pretty face was almost unrecognizable. He glared mutely down at them, his blood-blackened lips pressed together. Zhu had the disturbing impression that Chen had done something to his tongue to prevent any last-minute speeches.

The captains were the first ones killed. As far as executions went, it was quite humane—surprising, considering Chen's involvement. The man in question watched from the stage with the eye of a connoisseur of cruelty. The crowd was silent. With the mountain of bodies staring them in the face, not even Commander Wu's men could muster up any enthusiasm for the process. Sun stood stoically throughout: a man looking his fate in the eye, knowing that his only hope lay in his next life being a good one. His own death, when it came, was as quick as one might hope in such a situation. Still, Zhu was glad that Ma had been spared the sight.

As it turned out, there was no need for anyone to recalibrate their opinions of Chen's mercy: he had merely been saving his dramatics for Right Minister Guo. In front of the watching Red Turbans, Old Guo was skinned alive. Chen had clearly found some kind of inspiration in the many years he had watched and waited for his colleague's downfall. That death took a very long time.

Chen, who apparently believed actions spoke louder than words, left the stage as soon as it was done. Passing Zhu, he paused.

"Greetings to the Left Minister," Zhu said, subdued, and made her reverence at a ninety-degree angle. She clamped down on the nausea that was threatening the contents of her stomach. For all she'd known Right Minister Guo's fate, it was another thing to witness the manner in which it had occurred. She had the miserable thought that she had underestimated Chen's cruelty.

"Commander Zhu." Taking in the sight of her pale and vomiting men, Chen gave her an ambiguous smile. "I was sorry to hear of the recent deaths among your number. Truly unfortunate."

Zhu forced herself to focus on Chen rather than the smells and sounds around her. "This unworthy servant gratefully accepts the Minister's condolences."

"I mentioned before how impressed the Prime Minister and I are with the quality and dedication of your men." Behind him, the pile of corpses stared unblinking at the back of his head. "Well, Commander: since Yi is gone, this is your chance. Take his men and turn them into the force we'll need to take Bianliang." His black eyes stabbed Zhu. "I trust you'll do a good job."

"This servant thanks the Minister for the honor and opportunity!" Zhu bowed and stayed bent over until she was quite sure Chen had gone. Although it hadn't been what Zhu herself had intended, and it certainly wasn't what Ma had wanted, she had the ironic realization that it had been the better way after all. There were only two surviving Red Turban commanders, and Zhu was one of them; she now controlled almost half the Red Turbans' total strength. Chen had no proof that Zhu was anything but loyal, even if he might be keeping his ultimate judgment in reserve, and Zhu's men suspected nothing.

But as Zhu stood in front of that bloodied stage with Right Minister Guo's screams still ringing in her ears, she shuddered at the memory of those inhuman voices. *Who are you?*

She found herself searching desperately inside herself for any alien sensation that might harbor that red spark—the seed of greatness, pressed into her spirit by Heaven itself. But to her despair, there was nothing new to find. There was only the same thing that had always been there: the white core of her determination that had kept her alive all these years, giving her the strength to keep believing she was who she said she was. It wasn't what she wanted, but it was all she had.

For a moment she felt that old vertiginous pull of fate. But she had already launched herself in pursuit of it; there was no going back. *Don't look down as you're flying, or you'll realize the impossibility of it and fall.*

ANFENG, TENTH MONTH

It was raining outside, and the Prime Minister's throne room leaked. Zhu knelt quietly alongside Commander Wu on the spongy wooden floor, her robes soaking up the water like a wick. Wu, who hadn't spent the better part of his youth kneeling for hours, shifted and fidgeted like a wormy horse. The Prince of Radiance smiled unmoving from the dais, the Prime Minister beside him. There was a third of their number up there now. After Guo's death Chen had retitled himself the Chancellor of State and elevated himself appropriately. However much higher he planned to go, he would take those he trusted with him. *But he doesn't trust me completely,* Zhu thought. *I stayed out of his action against the Guos. He might not suspect, but neither have I proved myself—*

Chen said, "We have to tread carefully with Bianliang. Its governor may not command a strong force, but he has the strategic advantage. Although the outer wall is ruined, the inner wall still stands. If we give the governor a chance to secure that inner wall, I have no doubt he'll be able to hold us until rescue arrives from the Prince of Henan. The Prince's army may not be as strong as it was last season, given Yao River and now that Esen-Temur is no longer in the field"—they had received news, albeit belatedly, of old iron-bearded Chaghan-Temur's death in a hunting accident that past spring—"but if it comes to Bianliang's defense, then our chances of success will be very small indeed."

The Prime Minister said curtly, "Then we must take Bianliang swiftly—too swiftly for the governor to turn it into a siege situation." Unlike the Mongols, who specialized in sieges, the Red Turbans had no siege equipment at all.

"Then it must be a surprise. He must neither be prepared, nor have the eunuch general coming to his aid. We will need a distraction: an attack on something of such importance to the Yuan that they have no choice but to send the eunuch to deal with that instead. The Grand Canal would be the best such target." The canal, linking the north to the Zhang family's salt and grain, was Dadu's lifeblood. "While he's occupied there, we can launch a surprise assault on Bianliang and take it quickly."

Hearing this, Zhu tensed. She felt Wu do likewise. Although a decoy mission could be done safely, that safety depended on perfect timing. A Red Turban decoy force would have to engage the eunuch general at the Grand Canal until Bianliang summoned him to its defense, although ideally the speed of the assault would mean it would fall even before he got there. But if there was any delay at all in the assault force getting to Bianliang and starting the attack—then the commander of the decoy force would rapidly find himself running out of delaying tactics, in a very real engagement with the enemy. It was, Zhu realized, a test of trust.

Her stomach gurgled uneasily. A reaction to the idea of such an obviously dangerous mission—but then her unease deepened into a thrumming disquiet, and to her alarm she felt the sensation of inhuman eyes falling upon her from behind. For a moment the urge to bolt was nearly overwhelming. Zhu kept her eyes fixed rigidly on the dais, and counted shallow breaths. Her sinews burned from the effort of holding still. Gradually the feeling faded, until she wasn't sure whether it had actually been ghosts, or only her own paranoid memory of them. She relaxed, but her skin still crawled.

Chen gave her an avuncular look that made her think he'd seen her moment of fear. To the Prime Minister he said, "Your Excellency, the capture and subsequent defense of Bianliang will be no easy task. Please entrust this unworthy official with the mission of personally leading our forces into Bianliang." He looked down at Zhu and Wu, and made a show of contemplation. At length he said pleasantly, "Commander Wu will accompany me to Bianliang." His black eyes jumped back to Zhu. Despite the cruelties of which Zhu knew he was capable, it wasn't cruelty she saw in his expression, but an amused curiosity. "And Commander Zhu will lead the decoy mission to the Grand Canal."

It was only what she'd expected. Chen wanted to trust her, because he recognized her talents. But because he was the man he was, he was going to make her prove it. Zhu didn't know if following in Chen's wake as he rose to power would lift her to greatness, or if was only an intermediate step—but whichever it was, it was the path she had to take. She kept her head high, instead of bowing it with her usual deference, and let him read her intent. *I'll earn your trust.*

Chen smiled in acknowledgment. His small, neat teeth were a predator's nonetheless. "Don't worry, Commander. As a loyal, capable commander who has proved his worth to the Red Turbans time and again, I have every faith you'll succeed."

He swept out. The others followed, Wu with a look of naked relief. *He* hadn't been thrown into the fire. Zhu came last, her mind churning. Then stopped, startled: the Prince of Radiance was at the door.

The child regarded her. Behind his hat's motionless fall of jade beads, his round cheeks were as gently flushed as a summer peach. He remarked, "What did you do?"

It was the first time Zhu had heard him speak other than to make a public pronouncement. This close, she could hear his voice held the faint metal shiver of wind chimes. Gripped by the sudden terrible image of her own men dying from what she had done to them, Zhu said forbiddingly, "What do you mean?"

As if speaking of what was completely ordinary, he said, "To make the dead watch you."

Zhu stared at him in shock before she managed to regain control. The unease she'd felt had been real: ghosts had been watching her as she knelt. *And he had seen them.* In the decade she'd had her strange gift, she had never seen a single person betray a sign they might see what she did. Not a sideways glance, a startle in the dark. Nobody in all those years, except this child.

And, terribly, it made sense for him in a way it never had for her. The Prince of Radiance was a reincarnated divine being who remembered his past lives, and who burned with the power of the Mandate of Heaven. That he could see the spirit world seemed of a piece. Whereas the one time Zhu had thrilled in her power to see ghosts, the very next moment she had been turned on as an impostor.

A cold flicker ran over Zhu's skin like the touch of a thousand ghost fingers. She didn't bother hiding her disturbance. It was probably no different to any normal person's reaction to being told by a child deity that they were being watched by ghosts. Underneath it, though, her mind raced. What other strange knowledge did the Prince of Radiance have about the world? Could he tell, somehow, that she had the same ability as him?

Suddenly she was seized by the terrible conviction that he was about to say, *Who are you?* Sweat sprang out on her palms and the soles of her feet. Her body flushed hot and cold in alternating waves of alarm and dread.

But he only waited, as if genuinely wanting an answer to his question. At length two of the Prime Minister's assistants appeared in the doorway and, while bowing with every impression of great respect, somehow managed to convey a chiding attitude. The Prince of Radiance smiled gently at Zhu, and left.

"What?" Even in the single-candle illumination of their barracks room, Zhu could make out Ma's heartsick look. "You're going on a mission where the only thing keeping you alive will be *Chen Youliang*?"

"A decoy mission is probably safer than being part of the Bianliang assault force, so long as he doesn't deliberately hang me out to dry," Zhu said, feeling acutely aware of the irony of the situation. "I'm almost positive he won't. He knows I'll be useful to have around in the future, as long as he can trust me."

In Ma's face Zhu saw the anguished memory of Little Guo and Sun Meng, and all those others whose lives had fallen into Chen's hands. "What if something happens to change his mind when he's halfway to Bianliang?" Ma said. "You wouldn't even know if he decided to delay a day or two! That's all it would take to wipe your force out. It's too risky. You *can't*."

Zhu sighed. "And do what, run away? Where would that leave me? Our movement derives its support from the Prince of Radiance. The people believe in him as our true leader: the one who will bring the new era. Without him—without the people—I could perhaps win bits and pieces of the south by force, but I'd never be anything more than a warlord."

"Why can't that be enough?" Ma cried. "What else do you want that's worth risking your life for?" Her perfect willow-leaf eyes were wide with fear on Zhu's behalf, and Zhu suddenly felt a pang of such overwhelming tenderness that it felt like pain.

She took Ma's hand and interlaced their fingers. For a moment she saw the two of them as Heaven might: two briefly embodied human spirits, brushing together for a moment during the long dark journey of their life and death and life again. "Once you asked me what I wanted. Remember how I said I wanted my fate? I want my fate because I know it. I *feel* it out there, and all I have to do is reach it. I'm going to be great. And not a minor greatness, but the kind of greatness that people remember for a hundred generations. The kind that's underwritten by Heaven itself." With effort she ignored the gust that blew in through the cracks in the wall and made the candle hiss like an angry cat. The last thing she wanted to see right now was more ghosts. "I've wanted and struggled and suffered for that fate my whole life. I'm not going to stop now."

Ma stared at her, her face still. "You're not putting your faith in Chen. You're going to face the eunuch general and trust in *fate* to keep you alive?"

Zhu was suddenly struck by a vivid recollection of the eunuch general's stricken expression at Yao River as he realized what she'd done to his army. She had won at the expense of his loss and humiliation. And she knew, as clearly as if it were his own thought ringing in her head, that he would be determined to get his revenge.

She squashed the thought down. "Ah, Yingzi, don't give yourself a headache! I'm not even going to face him. I'm going to poke and tease and annoy him, and make him so furious that he'll be glad to be called away to a proper fight. Didn't you say the first time we met that I cause trouble? Don't bother trusting Chen or fate, if you find that too hard. Just trust in your first impressions of me."

Ma gave a watery laugh that broke into a sob. "You *are* trouble. I've never met anyone more trouble than you." When she looked down at their intertwined hands, her hair fell in two shining sheets around her face. Through it Zhu glimpsed her high nomad cheekbones, and the floating eyebrows signifying future happiness that every mother wanted their daughters to have. Ma was always exquisitely vulnerable in her worry. Zhu felt a bruised sadness that was like the shadow of future regret, from knowing that the pursuit of her desire would cause pain. More than she had already caused. She said gently, "I like that you care."

Ma threw her head up, her tears overflowing. "Of course I care! I can't not care. I wish I could. But I've cared about all of you. Little Guo. Sun Meng. You."

"You only like me the same as them? As *Little Guo*?" Zhu teased. "Don't I get any special consideration for being your husband?" Ma's tears caused that peculiar longing ache inside her again. She wiped away the tears with the back of her hand. Then, very carefully, she cupped Ma's cheek, leaned in, and kissed her. A soft, lingering press of lips against lips. A moment of yielding warmth that generated something infinitely tender and precious, and as fragile as a butterfly's wing. It was nothing at all like the unrestrained, half-violent passions of the body that Xu Da had described. It felt like something new, something they'd invented themselves. Something that existed only for the two of them, in the penumbral shadow of their little room, for the span of a single kiss.

After a moment Zhu pulled back. "Did Little Guo ever do that?"

Ma's mouth opened and closed. Her lips rested so softly against each other that they seemed an invitation for future kisses. Her cheeks were pink, and she was looking at Zhu's mouth from under her lowered eyelashes. Did she ache too? "No."

"Who did?"

"You," Ma said, and it sounded like a sigh. "My husband. Zhu Chongba—"

Zhu smiled and squeezed her hand. "That's right. Zhu Chongba, whose greatness has been written in Heaven's book of fate. I'll achieve it, Yingzi. Believe me."

But even as she said it, she remembered the accusing ghosts and the feeling of that awful, uncontrollable momentum: that with each choice and decision, she was slipping further away from the person whose fate that was.

Jining, their ostensible target on the Grand Canal, lay six hundred li due north of Anfeng on the northern tip of the vast lake that linked Jining to the canal's southern reaches. Zhu had them go slowly, taking their time to skirt the wetlands along the lake's western shore: she wanted to give the Yuan as much time as possible to see where they were going. The population fled ahead of them, so it seemed they were always traveling through an empty landscape in which everyone had been spirited away overnight. Coal mines, the industry of the region, lay abandoned with shovels scattered about their entrances. The empty towns they passed through clattered eerily with the sound of mills still turning under wind and water, pumping the bellows of cold forges. Black grime coated the houses and trees, and blew into their faces. Across the marshy plain to the west, hidden in the evening shadows at the base of mountains, were the Yuan's garrisons in Henan. And somewhere between there and here: the eunuch general and his army.

Zhu was on her rounds of the evening camp when Yuchun rode up. The boy had come a long way since Zhu's first meeting with the young thief. He had turned out to have an extraordinary talent for the martial arts, and had flourished under Xu Da's tutelage to become one of Zhu's best captains. Yuchun said now, "There's been an accident."

Contrary to Zhu's expectations, it actually *was* an accident, rather than the result of some argument about the kinds of things men usually argued about. The victim was in his tent being treated by the engineer Jiao Yu, who had picked up some medical knowledge through all his book-learning. It was an ugly sight, even for someone familiar with battlefield injuries. The man's face, raw pink with a shiny crust, resembled the chopped pork used to make tiger's mouth meatballs.

When Jiao was done, they stepped out of the tent. "What happened?" Zhu asked.

Jiao wiped the blood off his hands and started walking. "It's interesting. Come see."

They went a short way outside the camp, carefully avoiding one of the large sinkholes that peppered the region. When they came to a rocky outcropping, Zhu saw it: a flame burning inside a small cave, out of a crack in the bare rock.

"That water-brained idiot wanted to see what would happen if he put out the flame and relit it," Jiao said dourly. "It exploded. See how those rocks fell from the blast? He's lucky to be alive. He'll lose the eye, though."

"How does it work?" Zhu wanted to know.

"I don't suppose you've ever been inside a coal mine. You wouldn't like it. They're hot and dusty and wet, and the air is noxious. Take a torch below, the whole place goes up."

"So it's the coal dust that explodes?" The project she had given Jiao—to develop more reliable hand cannons—had given her an interest in things that exploded. No Nanren force was ever going to rival the Mongols with bows, but she liked the idea of a weapon that someone as untalented as an ex-monk could pick up and use.

"No. It's not dust coming out of those rocks, but noxious air. If you let it fill an enclosed space, like a mine—or even have enough of it that you can smell it—it'll explode if you light it, like fire-powder. But if it leaks out like water from a bucket, it's more like burning coal: it just makes a little flame like this."

It didn't seem useful, but Zhu filed it away. As they walked back to camp, she said, "I know you've worked hard on the hand cannons. Are you ready to make a test of it against the eunuch general? Or do you need more time?"

Jiao gave her a long look. Zhu had always had the impression that Jiao didn't really trust her. She remembered how he'd left Commander Sun's force to join her own. He was one of those people who made sure to hitch their fortunes to the one they thought would win. Someone who was perfectly loyal—until the day he wasn't. *He did choose correctly between me and Sun Meng*, Zhu thought, not entirely comfortably. She supposed it was a vote of confidence that he was still with her.

In the end all he said was, "You'll have your artillery unit. We'll be ready."

"If we wait too long before starting the engagement, he'll suspect we're just a lure," Xu Da said. "But the quicker we begin, the longer we'll have to last until he gets Bianliang's message to withdraw." They were in the house Zhu had chosen as their command post in a small town a dozen li east of Jining. When Zhu had climbed onto the roof earlier, she had been surprised and more than a little disconcerted to see Jining surrounded by the white fungal sprawl of the eunuch general's army. There had been nothing there the day before. The vibrating connection between her and that distant opponent churned her stomach like nerves.

She said slowly, feeling her way along that connection, "*We* won't be starting the engagement."

Xu Da raised his eyebrows. "He'll come here?"

"His last encounter with the Red Turbans humiliated him. There's no way he's not still angry. He won't want to stand still and wait for us to come to him, just so he can play defense." The truth of it rang inside her like the sound of a fingernail flicked against a blade.

"Ah well," Xu Da said cheerfully. "That reduces our options, but we can manage." Like all the other towns in the area, the one they occupied was unfortified. There weren't even enough trees in the area for them to put up a temporary palisade. "We'll hold here for as long as we can, then retreat and lead him on a merry chase."

There was a map on the table between them. Zhu used her finger to trace a line eastwards from their position to a long valley between two nearby mountain ridges. "This is our path." The valley's narrowness would force any pursuing army into a single column: a configuration that meant Zhu could engage with only a small front line, and fall back the minute she started taking casualties. "He'll see where we're going, though, and split his force. He'll bring his infantry into the valley in pursuit, and send his cavalry around to the other end of the valley to engage us as soon as we exit. But this"—Zhu tapped the lake that lay along the foot of the nearer ridge—"will keep them away for a while." Any force wanting to reach the far end of the valley would need to take a days-long detour around the lake's far shore.

"Chen Youliang's assault won't start for another three days, and it will take at least another two days for the eunuch general to get the message from Bianliang calling him for help. So if he starts the engagement tomorrow, we have to keep him busy for another four. That's doable. We can hold here for at least a day—two if we're lucky—and then we'll retreat to the valley. He'll get the message and withdraw before his cavalry ever makes it around the other side, so we don't need to worry about them."

Zhu stared down at the map. All logic told her to trust Chen, but she couldn't shake a deep uneasiness. Speaking of the eunuch general, she said, "He doesn't know this is pretend. He's going to give it everything he's got. He'll want to make us suffer."

"Let him!" said Xu Da, and his familiar grin filled Zhu with an intense fondness. Under the downwards slope of his eyebrows, his right eyelid creased a little more than the left. His hair, in the awkward stage between shaved and long enough to tie up, gave him a disreputable look. "I'm not afraid of a bit of suffering. Haven't ten thousand years of past lives brought us to your side to support you? Trust that I'm strong enough—that we're all strong enough."

His faith warmed her, even as she felt a stab of future pain. This was the price of her desire: to ask those she loved for their suffering, again and again, so she could get what she wanted. And at the same time she knew she wouldn't stop. She *couldn't* stop. If for a moment she stopped trying to reach that great fate—

Gathering herself, she said, "Thank you."

Xu Da smiled, as if he knew everything that had gone through her head. Perhaps he did. He came around the table and clapped her on the shoulder. "Come on, let's get some rest. If he's as beautiful as you say, I feel like I should get my beauty sleep so he can be distracted by the breathtakingly good looks of our side, too."

"There they go," Shao said as he came up beside Ouyang, his horse casually trampling the fingers of a Red Turban corpse lying in the middle of the street. Ouyang's army had departed

Jining at first light, and the subsequent battle against the rebels—if you could even call it a battle—had barely lasted two hours. Oh, the first time Ouyang had seen a dozen of his men drop simultaneously under a barrage of hand cannon fire, he'd been surprised. But when you had the numerical advantage, and most of those were conscripts, what did you care? You just sent in more men, then more after that, and eventually the rebels failed to reload in time or ran out of ammunition, and then they were done.

To the east, the rebels were fleeing towards the hills with a speed and coordination that suggested their retreat was pre-planned. Which of course it was. *A beautiful performance all around*, Ouyang thought sourly. The rebels were clearly trying to distract him from the imminent attack on Bianliang. And if he hadn't been playing along, it wouldn't even have taken him two hours to finish the job. But that wouldn't have been a good *performance*. For all that it was necessary, he hated it. It made him look stupid. And now to cap it all off he had to *chase* the rebels, a prospect about as enticing as the idea of deliberately sticking his hand into a rotten log so a scorpion could sting him.

Just a few more days. He tried not to think of what lay after that. "Send the cavalry battalions around to meet them at the other end," he ordered. "We'll take the infantry in pursuit."

His bad mood only worsened as they entered the valley. A narrow strip running between two towering cliffs, it was the strangest place he'd ever seen. In contrast to wintry Jining, it seemed a different world entirely. The ground was warm to the touch, like it would be around a hot spring—but there was no liquid water in sight. Instead they were passing through an uncanny desert, littered with rocks and bleached stumps. Wisps of steam emitted from cracks in the ground. Ouyang's men looked around uneasily. The steamy air muffled the sounds of their passage; even the crack of the subcommanders' whips on the conscripts had lost its edge.

Night was even stranger. The landscape was alive with hundreds of points of dull, pulsing red light, like embers under slow bellows. Men who went to investigate reported that the light was coming through cracks in the rock of the valley floor, as if the earth itself were on fire. They all slept badly, the valley cracking and groaning around them.

In the morning a layer of hot fog slowed their progress even further. The heat was rapidly growing intolerable, and the water they found tasted so foul that it was hardly any relief. Shao rode over, looking as miserable in his armor as a steamed lobster. "Where are they? Are they hoping to bother us to death?"

For the last hour Ouyang had had the sense that the rebels were lingering just out of sight ahead. Trying to ignore his ferocious headache, he said shortly, "I suppose they're planning an ambush."

"With those hand cannons again?" Shao scoffed. "And do what, take out one layer of our front line? They'd better try harder than that if they don't want it to be over in a day."

Ouyang didn't want it to be over in a day, either: it was too soon. He frowned and pressed his thumb between his eyebrows, which did nothing to relieve his headache. The smell didn't help. They were passing through a depression, the shape of which seemed to have trapped the air, and the place had a marshy reek as strong as last winter's mustard greens.

There was a warning shout. Ouyang peered through the swirling steam, expecting to see the rebel front line. For the first moment all he saw was a rocky outcropping, so camouflaged was the small figure in plain armor with a monk's gray robe underneath.

The monk. Everything in Ouyang's body seized in shocked recognition. His headache throbbed in double time. All this time, he'd had no idea the rebel commander he was facing was the monk. The memory of Yao River rose up as a wave of pure anger. The last time he'd seen this monk, his actions had set Ouyang on the path to his fate. Every day since then, Ouyang had felt the agony of that fate like a fatal wound. There might not be any escaping one's fate, but *it was that monk who had put it into motion.*

He was almost surprised that his fury didn't incinerate that slight figure on the spot. Taking revenge on the monk wouldn't do anything to change Ouyang's future, but it would be payment for everything he had suffered since Yao River. The idea of the monk suffering as Ouyang had suffered sent a sullen pleasure pumping through him, like the burn of a muscle taken to its limits. It could be one last thing to look forward to, before everything else began.

He had just opened his mouth to order the advance when the monk tossed something in the direction of Ouyang's front line. It hit the ground with a muffled clunk. In the moment of puzzled silence that followed, Ouyang heard it rolling downhill towards them.

Then the world exploded.

The explosion smacked Ouyang from his horse. Bodies and burning rocks crashed down around him. His ears rang so loudly that he could only tell men were screaming by their gaping mouths. Covered in ash, their bodies twisted unnaturally, they looked like demons stumbling through the smoke. Coughing, Ouyang staggered in the direction of his front line. *Which wasn't there.* There was only a vast burning pit, as deep as a ten-story pagoda. And all around it, in a blackened starburst of horror, was a wreckage the likes of which Ouyang had never seen in all his many years of war. Human and animal bodies had been torn apart and mixed back together. The ground was strewn with charred bones, pieces of armor, tangled swords, and helmets peeled apart like metal flowers. He stood there, hand pressed against his ribs and eyes streaming furiously, looking at the shattered flotsam of his army.

Someone limped up. It was Shao. Shao would probably survive the apocalypse like a cockroach, Ouyang thought uncharitably. He thought he should probably be thankful.

"What the fuck just happened?" Shao said, and for once Ouyang didn't care about his tone, the fact that he spoke Han'er, or that he addressed Ouyang as one soldier speaks to another. "That wasn't just a hand bomb. *The air was on fire.*"

"It doesn't matter," Ouyang said. His voice sounded muffled, like it was coming to him through the bones of his skull rather than his ears. The anger he had been feeling towards the monk only a moment ago had taken on a perfect clarity. He recognized it as pure, murderous intent. He hoped the monk could feel his ill will, even at a distance, and be tormented by it for every moment until Ouyang came for him. "Account for the dead, send the injured to the back, and continue."

To absolutely no one's surprise, the rebels were waiting for them on the other side of the burning pit. Ouyang led the push himself. The hand cannons spat their shrapnel, taking down a wave of men, but then they were upon the rebels in earnest. The monk's apocalypse might have caused Ouyang some losses, but he was a Yuan general: he knew how much it took for an army to lose its muscle memory of being a behemoth. His men, ten abreast with him at their center, flung themselves forwards as though they were still part of a thousand-man front line. And then it was all the chaos of hand-to-hand. Men stumbled and swung wildly; the fallen writhed and screamed; horses broke their legs in holes. Blood and red headscarves lent their bright color to the monochromatic landscape.

They fought until night fell. The next day when they awoke, the rebels had already melted backwards. Ouyang advanced until he found them, losing another layer of his front line in the process, and did it all again. Day by day, he was pushing the rebels towards their inevitable end: the plain beyond the outlet of the valley where, extremely soon, Ouyang's cavalry would be ready and waiting to crush them when they emerged from the protection of the valley's jagged terrain. For all that Ouyang knew that the pursuit was still nothing more than a glorified time-wasting exercise on his part, he found a genuine, savage delight in the rebels' mounting desperation as time went on. Their suffering was an appetite-whetting prelude for the far greater suffering he was about to enact upon their dog whelp of a leader.

The thought of *this* revenge, unlike the other, filled him with an uncomplicated, viciously pleasurable anticipation. *I don't* have *to end you,* he thought to the monk, *but oh: I will.*

"Something's not right," Xu Da said. "He should have gotten the message about Bianliang by now. Why hasn't he withdrawn?"

Zhu looked automatically at the waning moon, though the date felt hammered into her bones: they had been in the valley for four days, far longer than they'd thought they would have to be, and it was already two full days past the agreed time for Chen's attack to begin. She and Xu Da had climbed from the camp and were sitting on the crest of the right-hand ridge, although this close to the mouth of the valley it was barely more than a gentle mound. In front of them lay the darkened plain. Slightly to their right was a cluster of light, like a new constellation: the campfires of the eunuch general's cavalry battalions. By tomorrow those battalions would be directly ahead, waiting to meet them.

"It has to be Chen Youliang," Xu Da went on. Even in the space of days his face had thinned from the stress of their mounting losses. "Don't you think he wanted us to die all along?"

Despite her convictions, Zhu had started to wonder the same. She felt sick with tiredness. "Even if he wanted to get rid of me, there are so many ways he could have done it without losing my men as well." She sighed. "Strange as it is, I trust in his ability to murder creatively."

There was a scrabbling behind them. Yuchun, almost invisible in his dark armor, emerged onto the ridge and plonked himself down beside them. "So this is the end," he announced. He'd probably intended it to sound careless, but to Zhu it seemed uncharacteristically small and afraid.

For a moment none of them said anything else. Zhu reached inside herself and touched that strange resonance between herself and the eunuch. She remembered herself at twelve, looking down at him from the roof of the Dharma Hall, and the mysterious feeling of her own substance connecting to its likeness. And now somehow, because of that connection, his presence marked every critical junction in Zhu's progress towards her fate. He had destroyed the monastery and sent her to the Red Turbans. He had provided her with her first victory. And now—

In her mind's eye she saw his beautiful face that she had only ever seen from a distance. And all at once she knew what she had to do in order to keep moving towards her fate.

"Not the end," she said. "Not yet. There's one last thing we need to do."

Xu Da and Yuchun swiveled their heads towards her from opposite directions. Xu Da said, "*No.*"

"I don't think he ever received the message. That's why he hasn't withdrawn; he doesn't even know Bianliang needs his help."

"Even if that's the case! Even if he did believe you—"

"—he might just kill me anyway," Zhu said. But if she didn't believe in her fate, what else was there?

His expression stricken, Xu Da said, "Not you. I should do it."

"Do *what*?" Yuchun nearly screamed.

Zhu smiled at him. "Challenge the eunuch general to a duel. He seems the traditional type; he'll respect the challenge. That will at least give me the chance to speak to him face-to-face. I'll tell him what's happening in Bianliang. Then he can believe me or not."

After a long pause Yuchun said, "It should be me. If it's a duel then I'm the best man you have. That eunuch is better with a sword than both of you, and so am I. You know it!"

His loyalty was warming. *Trust that we're strong enough.* She said gently, "I know it. Ten-thousand-man Chang." It was a new nickname Yuchun had picked up somewhere along the way, when the men had realized he was as strong as (maybe not quite) ten thousand men. She patted Yuchun's shoulder. "If winning was the point, I would definitely ask you." She spoke to Xu Da, too. "But it's not about the duel. It's about convincing him. So it has to be me."

A wounded sound escaped Xu Da. Zhu reached out and took him by the back of the neck, that vulnerable part above the collar of his armor, and shook him gently. It gave her a possessive, protective feeling, like a leopard holding its cub in its mouth. She had no idea whether it was something Zhu Chongba might have felt for Xu Da or not. "Big brother. I'm counting on you to manage our escape as soon as his men show the first signs of withdrawing."

Xu Da relaxed his head back into Zhu's grasp. "And if they don't?"

There was no point fueling fear and doubt by thinking about what wouldn't happen. What *couldn't* happen, because of the sheer force of her belief and desire. Instead she sat up as tall as she could and slung her arms around both their shoulders, and together they sat watching the moon set over the endlessly burning campfires of the Yuan.

The armies assembled on the plain at dawn. Heaven looked down on them from a pale winter sky that seemed as brittle as a skin of ice. Zhu took in the sight of her small force of Red Turbans standing before the enormous expanse of the eunuch general's army, with its eerie front line of ghosts. She had compressed her fear and uncertainty so tightly that they were nothing more than the faintest tremble of water under the still surface of a deep lake. She took a breath and reached into herself, touching that point in the pit of her stomach where fate anchored, and let it pull her forward.

The other rode towards her under his own flag. Zhu felt the universe quivering around them as they entered the empty space between the armies. They were two things of the same substance, their qi ringing in harmony like twin strings, interconnected by action and reaction so that they were forever pushing and pulling each other along the path of their lives and towards their individual fates. She knew that whatever happened here, it wouldn't be him acting upon her, but each of them upon the other.

At the middle they dismounted and approached each other, holding their sheathed swords in their left hands. Zhu was struck anew by the eunuch general's crystalline beauty. *Flesh of ice and bones of jade,* she thought: the most exquisite form of female beauty. But for all that, there was no mistaking him for a woman. Where that smoothness should have been yielding, there was only hardness: it was in the set of his jaw, the arrogant tilt to his chin. His stride and bearing were those of a person who carried himself with the bitter pride of knowing that his separation came from being *above*.

The cool morning light drained the color from their surroundings. Their breath smoked.

"And so we meet." His raspy voice was instantly familiar. It had been stamped into Zhu's memory with fire and violence. *The last time I heard him speak, he destroyed everything I had.* "I admit, your challenge was a welcome surprise. After all that running and ambushing, I thought you'd make us grind it out to the end. Is there any particular reason you're so intent on making a public spectacle of your death?"

Zhu replied calmly, "I'd be a poor leader if I returned my men's loyalty of these last days by failing do everything I could to change the situation."

"Are you so certain of the possibility of change? It seems to me the outcome is inevitable."

"That may be. But are you sure it's the outcome you think? Perhaps you need more information to see clearly," Zhu said. Deep beneath her calm, she was distantly aware of her suppressed uncertainty reaching its peak. "For instance: you might like to know that this engagement is nothing but a distraction. Did you think we Red Turbans were so few? Our numbers have grown more than you've realized. As we speak, our main force is making its assault on Bianliang. I doubt I'm wrong in thinking that the loss of Bianliang would be a blow indeed to the Great Yuan."

Her attention on his face was as keen as a lover's, but he gave nothing away. "Interesting. But men will say anything to save their own skins. Indeed, if what you say is true, aren't you betraying your own side just for the chance that I might withdraw and go running to Bianliang? So you're either a liar, or a coward." He raised his eyebrows. "Which is more likely, I wonder?"

"Whether or not you believe me, can you risk not acting? Messages go astray. If Bianliang called for help but falls for lack of aid, who do you think will bear the blame for its loss?"

Now a shadow did cross his face. He said sardonically, "It's hardly the recipient of a lost message who should be blamed."

Zhu heard, unspoken: *But they* will *blame me.* The tremble in her depths subsided with relief: it was working. "But now you know. So the question is: What will you do with that knowledge, General Ouyang?" It was the first time she had ever said his name, and at the sound of it she felt that disorienting pull of fate more strongly than before, as if he were a lodestone to her needle. A sharp tang on her tongue tasted like the air before a storm. "Will you refuse to go—and afterwards like to explain why you failed to do everything possible to prevent the greatest symbol of Nanren power from falling into rebel hands? I can only imagine how unhappy your masters must have been with you after Yao River. What will they do to you for having lost Bianliang?"

As he considered the question a dense whiteness came pouring from his army, as supple as fog cascading down a mountainside. It flowed over the ground and encircled them. Before, his ghosts had never paid her any more attention than any other ghosts did. But now their absent black eyes watched her from over his shoulder, and she felt the hair on her neck rise as unseen gazes touched her from behind. Their murmur filled her with a numbed feeling of dread. Far above, the banners thwacked.

At length the eunuch general said, "That was an unpleasant homecoming, to be sure. It seems you know the situation well. But perhaps it's my turn to give you some information. So you can see the outcome clearly."

Being archers, Mongols didn't wear gloves. The closed hand he extended between them was bare. Like the rest of him, his hands evoked that tension of being both and neither: as fine-boned as a woman's, but scarred from a warrior's thousand small injuries. He opened his hand slowly. At first Zhu couldn't grasp what she was looking at. Then, staring down at that folded paper with its brief swirl of Mongolian script on its upper face, she felt a violent internal shaking, as of all her repressed emotions swelling in unison against the barrier of her willpower. She could have gasped with the effort it took to keep them contained.

Bianliang.

She had gambled everything upon the hope of his withdrawal, but now she saw clearly, just as he had promised. It had never been a possibility at all.

Instinctively she clamped down as hard as she could on that rising mass of disbelief and horror and fear. She crammed it back down until there was nothing for him to see but a glacial stillness that matched his own. She had been wrong, but being wrong wasn't failure—not yet. *And it won't be.* There was always another way to win.

He watched her with vindictive pleasure, as if he could sense how hard she was working to stay in control. "My thanks for your concern, but I know about Bianliang. This message from its governor came yesterday. It is indeed a frantic plea for help."

He knew and he chose not to go. She hadn't even considered that as a possibility. "But if you'd withdrawn when you first received it, you could have reached there in time—"

"Oh, please," he said. "We both know your plan was based on the assumption that if I withdrew upon receiving the message, I wouldn't make it to Bianliang in time to prevent its fall.

Which only shows you have no idea of my capabilities. Rest assured: if I'd wanted to get to Bianliang before it fell, I could have." Then, in response to whatever uncontrollable reaction he saw on her face: "Why didn't I? But esteemed monk: How could I pass up this chance to settle the score between us?"

Zhu thought, terribly, of those ten thousand drowned men. Even as she had known he would want revenge, she still hadn't grasped just how deep his hurt ran. The truth hummed in the connection between them. He hurt, and he was driven by it; it was the reason for everything he did, and his reason for being. *He's haunted by it.* Chilled, she said, "For the sake of revenge against me, you went as far as to let Bianliang fall?"

"Don't flatter yourself too much," he said bitterly. "Bianliang had to fall. But given this opportunity to finish things between us, I find myself pleased to take it." His black brush-stroke eyes bored into her with the promise of murder. "You caused my loss at Yao River, and started something I have no choice but to finish. Regardless of my own desires, you took the liberty of setting me on my path towards my fate." His delicate face burned with hate and blame. "So let me return the courtesy, and deliver you to yours."

He drew his sword. It sang as it came out of the sheath, and caught the icy light down its straight length.

And somewhere in the compressed depths of Zhu's emotions, there was panic. But for all that this didn't seem like the path to victory and her fate, it *had* to be. She drew herself up and let him see her: unshrinking and unbowed. "What is it you think you know as my fate?" she said. She was speaking to Heaven as much as she was to him: sending her belief, maintained with every particle of her will, up into that distant, jade-cold firmament. "Let me tell you my name: Zhu Chongba."

He answered coolly, "Should I know it?"

"One day you will," she said, and drew her sword.

※

In that instant before either of them acted, Zhu had the odd feeling of their flesh and blood having become immaterial—as if, in that single, shimmering moment, they were nothing but pure desire.

Then Ouyang struck.

Zhu threw herself aside with a gasp. He was faster than she'd imagined—faster than she'd have thought possible. She felt the shock of it clawing at the desperate, tiring part of herself that clung to Zhu Chongba's identity. It had already slipped, and she could *feel* the slide of it away from her, but there was nothing to do but hold on. *I have to keep believing—*

She twisted, and heard the whine of his sword as it sliced through where she'd been. She came down crouching, swinging the sheath in her left hand high for balance, then sprang forwards to strike. He deflected easily, then caught her next strike and held it. Their crossed blades slid along each other as they pressed in. The keening vibration set Zhu's teeth on edge. Her wrist screamed. She looked into Ouyang's beautiful porcelain face, and saw the curl of his lip. She was fighting for her life, and he was *playing*. But as terrifying as that thought was, there was hope in it. *If he could have finished me already, but hasn't, then I have a chance—*

But for all she tried, she couldn't see what that chance was. If he'd been as vain and fragile as Little Guo, she could have distracted him with wounding words. But how could you hurt someone who was nothing but pain? She flung him away, panting. It took all her strength. "You're a Nanren, aren't you?" she called, straining against rising desperation. "How can you fight for the Hu, knowing that every action you take against your own people is making your ancestors cry in the Yellow Springs? I have to wonder if you let Bianliang fall because, deep down, you know the Nanren cause is the right one—"

She broke off as he lunged forwards with a flicker of strokes in attack. She parried, hearing the clear tone of steel on steel alternating with the thump of his sword against her sheath. They flew across the ground, Zhu turning and skipping backwards with her heart racing faster than her feet. High and low and high again, but before she could recover from the last stroke he lashed her viciously across the ribs with the sheath in his left hand, then slammed his shoulder into her. She went spinning and hit the dirt lengthwise, and rolled just in time as he stabbed the ground where she'd been. She barely made it to her feet before he was on her again.

This time parrying was harder. It would all end well, because it *had* to, but her lungs burned and her feet stumbled rather than flew. Her heart felt like it was about to explode. A line of fire burst to life on her left arm as they fell apart for a single breath, then sprang back together. His strokes came fast and hard, and she could hear the awful rasp in her throat as she deflected and dodged and deflected again—

Then she twisted the wrong way, and the breath came out of her with a thump.

Why isn't he moving, she thought. In that first moment she didn't feel anything. Her hands were suddenly empty. She stared at him, seeing the amber flecks that made his eyes more brown than black, and groped blindly between them. Her fingers clenched around the sword in her lower body, and she felt its edges cutting her fingers and palm, and somehow *that* hurt. She would have gasped, but she didn't have the breath for it.

The tang of blood rose up between them as he leaned in. His lips almost brushed her cheek as he said, "I'm a Nanren, it's true. And I fight on the Mongol side. But I'll tell you the truth, little monk. *What I want has nothing to do with who wins.*"

He wrenched his sword out, and the world turned into a white shriek of pain. All the strength ran out of Zhu like water from a holed leather bucket. She staggered. He watched her expressionlessly, his sword lowered. It was glossed with blood. She looked down at herself, feeling a strange distance. *Such a small hole,* she thought, as the dark stain spread from under her cuirass. All of a sudden she was freezing. The agony radiating from that awful new center felt like the pull of fate magnified a hundred times—a thousandfold. And with horror, she recognized which fate she was feeling. Not the fate she'd been pursuing, the fate she thought she'd one day reach. *Nothing.* Under the physical pain, she felt an even deeper agony: a grief more intense than anything she had ever experienced. Had she even had a chance of the great fate, or had she been fooling herself this whole time, thinking she could be Zhu Chongba and have something other than what she'd been given?

She was as cold as she had ever been in her life, her teeth chattering with it, as her knees buckled. The world spun. Behind Ouyang's head she saw the flags that were the color of blue and red flames, and the empty face of Heaven. She looked into the void and saw the nothingness of herself reflected back from it.

His sword flashed.

She swayed from the impact. The cold had her by the throat. She had never imagined cold could be this painful. With a feeling of confused, abstract interest, she glanced down at the site of the impact and saw the blood spurting from where her right hand had been. It had been a clean cut, above the wristguard. The blood came and came, as red as the Mandate of Heaven, and pooled on top of the dust without sinking in. Her heartbeat echoed in her head. She tried to gather the beats, to count them—but the more she tried, the more they scattered. Finally a quiet lassitude stole in, calming and smoothing away the terror of the cold. She was being claimed by the nothingness, and it felt like relief.

She looked up at Ouyang. She saw him in silhouette: black hair and black armor against a night sky. Behind him were the dark shapes of his ghosts, and behind them: the stars.

"Zhu Chongba," he said, from very far away. "Your men were loyal to you, before. Let's see how loyal they are to you now, when all you can inspire in them is scorn and disgust. When you're nothing but a grotesque thing to be shunned and feared. You'll wish I'd killed you with honor." The shadow had swallowed her, and she was falling. It seemed as though a chorus of inhuman voices was speaking, but at the same time she knew it was only him: the one who had delivered her to her fate. He said, "Every time the world turns its face from you, know it was because of me."

PART THREE

1355–1356

18

ANYANG, ELEVENTH MONTH

It was a cold gray evening when Ouyang returned from Bianliang, which he had conveniently reached only days too late
to prevent from falling to the rebels. He had sent no notice of
his impending arrival, and came alone into the courtyard of
his residence. A faint dusting of snow fell and melted onto the
wet flagstones. For a moment he stood there, taking in the familiar cluster of buildings. It still seemed like Esen's residence,
not his own, and the sight of its unnatural emptiness shot pain
through him—as if Esen hadn't just moved to the other side of
the palace, but had gone.

A female servant passing under the eaves saw Ouyang
standing there and gasped loudly enough for him to hear from
the middle of the courtyard. In another moment he was surrounded, his servants stumbling in their haste to make their
greetings. As if his disgrace might somehow be alleviated by
them lowering themselves even further beneath him. It wasn't
exactly a kindness. He had lost Bianliang—and as much as they
pitied him for the punishments that presumably awaited, no
doubt they feared more for themselves.

One of them said, "General, will you like to send a message
to the Prince of your arrival? He requested immediate advice of
your return."

Of course Esen had known Ouyang would come in

unannounced. "Don't bother," Ouyang said curtly. "I'll pay my respects to him in person. Where is he?"

"General, he is with Lady Borte. If you'll let us send a message—"

The thought of Esen in his wife's quarters filled Ouyang with familiar disgust. "No, I'll go myself."

His servants couldn't have been more shocked if had he slapped them. *More like I slapped myself in front of them*, he thought viciously. They all knew the rule: no man save the Prince of Henan himself could enter the women's quarters of his residence. It was almost flattering that it hadn't occurred to them until this moment: that because Ouyang wasn't a man, he could go anywhere he pleased. *A privilege I never wanted.* He had never availed himself of it before; he had less than no interest in seeing Esen as the stallion amongst his mares. But now Ouyang seized his disgust, and twisted it until it burned like a fingernail dug under a scab. There was no avoiding this encounter. The angrier he was, the easier it would be to take this next step. Deep down, he knew the reason it seemed so hard was because this was the true point of no return. And the knowledge that there *was* a point of no return—that if he had been anyone other than himself, he could have chosen not to continue—was the worst thing of all.

Women's quarters were a foreign land. The colors and scents and even the feel of the air itself were all so alien that Ouyang's skin crawled. As he stalked down the corridor the female attendants startled at the sight of his armor, then relaxed as soon as they saw his face. Each time it happened his vicious feeling mounted. Women: twittering, perfumed, worthless things. He wished that his armor, with all its sharp edges and blood-metal smell, could actually hurt them. But instead they were hurting him with every one of their understanding looks intimating that he *belonged* here, in this female space. He burned with humiliation and anger and shame.

He was directed to an antechamber where hanging scrolls of Buddhist wisdom clashed with a suffocating array of chairs, side tables, and vases in the current blue-and-white style. Two maids opened the black-lacquered doors of Lady Borte's bedchamber and Esen emerged. He was fully dressed, but he had a loose-limbed air and his braids had been combed out. Ouyang's armor did nothing to protect him from the sight. It was one thing to know Esen had wives, and another to see proof of that life actually lived. To know that he had so recently touched another, and been touched. In this domain of women and children that would always be alien to Ouyang, Esen had a whole life of pleasures and intimacies and small sorrows. Ouyang's emotions nearly choked him: revulsion and scorn and jealousy, so tangled that he couldn't tell where one ended and the other began. Beneath it all was a piercing yearning. He had no idea if it was a yearning *for* or a yearning *to be*, and the equal impossibility of each of those hurt beyond belief.

Good, Ouyang thought viciously. *Let me hurt.*

He knelt. "Esteemed Prince, Bianliang is lost. This unworthy servant has failed you. Please give your punishment!"

Esen looked down at him. In his face was disappointment and a host of other emotions Ouyang couldn't identify. For all Ouyang harbored a tangle, Esen did too. It was new in him, and Ouyang grieved to know he had put it there. "Don't kneel," Esen said at length. "I'm not my father. I have no such expectation that you should abase yourself before me for a loss I myself would have made. Did you not at least defeat their decoy force? You did your best."

But Ouyang hadn't done his best. He hadn't even tried. He could have pleased Esen so easily, and he had chosen not to. To stave off guilt, he dug deep for his anger. *You did your best.* Esen's sympathy cut Ouyang's pride to the quick. He knew Ouyang better than anyone. How could he really believe that had been his best effort? All it showed was that Esen had forgotten the most important thing about him: that he was a Nanren.

Ouyang said, "Khanbaliq will not tolerate Bianliang being held by the Red Turbans. We have no choice but to retake it. Esteemed Prince, I would have your permission to go to the

Zhang family of Yangzhou to request their assistance with the endeavor."

"We have to retake Bianliang, that's true, but it seems I have more faith in your capabilities than you do. There's no need to go crawling to those wretched merchants," Esen said. He added, more quietly, "I know what you're doing, running from me out of shame. There's no need to. I have no blame for you."

You should *have blame.* Despite Ouyang's efforts to stay angry, pain and guilt threatened to undo him. He had to force himself to speak. "I had the opportunity to make the acquaintance of their General Zhang in Hichetu this past spring. Whatever his brother's reputation, General Zhang himself is more than capable. With his help, there will be no question of our victory."

"For pity's sake, get up! We shouldn't talk like this." Esen looked pained.

Ouyang's heart ached. *Why can't you make it easier for me to hate you?* "My prince, you should treat me as I deserve to be treated."

"And let that be the case, had you actually brought shame upon me," Esen said. "For years people have told me that the mere fact of having you as my general is shameful. I didn't believe it before, and I don't believe it now. I refuse to throw out my general, my best friend, for the sake of a loss that can be remedied. *So get up.*" When Ouyang still didn't move, he said, lower, "Will you make me command you?"

The room was too full of perfume. Ouyang's head spun. He was trapped in this nightmarish female space, where Esen was lord and king. And as with all the other inhabitants of this domain, Ouyang was Esen's too; he was mastered.

When Ouyang didn't move, Esen said very softly, "General Ouyang, get up. I command it."

Not a yank on the leash, but a touch under the chin: the words of someone who had never imagined refusal. And Ouyang obeyed. He stood, and felt a deep current of pleasure beneath his anger. It was the pleasure of a slave who wanted to please his master; the comfort of a chaotic world returning to order. And the very instant Ouyang realized that what he felt was pleasure, it blackened like a cut banana heart; it became disgust. He recoiled from the truth that he was the servile dog he had always been told he was. But even in the swamp of his self-loathing, he knew that if it had been possible for them to continue like that, he would have.

Esen said, "Come here."

Ouyang went. He was aware of the watching servants, and the telltale crack between the bedchamber doors. The thought of what they all saw pressed his humiliation closer. He stopped in front of Esen. Close enough to touch. The memory of Esen's fingertips on his face seared him. Part of him yearned for the debasement of that touch again, and an equal part hated Esen for having called pleasure and submissiveness out of him without even realizing what he had done. Each part hurt. The combined pain of them crushed him.

Esen regarded him with a strange intensity. "Go to Yangzhou if you feel you need to. But stop worrying about Bianliang. You'll win it back. And after you win it back—after you win me this war against the rebels—the Great Khan will reward us. I'll ask him to reward you with lands and a son you can adopt to carry your name. That's our future, don't you see? Our sons leading the Great Yuan's armies together. They'll take Japan and Cham and Java for the glory of the empire, and men will remember their names the way they remember the great khans." His voice rose. "Isn't that something you want? So stop blaming yourself and let yourself want it. *I'll give it to you.*"

Ouyang, staring at Esen in shock and anguish, saw he actually *believed* that vision of the future. At length he said hoarsely, "Then come with me to Bianliang, Esen. Ride with me as you used to. Let's win it together, so we can finish all of this and start towards our future."

He heard the servants' scandalized murmur: that he dared address the Prince of Henan so; that he dared ask more than was his right. As if the Prince of Henan could just leave his duties to his estate—and to his wives, who were still vying for that precious son. Ouyang could feel Lady Borte's resentment radiating through the bedchamber doors. *Choose me*, he thought, his eyes fixed on Esen's face, and felt sick.

Esen didn't answer immediately. His hand twitched, and Ouyang's breath stuck, but then Esen caught himself and clasped his hands behind his back. "It's snowing?" he asked abruptly. It was such a tangent that it took Ouyang a moment to realize there must still be snow in his hair. Esen was regarding him with an inwards, wretched expression, as of someone wrestling with a pain he had never expected to feel. "I suppose you wouldn't know, since you've been traveling. It's the first snow; it comes later than usual this year."

First snowfall, which lovers liked to watch together. All the things that Ouyang could never have were too present, like haunting ghosts. This was why he had wanted to be angry, so it could wash away everything else he might feel. But instead it was his anger that hadn't been strong enough, and had been drowned.

Esen said, still with that odd pain on his face, "If you want me there, I'll come."

He had always given Ouyang everything he wanted. Ouyang imagined the snow coming down outside, blanketing everything in its cold muffled stillness. If only he could take that blankness and wrap his heart in it, so nothing could ever hurt him again.

Lord Wang's office was more subdued than Ouyang had ever seen it. Esen might not have been able to strip Lord Wang of his titles, but his disfavor fell heavily upon him. Regardless of events, Lord Wang was still at his desk: loyal as ever to his work. Or perhaps just determined to exercise the only power he had left.

"Greetings, my lord." Ouyang bowed and handed over his request of resources for the upcoming siege on Bianliang. He had already tasked Shao with the preparations, so that they would be ready to depart as soon as Ouyang returned from Yangzhou.

Lord Wang scanned the list with a sardonic expression: Ouyang had made no attempt to economize. "You've outdone yourself, General. First you lose ten thousand men in what should have been a rout. Now your mistake sees the rebels put the Prince of Radiance on the historic throne of the last native dynasty to have power here in the north." His black eyes flicked up, inscrutable. "As the descendant of a traitor, you might want to be careful to succeed with your next endeavor, lest people begin to wonder whether your mistakes are caused by something other than incompetence."

Lord Wang was as nostalgic for the past as any full-blooded Nanren, Ouyang realized abruptly. If he knew that Ouyang had let Bianliang fall—

He dismissed the idea. It was only Lord Wang's usual jealousy speaking. "To ensure my success, my lord, you need merely fulfil my requests without argument. Or would you prefer that I petition the Prince of Henan to become involved? Given how little goodwill he bears towards you, it might not turn out in your favor. How much land do you have left? It would be a pity if he felt moved to take the rest of it away—"

Lord Wang rose, came around the desk, and struck Ouyang across the face. It was only as hard as one might expect from a scholar, but still enough to turn his head. When he turned back, Lord Wang said coolly, "I know you think you're better than me. In my brother's eyes, you certainly are. But I'm still a lord, and I can still do that."

The punishment for a Nanren hitting a Mongol was death by strangulation. But even had it not been, Ouyang wouldn't have struck back; Lord Wang's misery was all too apparent. His whole life was humiliation and the knowledge of his own uselessness. Ouyang saw a brief flash of another drained, agonized face: the rebel monk, staring in disbelief at the bleeding stump of his sword-arm. The monk faced a life as full of shame and impotence as Lord Wang's. It was a future Ouyang knew better than anyone. *The worst punishment is being left alive.*

He said, "Is that my thanks for saving my lord's life?"

"Such thanks should I give!" Lord Wang said bitterly. "Saved me, only so that my brother could blame me for dropping our father off a cliff."

Ouyang couldn't resist taking revenge for the slap. He said, cruel, "If only you had been stronger"—*if only you hadn't been a worthless scholar*—"you could have saved him."

Lord Wang blanched. "And for that I have never been forgiven." He went and sat back down behind his desk. Without looking up, he said harshly, "Take whatever you need. Do with it as you will."

Ouyang left, thinking it had gone surprisingly well. If Lord Wang's best revenge for Ouyang's part in his humiliation was a slap on the face, then there was nothing to worry about.

But for one troubled moment, he remembered Altan.

Anyang and Yangzhou were separated by well over a thousand li. Ouyang, speeding south down the Grand Canal on a cramped merchant boat, watched the scenery change. The winter-flooded plains under their shining yellow inundations gave way to a brisk bustle of human activity: peasants in the fields, marketplaces on the arches of bridges, industry. And then finally the mounds of gleaming white salt, stretching as far as the eye could see. The vast mercantile empire of the Zhangs, which had as its capital the great walled city of Yangzhou. The water brought them directly into it. The wide canals took Ouyang past high-walled gardens, under stone bridges, between the famous green and black mansions of the pleasure quarter. Every street was a spectacle of wealth. Ordinary citizens wore the bright silk brocades of the region; their hair was piled and pinned and adorned; they stepped down from palanquins that seemed to have been dipped in gold. It was a splendor.

Having witnessed this of Yangzhou, Ouyang had thought

himself adequately prepared for what to expect from the Zhang family's residence. But even he, raised alongside nobility, was shocked. The Great Khan's hunts might have displayed the finest things from the four khanates, but a certain Mongol simplicity ultimately prevailed. By contrast, Rice Bucket Zhang had built for himself nothing short of an imperial palace: the crass epitome of someone of incalculable wealth building on a region's centuries of tradition in producing and consuming every luxury of an empire.

In his gold and black–lacquered hall, the man himself sat upon a chair that gave every impression of a throne. It was warmer in Yangzhou than Anyang, but that did not fully explain the need for the array of maidservants who stood fanning him. His eyes, alighting on Ouyang, glinted with greedy curiosity.

When Ouyang finished his greetings, Rice Bucket Zhang gave a vulgar laugh. "So this is the eunuch my brother speaks so highly of! I see he neglected to mention some important details. I was expecting some soft old man." His gaze swept Ouyang from head to toe, assessing him in the same way one might judge the worth of potential new concubines on the texture of their skin and the size of their feet. "Here I thought the Mongols had no aesthetic tastes at all. I stand corrected that they put their most beautiful possessions at the head of their armies. What army of men would not be roused to protectiveness?"

"Big brother, I had heard General Ouyang from Henan had arrived—" General Zhang came in. "Ah, you did arrive safely," he said, seeing Ouyang, and gave him a warm smile. "Now that you have made your greetings to my brother, will you not accompany me to the reception room? We have prepared a welcome for you."

"I have received quite a welcome already," Ouyang said tightly.

General Zhang said as they withdrew, "I'm sure. Why do you think I came?"

"Your brother did say he thought I inspired protectiveness

in men." He had thought he could repeat the insult for humorous effect, but had misjudged his own capacity to detach himself from anger.

"Believe it or not, he does have some redeeming qualities. But I can see how you might not be inclined to give him the benefit of the doubt at the moment."

"I trust the judgment of those I respect."

Zhang smiled. "Don't respect me too much. I was not yet a man when he had his first successes. As the younger brother, I owe him much."

"Surely that's more than balanced now by what he owes you."

"Would that family and fate had the same rules as accounting," Zhang said. His mobile face, under its handsome tragic brow, made a series of expressions that Ouyang couldn't interpret. "But come, let's relax. Are you not now in the pleasure capital of the world? When traveling I always miss its charms. Music, poetry, the beauty of lanterns reflected in the lake in the evenings. Trust me: that Goryeo ribbon dance they like in Dadu is nothing in comparison."

"I must confess to lacking the education required to appreciate the finer entertainments," Ouyang said. In truth he thought the charms of most arts lay in certain obvious qualities of their performers. Since these qualities left him cold, he found them all equally tedious.

"Ah, our customs are different indeed. But I remember we both have drinking in common. The Mongols perhaps exceed us in their serious attention to wine, but I think we can satisfy you well enough."

He drew Ouyang into an intimate space where a table had been laid with an immense spread of dishes on fragile white porcelain. Even a soldier such as Ouyang could tell that the quality of the porcelain was such that a single plate was worth more than all his possessions put together. "Let us wait for— Oh, here he comes."

Rice Bucket Zhang came sweeping in and took the position

of honor. A few moments later a woman came in bearing a tray of cups and a ewer of wine. The many layers of her clothing rustled as she sank down to serve them. As she poured the wine she kept her head down; all Ouyang could see of her was her enormous sculptural hairpiece, pinned with gold and coral, and the milky skin of her wrist as she held her sleeve back to hand him the wine.

Rice Bucket Zhang looked on with proprietary pride. "My wife," he said carelessly. "The most beautiful woman in a city of beauties."

"My husband gives this woman too much credit," the woman murmured. On her downturned face, powdered as white as a moonlit vase, a hint of curved scarlet lips could be seen. "Please, honored guest, drink and be at ease."

She settled at Rice Bucket Zhang's side as he held forth without any need for the opinions of anyone else in the room. Ouyang and General Zhang applied themselves to the food and wine. Ouyang noticed that the other general's eyes strayed every so often to the woman as she attended her husband. When they finished, Rice Bucket Zhang belched and said, "Wife, will you not perform for us? A poem or a song?"

The woman laughed coquettishly behind her sleeve. "I have arranged some other entertainment for my husband. I hope it will please him." She tapped the door and it opened. A stream of girls came tripping in, attired in diaphanous gowns in the pale colors of eggshells and moths. Their faces were painted; their perfume insipid.

Rice Bucket Zhang said, leering, "Ah, you know my tastes well! Girls from your own house, are they not? I see the standard of its wares has not slipped." He looked at Ouyang and chuckled. "A shame, General, that you can't sample the true wealth and talents of this city. Though I've heard it said that palace women like eunuch lovers; having no personal needs they have only infinite patience. Strange for me to imagine!"

Ouyang saw the wisdom of General Zhang having had the servants take away his sword with his other belongings. He said as coldly as he could, "Patience is unfortunately not one of my virtues."

"Good, for I've never had patience for those of virtue," said Rice Bucket Zhang. "Virtuous women, I mean."

"I'm sure his ears and eyes can feast as well as any man's," the woman said. "I hope our guest will find the entertainment to his liking."

Ouyang gave her a sharp look, but she was already rising and withdrawing with little steps that made her sleeves flutter.

The girls sang for an interminable hour before Rice Bucket Zhang said, "So the Great Yuan comes seeking my support to retake Bianliang."

General Zhang excused himself, saying, "I will leave you to discuss the details."

"It will not only be to retake Bianliang, but to destroy the rebel movement entirely."

"Ah." Rice Bucket Zhang's attention, which had only ever been half on Ouyang, returned to the girls. "Then I give it. I hope the Great Yuan will recognize my loyalty. Without it, it occurs to me that it might find itself in trouble."

"Of course your contributions to the Great Yuan cannot be overstated."

"No!" Rice Bucket Zhang laughed. "No, indeed." To the girls he called, "More wine!" and several came and clustered around him like butterflies on a flower, pouring wine and giggling.

Ouyang was forced to sit there in a state of exquisite dislike while Rice Bucket Zhang fondled and leered at the girls as they sang and recited poetry, and poured drink after drink. After what felt like an eternity, Rice Bucket Zhang finally excused himself and rose stumbling, leaning on the girls who tittered and led him away.

Ouyang, returning to his rooms well past the third watch, found the long corridors dim. All down their length the servants sat asleep on stools outside their masters' rooms, their candles burnt down.

Not far from Ouyang's rooms a single door stood ajar, issuing a faint light. The stool outside was empty. As he passed, movement from within caught his eye. He glanced casually inside. Then stopped.

On the bed a naked man lay braced atop a woman. General Zhang's hair, as gracefully masculine as it had been in Hichetu, was still caught in its golden clasp and hairpins. Muscles shifted in his back as he moved, and the light slid in and out of the hollows of his lean brown flanks.

Under him was Rice Bucket Zhang's wife. Framed by her gleaming hair ornaments, pearl flakes winking from her cheeks, her face showed lazy performance. The man seeking his pleasure could have been anyone. To Ouyang it seemed there was no difference between her coy smiles and carefully timed whispers in her lover's ear than the faces of the whores his soldiers fucked. He watched the rhythmic bounce of her flesh, the growing sheen of sweat on General Zhang's back, and felt a flush of contempt.

General Zhang finished and rolled off. He pushed up on one elbow and looked down at the woman with unguarded fondness. Her revealed body was as delicate as a sheaf of white silk, finished with tiny scarlet bed-slippers that struck Ouyang's eye with the violence of opened flesh. She gave General Zhang a coy glance and took his free hand. Laughing lightly, she said something and tapped a fingernail in the middle of his palm. General Zhang's look softened further. Then, to Ouyang's surprise, light flared between their bodies: General Zhang was holding an orange flame on his palm. It had been as sudden as an entertainer's trick. The flame burned strong and steady, its strange orange light stealing the color from the room so the two people's bared skin turned gray and the woman's painted lips as black as charcoal.

Ouyang remembered the spurt of weak blue flame from between the Great Khan's knuckles. *The Mandate of Heaven.* It

made sense. The Mongols were losing the Mandate, so someone else had gained it. It was clear what it meant for the Great
Yuan's future. But although it was a future, it wasn't *his* future, so Ouyang's sadness was abstract and impersonal: nothing more than the sense of an ending.

There was a sound, and a lady's maid turned the corner into
the corridor with a washbasin and lantern upon a tray. Ouyang
hurried on. His footsteps were silent, but the candles along the
corridor bent slightly with his passing.

Though it was the depths of winter, the dull rags of last year's
foliage still hung on the branches of Rice Bucket Zhang's orchard. It gave the trees an ugly in-betweenness that reminded
Ouyang of molting animals. Not long past the appointed hour
he saw her: swaying slowly down the path towards him on her
tiny useless feet, her silk sleeves floating away from her body
like birds in flight. He found it surprisingly hard to reconcile
the image with the knowledge that she was the true power behind an empire, albeit a commercial one. He could have put his
hands around her throat and ended her in an instant.

"General Ouyang." Madam Zhang inclined her head in
greeting. Seeing her face closely for the first time, he noticed
her low cheekbones gave her appearance a slight fleshiness.
The white face powder failed to fully conceal the irregulari-
ties beneath; her perfume was distastefully strong. On her red-
lacquered mouth he could see a reflected dot of the sun.

She said, "Your reputation has you as beautiful as the Prince
of Lanling, and even more ferocious in battle. In daylight, I see
even more clearly that the former, at least, is true."

It was said the Prince of Lanling's face had been that of a
beautiful woman's, so he had worn a demonic mask into battle
to strike the proper fear into the hearts of his enemies. Ouyang
said, "Do you doubt the latter?"

The arch knowingness in her expression filled him with dislike. "Is the most effective general the one who fights best?"

"Perhaps you choose your generals for their effectiveness in other arenas."

Her painted eyebrows flew upwards. "I love that you don't disappoint! Eunuchs really are as petty as they say. He would be sad to hear you speak so; he has a certain respect for you."

"Had I not respect for him, I would never be meeting you."

"You're bad at these games, General. I imagine I'm not the first to tell you so. A cleverer man would make it less obvious that women disgust him."

"Don't flatter yourself to know me."

"Tell me: Who did you desire, when you watched? Him or me?"

Shame flushed through him. He said furiously, "You whore."

She gave him an appraising look, like a prospective horse-buyer. "It's true there are bitten-peach men who naturally prefer other men. I wondered if that was the case with you. But, no: I think you desire men because women remind you of everything you hate about yourself. That no matter what you do, what you achieve, you'll always be seen as more of a woman than a man. Weak. *Lacking.*" She laughed lightly. "Isn't that right? How tragic."

His private truth, on her lips. For a moment he was stunned. When the pain finally bloomed, it became a nucleus for his anger, like the imperfection in the base of a cup from which the bubbles rise. He hissed, "I thought the tragedy would be knowing that even a male child half strangled at birth has better qualifications than you do to rule. That no matter what you do, no matter what you achieve, you'll never receive the Mandate of Heaven, *because you're a woman.*"

Her composure was as immaculate as the glaze on a vase taken straight from the kiln. "The Mandate. Do you know orange is the color of burning salt? That's why the true color of fire is orange. Not blue or red. Salt is fire, and salt is life, and without it: even an empire falls to nothing." Ouyang's failure to produce a single crack in her veneer left him filled with impotent violence. "I may lack the qualifications to rule. But all I need is a man who has them. And as you've seen, I already have one of those." When she smiled, it was as sly as a stalking fox. "I have everything I need. Whereas you, General—you still need me."

19

ANFENG, ELEVENTH MONTH

Zhu came to. It happened so slowly and painfully that she had the feeling of being reconstituted out of nothingness. Even before she realized she was in Anfeng, in her own familiar bed, she was struck by the miracle of herself. She said, raspy with pain and astonishment, "I'm *alive*."

Ma was leaning over her in an instant, her face so drawn that it looked like she hadn't slept in a month. For all Zhu knew, it had been that much and more since the Grand Canal. "Ma Xiuying!" she said in delight. "I'm alive."

Ma greeted this statement with a furious look. She seemed tempted to strangle Zhu back to death. "How easily you say it! Do you even have any idea how close you came to not being alive? What we had to do—how many times we thought—"

She broke off, glaring, then to Zhu's surprise burst into tears. She said, weeping, "I'm sorry. I'm just so tired. We were so worried. We thought you were going to die! He might have spared your army, but he took it all out on you—" She had the sick, pasty look of someone whose heart was breaking to see another's suffering. Despite all the pain in her body, for one confused moment Zhu thought: *But I'm not suffering.*

Memories spooled through her like falling ribbon. Single moments, flickering faster and faster until they ran together into a nightmare version of reality. She saw the plain, and the dark forest of the Yuan army's spears. General Ouyang before her, as merciless as jade and ice. The flash of light from his sword; the banners frozen against the duck-egg dome of that winter sky. The silent, painless impact followed by the horror of reaching down and feeling the place where they joined. Her hand closing around the edges of his blade, as if that could somehow stop it from being inside her. Her hand—

When the world turns its face from you, remember it was because of me.

For those first few moments since awakening, Zhu had only been happy to be alive. Now, slowly and deliberately, she brought her consciousness to bear on her right arm. For an instant she thought she must have dreamt it, because it was still there. She was in pain, and all that pain was in her arm. She was wearing a glove of liquid fire. It ate through her skin, her flesh, until all that was left was her bones, outlined in white-hot agony.

Her right arm was under the blanket. She reached across her body with her left hand.

"Don't look!" Ma cried, lunging.

But Zhu had already twitched the blanket aside. She looked as dispassionately as she could at the bandaged stump a handspan below her right elbow. The sight seemed oddly familiar. It made her think of undressing in her storeroom in the monastery, and how the changed and threatening body she had uncovered had always seemed to belong to someone else. But this invisible agony-hand was undeniably hers, and so was the stump. The eunuch general had taken his revenge. He had mutilated her.

Her head spun. In all her years living someone else's life, she'd believed she was already operating at the highest pinnacle of difficulty—that she was working as hard as humanly possible to survive. She could never have imagined how it might become even more difficult yet. It felt as though she'd climbed a mountain, only to realize that all she'd climbed were the foothills and the real peak lay far above. The thought filled her with such a deep exhaustion that for a moment it felt like despair.

But as she stared at the rusty bandages, a thought wormed to the surface. *However tired I am, however hard it is: I know I can keep going, because I'm alive.*

Alive. She grasped that one true fact, the most important fact in the world, and felt the warmth of it summoning her out of despair. *He left me alive.*

What had he said, in that last awful moment? *You'll wish I'd killed you with honor.* He'd given her the worst punishment he could imagine. The mutilation of one's precious, ancestor-given body, and the knowledge of never again being able to hold a sword or lead men from the front line of battle: it was nothing less than the complete destruction of the pride and honor that made a man's life worth living. The eunuch general had delivered to Zhu Chongba the fate that would have destroyed everything he was, even more certainly than death. It would have made him nothing.

Zhu thought slowly: *But I'm still here.*

The eunuch general hadn't known he was acting on the body of someone who had never borne any ancestral expectations of pride or honor. Zhu remembered that terrible internal momentum: the feeling that she was diverging irremediably from Zhu Chongba, the person she *had* to be. She'd been so afraid of what it meant—that she wasn't Zhu Chongba and never would be, and that the instant Heaven found out she would be returned to nothingness.

Now she reeled with a realization that upended everything she'd believed about the world.

I survived—because I'm not *Zhu Chongba.*

"Why are you smiling?" Ma said, astonished.

For half her life Zhu had believed she was pursuing a fate that belonged to Zhu Chongba. She'd considered her successes as stepping stones along a path that only he could travel, towards an ending of greatness and survival that only he could have. But now she had succeeded, and for the first time in her life it had nothing to do with Zhu Chongba.

She thought of her mysterious ability to see the spirit

world—the ability she'd had since the moment she stood beside her family's grave and first gripped her desire to survive. The ability she shared with nobody else in the world except that unearthly child, the Prince of Radiance. Which meant they were, somehow, *alike*.

As she'd done so many times before, she turned her attention inwards. She dived deep into the mutilated body that wasn't Zhu Chongba's body, but a different person's body—a different substance entirely. She had always done this looking for something that felt *foreign*—for that seed of greatness that had been transplanted into her under the false understanding that she was someone else. But now when she looked, she saw what had been there all along. Not the red spark of the old Song emperors, but her own determination—her desire. Her desire that was so strong it overspilled the limits of her physical form and became entangled in the pulse and vibration of everything that surrounded her: the human world and the spirit world, both. Desire that burned white-hot. That *shone*. It shone with its own pure unceasing light, and for all that she knew it as intimately as any other part of herself, her realization of what it *was* stole her breath with joy. A white spark that would become a flame—

And it belongs to me.

Zhu was sitting up in bed, drinking one of Ma's medicinal soups by forgoing the spoon and drinking directly from the bowl balanced on her left palm, when there was a knock and Xu Da came in. He sat on the stool next to Zhu's bed and looked at her, his face softening into naked relief. "Little brother, you look good. I was worried."

Zhu took her face out of the bowl and put it down, which was aggravatingly hard to do without spillage. She smiled at him. She owed him her life, but that went without saying. She said instead, "Ma Xiuying said that after the eunuch general withdrew, you carried me all the way back to Anfeng by your-self."

"*Carried?* In my arms? That's a romantic image. What I did do was sit in a wagon beside your corpse-like body for six hundred li, praying for it to keep breathing. You're lucky I spent all my formative years in praying school." He spoke lightly, but sorrow rested on his face: he was remembering. Zhu realized how hard it must have been for him. For him and Ma Xiuying, both: the two people who loved her.

"You barely studied!" she said sternly. "It's a miracle the Dharma Master let you be ordained. But I guess you must have done something right, if Heaven couldn't refuse you."

"It wasn't just prayers that saved you." In the manner of a confession, he said, "I thought you were going to die."

"Seems a reasonable assumption, from what everyone's told me."

"I thought I could handle it until you got the fever. But I needed help—"

Zhu said calmly, "Who?"

"Jiao Yu. And he *did* help: he poked you full of needles and gave you medicine, and you pulled through," Xu Da said. He paused. "But now he knows. About you."

Zhu lay back gingerly. Her pain ballooned and throbbed. "Aiya. First you, then Ma Xiuying, and now Jiao Yu. Haven't you heard it only takes three people to tell of a tiger before every-one believes it?"

Xu Da had an ashen look. "I'll kill him, if you need me to," he said, low.

Zhu knew he would, just as she knew it would be the worst thing he had ever done. His other killings had no doubt earned him repercussions for his future lives, but the betrayal and murder of one of their own was something Zhu knew would haunt him in this life. The thought of his suffering sent a surge of angry protectiveness through her. She said, "He's still here?"

"As of this morning."

"Then he hasn't run, even though knowing my secret risks his life. It means he knows how important he is to my success. He thinks it's enough to protect him."

For all Jiao *was* valuable, her first instinct was to erase him. Years ago she had hesitated to do the same to Prefect Fang, but that was before she'd had blood on her hands. She could kill Jiao easily enough, and she doubted it would haunt her.

But the situation was different than it had been with Prefect Fang. Oh, Jiao's knowledge still made her skin crawl; it still felt like a violation. The wider release of that knowledge would still change her life in ways she couldn't imagine. But it no longer threatened what had been her greatest fear: that Heaven would find out that she wasn't Zhu Chongba and deliver her into nothingness. That fear was gone. She had faced nothingness, and lived when Zhu Chongba had been destroyed, and been seen by Heaven as nothing other than herself.

That meant Jiao's knowledge was only a matter of people, rather than fate and Heaven, and *that* meant it was something she could control.

She said grimly, "Leave him to me."

Even though Zhu only had two injuries (or three, if you counted the exit hole of the stab wound), the pain seemed to come from anywhere and everywhere. Worse, it was never the same pain: some days it gnawed, other days it throbbed and twisted. The only constant was her arm. That always burned. With her mind she traced the searing outline of that phantom limb. For some reason she could still feel her ghost fingers clenched around Ouyang's sword. *Live like your hand is on fire*, she thought wryly.

Ma came into the room with a bowl of medicinal paste and unwrapped Zhu's stump. Her hands were gentle, but the paste— "That smells *awful*," Zhu exclaimed, outraged. It had amused her to realize that Ma was sublimating all her worries and anger into making the healing process as uncomfortable as possible. It was a chastisement that took the form of increasingly pungent pastes, toxic soups, and pills that had grown as large as marbles. Since it made Ma happy, Zhu played her part by complaining. "Are you trying to kill me or heal me?"

"You should be grateful you're getting any treatment at all," Ma said, looking satisfied. When she finished with the stump she changed the rice-paper plasters over the wounds on Zhu's belly and back. Miraculously, she had been skewered without any of her vital organs being hit. Or perhaps not so miraculously: General Ouyang had wanted Zhu Chongba to live, after all.

Ma took the pulse in Zhu's left wrist. "You know, it's a wonder *only* Jiao Yu knows," she scolded. "Anyone who knows how to read a pulse can tell you have a woman's body."

It was funny, Zhu thought, to owe her survival to the same body that had been the source of so much terror. She remembered the relentlessness of its adolescent changes, and the sick, desperate feeling of being dragged towards a fate that would destroy her. She'd longed so intensely for a perfect male body that she'd dreamed of it, and woken up crushed with disappointment. And yet—in the end, she'd survived destruction precisely *because* hers wasn't a perfect male body that its owner would think worthless the minute it was no longer perfect.

Zhu didn't have a male body—but she wasn't convinced Ma was right. How could her body be a woman's body, if it didn't house a woman? Zhu wasn't the grown-up version of that girl with the nothing fate. They'd parted the moment Zhu became Zhu Chongba, and there was no going back. But now Zhu wasn't Zhu Chongba, either. *I'm me,* she thought wonderingly. *But who am I?*

Bent over Zhu's wrist, Ma's face radiated care and concentration. Despite everything that had happened, her cheeks still bore a trace of childhood roundness. The grain of her eyebrows was as perfect as if a lover's finger had traced them; her soft lips were so full their outline was almost a circle. Zhu remembered kissing those lips. The memory came with a scatter of sense-echoes: tenderness, and yielding, and the reverent gentleness with which one touches the warm curve of a bird's egg in the nest. She was surprised by the uncharacteristic desire to feel them again, for real.

"But Yingzi," she said, pretending seriousness, "there are so many more direct ways to know that than secretly measuring my pulse."

Zhu only saw it because she was looking for it: Ma's eyes dropped to the slight curve of her unbound chest. It wouldn't have meant anything had Ma not blushed brightly at the same time. *She likes this body,* Zhu thought, with an odd mixture of amusement and ambivalence. She had breasts; she knew that; and yet in a way they had never really existed to her because they *couldn't.* It was peculiar to have someone look at them—to *let* someone look at them—and know they weren't feeling horror, but attraction. *Desire.* It pinned Zhu into her body in a way she'd never felt before. It wasn't a comfortable feeling—but neither was it completely unbearable, as it would have been before General Ouyang's intervention. It seemed like something she could get used to, though she wasn't quite sure she wanted to try.

As if suddenly realizing her own lechery, Ma dropped Zhu's wrist and snatched up the nearest book.

"Is that one of the classics again?" Zhu moaned. "Usually when someone's lover is bed-bound, doesn't the other read love poetry instead of moral lecturings?"

"You could do with some morals," Ma said, flushing even more charmingly at the word "lover." Bodily qualms notwithstanding, Zhu could barely resist the temptation to kiss her again just to see how pink she could go. "And where do you expect me to find love poetry in Anfeng? If there'd even been any to start with, by now it's all armor linings. And which is the better use: arrow-proof armor, or sweet words whispered in your ear?"

"Without sweet words to believe in, who's going to go out into a rain of arrows?" Zhu pointed out. "Anyway, all the paper in the world wouldn't have saved me from our friend General Ouyang."

She realized belatedly that she'd spoiled the mood. Ma said with a sick look, "At least he left you alive."

"It wasn't mercy," Zhu said, gasping slightly as the pain of her arm slammed into her awareness. "He thinks the shame of being mutilated is worse than death. I suppose he was a cherished son, the kind brought up believing he should bring honor to his ancestral line. But then he was cut, and made to serve the very ones who did it, and he knows his ancestors would spit at him rather than receive his offerings." Then, slowly, because talking about her girlhood still felt wrong, she added, "But that's the difference between us. Nobody expected anything of me. Nobody ever cherished me."

To Zhu's surprise, the acknowledgment left her feeling lightened. It had never occurred to her how much strength she was expending on the effort to believe herself someone else. She realized: *He's made my path harder, but without knowing it he's made me stronger—*

After a long pause Ma said, low, "*I* cherish you."

Zhu smiled at her. "I don't even know who I am. General Ouyang killed Zhu Chongba, but I'm not the person I was born as, either. How can you know who you're cherishing?"

Rain drummed on the thatched roof. The mushroom smell of wet straw pressed around them with the intimacy of another's warm body under the blankets.

"I might not know your name," Ma said, taking Zhu's hand. "But I know who you are."

ANFENG, THE NEW YEAR, 1356

"Wah, it's so hot," Zhu complained, sitting upright on the edge of the bed. She was naked save for her bandages, and her sweat itched as it dripped out from under her arms and down her torso. "In the entire history of our people, do you think there's ever been a wounded warrior who died because he had a bath without being surrounded by enough braziers to roast a piece of pork? Tell me the truth, Yingzi. Is this just an excuse to get my clothes off?"

Ma looked up crossly from where she was peeling the rice-paper plasters off Zhu's stab wounds. "Oh, so I'm doing this for *my* benefit?"

"I'd wondered why you chose me instead of Sun Meng, since I'm so much uglier than he was, but now I know the truth: it's because I have breasts," Zhu said. She'd found that the more she said such things, the easier they were to say. "You took one look and knew I was the man for you."

"*Now* you're laughing about it. You lose a body part, and all of a sudden you're so eager to show off what extras you have?" Ma said, flushing, and yanked the plaster off.

Zhu howled obligingly, though it was all show. After nearly two months of recovery the only thing under the plasters were angry pink scars, the one on the front slightly larger than the back. It was as good an outcome as could have been expected. Even her stump was progressing. Not that it would have time to finish healing, Zhu thought ruefully. The New Year and Lantern Festival had both already passed, and she hardly expected the Yuan to wait much longer before trying to retake Bianliang.

While Ma tidied up, Zhu sat on the stool by the basin to wash. The once-familiar routine still felt strange. Not just using her left hand to do what she'd done a thousand times with her right, but for the newness of noticing herself. Her skin; her shape. For the first time since her adolescence she looked down at her body and didn't feel aversion, but simply the fact of herself.

These days she wasn't the only person looking at her body, either. Ma's embarrassed, sideways interest in her nakedness felt as intimate as a touch. For all that Zhu had never taken much of an interest in the business of rain and clouds, she liked the warm frisson of power that came from knowing another's private desire. It made her feel protective. A little mischievous.

She called with maximum piteousness, "Yingzi—"

"What?"

"Can you wash my left elbow?"

"As if an elbow needs special cleaning!" Ma said, pretending vexation, but came over and took the washcloth. Zhu sprawled as obnoxiously as possible so that Ma was forced to stand between her legs to reach. Ma's cheeks were flushed: she was very obviously aware of where she was standing and what she was doing. Her downcast eyelashes fluttered every now and then as she let out a breath she'd been holding.

Zhu's fond feeling intensified. Without thinking too much about what she was doing, she plucked the washcloth from Ma's hand and let it drop. Took Ma's right hand and placed it on her chest.

Ma's mouth opened silently. If it hadn't been for the brightness of her eyes, she might have looked stricken. Zhu followed her fixed gaze and saw Ma's hand resting on her own small left breast, the brown nipple just under Ma's thumb. Surprisingly, she did feel something at the sight. It wasn't her own feeling, but a vibration: the vicarious thrill of Ma's interest and excitement. But somehow it made sense that she would feel Ma's pleasure as she felt her suffering, because their hearts beat as one.

Smiling, she hooked her left hand behind Ma's neck and drew her down until she was sitting on Zhu's naked wet lap, and kissed her. As she felt the softness of Ma's lips against her own, and the shy slide of her tongue, Zhu felt that vicarious thrill strengthen until she wasn't sure that it *wasn't* something she wanted for herself. Desire, but another's desire running through her body, until she was as breathless as if it'd been her own.

After a while she pulled back, feeling slightly dizzy. Ma gazed at her, stunned. Her lips fascinated Zhu more than ever: slightly parted, with a wet shine that must have come from Zhu's own mouth. Despite all the pain Zhu had wrought on other bodies, it seemed the most personal thing she'd ever done.

She groped at Ma's waist for the tie that held her dress closed. It would only take a tug to undo, even for an awkwardly left-handed person. "You know, Yingzi," she said huskily. "I know how the business of rain and clouds works well enough, but I've never actually done it. I suppose we could figure it out together, if you wanted."

In answer Ma put her hand over Zhu's and pulled, and her dress fell open. Underneath she was gorgeous and glowing and sweating, and as she helped Zhu work her dress over her shoulders she said, smiling, "I want it."

"It can't have been true, that he meant to let Bianliang fall," Xu Da said, as a waiter came up the stairs of the drinking house and laid out bowls of snacks in front of Zhu and her gathered captains. "How could the Yuan possibly let us make Bianliang our permanent capital? It would be the next thing to admitting their empire is doomed. After he finished with you, he *did* immediately withdraw and go to Bianliang, even if Chen Youliang was already inside by the time he got there. Don't you think he said it because he was embarrassed at having been tricked?"

It was their first meeting in public instead of inside the temple. With no other Red Turban leaders in Anfeng, Zhu saw no point continuing her pretense of being an ambitionless monk—and it gave the useful impression that Anfeng was hers. In the days since resuming her leadership role, she had noticed a new tension between herself and her captains. They loved her for her sacrifice for them. And they were disgusted by and afraid of her new incapacity. For the moment their faith in her prevailed. They would follow her one more time. If she won, they might stay loyal. But if she lost—

They'll turn their faces from me.

And that was if Jiao and his knowledge of Zhu's *other* difference didn't upset this delicate balance before she even made it to the next battle. She shot him a glance, but his face was opaque as he hovered his chopsticks over the snacks before carefully selecting a cube of red-braised pork. *Meanwhile, I can't eat in public, because I can't even hold my bowl and chopsticks at the same time.*

"He said what he wants has nothing to do with which side wins," she reminded Xu Da. "But what that means for Bianliang is anyone's guess. There could be any number of reasons why he let it fall. For all we know, he wanted to pin the loss on a political enemy and now plans to retake it and cover himself in glory." But even as she said it, she remembered the way he had spoken about his fate. *You started something I have no choice but to finish.* His anger had been startling. Whatever his fate was, he wasn't happy about it.

"Commander Zhu!" A man ran up the stairs, saluted, and presented one of the tiny scrolls used for pigeon messages. "This just came in from the Chancellor of State."

Zhu nearly reached for Chen's message before remembering she had no way of holding open a curled-up scroll. Conscious of her watching captains, she said mildly, "Second Commander Xu, please read it."

Xu Da scanned the message. His face froze. After a beat he said, "The Chancellor of State writes of his concerns regarding the eunuch general's likely attempt to retake Bianliang in the window before summer. He requests Commander Zhu's assistance in defending the city until such time the Yuan withdraw for the season."

Zhu said, "And?"

"And if he's successful in holding Bianliang until summer—" Xu Da looked up at her. "He'll move against the Prime Minister, take the Prince of Radiance, and make Bianliang his own. He's inviting you to help him."

There was an intake of breath around the table. "Ah," Zhu said. The moment had the excitement of seeing the last portion of a map unrolled, revealing in exquisite detail what had been withheld. She smiled. "So our pain and suffering at the Grand Canal did earn us his trust. A rare and precious gift indeed!" That was why Chen had led the assault on Bianliang himself, instead of remaining in Anfeng. He had wanted to keep the Prince of Radiance within reach. Everything up until now had been part of one long game, and Chen had just made his first move to finish it. Zhu felt the white spark crackling within her: her future greatness that *would* happen, as long as her desire for it never wavered.

Xu Da observed, "With Bianliang behind us, and all of the Red Turban forces combined, we would make a genuine challenge for the eunuch general—if he does actually come. And if we can defeat him outright—what would stop us from taking all of Henan during summer? We could control the center and everything south of the Yellow River. If Chen Youliang has Bianliang as his capital, and the Prince of Radiance to give him legitimacy in the eyes of the common people . . . he won't just be the leader of a rebel movement."

In her mind's eye Zhu saw Chen standing bloody in the glow of the Prince of Radiance's Mandate. She said, "He wants us to help him become a king."

All eyes were on her. Xu Da said, "Will you?"

There was no question about going to Bianliang. That was where the Prince of Radiance was, and he was still the key to their rebellion's legitimacy in the eyes of the people. With that in mind, the question of who to support came down to who had the better chance of keeping the Prince of Radiance: Chen, or the Prime Minister. And Chen had already made his move.

She was viscerally aware of Jiao on the other side of the table, armed with his grenade of illicit knowledge. This was the opportunity she'd done everything for, but it was full of unknowns. The last thing she needed was a loose cannon of a captain running around. She could make a single decision he disagreed with, or even hesitate, and he would change to whichever side he thought would win. She wondered whether his knowledge had already diminished his perceptions of her. Did he consider her fundamentally weaker than before? If so, then the threshold at which he'd act would be even lower. If she wanted to win this game and achieve greatness, she would have to deal with Jiao before they left.

She looked around the table, catching each of her captains' eyes in turn and letting them see her determination. *Follow me one more time.* She lingered on Jiao. He returned her gaze coolly. She was disturbed to recognize an assessing quality to his look, as if he were peeling off her clothes and judging her based on something about her physical body. She had never been a target of a look like that before, and the shock of it filled her with an unfamiliar rage. She suddenly remembered the woman in Jiankang who had flown at Little Guo with the justifiable intention of murder. Zhu thought with bitter humor: *Big sister, I should have let you succeed.*

Breaking eye contact with Jiao, she ordered, "Make your preparations. As soon as we're ready, we ride for Bianliang."

20

ANYANG, FIRST MONTH

Despite its objectively vast size, the Prince of Henan's palace could be a surprisingly small place—running into people in courtyards or corridors was a given. Worst of all, Ouyang thought, was when you saw a person you would prefer to avoid on the other side of one of the palace's low rainbow bridges, and your meeting was inevitable. He ascended the bridge with a mental grimace; Lord Wang did the same from the other side. They met at the apex, under sprays of early-flowering apricots.

"Greetings to Lord Wang," said Ouyang, making a minimal genuflection.

The lord regarded him. He still had a bruised look about him, but there was a new sharpness to it. There seemed something in it specific to Ouyang, which disturbed him.

"So you're returned from Yangzhou," Lord Wang said. "I hear you successfully obtained the promise of their assistance. An unusual feat of diplomacy, for someone with not a diplomatic bone in his body."

"I thank you for the flattery, my lord, but no powers of persuasion were needed. They are subjects of the Great Yuan; they come willingly to its defense."

"What a lovely fantasy! While I'm sure my poor ignorant brother believes it, don't expect the same of me. In having told yourself so often that I'm worthless, have you forgotten what my domain actually is? I'm an *administrator*. I know far better than you the nature of business, and merchants. And I know they need more than the promise of praise to be persuaded into action. So I'm curious, General: What was it you offered in return for that assistance?"

A few petals fell and went swirling away under the bridge. Had Ouyang not already known how all this would end—*had* to end—Lord Wang's interest would have been concerning. He said tightly, "If my lord is interested, he may ask the Prince for the details of the negotiations."

Lord Wang gave him a level look. "Perhaps I will."

Ouyang bowed. "Then, my lord—"

Before Ouyang could brush past, Lord Wang said softly, "You think you understand me, General. But don't forget it goes both ways. Like knows like; like is connected to like. We've both seen each other's humiliations. *I understand you, too.*"

Ouyang froze. For all his anger at Esen for not seeing or understanding, the thought of being seen and understood by Lord Wang felt like a violation. He said, too forcefully, "We aren't alike."

"Well, I suppose in some respects you're like my brother," Lord Wang mused. "You think the only things of any worth are the things you yourself value. Does the world even exist outside your own concerns, General?"

"I've spent my life fighting for the Great Yuan!" Despite his best effort, Ouyang couldn't stop the bitterness from leaking out.

"And yet I care about it more than you, I think." Under the apricot flowers, Lord Wang seemed someone out of time: one of the elegant aristocrats of old imperial Lin'an. A scholar from a world that no longer existed. With a chill, Ouyang realized Lord Wang was making an accusation.

As he wedged past Lord Wang and continued on, the lord called from behind him, "Oh, General! I should tell you: I've decided to come along on your little expedition to Bianliang. Since it's my men and my money you're using, I would find it a shame if they were thrown away without achieving any good purpose."

The bitterness in Lord Wang's voice matched Ouyang's exactly. *Like knows like.*

Ouyang hadn't taken Lord Wang entirely seriously, but it was confirmed the moment he stepped into Esen's residence and found Esen looking grim and drunk. "Lord Wang came to see you," Ouyang stated. He already associated Esen's new type of bitter, miserable drunkenness with a recent encounter with Lord Wang. He clamped down hard on the thought of what had happened the last time Esen had come to him drunk after a fight with Lord Wang.

Esen said, "He claimed he wanted to come to Bianliang."

"Don't let him," Ouyang said immediately, sitting opposite. "You know the only reason he wants to come is to cause trouble." He didn't need to add: remember Hichetu.

Esen swirled his cup. "Maybe it's better to have him causing trouble where we can see it, rather than having him run around the estate without supervision."

"That makes it sound like the worst he's capable of is childhood pranks."

"We might come back to find he's sold the estate and gone to become a bureaucrat in the capital."

"That wouldn't be the worst outcome. But he can't; Bolud's family would destroy him," Ouyang said disparagingly. "They don't need proof he was behind Altan's exile. The suspicion would be enough to set them against him."

"I would back Wang Baoxiang over Bolud-Temur," Esen said, "as to who would survive longer in that jar of snakes. No, I don't *trust* him. Who would trust him, after what he's done to my father? But he's still my brother. Wish as I would, nothing can change that." Brooding, he gave a harsh laugh. "I hate him! And still I love him. Would that I could only hate. It would be easier."

"Pure emotions are the luxury of children and animals," Ouyang said, and felt the terrible weight of his own tangled emotions.

"But perhaps this is an opportunity," Esen mused. "For him to make amends and seek my forgiveness. What better place for it than on campaign, as when we were boys? I do want to forgive him! Why does he make it so difficult?"

"Wang Baoxiang killed your father. What forgiveness can you have for that?" It came out more harshly than he'd intended.

"Oh, fuck you!" In a sudden rage Esen flung the wine ewer across the room, shattering it. "You think I don't know that? Curse your literal-mindedness. Why can't you humor my fantasies just for a moment? I know it can't be the same. I know it won't be the same. I know I'll never forgive him. I *know.*"

When Ouyang didn't respond, Esen observed, "You don't kneel." He fumbled around on the table and found another ewer with some wine still in it, and poured himself a refill.

Ouyang was hit by the memory of his return from Bianliang. He'd knelt then only because he'd thought it would make him as angry as he needed to be. But now there was no need for anger: everything was already in motion, and it would unfold regardless of what Ouyang did or felt. If he knelt now, it would be because he wanted to. The thought filled him with hot shame.

He said, low, "Do you want me to?"

Esen's cup of wine sloshed onto the table. When he glanced up at Ouyang it was with a sick, hungry look that pulled between them like a physical connection. Ouyang heard Lord Wang's voice: *You and Esen are two unlike things.* Like and unlike: the tinder and the spark.

But then Esen's gaze dulled, and he looked back at his wine. "I apologize. I gave you liberty to be honest with me a long time ago."

Ouyang's churning emotions made him feel like a sailor on a typhoon-tossed ship, clinging to every moment of life while knowing there was nothing for him beyond the blackness of the deep. He said woodenly, "You're the Prince of Henan. Don't apologize."

Esen's mouth thinned. "Yes, I am." Spilled wine spread on the table between them. "Go. Get some sleep. Be prepared for our departure."

Ouyang withdrew and made his way to his own residence. Absorbed in painful thoughts, it was an unpleasant surprise to look up and find Shao and a handful of his battalion commanders waiting for him in his reception room.

"What is it?" He spoke in Han'er, since all those waiting were Nanren. The language never ceased to feel strange to his tongue. It was only another thing that had been stolen from him.

Commander Zhao Man, whose filigreed drop earrings lent a certain delicacy to an otherwise thuggish appearance, said, "General. Is it true Lord Wang will be accompanying us?"

"I was unsuccessful in dissuading the Prince from the idea."

"He's never come out before. Why now?"

"Who knows the workings of Lord Wang's mind?" Ouyang said impatiently. "It can't be helped; we will have to accommodate him."

Shao said, "Lord Wang is dangerous. What happened to Altan—"

"It's fine," Ouyang said, holding Shao's eyes until the other looked away. "The Prince stripped him of most of his power even here in Anyang. With regards to the military, he has none. What threat is he to me?"

"Lord Wang is no fool," someone else muttered.

"Enough! Having him with us or not has no bearing on the situation," Ouyang said, scowling, and left them muttering. He couldn't bring himself to care about Lord Wang. All he could do was keep moving forwards under the assumption of success. Dwelling on what might be, or what could have been, was the path to insanity. For a moment he had a sense-flash of Esen—not one particular memory, but something stitched together from every moment they had spent together: the feel of his body, his particular smell, his presence. It was intimate and completely false, and it was all Ouyang would ever have.

Bianliang, on the doorstep of the Yuan's northern heartlands, was a mere three hundred li south of Anyang. There were no mountains on the way, nor treacherous river crossings. A determined Mongol with several horses in his string could have covered it in a day. Even for an army it *should* have been completely straightforward. Ouyang surveyed the battalion's worth of supply wagons mired axle-deep in the bog and thought: *I'm going to kill him.*

"This has gone on long enough!" Esen said, when Ouyang told him during their nightly debrief. He spat out the shell of a roasted melon seed as though aiming it at Lord Wang's head. "Oh, I know you warned me. More fool I am, to hope against hope for a change in his nature, that he might actually try to be useful. Better had I wished for horses to fall from the sky! This is only what I should have expected all along: that he should try to *bother me to death.*" He leapt to his feet and stood before his father's sword on its stand, which he bade the servants put out every night when they erected his ger. "What should I do?"

It wasn't entirely clear whether he was asking Ouyang or his father's spirit. Ouyang, who wanted nothing less than for Chaghan's spirit to give its opinions, said shortly, "Punish him."

As he said it, he was startled by an internal feeling that was like a bell being rung by the vibration of its likeness far away. He remembered kneeling before Esen, seeking to be humiliated so that his hate could fuel what he needed to do. The only point to Lord Wang's pranks was to seek his own humiliation at Esen's hand. Ouyang thought uneasily: *But if that's the case— what does he need to do?*

Esen stalked over to his door guards and issued curt instructions. Ouyang put aside his bowl of noodle and mutton soup and rose, intending to leave, but Esen returned and pressed him back down. "Stay." He wore an uncharacteristically vicious look. Another might think it the look of someone girding for battle—except that Ouyang, who had actually seen Esen before battles, knew it was worse. There was something of Chaghan in the expression, as if Esen had actually succeeded in calling up that angry old spirit. "Let him have you witness his shame. Is it not your army too?"

"He won't thank me for it." *We've both seen each other's humiliations.*

"He won't thank me for what I'm about to do, either."

Lord Wang came in a few moments later. Two weeks on the road had turned his milky indoors complexion the color of an etiolated bamboo shoot. He sank onto the tiger-skin rug, giving Ouyang a poisonous glance as he did so, then said in a coquettish tone designed to infuriate Esen, "Do give me a drink, dear brother. It will soften the impact of the splendid berating I can see you're about to deliver. Or have you and your lapdog drunk it all already?"

"Wang Baoxiang," Esen said savagely.

"Brother!" Lord Wang clapped. "Congratulations! You've captured his tone exactly. Ah, it's like hearing our father's spirit. What have we been mourning him for when he's right here with us? Look: you've given me chicken-skin."

"Is this your whole purpose for being here? So you can prick me with your petty inconveniences?"

Lord Wang sneered. "Far be it for me to disappoint your expectations."

"I don't—you've well earned my distrust!"

"Ah, of course, I forgot. Since *you* managed to be the perfect son, there was no reason why I couldn't have been too. How selfish and willful of me to deny our father that satisfaction. Did I not do all my wickedness deliberately, out of love of seeing him hurt? How I must have wished for his death!"

Esen regarded him coldly. "Wang Baoxiang, I will not tolerate your interference in the operations of this army. Let this be your warning." He called, "Enter!"

The two young guards came in, their arms filled with books.

Without changing expression, Esen plucked a book from the nearest guard and tossed it into the fire. The guards began feeding the books in one by one. The sacred hearth flames rose up, whirling the ash, and the ger filled with the smell of burning paper. Ouyang saw Lord Wang's face drain of blood. It was such a drastic reaction that Ouyang was reminded of the stricken look of the first man he had ever killed.

Lord Wang said, terrible, "I see you have our father's cruelty in you, too."

A commotion outside startled them, and an attendant burst in. He made an anxious reverence and stammered, "Prince! Please come! Your favorite horse—it is—"

Still white-lipped, Lord Wang gave an ugly laugh. "His horse! Oh, the pity."

"If you dare have—!" Esen, already snatching up his cloak, directed a sick look of suspicion at Lord Wang.

"What, brother? Been cruel too? Rest assured: if I wanted to hurt you, you'd know."

His face pinched in fury, Esen turned and ducked out. The guards followed. Ouyang and Lord Wang were left alone with the books softly collapsing in the fire, the horse screaming in the distance.

Ouyang watched the firelight playing off Lord Wang's down-turned face. There was a strange, ill satisfaction there, as if Esen had proved something Lord Wang wanted—but in having proved it, had killed some other part that was still holding out hope.

Lord Wang hissed, "Get out."

Ouyang left him staring down at his burning books. It was a pitiful sight, but Ouyang's guilt had nothing to do with Lord Wang. It was Ouyang's betrayal that had turned Esen's pure-heartedness into something capable of cruelty and suspicion. For so many years Ouyang had viewed Esen's uncomplicated joy in life with jealousy and admiration and scorn and tenderness, and now it was gone.

⁂

It had been a grim morning, and everyone knew they would likely be halted the rest of the day due to the Prince of Henan's bad temper. The horse had died—a twisted intestine—and Esen had spent the hours afterwards furious and grieving. Despite his suspicions of Lord Wang, the illness had already been verified in autopsy: it was simply one of those things that happened.

"Why should a man cry that much over a horse?" Shao said, flipping a black weiqi piece across his knuckles. They were in Ouyang's ger. Outside, befitting the mood, it was raining.

"His father gave it to him," Ouyang said, placing his own white stone. He hated speaking about Esen to Shao, as if Esen were only an enemy. He made himself do it anyway. He had the image of his relationship to Esen being a thin strip of metal that Ouyang was deliberately bending back and forth. Each time it bent, it hurt. Maybe it wouldn't hurt after it finally snapped, but Ouyang couldn't make himself believe it.

Shao said, "Where are the others? They're late."

As if on cue, the flap lifted in a gust of wet rain and Commander Chu ducked inside. Without preamble he said, "General: Zhao Man is missing."

Ouyang looked up sharply. "Details."

"Nobody in his command has seen him since last night. He appears not to have slept in his ger."

"Deserted?" Shao asked.

"Could be, sir." Chu jumped as the flap opened again and admitted the other battalion commanders. They came and knelt around the forgotten game of weiqi, which Shao had been winning.

Commander Yan said, "General. Is it possible he spoke?"

"To whom, and for what?" Shao snapped. "Unlikely."

"Even so, we need to consider the worst-case scenario."

"Clearly the worst-case scenario hasn't occurred, if we're sitting here talking about it," Ouyang said. He spoke quickly, convincing himself as much as the others. "Isn't the point of speaking to be rewarded? Why would he desert with nothing but the clothes on his back? No. Tomorrow we'll find him fallen from his horse somewhere; that's all there is to it."

Shao said, "We continue."

Commanders Chu and Geng nodded, but Yan and Bai exchanged glances. After a moment Yan said, "Respectfully, General, I'm not convinced. You may be correct, but the uncertainty concerns me. More and more there are things we don't know about this situation. How can we proceed with confidence?"

Commander Bai said in his scratchy voice, "I agree with Yan. We should wait."

"No; it's too late for that," Ouyang said, noticing the glances the others exchanged as he said it. It was the careful way people treated someone gripped by an idea to the point of acting past all rationality. "If there are those who do not wholeheartedly believe in the success of the endeavor, you may disengage from it. In the event of failure you will not be mentioned. I ask only your silence."

Yan and Bai looked at each other again, and then Yan said, "I see no benefit in us speaking of it."

"So then we part ways," Ouyang said, turning back to the game.

"Be well and have success, General," said Yan, rising and bowing. "I hope for your sake I'm wrong."

Ouyang placed another stone without really seeing it, and was aware of Shao pursing his lips in dissatisfaction. He thought Shao might argue with him, but after a moment he placed a stone without saying anything. Ouyang, looking down at the board, felt a creeping suffocation. Shao's black pieces were throttling the white, pressing ever inwards in a spiral that left no place for escape.

Ouyang looked furiously at the bodies. Yan and Bai had been discovered that morning in Yan's ger, lying in puddles of their own vomit. Despite his anger he kept his face carefully blank.

He was conscious of Shao hovering in the penumbra of his peripheral vision.

"What's the cause of this?" Esen demanded, equally furious. The deaths of men in battle never affected him, but death within his own camp—after a night spent watching his beloved horse die in agony—had made him raw. He turned a hard look upon Lord Wang, who had been drawn like a floating gerfalcon to the sight of prey below.

Mustering blandness, Ouyang said, "We've lost a few men lately from a particularly virulent strain of illness from bad food. We had thought the source identified, but it may be that some tainted products remain. The fact that Yan and Bai died together, after eating and drinking, suggests a common cause."

Esen shook his head impatiently. "Coming so shortly after the disappearance of Commander Zhao? It can't be a coincidence. Call the physician!"

The physician arrived and knelt by the bodies. He had recently replaced an older man in the position, and was familiar to Ouyang only by sight. With a sinking heart, Ouyang saw that the man worked methodically, indicating some experience. Shao, no fool, would have used an uncommon poison, knowing that only court physicians made that subject their specialty. But it was a gamble Ouyang wouldn't have made himself. He thought grimly: all that has been traded is the uncertainty of Yan and Bai's silence with the uncertainty that their bodies will speak for them.

As the physician rose from his examination, Ouyang felt a chill at the sight of Lord Wang watching him with an ironic pinch on his thin mouth, as of a man receiving his validation of something already known but not desired.

"Esteemed Prince." The physician made a reverence to Esen. "Based upon my examination, I believe these deaths to be natural."

Esen frowned. Beneath his mask of control, Ouyang felt surprised relief. Shao, at his side, breathed out. But not in relief. No, thought Ouyang: it was the satisfaction of having one's fool-hardy assumptions validated. Shao had never doubted at all.

The physician continued, "I can find no traces of foul play, of violence or poison. It may be as the General guessed. The symptoms are consistent with a rapid illness of the kind commonly caused by bad food."

"Are you certain?"

"Superficially there is a resemblance to poisoning, since bad food is in and of itself a kind of poison. But upon examination the situation is clearly distinct." The physician rose. "Esteemed Prince, please accept it as my informed opinion of the matter."

Esen's face remained clouded, but after a moment he said, "Very well. Conduct the burial. This matter should not stand in the way of our normal preparations. Tomorrow, we will travel the usual distance. Prepare yourselves!" He left abruptly.

Lord Wang drifted over to Ouyang. His catlike mien of sat-isfaction was red-rimmed, and despite his immaculate hair and gown he seemed harrowed—as if he hadn't slept a wink since Esen's mistreatment of him two nights before. "How careless. Losing all these commanders right before a critical battle? I would worry about morale."

Ouyang said cuttingly, "Save your worry for your own mo-rale, my lord. Saddle sores losing you sleep?"

Lord Wang shot him a caustic look. "I'd say I was being haunted by my sins, but then I remember how many sins *you* have and it doesn't seem to have stopped you from sleeping, has it?" Then, to Ouyang's shock, his eyes suddenly slid past Ou-yang and his thin lips pressed together in bitter incredulity. The familiarity of that glance turned Ouyang to ice. The thing that animals could see, that made candle flames leap in his pres-ence, was behind him. And now, somehow, *Lord Wang could see it.* Ouyang's skin shrank in horror. He knew it wasn't some-thing he had simply missed about Lord Wang during all the years they had known each other. This was new. Something about the lord had changed since that night in Esen's ger, and he had no idea what it meant.

He must have displayed some reaction, because Lord Wang's mouth pinched tighter. "A pity, General, that good commander material is so thin on the ground. They were three of your best leaders, weren't they? And with time being so short, I imagine it's going to be hard to cultivate the kind of trust you need for this critical engagement."

"I have men enough I trust," Ouyang said shortly. A cold sweat crept and prickled under his armor.

"Do you? For your sake I hope so, General. A lot is riding upon Bianliang. Since I'm not sleeping anyway, perhaps I should spend a few of those hours praying for a good outcome."

"Pray all you like," said Ouyang. "It won't make a difference."

"Well, obviously *your* prayers wouldn't. Which deity or ancestor is going to listen to a filthy eunuch? They might listen to me. But it's true: I do feel more comfortable putting my faith in the efforts of my own hands." Lord Wang's humorless smirk held the sharp edge of a blade, and it unsettled Ouyang that he couldn't tell which direction it faced. "Plan well, General. I would hate to see you fail."

21

ANFENG, SECOND MONTH

Ma lay in the lamplight, Zhu's head between her legs. They had been at it so long that friction was long gone—the slickness of Zhu's fingers inside her was so flawless that their movement seemed invisible. "More," Ma said, arching. "More—"

Somehow she knew Zhu was smiling. Zhu increased her fingers to all five in a wedge, pressing in. Stretching in an incremental penetration. Ma felt *that*. It hurt; it was an all-consuming pleasure that seemed familiar and new at the same time; it was everything in the world. She heard her own voice, crying out.

"Should I stop?"

"*No.*"

Ma could imagine Zhu's smile, mischievous and intent, with that edge of detached curiosity that never went away even in the rawest moments between them. Zhu pressed her hand deeper, up to its widest part. Easing in confidently, bit by bit, as Ma panted and whimpered around the stretch of knuckles. When Zhu paused, Ma realized she had lost the ability to form individual thoughts. She was only sensation. Pain and pleasure, pleasure and pain. She had no idea how long the pause had been by the time Zhu moved again. In, or perhaps out—then Ma spasmed helplessly around Zhu's hand. She was so stretched her muscles fluttered rather than clenched. She gasped and shuddered, feeling the rock-solidness of Zhu within her.

"Still good?" Zhu's voice floated up to her. Her tongue glided lightly over Ma's sensitive point, wringing from her a gasp and another round of subdued fluttering. When the flutters subsided Zhu pressed in again, and Ma cried out at a sensation that was too big to contain, and then Zhu pushed one last time and sank inside to the wrist. Ma lay shuddering around it, drawn out of herself by that beautiful terrible ache, muscles all over her body twitching in discordant sequence like the creaking of metal as it cooled.

"I feel like I could take all of you, however much you give me." She barely recognized her own voice.

Zhu chuckled. "You've taken it all already." Her head dipped, and Ma felt her tongue brushing between her legs again. She licked a soft repetitive stroke, over and over until Ma's oversensitive shivering turned into shudders: an exhausted rebuilding. All she could do was writhe weakly against Zhu's mouth, her heart beating in the thin skin stretched around the penetration of Zhu's hand. There was an occult thrill to it: that she could take Zhu in, and hold her within her body, as if she were the only person in the world with that peculiar power.

I would take Zhu forever, Ma thought, terrified. What could this be other than love, this surrendered feeling of her heart beating around Zhu's hand? Zhu, who could hurt her, but chose not to—who in filling Ma's body was as intimate as any person could be, and yet who at the same time was always moving away from her in pursuit of her own greatness.

Zhu withdrew her hand in a slow, twisting slide. Ma moaned; Zhu's tongue slipped faster against her. She floated above a distant feeling of arousal—and then, without realizing she'd even been chasing it, peaked one last time with a choked sob.

Zhu wriggled up the bed with an undignified one-and-a-half-armed flailing, and lay next to Ma with a look of smug accomplishment. She never needed anything from Ma in return, which made Ma slightly sad. Even if Zhu had wanted it, though, this time Ma wouldn't have been of any use: she was too exhausted to even turn her head for a kiss.

Later, she was dimly aware of Zhu getting up—eschewing trousers in favor of a robe that could be slung on without needing to be tied—and going to her desk where she practiced doing simple things left-handed. The flare of lamplight behind Zhu's bent head made Ma's eyes ache. Suddenly the sight of her, silhouetted by light, filled Ma with an unbearable pang of distance. She wanted to run to Zhu and take her in her arms, to turn her from silhouette back into a real person. But even as she watched, Zhu's details faded further as she receded into that terrible, intensifying light—

Then Zhu was sitting on the edge of the bed, and the light was only daylight. Her left hand was warm on Ma's shoulder. "Hey, Yingzi." She smiled down at Ma: genuine and fond, with the faint surprise that struck Ma with the usual punch of delight. She loved that Zhu, always so self-possessed, was still a little bit baffled by her own happiness at finding Ma in her bed. "Will you help me put my armor on? There's something I need to do."

The door of Jiao's workshop was wide open despite a brisk wind through the streets. Zhu went inside. She was immediately plunged into gloom: the cavernous space lacked even a single candle, though it was pleasantly warm from the foundry next door. There was an overpowering aroma of cast iron and sticky old grease, shot through with the sharper smells of some mysterious alchemy. Zhu felt the urge to sneeze.

Jiao was sitting hunched over a table, weighing powders on a tiny scale. When she blocked the light from the doorway he squinted up at her like a bad-tempered bamboo rat.

Zhu said, "You'll go blind if you keep working in the dark. Afraid you'll explode if you use a lantern?" She was wearing her usual combination of armor over old gray robes, now with her right arm slung across the front, and she wondered at the odd silhouette she must make. Neither a warrior nor monk; neither whole nor incapacitated. And what else did Jiao see? A man or a woman, or something else entirely?

Jiao pushed back from the table and wiped his blackened hands with an even blacker cloth. "I wondered when you were going to turn up." His eyes flicked to the curved saber she had taken to wearing in place of her normal sword. Not that it was anything more than a decoration. She didn't have either the strength or the coordination to wield it with her left hand, and no doubt Jiao knew that as well as she did. She had always found his gruff superiority entertaining, but now there was an edge to it she disliked: a superiority not by virtue of his learning, which she respected, but by virtue of what he was. *A man.* He said, "I presume you're not here to kill me."

She saw his confidence. He knew that if it *had* been her intention to kill him, she'd have done it long before. And because she hadn't, he thought she was afraid. He thought he was the stronger.

"Do you think it's because I couldn't?" Zhu inquired. "Because of the arm, or because of what you know?"

"You tell me."

There was cold-blooded calculation in his eyes. He was weighing her up against the others: Chen, the Prime Minister, General Ouyang. And Zhu was already diminished in his eyes. If he were to choose against her, she knew he would sabotage her as much as he could before leaving. *It's what I would do.*

Zhu's stump throbbed in time with her heartbeat, as steady as a water clock. "You think you have power over me because you know a secret. But you don't."

"It's not a secret?" Jiao raised his eyebrows.

"It's a secret without value. Tell it to whoever cares to listen, and I'll still do exactly what I plan to do, and get what I want. You think I can't overcome being exposed, when I've overcome everything else in my way?" The eunuch general had made her into the person she needed to be—and now her fate could never be denied to her on the basis of who or what she was, because everything she needed to achieve it was within her.

"I'm not afraid of what you know," she said. "How can something like that stop me, destroy me, when nothing else has?" She took a deep breath and reached for the white spark that was the seed of her greatness. "Look at me," she commanded, and Jiao's chin jerked in unthinking obedience. "Look at me and see the person who will win. *The person who will rule.*"

She extended her closed left hand, and *desired*. She felt a disconcerting sensation of opening—of connecting to the world and everything it contained, alive and dead. To everything under Heaven. She gasped as the power ran through her. In an instant the seed of brightness inside her was a blaze, blasting her clean of every other thought and feeling until all that was left was the blinding, ecstatic pain of looking into the sun. She was burning with it; she was on fire with her belief in her own shining future. It was agonizing. It was glorious. She opened her hand.

Light sprang out, faster than thought. A merciless white blaze that blew out every shadow; that raked the dusty gray secrets out of the recesses of Jiao's workshop, and sent Jiao recoiling with a shout. The unyielding light pouring from Zhu's palm washed the color from him until he was as ashy as a ghost. His first reaction was terror: he saw a real flame that would explode them both into their next lives. With a twist of satisfaction, Zhu watched as his second reaction took hold: the realization that it *wasn't* a real flame, and his ensuing struggle with the impossibility that was all that remained.

After a moment, still breathing heavily, Jiao leaned forwards with obvious effort and took up his scale. That was all the capitulation she got. He was too superior to bow, even in defeat. With his head down over his powders, he said in the manner of someone making a casual inquiry, "That isn't the color of any dynastic Mandate of Heaven recorded in the Histories."

Zhu closed her hand around the white flame. Afterimages danced in front of her eyes in the restored darkness. Her body thrummed with energy. "It's not a color," she said, and felt the truth of it ringing out like a promise of the future. "It's radiance."

Zhu's force left Anfeng two days later and reached Bianliang on a darkening afternoon. Even Jiankang, that seat of kings, had been smaller: Bianliang's inky mass reared in front of them like an oncoming storm. And that was only the inner wall. Zhu had made camp five li to the south, but even that still lay inside the ruins of the outer wall. That whole vast area between the two walls, and even outside the outer wall for another ten li, had once been covered by the mansions of that sprawling imperial capital. But since that time the unchecked Yellow River had flooded the area so often that the wooden buildings had melted back into the ground as if they had never been. Now there was only barren marsh, ghosts, and the call of herons.

A lonely landscape, but they weren't alone. It had been a closer race than Zhu had thought it would be, given how much further she had to travel, but General Ouyang had still won. East of the inner wall, his encampment was a city in and of itself. Its torches cast a golden glow over Bianliang's stone ramparts. A line of trebuchets lifted their tall heads in silent regard of the wall in front of them.

Xu Da said, "According to Chen, he arrived on the sixth day of this month."

"Four days, then." Zhu had thought she was sufficiently recovered, but the journey had left her feeling paper-thin with exhaustion. Her right arm ached from being bound across her chest, and her back hurt from riding lopsided. No doubt her arm would be useful again one day, but for the moment it was as though she'd lost the entire limb. Its absence gave her an unsettled feeling of blindness on her right side. She often caught herself twisting to the right, as if to see. "But he hasn't used his siege engines yet, despite having such a limited window. Why?"

"He did have to bring the trebuchets in pieces from Anyang. Maybe they aren't all assembled yet."

"Maybe," Zhu said, unconvinced. Turning inwards, she sank past her exhaustion into that faint vibration that was the sense of some distant self. The shivering entanglement of their qi seemed as intimate as the breath shared between lovers. And now that he had helped her become who she needed to be, they were more entangled than ever.

He wasn't waiting out of simple incompetence, she thought. No; it was something else. She remembered the circle of his watching ghosts as they fought. Of all the people in the world, he was the only one she'd ever seen who was *haunted* by ghosts. Who were they, and what did they want from him? And why were there so many of them? It was if a whole village had been wiped out in a single act—

Distantly, she heard the Prime Minister saying: *Under the old rules, a traitor's family was executed to the ninth degree.*

General Ouyang, a Nanren slave of Mongol masters, whose only pleasure seemed to come from revenge. Who had told her a truth about himself when his sword had been sunk inside her: *What I want has nothing to do with who wins.*

All of a sudden, she knew why he waited.

Xu Da was giving her a look of forbearance from beneath lowered eyebrows. "You have an idea."

"I *do.* And you're not going to like it." Zhu was surprised to find she had broken out in a cold sweat. She wasn't afraid, but her body was; it remembered pain. She bit down on a gasp as her phantom arm flared in agony. "I have to meet General Ouyang again."

After a beat Xu Da said in a measured tone, "*Meet.*"

"Just speak to him! Preferably this time without being skewered." Beneath her pain she felt General Ouyang's presence in the distant Yuan camp like a coal in the heart of a fire. *Understanding fire doesn't mean it can't still burn you.* "And it has to be now."

"Last time you *had* to face him," Xu Da protested. There was fear on his face, and remembered pain. "This time we have other options."

Zhu smiled with some effort. "Remember what the Buddha said? Live like your head is on fire." Instinctively, she knew her desire could never be satisfied by hanging on to Chen's ankles as he rose. But if she wanted more than the scraps of power he might toss her, she would have to jump into the fire.

She squeezed Xu Da's shoulder fondly with her left hand. "He didn't destroy me last time, and that's all that matters. So whatever happens this time—" She felt a thrill of rightness, even sweeter than anticipation. "It will be worth it."

General Ouyang's problem, Zhu mused as she slipped through the dark space between their two armies, was that he lacked Chen's imagination. *If you really wanted to make me useless, you should have cut off all my limbs and kept me in a jar like Empress Wu did with her enemies.* Once she was inside the Yuan's perimeter it took her no time at all to find his flag-crowned tent standing alone on the outer edge of the command cluster. It seemed entirely characteristic of him that he should keep himself apart despite the inconveniences it caused. *And the diminished security.*

The round Mongolian tents seemed big from the outside, but on the inside they were gargantuan. Or perhaps it was just the empty space that gave that impression. Except for all the braziers (which, added to the central fire, made it rather too warm) and the multiple hides layered over the springy woolen floor, General Ouyang's living space was as utilitarian as Zhu's own room in Anfeng. Two sets of armor hung on stands, next to an empty stand that presumably belonged to the set he was wearing. A stack of rectangular cases held bows and arrows. There was a chest of clothes, and another of small tools and the assorted bits of leather one keeps about for fixing tack. A bow-legged low table covered with papers lined in running Mongolian script, with a helmet on top like an oversized paperweight. A washbasin and simple pallet dressed with a felt blanket. Bare as the space was, it still carried something of *him*, which surprised Zhu more than it should have. For all she understood him, she had never really thought of him as having an ordinary aspect: of being a person who slept and ate, and had preferences about his clothes.

There was a murmur of ghosts outside. Zhu braced herself as the doorflap brushed aside and General Ouyang stepped over the threshold board, bareheaded with his sheathed sword held loosely in his hand. When he saw her he stopped and stood very still. The connection between them rang deafeningly in Zhu's head. She had taken off her sling before coming. Now, slowly and deliberately, she spread her arms to the side. Her left hand open and empty. Her right arm ending in a bandaged stump. She let him look. Let him see what he had done.

For a moment they just stood. The next, she was pinned against the tent wall with General Ouyang's studded leather wristguard crushing her throat. She choked and kicked. Despite his small size, she might as well have tried to free herself from a statue's grip. The scratchy tent fabric bowed outwards under their combined weight. He leaned in and whispered in her ear, "Wasn't losing one hand enough?"

He let go. As she crashed down she instinctively caught herself—with a hand that wasn't there. The world flashed red as she smashed down chin-first with a strangled scream. After that she could only writhe and gasp. In the way in which pain renders everything else unimportant, she was vaguely aware of General Ouyang standing over her. The tip of his sword pricked her cheek.

"Take what you like," she ground out. "It takes more than that to destroy me."

He crouched by her head with a creak of armor. "I'll admit to some surprise that you're still around. Your men must be pitiful indeed, to follow a cripple into battle." There was something else under his viciousness. *Envy.* Zhu remembered the whips, and the cruel ease with which he had squandered his conscripts. His men despised him, and he hated them; he had probably always led through fear, because he had to.

He took the lip of her helmet and lifted her head up so they were eye to eye. Even in her pain she marveled at the dark sweep of his lashes, and the fine brushstroke of his brows. As if he had some idea of her thoughts, he mused, "Apparently being as ugly as a cockroach makes you as resilient as one, too. But there are certain things nobody comes back from. Shall we try them, one by one?"

Zhu said between pants, "And not even hear my offer first? Surely you're curious as to why I came."

"What can you have that I could possibly want? Especially since you've already given me the opportunity to kill you."

An opportunity for an opportunity. A more specific agony radiated up her right arm—the pain of her phantom hand still cutting itself to the bone around his blade. She wondered if she would ever be able to let go. "You haven't attacked yet because you're waiting for reinforcements to arrive. But since you let Bianliang fall in the first place, your reinforcements are for some purpose other than taking it." She glanced over his shoulder at the crowding ghosts. They were still watching, but the sight of them no longer provoked fear. They filled the tent, pressed close like a murmuring audience before the start of a play. He didn't know they were there, but at the same time he *did* know—the knowledge of it was in the very fabric of his being, because everything he did was for them. He was a man in his own invisible prison, walled in by the dead. She said, "A purpose that has nothing to do with the Red Turbans at all."

He turned as if compelled to follow her gaze, and laughed in horror as his eyes met emptiness. "What do you see there, that tells you about me?" He released her helmet and sank back on his heels with an incredulous expression. "It's true, though. I do have reinforcements on the way. They'll be here tomorrow morning. And while they're not *for* you, they'll do against you very well. Since you and your pitiful little army turned up just in time to be in my way."

"What if I told you our goals are compatible? Help me get the Prime Minister and the Prince of Radiance out of the city, and I'll take my army and leave you to do whatever you're planning, without interruption."

He regarded her. "I presume you realize how much I dislike you. Wasn't the part where I said I wanted to kill you clear enough?"

"But there's something more important to you than anything you feel about me. Isn't there?" Zhu got up with a stifled grunt of pain, took the pigeon message from her armor and proffered it to him. When he made no move to take it, she said, "Can you read it? It's written in characters."

"Of course I can read characters," he said, as insulted as a wet cat.

"I'm not sure you'll be able to hold a scroll open and keep your sword on me at the same time," Zhu observed. "Trust me on things that are hard to do one-handed."

He glared at her as he rose, sheathed his sword, and took the message.

"It's from our Chancellor of State, Chen Youliang," Zhu explained. "If I can get this message to the Prime Minister, he'll know Chen Youliang intends to betray him. Then he'll come to me out of Bianliang of his own accord. As soon as I have him and the Prince of Radiance, I'll withdraw from the field. You won't have to waste any men or effort fighting me."

"And if your Prime Minister gets the letter but decides to handle the matter himself? Once my reinforcements arrive, my hands will be tied. Whether or not you get what you want—if you don't withdraw, I'll be forced to attack."

"That's a risk I'll take."

"How lucky your Prime Minister is to command such loyalty." His beautiful face was sour.

"Loyalty?" Zhu held his eyes and smiled. "Hardly, General."

After a moment his mouth turned down with bitterness. "I see. Well, I have no loyalty either. And on the scale of bargains I've made lately, this is nothing." He gestured for her to get up. "If you want to send that message to Liu Futong, I know a way. You may not like it."

"I'll hear it."

"That point you see above the city's walls is the top of the Astronomical Tower. The past three mornings running, your Prime Minister has gone up there to survey my camp. Have him ascend the tower tomorrow morning to find an arrow waiting for him with Chen's letter. Will that not serve?"

Zhu regarded him. "So someone needs to shoot an arrow into the upper level of the Astronomical Tower. In the dark. From outside the city. I only have one letter."

"Trust that I'm Mongol enough to do it," General Ouyang said sardonically.

If he failed, the arrow would fall somewhere else in the city. It would be found and reported to Chen, who would know whose side Zhu had chosen. But Zhu wouldn't know that Chen knew. She would be waiting on the battlefield opposite General Ouyang, and the Prime Minister would never come, and then he would kill her. She would be risking all the potential the white light signified, for the chance to fulfil it completely. Everything or nothing in this one chance to defeat Chen.

She was no longer afraid of nothing, as she had been, but neither was it something she wanted to run towards. Anticipation made her break out in chicken-skin. "Do it."

"I already knew you were foolhardy. But you'll really gamble your life on the one who nearly killed you?"

"You didn't nearly kill me," Zhu corrected. "You freed me." She stepped closer, forcing him to see her. Despite all the pain he had caused her, she didn't hate him. She didn't pity him, either; she simply understood him. "At our last meeting you said I set you on your path towards your fate, and you promised to deliver me to mine. But just as you know your fate, I know mine. You didn't give it to me then, because that wasn't the moment for it. *This* is the moment. *So do it.*"

Fate. His face contorted as though the word had struck him. Zhu had always thought that whatever his fate was, he didn't want it. But now, startled, she saw the truth: as desperately as he didn't want his fate, and he feared and hated the idea of it—he wanted it just as much.

Zhu thought of the original Zhu Chongba, motionless in bed with the quick of life gone out of him. He hadn't wanted his fate, either. *He had given it up.* Her eyes slid over General Ouyang's shoulder and met the stares of his ghosts. She had wondered, before, what bound them to him. But it was the opposite: he bound himself to them. That was his tragedy. Not being born to a terrible fate, but not being able to let it go.

And just for that moment, she did pity him.

As if aware of her sentiment, he jerked his face away. He went to the rectangular cases and selected a bow. A single arrow. As he left he said, blisteringly dry, "If you want your fate, then stay here."

He was gone a long time. Time enough for him to have gone to the Prince of Henan and shown him Chen's message, or done anything else. Perhaps he had never intended to try to make that shot. The more Zhu thought about it, the more impossible it seemed. The watch called, and despite herself she felt her stomach sink.

Then the doorflap swung inwards, making her jump. "It's done," General Ouyang said shortly. The murderous look he gave her said he still held her partly responsible for his fate and whatever personal horrors it contained. "I'll give you until midday tomorrow to take your men and leave, with or without your Prime Minister. If you're still here after that, all bets are off. *Now get the hell out of my ger.*"

Zhu sat on her horse at the head of her waiting army. For the sake of appearances she was wearing the saber, which even after diligent practice she could still barely draw from its sheath in one clean motion. *It's like I'm a hapless monk all over again.* She wondered if her captains realized how truly incapable she was. Everything about this encounter was appearances. Just as the Mandate itself was only appearances. The Prince of Radiance's Mandate of Heaven could rouse an army to follow it, but that was because it was fused with the belief that he would usher in a new era. Her own Mandate, unbacked by any such beliefs, was nothing more than a light.

Yet.

For it to be more than that, she would have to make it through this encounter. And for all that this encounter was appearances—at the same time it was as real as life and death.

Mist swirled over the plain. As it shifted she could make out geometric shapes far above, like a glimpse of the Jade Emperor's realm in the sky. The straight edge of ramparts; the tops of Bianliang's famous Iron Pagoda and Astronomical Tower. Both that upper world and the one below were completely silent.

A breeze came up off the Yellow River. The mist moved and thinned. Zhu looked at the pale, determined faces of her captains, staring eastwards through the mist in the direction of the Yuan camp. So much of this moment depended on their trust in Zhu. And her own trust lay in a perilous stack of unknowns. On General Ouyang actually having done what he'd said. On him having made that impossible shot. On the Prime Minister having found the letter, and his response.

I just need their trust for this little bit longer.

There was a hoarse, muffled cry. "Commander Zhu—!"

The mists had lifted enough for them to see their surroundings. To the east there was the expected sight of the Yuan camp, swirling with activity. To the west—

At first glance one could have mistaken the prickle of vertical lines for a winter forest. But not a forest of trees. *A forest of masts.* In the middle of the night a navy had sailed up the Yellow River, and even now was disembarking an army.

"Yes," Zhu said. "The Yuan called the Zhang family of Yangzhou to their aid."

She watched the dismay dawn on their faces. They knew what it meant: they were pinned between the eunuch general to the east, and the Zhang forces to the west. They knew Chen would never send troops out now. He and the Prime Minister would hunker down and hope to withstand the siege until summer. They would leave Zhu outside to be slaughtered.

She thought urgently: *Trust me.*

Just then there was a mechanical spasm in the Yuan camp, and a projectile splashed against the eastern wall. After a moment they heard a low boom like distant thunder, and a thick column of black smoke rose from the wall. It hadn't been a rock—it was a *bomb.* A second trebuchet released, then a third. Their lashing arms inscribed arcs across the sky like the spinning stars. Zhu could feel each explosion deep inside her gut. She tried to imagine what was happening in the city between Chen and the Prime Minister. Who would end up betraying whom, now that everything had changed?

Light from the explosions washed over her captains' faces. "Wait," she commanded. It was like holding back restive horses. She could feel her control of them slipping. If even one of them broke and ran, the others would follow—

There were no shadows under that flat sky. The morning mists burned off as General Ouyang's army emerged from their camp and began assembling at the far end of the plain. Mounted units rotated into position on the wings. *I'll give you until midday,* he'd said. It was nearing midday, and still nothing had come out of Bianliang. Helplessly, Zhu watched the parts of his army flowing together into a seamless, motionless block. *Waiting.* Only the flame-blue banners moved overhead. In the awful stretched moment that followed, Zhu thought she could hear the drop of the water clock. A dripping that came ever slower, until the last drop came and there was only a terrible suspended silence.

Into that silence fell a single beat. One drum, beating like a heart. Then another picked up the rhythm, and another. From the west, an answering cadence. The Yuan and Zhang armies speaking to each other. Readying themselves.

Xu Da rode over to Zhu. The other captains' heads swiveled to watch. Jiao's head turned the quickest. Showing him the Mandate had convinced him to follow her—then. But that had been in the safety of Anfeng. Now she remembered how he had abandoned them at Yao River—how, in practical matters of life and death, he placed his trust in leadership and the numerical advantage. She could feel his faith in her hanging by a thread.

Xu Da said, low and urgent, "It's already midday. We have to go." And with a blow of pain that hit her directly in the heart, she saw he doubted too.

She looked past him to that distant Mongol army. It was too far away for her to pick out individuals. Was that shining speck in the middle of the front line General Ouyang?

And still there was nothing from Bianliang.

The cadence of the drums grew frenetic. Their ever-quickening beat generated a pressure that set their teeth on edge; at any moment it would burst and spill two armies on Zhu. They would be her annihilation. But Zhu had felt annihilation before. She had feared it her whole life, until she had *been* nothing and come back from it.

She looked back at Xu Da and forced a smile. "Have faith in my fate, big brother. How can I die here, before anyone knows my name? I'm not afraid."

But *he* was afraid. She saw the burden she was placing on his love and trust to ask him to stay when it must seem that all was lost. Despite their shared childhood and years of friendship, she realized she didn't know what he would choose. The cords in his neck stood out, and her heart fluttered. Then, after an interminable moment, he said quietly, "It's too much to ask for an ordinary man to put all his faith in fate. But I have faith in you."

He followed her as she rode the length of her lines. As her men turned their pale faces to her, she looked each in the eye. She let them see her confidence—her shining, unshakable belief in herself and her fate and the brilliance of her future. And as she spoke she saw that confidence touch them and take hold, until they became what she needed. What she wanted.

She said, "Hold. *Hold.*"

The roar of the drums was continuous now, unbearable. And then it happened. *Movement.* Two converging armies: infantry leading in the west, cavalry in the east. At the sight Zhu felt a peculiar stillness descend upon her. It was a wall built of nothing more than belief, and deep down she knew it was taking every scrap of her strength to keep it there between herself and that approaching horror. General Ouyang's cavalry formations were spreading as they advanced until it seemed that men were riding abreast towards them across the entire width of the horizon. Under a field of rippling banners their spears and swords glittered: they were a wave endlessly renewed from behind until they formed a dark ocean surging towards them. Even across that distance its voice reached them: a swelling roar of human and animal sound overlaid on the beat of the drums.

Zhu shut her eyes and listened. In that instant she didn't just hear the world, but *felt* it: the vibrations of every invisible strand that connected one thing to another, and drew each of them to their fates. The fates they had been given and accepted—or had chosen for themselves, out of desire.

And she heard the moment the sound of the world changed.

Her eyes flicked open. The drums in the east beat a new pattern, and the west responded. The Zhang army wheeled around in a great curve like swallows changing direction. They left the trajectory that would have taken them into collision with Zhu, and went to Bianliang's western wall, and were sucked through an opening with the swiftness of smoke up a chimney.

And *there*—a single figure on horseback floating across the plain towards them, from a gate that had opened on the city's south side. Her captains shouted in surprise, and a pinprick of emotion bored through Zhu's detachment. Tiny, but painful because its very nature admitted the possibility of failure:

Hope.

Even as the figure from Bianliang approached, General Ouyang's army was still bearing down on them. Across the shrinking distance Zhu could just make out the rider on the black horse in the center of the front line, a shining pearl in the dark ocean. The flat light blazed from his mirrored armor. Zhu could imagine his braids flying beneath his helmet, and the naked steel in his hand.

She couldn't tell who would reach them first. She had lost her detachment without realizing it, and now she was nothing more than a thrumming speck of anticipation. The rider from Bianliang seemed to inch forwards, and she couldn't remember the last time she had breathed. And then, *finally*, he was close enough that they could see who he was. Who *they* were. Zhu had *known*, and yet all the breath came out of her in an explosive burst of relief.

Xu Da urged his horse forwards in a gallop, coming around beside the Prime Minister's lathered horse and scooping the Prince of Radiance off his pommel. Zhu heard him shouting to the Prime Minister, "I'm just behind you! Keep going—run!"

General Ouyang's army crested in front of them like a wave about to break. Just as Zhu kneed her horse around, she saw a flash of his beautiful, hard face. The connection between them keened. As with any two like substances that had touched, she and the eunuch general were entangled—and no matter how far apart they might range, she knew the world would always be trying to bring them back together. *Like belongs with like.*

In what circumstances, she had no idea, but she knew: whatever General Ouyang's dreaded and desired fate was, he still had enough of its path left to travel that they would meet again.

Goodbye, she thought to him, and wondered if he was alive enough inside to feel that tiny message. *For now.*

Turning to her men, she shouted, "*Retreat!*"

Zhu pushed them hard for two hours, then called the halt. General Ouyang hadn't pursued them, even though he could have caught up with her trailing infantry units easily enough. It was only because he'd had better things to do, but she sent him a small thought of gratitude anyway.

She dismounted awkwardly and went over to Xu Da as he lifted the Prince of Radiance from his horse. Xu Da wore a ginger look that she understood perfectly. There was something about the child that provoked unease. It was like seeing someone's knee bending the wrong way. Even now, despite everything that had happened inside and outside Bianliang, the Prince of Radiance still wore that same graceful smile.

Prime Minister Liu came over, limping from exhaustion. His robe was stained and disheveled, and his white hair was coming out of its topknot. He seemed to have aged ten years since Zhu had seen him last. She thought with some humor: *Probably so have I.* "Greetings to the Prime Minister," she said.

"Commander Zhu! It's thanks to you that I was prepared for that traitor Chen Youliang." The Prime Minister all but spat Chen's name. "As soon as he saw those ships, I knew his intention: he was going to betray me that very instant. He was going to take the Prince of Radiance and flee! But I beat him to it." He laughed harshly. "I opened those gates myself, and I left that betraying piece of dog shit to his fate. May those Hu bastards kill him painfully so he can eat bitterness in hell and all his future lives!"

Zhu had a refreshing vision of how Chen must have looked when he realized he was alone inside Bianliang with an army pouring in on top of him. She said, "He must have been very surprised."

"But you—you were always loyal." The Prime Minister's glance skittered to Zhu's right arm. "None of those other commanders knew the meaning of loyalty and sacrifice. But you sacrificed yourself to the eunuch general so we could take Bianliang. And just then, you waited for me. Ah, Zhu Chongba, what kind of reward can there be for a person of such quality as you?"

Zhu looked into the Prime Minister's rheumy, bitter eyes and felt a peculiar impulse to absorb every detail of him. She took in his bluish lips and papery old man's skin; the coarse white hairs on his chin; his cracked and yellowing fingernails.

It wasn't because she cared, she thought. It was only a reflexive acknowledgment of someone else who had desired.

But for all the suffering the Prime Minister's desire had caused, in the end his desire had been curiously fragile. He had let go of it without even realizing.

Zhu took the small knife from her waist. Her left hand was useless for the battlefield, but perfectly adequate for the single backhand stroke that cut the Prime Minister's throat.

The Prime Minister stared at her in surprise. His mouth formed inaudible words, and the scarlet blood bubbled up until it overflowed and ran down to join the thick stream from his neck.

Zhu told him calmly, "You never saw what I am, Liu Futong. All you saw was what you wanted to see: a useful little monk, willing to suffer for whatever purpose you put him towards. You never realized that it wasn't your name they were going to call, exhorting you to reign for ten thousand years." As the Prime Minister fell facedown in the dirt, she said, "It was mine."

BIANLIANG

Ouyang led his army back to Bianliang at a walk. A black pall of smoke hung sullenly over the city, and its gates hung open in a perverse invitation to entry. When midday had passed Ouyang had been convinced that the young monk had failed, and it hadn't been much of a surprise. Even with his own contribution, what chance had such a plan ever had? He could only suppose that its success had been the mysterious action of Heaven granting Zhu Chongba his fate.

A messenger met them halfway. "General! General Zhang has Bianliang under control, but the rebel Chen Youliang has escaped through one of the northern gates and is currently fleeing with several hundred men. General Zhang asks if he should pursue?"

Ouyang was suddenly sick of everything. It was strange how, having struggled against the rebels his whole adult life, all it took was an instant for them to cease to matter. "No need. Tell him to make his priority clearing and securing the city."

Later, when he passed Zhang's guards at the central southern gate and came into the city, the work of clearing was well progressed. He found the other general overseeing his troops as they went through the piles of dying rebels, killing them where they lay.

"That went easier than expected," Zhang said, smiling in

greeting. "Did you know they'd open that western gate from the inside?"

"I did have a small conversation with one of the rebel commanders last night, though I wasn't sure if it would work out as planned."

Zhang laughed. "That one-armed monk in charge of their outside forces? How did he manage to influence what happened inside?"

Ouyang said sourly, "Heaven smiles upon him."

"Ah well, maybe he earned his luck through prayer and virtuous works. Although—he can't be a real monk, can he?"

"Oh, he is. I destroyed his monastery."

"Ha! To think that years later you would be working together. You never can tell when people will come in handy, can you? I'll have to tell Madam Zhang to keep an eye on him in the future. I suppose if you hadn't had us here, he could have mounted a flank attack while you faced the rebel forces out of Bianliang. In that case he might have stretched you quite well."

"Then I particularly owe you my thanks for being here." Ouyang tried to smile, but it felt dead on his face. "And I have need of you yet." He touched his horse forwards. "Come. Let's not keep the Prince waiting."

The Yuan's governor of Bianliang had made little use of the old palace, which lay inside its own wall in the center of the city. Obsessed with the symbolism of taking their historic throne, the rebels had ended up occupying nothing but ruins. There was no regaining the past, Ouyang thought bitterly. He knew that as well as anyone.

The red-lacquered palace gate, for centuries the sole passage of emperors, hung from its hinges like broken wings. Ouyang and Zhang rode through and gazed upon the blackened earth of the once-magnificent gardens. The wide imperial avenue arrowed before them. At its end, floating atop marble stairs, rose the Emperor's pavilion. Even a century after its last inhabitant's departure, the milky facade had a luster; the curve of its roof glittered like dark jade. On those shining white steps, dwarfed by the scale, stood the Prince of Henan. Esen's face was flushed with triumph. The warm spring wind swept his loosened hair to the side like a flag. Arrayed before him on that vast parade ground were the assembled troops of Henan, with Zhang's men behind. Together they made a great murmuring mass, victorious in the heart of that ancient city.

As soon as he saw Ouyang approaching, Esen called out, "General!"

Ouyang dismounted and made his way up the steps. When he reached the top Esen grasped him warmly and spun him around so they looked together upon the massed soldiers beneath. "My general, look what you've given me. This city, it's ours!" His joy seemed to expand past the bounds of his body and into Ouyang's own. Ouyang was captured by it, vibrating helplessly with it. In that moment Esen seemed breathtakingly handsome: so much so that Ouyang felt a sharp ache of incomprehension. That someone this perfect, so alive and so full of the pleasure of the moment, could *be*. It hurt like grief.

"Come," Esen said, pulling him towards the hall. "Let's see what they were so eager to die for."

Together they crossed the threshold into the cavernous dimness of the Hall of Great Ceremony. A shadow drifted in behind them: Shao. Opposite the main entry, another set of doors opened to a bright white sky. Atop a short flight of stairs at the end of the hall, dingy in the shadows, was the throne.

Esen said, puzzled, "That's it?"

That seat of emperors, the symbol that the Red Turbans had so desperately sought, was nothing but a wooden chair scabbed with gold leaf like the fur of a mangy dog. Ouyang, watching Esen with an ache in his heart, realized afresh that Esen had never been able to understand the values that made other people's worlds different from his own. He looked but couldn't see.

The light at the door dimmed as Lord Wang swept in. His beautifully tooled armor was as pristine as if he had spent the day in his office, although under his helmet his thin face was even more drawn than usual.

As if hearing Ouyang's thoughts, he said scathingly to his brother, "You betray your ignorance in less than a sentence. Can you really not comprehend what place this city occupies in their imagination? Try, though! Try to imagine it at its peak. Capital of empire; capital of civilization. A city of a million people, the mightiest city under Heaven. Daliang, Bian, Dong-jing, Bianjing, Bianliang: whatever its name, a city that was a marvel of all the world's art and technology and commerce, in-side these walls that withstood millennia."

"They didn't withstand us," Esen said.

Through the back doors, far away and far below, Ouyang thought he could see the northern edge of the ruined outer wall. It was so distant it was almost one with the line where the sil-ver floodwaters merged into the same-colored sky. He couldn't imagine a city so large it could fill that space, the empty breadth encompassed by those ruined walls.

Lord Wang's lip curled. "Yes," he said. "The Jurchens came, and then we did, and between us we destroyed it all."

"Then they must have had nothing worth keeping." Esen turned his back on his brother, strode out the back doors and vanished down the steps.

Lord Wang had a still, bitter expression. He seemed lost in thought. The lord's thoughts might have been opaque to Ou-yang, but his emotions never were. It was probably the only way in which he resembled his brother. But whereas Esen never saw any point in hiding what he felt, it was as though Wang Bao-xiang felt so intensely that despite his best efforts to conceal them, his emotions always penetrated the surface.

Lord Wang suddenly looked up. Not at Ouyang, but past him to where Shao had taken a leisurely seat on the throne.

Shao met their eyes coolly, his naked dagger in his hand. As they watched, he scraped the throne's flaking gold leaf into a cloth. For all that the movement was casual, he never took his eyes off them.

A flicker of contempt crossed Lord Wang's face. After a moment he turned without further comment, and made his way down the back steps in the direction his brother had taken.

As soon as he was gone, Ouyang snapped, "Get off."

"Don't you want to know what it feels like to sit up here?"

"No."

"Ah, I forgot." Shao spoke so flatly it verged on rudeness. It seemed, at that moment, that his true voice emerged. "Our pure general, free of the base cravings for power and wealth. Who has none of the desires of a man, save one."

They stared coldly at each other until Shao tucked the cloth away, rose without haste, and went out through the great front doors to the parade grounds. After a long moment, Ouyang followed.

Esen stood at the broken end of a marble causeway, looking out. He assumed there had been a pavilion there once, suspended above the lake. Now there was no lake. There was not even water. In front of him the ground burned as pure red as a holiday lantern. A carpet of strange vegetation stretched as far as his eye could see. The palace walls were out there somewhere, hidden by a lingering haze, but instead of stone ramparts Esen only had the impression of something very bright and very distant: the shimmering floodplain, or perhaps the sky.

"It's a kind of shrub that normally grows near the sea." Baoxiang came up beside him. For the first time in a long time Esen didn't feel rage upon seeing him. It felt as though they were floating in this strange place, their enmity washed away on a tide of memory. Baoxiang followed Esen's gaze outwards. "These were the imperial gardens during the reign of the Northern Song. The most beautiful gardens in history. The imperial princesses and consorts lived here in jade pavilions, surrounded by perfection. Lakes with rainbow bridges; trees that blossomed as thick as snow in the spring, and as golden as the Emperor's robes in autumn. The Jurchens deposed the Song, but at least their Jin Dynasty recognized beauty, and preserved it. Then the first khan of our Great Yuan sent his general Subotai to conquer the Jin. Subotai had no use for gardens, so he drained the lake and cut down the trees with the idea of turning it into pasture. But no grass ever grew. It's said that the tears of the Jin princesses salted the ground, so the only thing that can grow here is this red plant."

They stood there silently for a moment. Then Esen heard the screams.

He already had his sword in his hand when Baoxiang said, "It's too late."

Esen stopped dead. Cold terror crushed his chest. *"What have you done."*

Baoxiang gave him a twisted, humorless smile, and for some reason there seemed to be hurt in it. Outlined there against the bloodred landscape, the silver detailing of his helmet and armor were burnished with crimson. "The men loyal to you are dead."

Esen's rage crashed back into him. He lunged and slammed Baoxiang against the marble railing. Baoxiang's back met it with a crack as Esen shoved his forearm against his throat; the silver helmet went tumbling over the side.

Baoxiang coughed, his face reddening, but he maintained his composure. "Oh, you think—? No, brother. This isn't *my* plot against you."

Esen, wrenching himself around in confusion, saw movement within the doors of the great hall. A figure descended the steps, armor covered in blood, his sword in his hand.

"No," said Ouyang. "It's mine."

Ouyang came down the steps with Shao, Zhang, and the other Nanren battalion commanders behind him. He let them surround and separate Esen and Lord Wang. Esen stared at Ouyang in stunned silence, Shao's sword at his throat. His chest rose and fell quickly. Ouyang felt those breaths like the hammering of an iron spike through his own chest: an agony in the very quick of him. When he finally tore his eyes away from Esen, it felt like ripping out a piece of himself.

Zhang was holding Lord Wang. The lord, composed despite the hectic flush coloring his cheeks, met Ouyang's eyes with a slitted, wary gaze. A bead of blood welled on his neck above Zhang's blade. Scarlet against his pale skin, it drew Ouyang's eye: he saw the flutter of pulse in the bluish hollow of the throat, the bared ear with its dangling earring—

Lord Wang gave a biting smile.

Zhao Man's filigreed earring, gleaming in the flat white light, at Lord Wang's ear. Commander Zhao, who had been found by someone else the night he walked into the Prince of Henan's ger to betray them.

Into the terrible stillness, Ouyang said, "*You knew.*"

"Of course I knew." Despite his uncomfortable position, Lord Wang managed diamond-edged disdain. "Didn't you listen when I told you like knows like? You hid behind that beautiful mask, but *I saw you.* I knew what was in your heart long before I saw your—" He bit down on a word, then continued, "Were you really fool enough to think your success was due to good luck and your own capabilities? You can't even control your own men. Commander Zhao ran to my brother to tell of your treachery, and the only reason he didn't succeed was because I was there to stop him. And when you poisoned your own commanders—no doubt because they lost trust in you—that physician would have told the truth had I not guided his tongue." A spasm of detestation crossed his face. "No, indeed, General: not luck. Any success you have is due to *me.*"

Next to him, Esen made a dreadful, choked sound.

The color drained from Lord Wang's cheeks. But he said unflinchingly, "I'm not Chaghan's true son. You have no blood debt against me."

Ouyang clenched the hilt of his sword. "Perhaps I'd like you dead anyway."

"For the sin of understanding you? Even if it could not be

him," Lord Wang said, "you would think you would be grateful for one person in the whole world to do so."

Agony lanced through Ouyang. He looked away first, hating himself. He said harshly, "Go."

Lord Wang shrugged away from Zhang and turned to Esen. Raw emotion showed on those strange features that were a mixture of Mongol and Nanren. And perhaps Lord Wang had spoken truly when he claimed his likeness to Ouyang, because at that moment Ouyang understood that emotion perfectly. It was the wretched, propulsive self-hate of someone determined to travel the path he had chosen, even in the knowledge that its end holds nothing but ugliness and destruction.

Esen's jaw was clenched and the tendons stood out in his neck, but he didn't move as his brother leaned in close. The emotion that Ouyang had seen had already vanished. In the tone of someone feeding an audience's eager contempt, Wang Baoxiang said, "Oh, Esen. How many times you imagined my betrayal. How willing you were to think the worst of me. Why aren't you happier? I'm just being who you've always thought I was. I'm giving you the ending you believed in." He lingered for a moment, then pulled back. "Goodbye, brother."

"Let the Prince go," Ouyang ordered as soon as Lord Wang left. He looked out at that dry red lake, and the shimmering silver mystery beyond, and felt a receding tide carrying him away from his pain. Without turning, he said distantly, "More of them than I thought stayed loyal to you."

There was a long silence. Eventually Esen said, his voice cracking, "Why are you doing this?" .

Involuntarily, as if the foreign sound in Esen's voice summoned the response out of him, Ouyang looked at him. And the instant he saw the depth of hurt and betrayal in someone he loved, he knew he would never survive this. The pain rushed back into him, and it was so great that he felt himself consumed by the white-hot fire of it. When he tried to speak, nothing came out.

"Why?" Esen stepped forwards ignoring how Shao and Zhang tensed on either side of him, and suddenly cried out with a vehemence that made Ouyang shudder, "*Why?*"

Ouyang forced his voice out, and heard it break. And then he was speaking and couldn't stop; it was that same awful momentum that powered everything he had put into motion and couldn't have stopped even if he had wanted to.

"Why? Do you want me to tell you why? I was nearly twenty years by your side, Esen, and for all that time did you think I'd forgotten how your father slaughtered my family, and his men cut me like an animal and made me your slave? Do you think for a moment I *forgot*? Did you think I wasn't even man enough to care? Think me a coward who would dishonor my family and ancestors for the sake of staying alive like *this*? I may have lost everything important to a man, I may live in shame. *But I am still a son.* I will do my filial duty; I will avenge my brothers and uncles and cousins who died at the hands of your family; I will avenge my father's death. You look at me now and see a traitor. You scorn me as the lowest form of human being. *But I chose the only way left to me.*"

Esen's face was full of grief, open like a wound. "It was you. You killed my father. You let me think it was Baoxiang."

"I did what I had to do."

"And now you'll kill me. I have no sons; my father's line will be extinguished. You'll have your revenge."

Ouyang's cracking voice sounded like someone else's. "Our fates were sealed a long time ago. From the moment your father killed my family. The times and means of our deaths have always been fixed, and this is yours."

"Why now?" The pain on Esen's face was the sum of all their memories; it was a palimpsest of every intimacy they had ever shared. "When you could have done it any time before?"

"I need an army to take me to Khanbaliq."

Esen was silent. When he finally spoke, it was laden with sorrow. "You'll die."

"Yes." Ouyang tried to laugh. It stuck in his throat like a salty sea urchin. "This is your death. That is mine. We're fixed, Esen." The saltiness was choking him. "We always have been."

Esen was coming apart; he was spilling grief and agony and anger, like the invisible radiance of the sun. "And will you stand and kill me stone-faced with nothing but duty in your heart? I loved you! You were even closer to me than my own brother. I would have given you anything! Do I mean no more to you than those thousands I've watched you kill in my name?"

Ouyang cried out. It sounded like a stranger's sound of grief. "Then fight me, Esen. Fight me one last time."

Esen glanced at his sword, lying where Shao had flung it.

Ouyang said viciously, "Give him his sword."

Shao, picking it up, hesitated.

"Do it!"

Esen took his sword from Shao. His face, downturned, was hidden behind the fall of his unraveled hair.

Ouyang said, "Fight me!"

Esen raised his head and looked squarely at Ouyang. His eyes had always been beautiful, the smooth shape of them balancing the masculine angles of his jaw. In all their long relationship, Ouyang had never known Esen to feel fear. Neither was he afraid now. Strands of hair clung to the wetness on his face, like seaweed draped over a drowned man. Slowly, deliberately, Esen raised his arm and let the sword fall. "No."

Without breaking eye contact, he reached up to unlace his cuirass. When it was unlaced he pulled it over his head and threw it aside without looking to see where it fell, and walked towards Ouyang.

Ouyang met him halfway. The sword, going directly into Esen's chest, held them together. As Esen staggered, Ouyang wrapped his free arm around him to keep him up. They stood there chest to chest, in that cruel parody of an embrace, as Esen gasped. When his knees buckled, Ouyang sank down with him, cradling him, pushing his hair out of the blood coming from his nose and mouth.

All Ouyang's life he had believed he was suffering, but in that instant he knew the truth that every past moment had been a candle flame compared to this blaze of pain. It was suffering that was lit around without shadow, the purest thing under Heaven. He was no longer a thinking being that could curse the universe, or imagine how it could have gone differently, but a single point of blind agony that would go on unending. He had done what he had to do, and in doing so he had destroyed the world.

He pressed his forehead to Esen's and cried. Underneath them the blood pooled, then ran out across the marble bridge and off the side into the red ground.

Ouyang stood on the palace steps above his army. The bodies had been cleared, but the white stone of the parade ground was still covered in blood. Here there was no camouflaging earth: it spread in great blotches and streaks, smeared under the men's boots. Above, the white overcast sky was the same color as the stone.

Ouyang was soaked in blood. His sleeves were heavy with it, his hands gloved in it. He felt exsanguinated, as cold and still inside as ice.

To the grim-faced, silent crowd of Nanren faces, he said, "We have been subjugated, enslaved in our own country, forced to watch barbarian masters bring our great civilization to ruins. But now we fight for our *own* cause. Let our lives be the currency by which the honor of our people will be avenged!"

It was what they wanted to hear; it was the only thing that would have ever motivated them to follow someone like him. As he spoke to them in Han'er, he realized he might never speak Mongolian again. But his native language held no comfort. It felt like a cold leather glove that had been prised from a corpse. His Mongol self was dead, but there was no other to take its place, only a hungry ghost containing the singular purpose of revenge, and the inevitability of its own death.

He said, "We march to Dadu to kill the Emperor."

23

ANFENG, THIRD MONTH

The news about Bianliang reached Ma in a letter, from Zhu but written in Xu Da's hand. The letter spoke of Chen's defeat ("regrettably overcome by the superior combination of General Ouyang of the Yuan, and the forces of the merchant Zhang Shicheng") and Prime Minister Liu's death ("an unfortunate accident in his flight to safety"). Prior to his death Liu had received the Buddha's blessings for having saved the Prince of Radiance, whom he had passed into Zhu's own protection. Zhu trusted that his loyal and honorable wife, Ma Xiuying, could make the preparations for a suitable welcome for the Prince of Radiance on his imminent return to Anfeng.

It was the first time Ma had received a letter from Zhu. Her relief at Zhu's triumph was tinged with a peculiar sorrow. The formal language of letters captured nothing of Zhu's voice; it could have been written by a stranger. Any man providing instructions to his dutiful wife. Erased by the literary phrases was not only the truth of what had happened at Bianliang, but some truth of Zhu herself. Ma had never minded before that the public saw Zhu as a normal man. What other way could there be? But Zhu had promised to be different with Ma, and the loss of that difference in private correspondence hurt more than Ma could have anticipated. It felt like a betrayal.

Ma made the arrangements. Dutifully. But she felt no need to be among the throngs from all over the countryside that pressed into the center of Anfeng to watch the Prince of Radiance's return. She stood at the upstairs window of the Prime Minister's mansion—Zhu's, now—and looked onto that field that had seen so much carnage. It was dusk as the Prince of Radiance's gleaming palanquin was borne in, flanked by Zhu and Xu Da. Neither of them seemed changed. Zhu still wore her usual armor over her monk's robe. Ma knew exactly what that modest appearance was for: she was taking every care not to look like a usurper. By accepting the power granted to her by the Prince of Radiance with grace and humility, Zhu could cement the ordinary people's impression that she was the legitimate leader of not just the Red Turbans—but the entire Nanren movement against the Mongols.

The Prince of Radiance ascended the stage and took his throne. Ma watched Zhu kneel to receive the benediction of that small outstretched hand. The red light of his Mandate flowed from his fingertips into Zhu, consuming her kneeling figure in a corona of dark fire. Ma shuddered. For a terrible moment she thought it might not be the leadership that the Prince of Radiance was bestowing, but a death sentence. In her mind's eye she saw Prime Minister Liu wreathed in that same fire. Like Zhu, he had desired and been ambitious—and despite his best efforts, he still hadn't been able to keep control of that unearthly power that was the basis of his leadership. How could Zhu avoid the same fate?

The bonfires and drums roared all night long. It was the voice of the end of the world—or perhaps the new one, already come.

A knock at the door awakened Ma from a disturbed sleep. The drums were still pounding. A rosy glow, brighter than the Mandate, poured through the open window: firelight rolling over the underside of low clouds.

Xu Da was standing in the hallway with the Prince of Radiance beside him. Xu Da inclined his head to Ma and said with odd formality, "Commander Zhu requests your assistance." Behind him Ma saw other figures recessed in the darkness. Guards. Zhu had never bothered with guards before, being of the opinion that she had little to interest anyone. But possession of the Prince of Radiance changed everything. She saw that Xu Da's eyes were warm, even as he maintained the expected propriety: "I'll see that you're safe, so please take your rest. The commander will come when he can."

The Prince of Radiance stepped in. Xu Da shut the door, and Ma heard him issuing directions outside. A shuffle of booted feet in response. They were guarding an asset, not a person. For the first time, Ma looked closely at the Prince of Radiance. Lit dimly by the window, his round-cheeked face had the unearthly quality of a bodhisattva: serene and not quite present. Ma's skin crawled. It was the look of someone who remembered every one of his past lives: ten thousand years or more of unbroken history. How could anyone bear all that pain and suffering? Even in this one life, he had surely seen too much in the Prime Minister's keeping.

Ma found tongs and the pot of coals for lighting the lamp. As she picked up a coal, the Prince of Radiance looked out the window and commented, "So many ghosts tonight."

Ma jumped, losing the coal. Hearing him speak was as unnerving as if a statue had bent down to touch her as she knelt before it. "What?"

"They came to watch the ceremony."

A cold finger of dread traced Ma's spine. She imagined the space between the stage and the crowd filled with ghosts: their hungry eyes fixed upon Zhu as she burned.

The Prince of Radiance's otherworldly gaze drifted back to her. As if knowing the question on her tongue, he said, "Those with the Mandate of Heaven are more attuned than others to the threads that connect all things and make up the pattern of the universe." Adult words, from a child's mouth. "The dead awaiting their rebirths are no less a part of that pattern than the living. To us the spirit world is as visible as the human world."

Us. He must mean himself and the Emperor—but with shock, Ma remembered something she had dismissed as a dream. Zhu's voice, fractured and distorted through the lens of fever: *I can see them coming.*

She couldn't handle the implication; it was too big. It felt like staring into the sun. Rather than dwell on it she fumbled with the tongs and managed to light the lamp. The scent of the warming oil mingled with the scorch and sulfur of spent fireworks from outside. The child watched her lid the coal pot and stow it under the table. In the same conversational way he had spoken of things beyond normal comprehension, he said, "Liu Futong was never going to rule."

Ma froze. If what he said was true, and he could see the pattern of the world, could he read their fates as easily as someone else might read a book? She said uneasily, "Then who? Is it Zhu Chongba?" A wash of foreboding changed her mind. "Don't answer that. I don't want to know."

The Prince of Radiance regarded her. "Even the most shining future, if desired, will have suffering as its heart."

Ma's newly lit lamp flame shrank and turned blue, and drowned in the pool of its own oil. It was only that the wick had been too short—but as she stared at the stream of smoke rising in the dark, all the hairs on her arms stood up. She saw the faces of all the ones she had loved and lost. How much more suffering was even possible?

Since there didn't seem to be anything else to do, she put the child to bed and lay next to him. When it seemed he had fallen asleep, she glanced across at him. She was surprised to see his serenity had transformed into the perfectly ordinary sweetness of a sleeping child. Ma looked at his round cheeks and small parted lips, and felt an unexpected push of tenderness. She had forgotten that despite being a bodhisattva, he was still human.

She didn't think she had slept, but then someone was leaning over her in the darkness.

"Move over," Zhu said. Her familiar voice slid over Ma as

warmly as a blanket. "Isn't there room for me? You two are taking up all the space."

Ma awoke to daylight showing through the window-paper. The Prince of Radiance, to all appearances an ordinary child, was still asleep on her side of the bed. On her other side Zhu lay drowsing with her head on Ma's arm. Sometime on the way back from Bianliang she had stopped shaving her head. The dense regrowth made her look surprisingly young. The ends ruffled softly against Ma's fingertips. She stroked again, feeling lulled. In the space between those two trusting bodies, the edges of the world felt warm and rounded.

"Mmm," said Zhu. "I don't think anyone's ever done that to me before." She roused and rubbed her head against Ma's stroking fingers. "It's nice. When my hair's longer, you'll have to do my topknot for me." Her stump, dressed in a fresh bandage, lay on top of the quilt.

"Touch-starved?" Ma teased. It was unusual; Zhu always seemed as self-contained as a geode. "Are you telling me you didn't pick up any concubines along the way to pleasure you?"

"I was sharing a tent . . ." Zhu rolled onto her back and stretched.

"With Xu Da," Ma said. "The most notorious lover of women in half a province. He'd probably have aided and abetted. Found a girl you could share." After a moment of staring longingly at the curve of Zhu's clothed breasts, she stroked them with a mildly guilty feeling. For all Zhu claimed not to mind being touched, Ma had always thought she was making some conscious effort not to tense. But now to Ma's surprise, Zhu accepted the caress with every impression of relaxation. Comfortable in her body, for the first time since Ma had known her. Something had changed.

"Jealous as everyone is of the fact that I've seen Xu Da naked," said Zhu, amused, "I'm happy to go the rest of my life

without it happening again. Even apart from that, I wouldn't;
you'd mind."

"You can do what you like."

Zhu gave her a knowing smile. "Don't worry, Yingzi. I'll ask
first before I take a concubine."

"Oh, so you *are* planning on one?"

"You might like it. Someone else to sleep with. Novelty."

"I don't want to sleep with your concubine," Ma said, refusing to explore why the idea felt so distasteful.

"Ah, it's true: she'd probably prefer men. I suppose she could
always take a lover." Zhu turned her head to grin at Ma. "You
know, Yingzi, I wasn't planning on getting married. You were
an accident. But as it happens—I'm glad of it."

Zhu reached over and they held hands, left and left, chaste
because of the child.

After a while Zhu released Ma's hand and said, "Just so you
know, I'm not going to be around for long. I want to retake Jiankang."

It hadn't even been half a day. How quickly Ma had allowed
herself to fall back into the comfortable illusion of intimacy.
Now she regretted it. "You won't stay awhile?"

"This is my opportunity." Zhu sounded honestly regretful.
"I have uncontested leadership of the Red Turbans, and popular support thanks to the Prince of Radiance's blessing. I have
Anfeng. It has to be Jiankang next. Little Guo wasn't wrong: we
need it if we want to control the south. And if we don't take it—
Madam Zhang will." Zhu made a face. "Should I be calling her
the Queen of Salt now? What an odd title. Queen of Salt. I suppose I just have to get used to it. Queen of Salt."

"Stop saying Queen of Salt!" Ma said, exasperated. "What
do you mean, Queen of Salt?"

Zhu laughed. "Now you're the one saying it. I suppose you
haven't heard. The Zhang family—Madam Zhang, in other
words—supported General Ouyang's move against the Prince
of Henan. She wanted to strike a crippling blow to the Yuan before breaking away from it." Zhu flung her arms out melodra-

matically, which made her abbreviated right arm stick out like the wing of a steamed chicken. "*Quite* the blow. Henan is completely destroyed as a military power. Now the Zhang family claims sovereignty over the entire eastern seaboard, and Rice Bucket Zhang is calling himself the founding ruler of the Kingdom of Salt."

"So the Yuan—"

"Lost access to their salt, grain, silk, and everything else that travels along the Grand Canal, overnight. They'll be *furious*," Zhu said cheerfully. "They'll have to send out their central army from Dadu to put her down. She'll give them a run for their money. Especially since she *has* all the money."

"And the eunuch general?"

"Holed up in Bianliang, but who knows for how much longer given the size of his grudge against the Yuan. Apparently he's bitter about the circumstances in which he lost his—well, you know." Unexpected sympathy flashed over Zhu's face. "I wouldn't say he's a *fun person* to be around, but he helped me. I'm grateful to him."

Ma hit her. "*He cut off your hand.*"

Zhu smiled at her indignation. "Why should I hold that against him, if in the end we both got what we wanted? Even if it does mean you're going to have to do my hair and tie my clothes and wash my left elbow for the rest of our lives."

"Is that all your ancestor-given hand is worth? If you wanted to trade it in," Ma said tartly, "he should have at least killed Chen Youliang as part of the bargain."

"Ah well, you can't have everything," Zhu said philosophically.

News of Chen Youliang had reached them both. He'd ended up in Wuchang, upriver on the Yangzi, with a few men scraped together out of the Bianliang fiasco and a newfound hatred for both monks and eunuchs. Without the Red Turban name or popular support, he was barely more than a bandit leader. But everyone knew you underestimated Chen at your own peril.

On the other side of the bed, the Prince of Radiance smiled

in his sleep. Almost involuntarily, Ma reached out and touched his smooth, warm cheek. It had been a long time since she'd slept in the same bed as a child; she was surprised at the power of her yearning to hold a little body.

Zhu said, "Fond of him already? He has to come with me to Jiankang, though."

Ma drew the child into her arms, enjoying the soft feel of his skin against hers. "After that, let me look after him again."

"It's a good thing one of us is maternal," Zhu said, and smiled wryly.

"Jiankang!" said Xu Da. He and Zhu sat on their horses and looked down at the city on the far bank of the Yangzi. The hill they had climbed was part of a tea plantation, with apple trees scattered here and there between the rows. The smell of the bushes wasn't exactly like tea, but a distant cousin of it: unfamiliar in and of itself, but somehow bringing the thing to mind.

"The place where the dragon coils and the tiger crouches," Zhu said, recalling long-ago history lessons. "The seat of kings and emperors—"

On Jiankang's far side, bald yellow hilltops breached the afternoon haze like islands. The vast eastern lands of Madam Zhang. There, invisible in the distance, were her fertile fields; the canals and rivers and lakes. Shimmering mountains of salt, ships with their ribbed sails like cut-open lanterns, and then finally the sea itself. Having never seen the sea, Zhu thought of it as a river made endlessly wide: smooth golden waters stretching to the horizon, with storms and spears of sunshine racing across its face. To the north there was Goryeo and Japan; to the south, pirates and Cham and Java. And that was just the tip of the world—a fraction of the mysterious but perhaps one day knowable lands that filled the space between the four oceans.

Xu Da said, "This isn't the end of it, is it? When we take Jiankang."

"Do you want to stop?"

Apple petals fluttered down around them. On the river below, sails progressed as placidly as floating leaves. He said, "No. I'll follow you, as far as you want to go."

Zhu looked down at Jiankang, and thought of standing with the Abbot on that high-up terrace, staring with fascination and fear at the outside world. What she had seen had seemed so vast that it was strange to think it had only been the Huai plain. Even the person who had stood there had been different: not the person she was now, but someone living in the shadow of that hungry ghost, Zhu Chongba. Looking back she saw herself like a chick within an egg, not yet hatched.

Somewhere far away, flags banged. It sounded like the voice of Heaven itself. "Big brother, this is just the beginning." Within her she felt a glorious, swelling sense of the future and all its possibilities. A belief in her fate that shone brighter and brighter until the darkest cracks of herself were split open by light; until there was nothing left inside her but that radiance that was pure desire.

She didn't just want greatness. She wanted the world.

The breath she took felt like joy. Smiling with the thrill of it, she said, "I'm going to be the Emperor."

Dusk fell while Zhu's force was still picking their way down the steep road to the Yangzi River. Zhu had ridden ahead, and now when she looked back she saw the dark cliff face veined with flickering lantern-light. Perhaps that was what their own lives looked like from Heaven: tiny pricks of light, constantly blinking out and reappearing in the endless dark flow of the universe.

"Come, little brother," she said to the Prince of Radiance, who was sitting quietly beside her on his pony. Even after days of travel his skin seemed to glow. Nothing surprised or stirred him as far as Zhu could tell, although sometimes gentle contemplation swept across his face like a rain shower seen at a distance.

They rode a short way to where a grove of weeping willows leaned over the water. Zhu dismounted and looked at Jiankang shining on the far bank. "Ah, little brother. After generations of struggle, we're finally on the cusp of change. Your arrival promised the beginning of a new era, and over there in Jiankang—that's where it will happen."

The child dismounted his pony and stood silently beside her in the dusk.

Zhu said conversationally, "You told my wife Ma Xiuying that Prime Minister Liu was never going to rule."

"Yes."

"Liu Futong thought it would happen for him simply from the fact of having you," Zhu said. "He borrowed your power to win him the people's faith, and he thought that would lead him into greatness. But when it came down to it, he never wanted it enough." Crickets chirred in the deepening gloom under the trees. "I don't think Liu Futong was born with greatness in him. But that shouldn't have mattered. If you want a fate other than what Heaven gave you, you have to *want* that other fate. You have to struggle for it. Suffer for it. Liu Futong never did anything for himself, and so when I took you away from him, he had nothing. He became nothing."

The child was silent.

Zhu said, "I wasn't born with the promise of greatness either. But I have it now. Heaven gave it to me because I wanted it. Because I'm strong, because I've struggled and suffered to become the person I need to be, and because I do what needs to be done."

As she spoke she wrapped her hand around the hilt of her saber. It did need to be done; she knew that much. When there were two Mandates of Heaven in the world it was the fate of the old one to end, so the new era could be born.

And yet.

As Zhu stood there in the darkness, she thought of Ma holding the child, her face suffused with care for that small life. Ma, who had always urged her to find another way.

But this is the only way. Light from Jiankang's distant

torches gilded the river waves as they came in against the bank with a slow, regular slap. *It's the only way to get what I want.*

For so long, she had chased greatness just to survive. But without Zhu Chongba, that reason no longer existed. With the sense of dredging up something she didn't particularly want to look at, Zhu thought slowly: *I don't have to do this. I can leave, and go anywhere and be anything, and still survive—*

But even as the thought came to her, she knew she wouldn't give up greatness. Not for a child's life, and not even to prevent the suffering of the people she loved, and who loved her.

Because it was what she wanted.

The rising moon lit the Prince of Radiance's profile as he gazed out over the water. He was smiling. The moment felt like an indrawn breath: a stillness containing the inevitability of the outbreath.

This is what I choose.

His eyes still fixed on that distant shore, the Prince of Radiance said in his fluting, unearthly tones, "Liu Futong was never going to rule. But neither will Zhu Chongba."

There was a rustle in the willows, and Zhu knew if she looked she would see the hungry ghost that had been her brother. Unremembered all these years, because his name had been taken by someone who lived. "No," she agreed. She drew her saber and heard the familiar sound of the blade rushing smoothly against the sheath. Her left hand was stronger now, and it didn't shake. As the child started to turn, she said softly, "Keep looking at the moon, little brother. It will be better that way. And when you're reborn centuries from now, make sure to listen for my name. The whole world will know it."

JIANKANG, FIFTH MONTH

Nearly two months after Jiankang's second, more uneventful, capture by the Red Turbans, Ma received word that she should join Zhu in Jiankang. If you weren't an army, it was only a few days' ride from Anfeng. Crossing the Yangzi's lazy summer flow, Ma marveled at the sight of a city verdant with foliage, its streets bustling with industry. Only here and there were still the burned buildings from Little Guo's first attempt at an occupation. That already seemed a lifetime ago. The sun sweltered as she and Chang Yuchun, her escort, rode past thrumming oil mills and silk workshops and into the center. A clutch of modest wooden buildings crouched around the stone parade ground that was the sole remaining evidence of the ancient dynasties whose rulers had been enthroned there. Yuchun gave the buildings a jaundiced look and said, "Commander Zhu said he's planning to build another palace. Something more fitting, with a nice stone wall and everything."

Ma said, "Fitting—for the Prince of Radiance?"

An awkward expression flitted over Yuchun's face. "Um."

"What?"

"There was an acci— Well, anyway, the mourning period has finished. We observed a month. For—but we don't call him the Prince of Radiance anymore. Commander Zhu gave him a proper temple name. I've forgotten it; you'll have to ask him." Catching sight of Ma's face, the youth looked alarmed. "What's wrong?"

The depth of Ma's grief and anger surprised her. For all that the Prince of Radiance featured in some of her worst memories, it was only the most recent that came to her: the protectiveness that had risen up in her as she held that small warm body against her own. The thought that he had been dead for so long, without her even knowing, somehow made it worse.

She followed Yuchun numbly into a hall where Zhu stood in a group of men. Then everyone was gone and Zhu was alone in front of her with a serious expression. Apparently she knew better than to touch Ma right then, because she just stood there with her arms by her sides and her left hand open. What was that gesture? A plea for forgiveness, or simply an acknowledgment of Ma's pain?

The witnesses gone, Ma's tears overflowed. "You killed him."

Zhu was silent. Ma, reading her face, exclaimed, "You don't even deny it!"

After a moment Zhu sighed. "He served his purpose."

"Purpose!" Without having consciously worked to fit the pieces together, Ma realized she already had the whole picture. "The only thing you needed him for was to hand you power. You had to make sure the people accepted you as our rightful leader. After that—anyone else would have still needed him for his Mandate, so they could rule. But you don't need him for that, do you?" She said bitterly, "Because you have the Mandate, too."

She felt a slap of satisfaction at Zhu's surprise. "How did you—"

"He told me! He said that people with the Mandate can see the spirit world. And I already know you can see ghosts." She flung the words at Zhu. "So what did you do, throw him in the river like an unwanted kitten?"

Zhu said, very controlled, "It was quick, if that makes you feel better."

"It doesn't!" She thought of that brief moment of domestic joy she had felt that morning with Zhu and the child in her bed. Even that hadn't even been real, because Zhu had known all along what she planned to do. She said painfully, "How is this better than anything Chen Youliang would have done? You said you'd be different. You *lied* to me."

Zhu said, "I had to—"

"I know!" Ma screamed. "I know, I know! I know *why*." She felt a sharp internal pain: her heart twisting into a thousand loops. "You say you want me for my feelings, my empathy. But when you did this, did you even stop to think about how it might make me feel to bear witness for what you think is justified? Or did you know, and not care that you were being cruel?"

Zhu said quietly, "I didn't mean to be cruel. I'm different from Chen Youliang in that, at least. But I want what I want, and sometimes I'm going to have to do certain things to get it." The uneven indoors light gave the hollows and points of her face the exaggeration of an actor's mask. There was regret there, but it wasn't regret for the child—but for Ma herself. "I promised you honesty, Ma Xiuying, so I'll be honest with you. I'm not going to stop until I rule, and I'm not going to let anyone stop me. So you have two choices. You can rise with me, which I'd prefer. Or if you don't want what I want—you can leave."

Ma stared at her in anguish. In that ordinary, ugly little body was a desire so fierce that it scorched and blistered those who came near it, and Ma knew that pain was something she would have to endure over and over again for the transgression of loving and choosing Zhu. It was the price of her own desire.

For Zhu, Ma's pain was worth it.

But for me, will it be?

The golden flags arrowed down Jiankang's graceful avenues, coming together into that gleaming, pulsing point of light in the heart of the city. The palace's parade ground glowed gold under the sun that beat down mercilessly on the roaring, cheering crowd.

Encased in golden armor, Zhu stepped out onto the top of the palace steps. The sight of her subjects filled her with an expansive tenderness, as of the man who looks down upon the world from a mountain and feels suspended within himself the fragility and potential of all that lies beneath. Alongside it was her awareness of all the suffering and sacrifices it had taken to get her here. She had been nothing, and lost everything, and become someone else entirely. But now there was no longer anything to be afraid of, and the only thing ahead of her was her shining fate, and joy.

She thought: *I've been reborn as myself.*

This time when she reached inside for the light, it came as naturally as breathing. The radiance rushed out of her: an incandescent flame burning from her body and armor, as though she had transformed into a living being of fire. When she looked down at herself, she was greeted by the strange vision of her missing right hand gauntleted in white fire. Apparently the flame followed the outline of what she *thought* her body was. Her phantom hand made visible as it burned with white fire and white pain. It seemed fitting.

Above the crowd's heads, golden flags bore the city's new name. *Yingtian:* a name that claimed its connection to Heaven. And Zhu herself was making that same claim with her own new name. The name of someone who refused any future other than one in which she made history; the name of one who would change everything. *The greatest omen of a nation's future.*

As Zhu called down to those waiting faces, she heard her own ringing voice almost like a stranger's. "Behold me as Zhu Yuanzhang, the Radiant King. Behold me as the one who will lay waste to the empire of the Great Yuan, and expel the Mongols from this land of our ancestors, and reign in unending brightness!"

Remember me, and say my name for ten thousand years.

"Behold the Radiant King!" came the soaring response, and as the echoes faded the crowd fell to its knees with the long sigh of bodies folding upon themselves.

From that vast human stillness, a single person rose. A tremulous quiver went through the crowd. Zhu caught her breath in surprise. *Ma Xiuying.* She hadn't seen Ma since that terrible conversation, days ago, in which Zhu had given her the ultimatum. Zhu hadn't wanted to ask after her afterwards, in case it was true: that it had been their goodbye, and Ma had already left.

Ma was wearing red, the color of what had been ended so that Zhu could build the new. It felt like a castigation: *Don't forget.* Her gold-embroidered sleeves draped nearly to the ground. Her upswept hair, as high again as her head, was crowned with hanging silk ribbons and golden threads that swayed as she walked. In silence she made her way between the bodies prostrated on the stone. Her skirts flowed behind her like a river of blood.

At the foot of the stairs, Ma knelt. She was all smoothness and softness in the pool of her madder-dyed silk—but under that surface she had her own kind of strength: a compassion as unyielding as an iron statue of the Goddess of Mercy. Zhu looked down at the naked line of Ma's bowed neck, and her chest fizzed with oddly sharp relief and gratitude. It hurt in the way that pure beauty hurt. She had told Ma what she preferred, but she hadn't realized how much she *wanted* it.

"This woman addresses the Radiant King." Ma spoke strongly enough for the whole crowd to hear. For Heaven itself to hear. "I pledge to stand beside my husband for every step of his journey, even should it take ten years and ten thousand li. And at its end, when he begins his reign as the founding Emperor of our new dynasty—I will be his Empress."

Zhu heard the unflinching demand in Ma's voice: for Zhu's own loyalty, and honesty, and difference. As Zhu stood looking down at her, she suddenly saw how their journey would go: Zhu's desire propelling them higher and higher, until there was nothing left above them but the dazzling vault of Heaven. And for Ma every moment of that ascent would be compromise and heartache and the gradual erosion of her belief that there was always a kinder way. That was the price Ma would pay—not just for Zhu's desire, but for her own. Because she loved Zhu, and wanted to see her rule the world.

Zhu's heart ached. *I'll make it worth it, for both of us.*

She looked out at the crowd, and tried with all her effort to impress the sight of them into her memory, so she might not lose it: Ma, and Xu Da, and her captains, and behind them the tens of thousands of others who would follow her, and die for her, until she achieved her desire. "My future Empress," she called, and the words left her throbbing with the sweet potential of what was to come. "My brother commander, my captains; all my loyal subjects. The world is waiting for us."

She lifted her arms and let the pure white light stream from her until their folded bodies were bathed in a brightness to rival that of the sun. From inside the coruscating aura of her own radiance the spectacle of them was a vision of the future. It was the most beautiful thing Zhu had ever seen.

She said joyously, *"Rise."*

ACKNOWLEDGMENTS

This book began life during a series of brainstorming sessions with friends, in which we all decided to write the books we longed for but could never find. I'm not sure any of us realised then how long a journey it would be, but guys: *we did it*. To those who were there from the beginning: thank you from the bottom of my heart. Vanessa Len, for trudging every step of the way with me towards the finish line, and for understanding the joys and frustrations of being a mixed-race member of the Asian diaspora. I'm delighted beyond all measure that we'll be debuting together in 2021. C. S. Pacat, for inspiring us to delve deep to find our stories; for your endless support and counsel; and for your inability to lie about art. Beatrix Bae, for hosting that very first session, thereby starting the food arms race that left the rest of us mentally broken, and then taking us back and feeding us delicious soup.

Anna Cowan, what a good friend to have found! Thank you for being my K-drama partner in squee during the hell year of that first draft, and for your pithy character insights. I'll never think of Ouyang's sword the same way again.

My indefatigable cheerleader with a brain as big as a planet, my agent Laura Rennert: I can't thank you enough. Like a martial arts master in a training montage, you said, "Again! But better!" even when I thought I was too exhausted to keep going (although unlike a real sifu, you always said it in the nicest possible way). This book is immeasurably better because of you. Thanks also to your wonderful team—Paige Terlip, Laura

Schoeffel, and Victoria Piontek—and the rest of the Andrea Brown Literary Agency.

My very first editor at Tor, Diana Gill: thank you for your enthusiasm and tireless in-house support for this book. I still can't quite believe the Tor logo I saw on my treasured fantasy paperbacks will be on the spine of something I wrote. Will Hinton, Devi Pillai, and the entire team at Tor, including the freelancers: thank you for your magnificent efforts, including the many that went unseen from my end, to bring this book into the world.

Bella Pagan and the wider Pan Macmillan team: many thanks for your warm welcome to the world of publishing, and your enthusiastic and dedicated work bringing my book to the Commonwealth and, particularly, Australia.

Thank you to the Otherwise Award: the 2017 Fellowship gave me vital encouragement when I still had many miles to go.

Thanks to the delightful Ying Fan Wang for help with names and pronunciations. (Any remaining infelicities are, of course, my own.)

To Cindy Pon, Jeannie Lin, Courtney Milan, and Zen Cho, whose genre books with Asian protagonists made me believe it was possible for my own to be published.

To the patient and welcoming authors in the group chat, who answered my questions and shared in yay and woe alike during this long journey towards publication.

To my mother, who always encouraged my writing.

And thank you to my two nearest and dearest: John, for years of unwavering support despite my refusals to let you read the manuscript, and for arguing that at least *one* of the male characters should be a decent human being; and Erica, for sharing time and attention with an older sibling who happens to be a book.

Finally, I would like to acknowledge the Wurundjeri people who are the traditional custodians of the lands on which I wrote the final drafts of this book.